I0712707

VEIL HAVEN

A NOVEL

VEIL HAVEN

Edited: Amanda Brown
Formatting: Enchanted Ink Publishing
Cover Design: Aprampar
Illustration: Sarah Navin

ISBN: 979-8-9889654-0-4 (Paperback)
ISBN: 979-8-9889654-1-1 (Hardcover)
ISBN: 979-8-9889654-2-8 (eBook)

WWW.VEILHAVEN.COM

For my family, my friends, my community,

and anyone who has lost someone along the way.

VEIL HAVEN

A NOVEL

ANNE M. KELLEY

CHAPTER 1
The Abandoned Carnival

My mind's eye moves through Veil Haven like a storm-burdened breeze. *Someone is trying to outrun a Mothman. Someone is baking sugar cookies. Someone is hoping the thing they buried stays dead. Someone is cuddling their cat. Someone is fishing along the Black River.*

As the sunset glows through the mountains while I drive, I sing out of tune to no one while the October air flirts with my short hair. Speeding down this backroad to pick up Josie, I pass a Not-Deer crossing sign without a second thought. I'm hardly caught off guard when that very cryptid saunters onto the road.

My tires wail as I swerve across the yellow line to avoid it.

At a glance, the creature could be an injured buck, but the best indicator of a Not-Deer, since they take many forms, is that they look like deer but *wrong*.

This buck drags its feet as it hobbles on one side, and its neck is curved at an uncomfortable angle. But as I readjust in my lane and drive on, the Not-Deer's body shapeshifts in the reflection of my mirrors.

The deer's neck extends further and further, its antlers grow in jagged shapes, and its unhinged jaw reveals a mouth full of jagged teeth. It chases after me with a horrifying speed despite its broken legs, and... oh, it's grown a few more legs now. Nice.

But as I speed around another bend, it realizes I'm not worth the trouble.

"Stupid cryptid." I laugh.

It's much easier to ignore the dangers of our world than worry about them nonstop. Otherwise, you'd never leave the house. Or your bed. I mean, there's always something watching you. Even if it's just me.

Someone laughs with their friend. Someone cuts lemons for a garland. Someone is being followed. Someone is foraging for mushrooms. Someone is putting up their Halloween decorations.

My entire life revolves around the present, which is an anomaly in Veil Haven. They call me omniscient, but that's not really how it works. Sure, it might take another breath to say, "That's the girl who can see everything happening in the present," but at least it's not some weird fear-mongering propaganda.

People act like I'm all-knowing, but I can't see the future, and I definitely can't see the past. I can't even remember what I had for dinner two nights ago. How am I supposed to remember what thousands of people did three hours ago?

My ability has been described in hundreds of ways. It's like a fog that permeates everything, or a million invisible eyes all over town, or maybe I can only see through the eyes of other people—which isn't true—or that I'm astral projecting, or, well, the examples go on and on.

I think my favorite explanation is that I'm simply a narrator. I'm the person who's aware of everything happening. Everyone is the main character of their own story, and I'm just in the background doing my own thing. Because I am.

I couldn't care less about someone's infidelity, the drama between friends, or the politics of the sewer rats. But that's what makes me so useful to The Watchers. That's why the director chose to "adopt" and raise me after my parents were killed when I was a baby. And why he allowed Chief to aid in my development, too.

Director Capaldi gave me a house to grow up in, a car when I turned sixteen, and a salary to pay for everything else. He let me be an extra eye for The Watchers so I could help keep Veil Haven safe from those who would do it harm.

But even though everyone has teachers and the training facilities to help them control their abilities, I'm the first "omniscient" person in Veil Haven's history. It's a learning curve for all of us.

I brush the black hair out of my blank white eyes as my car shrugs up Josie's steep gravel driveway. Living in the mountains isn't for everyone, but when the woods become this gold and scarlet tapestry, it makes the added dangers worth it.

Josie's modest ranch house hides snuggly in the shadow of the mountain as its tiny warm windows hint at the family cramped inside. Her mama is waving at me from the kitchen as she clears the table from dinner. I wave back with an extra wide smile. This is a woman whose bleeding heart has made me feel like a relative of her family since I became friends with Josie.

The screen door squeals open and slaps shut as Josie hurries out with her signature yellow flannel and muddy camo boots. Her vibrant hazel eyes and bright smile can make anyone overlook her chipped front tooth.

As she literally bounces into my car, she strangles me with a hug. "I can't believe the abandoned carnival is back!" Her mountain drawl contrasts to my lack of one. "And you're sure all the noise won't be too much for you?"

I laugh. "Yeah, if I can handle football every Friday, I can handle the best fall activity. Besides, the carnival music is playing nonstop in my head, so it's about time we get to go." I lean against her shoulder for a moment. "But thank you for thinking of that like always."

"What else are friends for, girlie?" Josie hums, hugging me again.

I'm grateful my inner circle understands how my ability works, but I wish everyone else did too. Maybe then people wouldn't dislike me so much.

Nobody likes somebody witnessing all their private moments and secrets. But most of the time, I'm overwhelmed by the noise of it all, so I push the world to the periphery of my mind.

If you saw thousands of moments overlapping in your head nonstop, you'd want to put it somewhere else too.

I back out of Josie's driveway and begin our descent back to civilization to pick up Lydia. In the meantime, I listen to Josie recount her latest training session and all the past memories her teacher had her dig up in hopes of honing her already impressive skills.

When we pull up to Lydia's mansion in the richest neighborhood in Veil Haven, she quickly slides into my car. Her orange and jasmine perfume fills the backseat as she greets us, flipping her freshly straightened hair over her pink puffer jacket.

"Thanks for picking me up. Yes, I'm still on car probation."

"I told you textin' and drivin' was a bad habit," Josie teases. "But I *am* glad the only thing hurt was your car."

"Expensive car," I add, shifting into reverse.

Lydia rolls her eyes. "I've been working at the Foodie Mart since the spring! You'd think my punishment would be over."

"At least the store likes you."

"So true, Ash." She crosses her arms. "It's such a relief the sentient building that eats people appreciates my presence."

I grin. "It has good taste."

Josie squints at Lydia, trying not to laugh. "Did you go to the tannin' salon again?"

"You're officially darker than I am." I cackle.

Lydia laughs dryly and pushes both our shoulders. "Someone has to keep the color in our lives."

As we cut through downtown, we pass the town hall where I regularly visit our mayor whenever The Watchers need me to speak to their representative. The only people who work directly with The Watchers are Winona, our mayor, and Police Chief Mun.

I used to, but we had this big fight a few years back and I haven't spoken to Director Capaldi since. He was always kind of distant when he helped raise me, but now he's really stepped into the absentee father role—adoptive or not.

The giant white building sticks out like a sore thumb as it towers above the humble brick buildings of downtown. The circular window overlooking Main Street like an ever-watching eye is the finishing touch to the most ridiculous and pointless building in Veil Haven.

We cross the Black River and drive deeper into West Veil Haven as the road turns slowly to gravel and then grass as it leads to the tree line.

The abandoned carnival hums to life for an unknown amount of time every fall. Despite the generous warnings to never go near the woods, everyone decides the carnival gets a pass. So long as you don't go off the grounds.

Nobody knows when the carnival started or how it operates. We are raised not to ask questions, after all. There are no attendants, no guards, no guides—only partially rusted antique rides overgrown with vines and muted tarps speckled with holes.

We park on the grassy lot and slide out of the car just as the commercials start playing over the radio. *At the Shady Pines Aftercare Facility, we take care of all your poltergeist needs. When you don't have the time or energy to support the ghost in your life, we will.*

"I can't wait for my fried cappuccino," Lydia says, readjusting the cami crop top under her designer jacket.

Josie and I recoil at the thought of it.

"Don't do me like that." She wags her manicured finger. "I watch you two scarf down fried Oreos and funnel cakes like animals."

"But to drink it?" Josie gags. She rolls up her flannel sleeves before tightening the laces of her mud-stained boots.

"It's pretty disgusting," I tell her, brushing a bug off my iridescent leggings.

Lydia adjusts the diamond stud in her Roman nose. "Then why do they sell it? People must like it if they sell it every year."

They look at me to confirm my ever-present knowledge, and I resign with a sigh. "A surprising amount *is* ordered."

"See?" Lydia boasts.

Josie laughs. "Then you're all gross!"

As we get out of the car, Lydia pauses as she stares at a pile of spilled popcorn on the ground. A chill runs down her spine as an impossibly distant, wispy voice speaks only to her.

Josie and I realize she's communing with a deity. Though communing makes it sound like a two-way street, and Lydia doesn't quite have that grasp on her ability yet. Being a mouthpiece is a hard ability to train, but with enough practice and focus, she'll be able to not only understand the messages she receives but to even ask for them.

"Everything okay?" Josie asks.

"Yeah." Lydia scoffs, motioning to the popcorn. "It says: When feeling overwhelmed, sometimes the best reaction is to walk away."

I nudge her. "Very wise."

She rolls her eyes, grinning. "What can I say. There's advice everywhere I look."

"But will she listen to the advice is the real question, folks," I tease.

Josie takes Lydia's other arm and we walk side by side toward the carnival entrance.

Despite the otherwise unnerving atmosphere of weather-worn tents, rusted rides, muted colors, and too-bright lights to make up for the many burnt-out ones, the abandoned carnival is one of the best places in Veil Haven.

No tickets are needed for the carnival because, again, it's a kidnapping scheme, but the nostalgia pulls us in all the same.

The slow, out-of-tune melody hums through the trees welcoming everyone to come closer, have fun, eat greasy fair foods, and let your guard down. It's not run by ghosts, but by mysterious shadowy beings formed from the forest and forced to stay here. People call them Carnies, though it's unclear if that's because of the carnival or their carnivorous behavior.

The first things we pass are the Ferris wheel flushed with ivy and the swing ride painted with vintage scenery. Edison bulbs strung between the trees turn everything gold, and lights from the rides cast warm shadows under the pink sunset sky.

The autumn fireflies illuminate the dark outside the carnival, and anyone who looks out there long enough could swear those little yellow flashes start to look like eyes.

I find the familiar faces of Logan and Hayden as they stand in the entrance area. They're the stars of the football team. If you aren't impressed by their sportsmanship, you just might be drawn to their good looks. At least, that's how everyone at school treats them.

Hayden's warm copper skin glows under the lights and makes his bedroom eyes that much more compelling to anyone passing by. His cool smile accentuates his high cheekbones while he "mindlessly" rustles his black hair. In case it isn't obvious, he's obsessed with himself and anyone who glances in his direction. Though that leads to an arsenal of hilarious facts about Hayden, like how the mayor created a rule outlawing anyone from being shirtless downtown because of him.

Logan, on the other hand, is Veil Haven's golden boy. Unabashedly kind, genuine, and grounded, he's one of my oldest friends along with Josie and Lydia. Logan is one of those lucky people who can't help but be popular. He has wavy blond hair that touches his ears and blue eyes. People consider him to be the best quarterback the Mothmen have seen in decades, and his ability to see the future doesn't add to his skill.

Someone's dad gives Logan a handshake as he passes the pair, congratulating him on the latest win and wishing him luck for tomorrow's game. He celebrates Hayden too when he recognizes the running back's number on his letterman jacket.

They smile awkwardly and laugh as the family man moves on.

That same family comes our way as they're leaving, but when they see my blank white eyes and recognize who I am, they clench up a little and give me a wide berth. My eyes are instantly recognizable. I'm not the only one whose ability has altered their body in some way, and I'm not the only person with unique eyes, but something about the lack of pupil and iris always makes people uncomfortable.

I can see the same as anyone else. My white eyes are mainly difficult for other people. They don't know where to look or where I'm looking. I guess I've adapted to be more obvious with my body language. Still, as this family obviously avoids me, I shift my body so they think I haven't noticed their glares.

Josie and Lydia don't seem to notice.

I ignore the family and focus on Logan and Hayden, who seem to be waiting for us despite not having any plans to meet up. But knowing Logan, this is just what's supposed to happen tonight.

Lydia follows my gaze and stops on Hayden. She cocks her hip. "No warning, huh?"

"Your spirit guides didn't say anythin'?" Josie jokes.

I smile deviously as I jog away before she can hit me. "I thought you were over him." I see her scoff and shake her head as I approach the boys.

"Ash, hey!" Logan hugs me. "Nice sweater. It's very grandpa of you."

"Thanks." I tug on the extremely detailed oversized sweater. "So, are we right on time?"

"Always."

Hayden is already checking over my shoulder and catching Lydia's daggers. His dark eyes light up as he smirks and waves.

"Give it a rest, Hayden," I tease.

"Oh come on. We're just having a little fun." He smirks as we walk their way.

"I think that was the problem in the first place."

As we agree to play games before Lydia or Hayden can open their mouths, Josie and I are already running off to the nearest stall, my black hair dancing around my jaw.

As we move together as a group, Hayden keeps prodding Lydia. And she nearly punches him before Josie distracts them both by knocking over the pyramid of jugs and getting one of those wiggly armed plushies.

"Woohoo! In your face!" Josie celebrates as she ties the Jacka-lope around her neck. She bounces between me and Lydia as she playfully flexes.

Lydia tries not to laugh as she pushes Josie into me. "It's not even that hard."

"Then beat my score," Josie dares, handing her a ball.

Lydia throws the baseball so hard her feet slip on the crabgrass and she loses her balance.

Josie catches her, laughing. "M'lady."

When Lydia realizes Hayden is laughing so hard he's clutching his sides, she eyes him dangerously. "Are you serious?"

"Serious about you." He grins.

Lydia throws her hands up. "I don't know why I try." Her mousy brown hair shifts over her shoulders as she threatens to leave.

"Okay, hold on. Hold on." Hayden moves in front of her. "If I promise not to bother you, will you learn to have some fun?"

She glares at him. "As if you've ever kept your promises before."

Logan and I *Oooh* as Hayden smirks to cover his embarrass-ment.

Lydia struts away dramatically.

Josie considers going after her, but I convince her she needs the space.

Hayden's shoulders drop slightly before he scoffs and straightens his back. He waves her off. "Her loss."

We've seen this interaction play out many times, and instead of prodding him further, we agree to just refocus on the game at hand.

But I stand at their backs and watch Lydia disappear into the crowd. Logan nudges beside me as I do.

"Do you know how hard it is to not just coach him and tell them to go for it?" I ask him.

Logan and I don't need our abilities to know how our best friends feel about each other, as complicated as they make it. An eruption of celebration moves our gazes toward some water game before shifting back to the crowd.

He crosses his arms contently. "Waiting is the hardest part."

How could I forget who I'm talking to? Logan, the oracle, the boy with a crush of his own. Where I can assume how people feel now, he knows how happy they are in the future—his own happiness, too.

"You know, Shakira is wandering around with her family. I could accidentally run into her if you'd like."

I watch her with my mind's eye as she brushes powdered sugar off her jeans and laughs with her siblings. Her bright smile makes the carnival lights look dim.

Logan smiles at the mention of her name but looks away, unfurling his arms. "You should let it happen naturally."

"Oh, so it does happen." I smirk.

My mind's eye suddenly takes me out of place. The carnival falls away like a distant hum as it's replaced by the faraway deep woods. I expect the Wildwoods to be quiet compared to the carnival but it's full of energy.

I haven't looked at this cryptid haven in a long time, let alone been redirected here by something so eye-catching.

Every herd of six-eyed deer lines the edge of our world at the densest section of the Wildwoods. Seeing so many of the same cryptid in one place makes my skin crawl. It's so unnatural. The harmless cryptids seem agitated as they cast long glances at one another, communicating some sort of deep understanding.

But in a single breath, I watch as every six-eyed deer charges forward, crosses the threshold of our world, and disappears into the Void. They blip off my radar in a rush of noise and I'm frozen stiff.

My mind's eye pulses as chills roll over my frame.

Veil Haven is one of the five towns hovering in the center of the windless plane of Void and stars. The only thing that connects these worlds are portals found at the center of each town. Ours is in the park. It's a glowing green doorway. But voidwalkers like the six-eyed deer can simply leap off the edge of the world and run out there to do whatever voidwalkers do.

But for an entire species of deer to leave all at once is unheard of. Why would they do that?

In the same moment this happens, Logan is still talking. "Yeah, it's going to be a good night." But as I come back to myself, I watch him recognize the quirk in my brows and my distant stare. He knows I've seen something. He leans closer, his hand on my shoulder.

"Ash, what is it?"

I refocus on my present, the noise of the carnival crashing through my mind's eye like whiplash. I wince.

"All the six-eyed deer just left Veil Haven." I sway a little, feeling lightheaded.

He cocks his head. "Is everything okay?"

"Yeah, it's fine." I swallow the dread of not knowing what's happening and focus on my friends again. "Just cryptids being weird." I force a smile and we move on.

"We should ride some rides," Hayden suggests. "I can't upset Lydia if she's not with us, and she definitely doesn't like rides."

A few years back, when Lydia rode the Gravitron, she threw up on our old middle school teacher, who was unfortunately strapped beside her. And then the year after, thinking it was a fluke, she threw up on the rollercoaster, too. She's never lived it down... well, we've never let her.

Josie jumps in place and points her finger to the sky. "True enough!" But as we decide what ride to go on, she quietly gives Hayden friendly advice. "You shouldn't crowd her, and you definitely shouldn't make fun of her. You know how sensitive she can be. And just, don't be..."

"Too much?" Hayden offers.

"Well, no, but..." Josie kindly trails off.

Hayden raises his brow, as if the realization finally sinks in. "Why are you helping me?"

"Because we're sorta friends." She lightly punches him in the shoulder. "It's important to have a healthy, uhm... equilibrium?"

I jump in between them. "Do you mean ecosystem?"

"Yes!" Josie declares, poking me and then Hayden. "We're all friends here. One big ecosystem."

"You're sweet as ever, Josie," Logan says, walking up beside her.

"If you ever tell Lydia I gave y'all any sort of help..." She looks between the boys. "I will destroy you."

"Or *she* will." I laugh.

My mind's eye catches a young couple eager for devious privacy as they sneak around the back of one of the game stalls. They're putting space between them and the rest of the carnival—and only inches between them and the boundary of the woods.

She clutches his jacket lapels as his hands wander across her body. They lose touch of where they are and how far they've moved, but it's too late to realize their mistake.

They assume the carnival noise dipped because of their intense focus on each other, but they become frozen in place as the Carnies surround them.

The shimmering inhuman figures are dressed in tattered attendant jumpsuits and clown costumes. Their gaunt, hollow faces mimic what might've been human once. But they're so hungry now. And this is an easy meal.

The couple can't even scream before they are consumed in a soundless feast.

I walk onto the ride, watching my step as we go.

The two teens are lost to the woods. Not even their bones or clothes are left behind. But that's Veil Haven. People disappear or die all the time. I learned early that I can't involve myself with every horrible thing that happens. The world moves on. People do it every day without knowing, so why should I be burdened by it?

Josie says something to me and I laugh, readjusting my own present as I strap into the whirling ride.

We spill out of the exit, still dizzy from the rounds, when someone jumps on Logan's back. He smiles wide and spins her around before letting her go. I imagine these are the moments that make his ability worth it. The satisfaction of that future glimpse finally colliding with the present and him stepping into it ceaselessly.

Shakira lands on her feet and throws her long, gold accented braids out of her face. "I didn't know y'all were gonna be at the carnival. We should've just planned somethin'."

"All things in time," Logan says.

"I should've known you knew." She grins.

All things in time. Logan must know when they become official. I wonder how long he's known and how much longer he'll have to wait.

Everyone knows they have a thing for each other. With that look in his soft blue eyes, I know he'll spend eternity waiting if that's what it takes. To know one's destiny is a powerful, heart-wrenching thing. But his glimpses into the future are enough to make him wait. And enough for her to wait on him.

Lydia finds us with strides, sucking down her deep-fried cappuccino. Her face lights up when she sees Shakira and throws her arm around her. "Hey, girl, when did you get here?"

"I came with my family," she says. Her mountain drawl is even thicker than Josie's. "Saw y'all gettin' on the ride before I could say anythin'."

"You should join us," I suggest. "We could go on more rides."

"I'll pass," Lydia says, a hand on her stomach.

"Maybe you throw up because you drink those awful things," Josie suggests.

"Y'all go ahead. I'll stay with Lydia," Shakira says before winking. "We have to catch up anyways."

As we wait in line for the wooden roller coaster, I sense the forest come to life.

In a breath, the entire world shifts and bends as every sentient being focuses on me. I am intoxicated by the rush of secondhand power. The recognition of this pulsing energy is impossible to forget, and the familiarity of it makes my stomach clench.

Through the inescapable noise of the carnival comes a soothing disembodied voice only I can hear—a voice I haven't heard since I was a child.

"Ash..." it hums softly. *"Come back to me. We have so much to discuss."*

I swallow sharply, feeling claustrophobic under its ubiquitous attention. The Forest Eye hasn't tried to reach out in years. Not after we fought. Not after I left the woods for good. And I find my cheeks flush with heat as I ball my fists and glare at the trees.

I send my thoughts loudly around me, *Leave me alone!*

A nearby telepath looks at me funny but moves on.

"It's been so long," the voice continues, half-taunting, half-hollow. A parent at patience's end. *"And you can't run forever..."*

The pressure of its gaze on me makes my knees buckle. My entire body itches like a battery trying to be jumpstarted. As I look around, it feels like my insides are vibrating.

I'm in line with my friends and there are trees everywhere. The Forest Eye could wrap a vine around my waist and drag me into the woods before anyone could blink. I'm becoming more lightheaded as the seconds pass.

I need to get out of here.

I swallow the tension building in my throat, hoping to stall the sound of my discomfort, and bite back the anger.

"I, uh, have to go."

Josie takes my hands and asks what's wrong, but I don't have the energy to explain. I play it off as some immediate work I have to do for the police. The others don't try to stop me. Josie hugs me goodbye, saying she and Lydia will catch a ride home with Shakira, and finally, I'm leaving.

As I speed walk through the crowded pathways, my itch is soothed, if only a little. I glare at the trees as its secondhand power still washes through my being, trying to make me feel airy and safe. But as I grind my molars, I'm reminded of what the Forest Eye did to me the last time we were together. And how I vowed it would never get the opportunity to manipulate me again.

"We need to talk, Ash."

My blood boils as all our sharp memories resurface—the tension, the heartache, the manipulation. *There is no* we *anymore,* I shoot back.

Can't I have one simple night? God forbid I go anywhere near the woods without it watching me, but now this?

As I trek back to my car, I watch some poor kid chase his sister behind a game stand.

The carnival noises slow as they step off the grounds. They pause beside one another, the forest towering around them as the shimmering Carnies rise from the shadows. The carnival lights dim in the background as they clutch one another, terror rising in their chests.

The kids are paralyzed, their voices stolen from them, and in an instant they are consumed by the shifting shroud of mythical beasts. The carnival music skips a beat as everything beyond the grounds goes black with shadows.

I shake my head and let their mother's increasingly worried cries fall to the background.

With a steady breath and a white-knuckle grip on the wheel, I leave the tree line and head home to put that voice and all the noise behind me.

CHAPTER 2
THE BOY WHO FINDS DEAD BODIES

I watch my friends for the rest of the night and laugh with them from the comfort of my bed. The fairy lights in my room cast a warm glow over everything. The walls are even more packed with posters and photos than my living room, relics from my childhood half-hidden under new interests.

I've collected many things over the years, anything to keep my walls from being boring and bare—from art and posters to rusted metal work rescued from abandoned buildings, and photos of my friends. I have so much color and movement inside my head it might as well reflect in my home.

The window beside my bed is undecorated so I can lean out of it and talk to the Void. I'm not the only one who speaks to the sky god, but they still seem lonely. Between the two nature gods, the Void is kinder. They care about humanity. They are a direct foil to the Forest Eye. It's a shame they can't interact with us like the cryptid god can.

The midnight sky has darkened to burgundy as the rainbow stars spill over the mountains like a river. I trace the dark faraway ridges on the glass, but when small balls of light flare on the mountains, my throat tenses. The Mysterious Mountain Lights.

They only appear on the distant ridge of the west woods, right where I'd be able to see them from my window. It seems like every other house in Veil Haven misses these lights. They're obscured by the hillsides, treetops, other houses, or whatever else.

One of the first times I remember seeing these lights was when I was with my neighbor Kane. We were kids, and he snuck over to watch some TV movie marathon late at night. I can't remember what he thought of the lights, or if I tried to explain how weird they seemed. But I guess some mysteries are supposed to be left unsaid.

Our friendship fell apart years ago but he still lives next door. I see him regardless, but the better days are when he ignores me completely. Kane blamed me for his uncle's disappearance and told everyone who would listen. That was the only rumor people needed to turn their backs on me. It felt like the world was never going to be the same when I was younger, but staring at the Mysterious Mountain Lights now, it's comforting to know some things really don't change.

For the most part, I can't tell if people don't know about them or if they're choosing to ignore them. It's a hard line to determine sometimes, though it's the best survival technique. *If you see something, say nothing.*

If I didn't know any better, I might think the lights are from somebody's house or maybe a set of light posts flickering along the road. But nobody lives in the west woods, and there are certainly no roads.

The Mysterious Mountain Lights are an itch that picks my brain. A terrible blindness lies there, like binoculars with one lens blacked out. Whenever I stare at the mountain lights, my mind's eye assures me nothing is there, my omniscience and my physical eyes refusing to agree. But they're real, they're right there glaring at me like some punchline I can't understand.

The tiny white dots flicker like flames consumed by their own wick. About as soon as they flare up, they die out, and the mountains return to a dark ridge cutting into the starry burgundy sky.

As the carnival crowds tire of testing their luck, the abandoned carnival begins to live up to its name. Soon enough, everyone finds themselves getting ready for bed, and I, too, shuffle beneath my sheets, falling asleep.

As the world shifts to its night crew, the cryptids stir from the trees and creep into town where only the bravest or dumbest remain. Visions of town pass through my mind's eye even now. Every night as I rest, the world sinks into a haze while my mind's eye picks one event at a time to focus on. I'm stuck watching whatever is exciting enough to grab my attention.

I hear the night in hushed tones.

Some people use the night to their advantage while others use it for clumsy matters. Hayden uses his nights for both, and no one is more well-versed than he is.

Hayden's ability comes with the affliction of purposeful insomnia. Known as a death spotter, he is sworn to find the dead wherever they call to him. When he's awake, he's less susceptible, thus the choice to stay awake as long as his body can take it.

He sits upright and shirtless in bed and I'm reminded why Lydia is so infatuated with him. It might seem strange, but I've seen every naked body in Veil Haven. I can't help it. Lydia made a comment once about how she wouldn't be able to do it—seeing all those hot, perfect bodies doing all sorts of marvelous things. For me, the idea of sex is no idea at all. It's just another thing that falls to the background with all the other noise. Hayden and his athletic body are no exception.

While I have become very familiar with everyone over the years, I can still only witness what is happening in real time. When you people-watch long enough, anyone can assume how someone feels and take a guess at their intentions.

But with enough focus, and a lot of practice, I *can* witness what's going on inside someone's head. It's easier to practice with my friends, who I've obviously grown familiar with. When it comes to strangers, I need time to watch them before I can worm my way inside.

That's why the director would give me people to watch in advance of their wrongdoings. But with all the surveillance devices, The Watchers know more than I do. That might be why I haven't gotten any direct work in a while. That and something about "letting me be a kid while I still can," as if that's ever been reason enough before.

I naturally hyperfocus on people but it *is* my job for The Watchers. It's hard to shut it off when I'm always supposed to be on alert. Ever watchful. But whatever.

Hayden's bedroom is decorated with explicit posters as empty bottles and dirty plates scatter the floor. He's always lived more like a college student than a high schooler. Though I guess they're just as fluent in staying up late.

Hayden gets a text from his friend asking him to come out, but he's too preoccupied scrolling through Lydia's socials.

He stares at her for a long time, studying her smile and the way her hands lie on the exposed waist of her cheerleading uniform. She posted this earlier today, reminding everyone to see her fly atop the pyramid at tomorrow's game.

Lydia and Hayden didn't date. Lydia and Hayden were never officially a thing. Lydia fell in love with Hayden after their third hookup when he didn't want anything serious. That's what he told her, at least, and at the time, I think it might have been true. Yet here he is, swiping through her socials at 3:14 in the morning.

He finally notices the text from Prickly Pear inviting him to meet up with their other friends at the Stoplight Motel. He doesn't have to say why. Hayden leans into his pillow with a sigh and responds.

It's game day tho.

Prickly promptly responds. *Come on, man, we have the goods tonight.*

His eyes beg him for rest, but he keeps looking at the message. At this point, it's almost obvious he's going to the Stoplight Motel. Hayden doesn't have the best impulse control, and his nighttime habits of pushing himself to either stay awake or dull his senses kick in.

He texts Prickly back. *It's never too early to pregame. I'll be there in fifteen.*

He throws on a shirt, grabs his keys, and makes his way to his car. Security cameras around his house catch him leaving in full control of himself. He waves at them to make a point. Usually they film him sleepwalking to the call of a nearby corpse but not tonight.

He drives out of the maze of his neighborhood and turns onto the twisting road that avoids the hospital. This backroad is notorious for its sharp bends, outdated guard rails, and elevation drops. It isn't the easiest route, but it's Hayden's best bet to avoid the hospital's morgue.

Regardless of the dark twisting road, he drives twenty over the limit, the humming beat of his radio trailing behind him.

He sees the reflective eyes of deer and other things watching from the woods, but the blood drains from his face when he begins to feel lightheaded—the first sign of his trance.

He forgot about the roadkill. He assumed someone would've cleaned it up by now, but they haven't. It's been on the left shoulder for four days.

He curses and beats against the steering wheel.

Hayden presses the gas, turns on the high beams, and puts his music on full blast. But the tension clutches his body anyway. It creeps under his skin until he slowly goes numb, grows tired, and begins to swerve. He tries to ground himself by shaking his head and arms while shouting the lyrics, but he is quickly approaching the bend and the dead deer calling for him.

He should slow down.

He doesn't.

The numbness crawls down his neck and makes his hair stand on end. The corners of his vision darken into a tunnel of focus. He locks on to the deer with perfect clarity.

Maggots squirm in the thick of it, licking the ribcage white as they burrow deeper into the moist flesh of its intestines. Blackened gore spills from the deer's mouth and neck while its legs are pinned awkwardly under it. Parts of its pelt have been peeled away by skull-headed vultures.

Hayden sees its missing tongue and pecked-out eyes as his breathy singing devolves into a distracted hum. He passes the corpse as quickly as he approached it but his eyes are still glazed over. He looks back at the deer as his hands slowly turn the wheel. He isn't slowing. The bend begins to sharpen. He crosses the yellow line.

The bass drops, and it shakes him out of his trance.

He readjusts across the center line and slows as he takes the bend, putting more and more distance between himself and the roadkill. He sighs with shaking hands, keeps the music high, and drives until he reaches his destination.

Hayden drives into the Stoplight's parking lot and scrapes the undercarriage of his car on the pavement. The motel's sign glows softly, welcoming visitors with a vacancy sign missing the V. The building stands out from its gray-brick neighbors with a green roof and a large blue pastel stripe running beneath it.

The motel wraps around a pool in the center of the parking lot, though the pool hasn't been filled in decades. The giant crack in its foundation prevents anything more than puddles even in a heavy rainstorm. I'm not sure what caused that crack but a human finger bone is wedged down there, calcified by chlorine—a left ring finger, I think.

Hayden parks beside the lifted red truck like he always does and smiles at the light peeking out from room 119. He's been here enough to know where his boys stay.

When he knocks on the door, he isn't greeted at first. But when he shouts his name, the door opens surprisingly quickly. Stale-smelling smoke curls into the night as a large man with ficus leaves for a head fills the entrance.

After an intimidating pause, they both melt into laughter and pat one another as Hayden moves inside.

But something happens. Not to Hayden, but to me.

I'm waking up as if some ethereal force is pulling me back to my body.

I open my eyes and the world hits me in one loud burst. I jolt under my covers, nails scraping the bed as I catch my breath.

It's not four in the morning. It's seven, and Hayden is asleep in his bed and—

My attention snaps to a neighborhood road above downtown.

A family is moving into a previously abandoned Victorian house.

I sit up tense as I focus on this family. I've never seen them before. They didn't exist before I fell asleep and now they're half-unpacked in a house that isn't theirs?

My thoughts devour me, chills rolling down my back.

I see a wheelchair-bound woman, a boy about my age, and two young girls.

I don't know anything about them. I don't know *them*.
They're not from here.

My face flushes with heat. I crash on the floor getting out of bed, my ankle caught in the sheets. I grab the first clothes I find and throw them on, hobble downstairs, and grab my keys.

I don't know what happened—which is unheard of—*and* I don't know who these people are. *Or* where they came from.

No. No, this isn't good.

Nobody moves into Veil Haven.

The only visitors we get are football teams from the other towns across the Void. But they only arrive before games and they certainly don't bring friends or family.

This isn't right. Why aren't The Watchers stopping them?

I turn my attention to Winona, our mayor, whose purpose is to do nothing but also to at least do *something* if someone breaks one of the most important laws we have! This has never happened before. Not even the police seem bothered. Chief doesn't even seem aware. And what about The Watchers? What happened to protecting Veil Haven at all costs?

I return my attention to the new family as I drive to town hall. My palms sweat as I white knuckle the steering wheel.

The taller of the two young girls huffs and leans against the side of their U-Haul. "Markus, I'm tired. I don't want to do this anymore."

The large boy walks down the front yard steps and looks at her with tired eyes, running a hand over his thick, twisted hair. He rests against the trailer and cups her cheek softly.

"I'm tired too, Kyah. But the sooner we move in, the faster we can all rest."

"This place smells like old people," the smaller sister drones, sliding out of the U-Haul with a tiny box.

"I know, Jarissa, but you can't talk bad about this place." He faces the towering Victorian. "Whether we like it or not, this is our new home."

CHAPTER 3
A BEGGING TO BE BELIEVED

I park sideways in the nearest spot to the entrance of the giant white building and rush inside, nearly forgetting to shut off my car.

My ears ring as the town floods out of my periphery.

Someone is singing to their plants as they water them. Someone opens a birthday card and pretends not to notice the money falling out. Someone meal preps for the week. Someone unsuccessfully pinches the contact lens in their eye and panics, thinking it'll be stuck there forever. Someone has been hypnotized by a Black Dog to play fetch with it. Someone drives by a dead deer on the side of the road and laughs at the GET WELL SOON balloon tied to its hoof.

Inside the town hall, I'm met by a grand staircase covered in a long red rug. The few government employees who wander in from the halls on either side of the foyer choose to ignore me. Everyone knows me here, namely because no other teenager is going to be willingly in town hall as often as I am.

I rush up the stairs and head through a twisting maze of hallways.

Halfway to the mayor's office I catch a glimpse of a nameless cryptid. The pinkish-white humanoid skitters across the ceiling as if surprised by the company. The dim lights accentuate its glowing degloved flesh, as if making a point of its pale pink muscular body. It's almost human in form but lacks any proper face or skeletal shape. When I make eye contact with it, the monstrous "man" simply shuffles away, and its glow is consumed by the shadows of the dead end hall.

I scoff and shake my head at the classic Veil Haven experience. There's always something shuffling about.

All sorts of government agencies and offices are in town hall, which means the building is basically purposeless. This government—the government we're allowed to talk about and interact with—is just the face of the far more powerful system really running Veil Haven.

The Watchers take care of us, keep us safe, and do all the unsightly tasks that would only burden the average person, let alone a public servant. The Watchers thought it would be nice to give people with a sense of justice something to do. It keeps them occupied.

The mayor's position is pointless in terms of leading our public government but is instrumental as the representative for The Watchers. Somebody has to visibly lead the people, and it surely isn't going to be the director.

As I finally reach the hallway leading to the massive double doors of the mayor's office, Winona's secretary doesn't stop me. I actually don't know what he does. Except smile.

Winona would be a junior in college if being the mayor wasn't a full-time position. This makes her the youngest person working for the government besides myself and interns.

I push through the double doors and Winona jumps in her seat, dropping her phone hard on her desk.

"God, Ash! What is it?"

Purple petunias bloom where her head should be, creeping across her shoulders, down her back, and along her breast like a delicate shawl. As I enter, the flowers stir toward me like dozens of eyes shifting to attention.

"Oh, sorry." I hurry across the room as the doors close softly.

Her office is filled with natural light, and the circle window at her back encircles her like a halo.

Her office is about what you'd expect a high officer of the government's office to look like: sprawling bookcases filled with ancient, boring texts, antique paintings hung in ostentatious golden frames, and random government-themed knickknacks on mahogany furniture.

Winona and I look out of place here, yet we're exactly where we belong. Winona most of all. She's the perfect apathetic person to be The Watchers' representative.

I approach her desk with wide white eyes, my bedhead wild. "Do you know about the new family on Dupont Drive?"

Winona's petunias stare at me as she rolls her shoulders. She sinks into her chair and her dark purple flowers settle cooly along her chest. She inspects her phone for cracks before folding her hands on her desk littered with loose papers.

"Ash, you have nothing to worry about. The Jacksons are just a normal family."

My hairs stand on end. "Where did they come from? Did they just drive through the portal in the park?"

"Yes, obviously. They came from Fox Falls." Her petunias sway as she shifts in her seat.

"Winona," I whisper like a warning, "I didn't see them come into town."

She seems to sense the gravity of my message but her understanding vanishes just as quickly. "They came in the middle of the night. You were just sleeping."

"But you know I still see the town in my sleep."

"I know you hyperfocus," she reminds me.

I step back. "I assume something like this would grab my attention."

"Ash, take it from someone who actually dreams. You can't expect precision when you sleep." She moves some of the papers around aimlessly. "The family is supposed to be here. We are welcoming them into our town."

I scoff and look around as if hoping some invisible force will take my side.

The other end of the room overlooks the lake. The navy sky reflects on the glowing turquoise water as the sun rises.

Looking back at Winona I scan the colorful downtown buildings at her back—the autumn trees, the people milling about—and when I catch the clock tower at the opposite end, it chimes. The clock tower always chimes when you acknowledge it. I'm surprised to hear it this far away.

Dozens of questions are flying through me at Winona's assurance but all I can manage is, "Why?"

She leans into her creaking, oversized leather chair. "More diversity, more business, more culture, more inclusivity—take your pick. We're trying something new."

I laugh abruptly but shuffle under her gaze as a couple of petunias rise skeptically. "Sorry, I thought you said the town was trying something new."

Winona stares at me.

I gawk. "But sticking to tradition is how we *do* things. We keep everything the same as it's always been. Veil Haven doesn't change."

"Ash, this is happening. If you were supposed to know, you'd know."

I straighten my back as my heart pounds. Knowing that this is supposed to be happening doesn't make it any easier.

"I don't know anything about them." I sound as deflated as I feel.

"Learn the old-fashioned way," Winona suggests. She checks her phone then looks at me, humming as her petunias flutter. "I hear one of them is your age."

"But, Winona—"

"You aren't needed on this matter, Ash." I hear the grit in her voice, the sharp, hidden message behind her words. *Stop asking questions.*

I clench my jaw.

"You need to get to school." She returns to scrolling on her phone and my warm welcome expires.

Except I don't move. My shoes feel lined with lead. My head is ringing as it swims with unanswered questions. "If you let me in on what's happening, I can help. You know I always help. Maybe the director wants to talk to me?"

Her petunias look at me too quickly and I swear I catch a flash of fear, maybe pity, but it melts back into her apathy as the flowers relax on her shoulders. "If he wanted to talk to you, he would talk to you. You know that."

I run my fingers through my hair, working out some knots as I stand there like a child shunned by her father. It's something I should be used to. The director and I haven't spoken in years. Not since our fight. Not after I disconnected the rotary phone.

I stare at the matching phone on Winona's desk, propped teasingly in the corner. He's just a phone call away. He's behind every hidden camera. But he's still a world apart.

"Is there anything else?" She sighs, not looking away from her phone.

I don't say anything.

"I'll see you later, Ash." She doesn't even look at me.

I hold my breath on the way out and close the doors behind me. Her secretary watches me leave with a shallow, fake smile, and I drop my shoulders when I'm alone in the maze of hallways. I tuck my hair behind my ears and pick at a pimple on the side of my face. Before I know it I'm back in the parking lot.

It's airish today. The wind pushes away the fading warmth of our late summer. The mountains are quickly fading into soft yellows, but not even autumn can distract me from this.

Someone checks their reflection in a stranger's car mirror. Some-one is making a goodies basket for their boyfriend's birthday. A Cloud Person's altocumulus head makes their dog want to play with them, the spotted, globular clouds always a sign their master is in a good mood. Someone shows a new witch the best way to cleanse their space before communing with deities. Someone plays the mandolin in the woods and watches the kinder cryptids dance.

My cheeks flush with heat despite the cool breeze. I'm left feeling strange.

Winona has always been harsh but this feels different. I mean, this is the weirdest thing that has ever happened, and they're just allowing it?

I decide to head to the police station. I know I can get better answers from Chief.

The tan brick building covered in deep green clumps of moss used to mean more to me, but now I'm only here when Chief is around. I used to help the police all the time until the officers got jealous of me or became scared that they would lose their jobs since a child was doing it better than the entire force.

At one point, it even felt like I had a family with Chief and his wife Iliana. But that changed when they had kids of their own. In Iliana's mind I am Andrew's work daughter, some strange bastardization. Despite all the kindness she once had for me, the intention to keep me away from her family is wedged between her ribs like a mother's survival instinct. I guess she believes the rumors about me.

Chief Mun, of course, is blissfully unaware. So now I only catch him when he's alone at work. It's not the best feeling in the world but who else do I have?

I park and clutch the wheel to steady my nerves before going inside. A family of pigeons live on the roof of the station and will occasionally fly at officers' service weapons. We have no idea why. I see them perched up there now and wonder if they recognize me.

I press through the glass swinging door and ignore the receptionist like she does to me.

The inner layout of the station is basic, one large room filled with desks, Chief's corner office, and two jutting hallways. One leads to the cells and interrogation rooms while the other leads to the morgue, meeting rooms, storage spaces, lockup, and so on.

Chief Mun keeps his blinds closed. He doesn't want people knowing he's in there watching cat videos and purposely ignoring all his duties.

Some officers eye me as I enter, but I ignore them and open Chief's door.

"Ash." He catches his breath. "What have I told you about knocking?"

I stand in his doorway. "Oh, right. Sorry." I close the door and ignore his plea as I sit in one of the two uncomfortable chairs in front of his desk.

Police Chief Andrew Mun has a chronic kindness about him, which doesn't fit with his field of work. He's the last stop in halting every attempt to rescue the missing, the first man you see in matters of grave importance, and the closest thing to The Watchers on a good day.

Being the front man for the security of town is a job that can easily change you, and I suppose it has. Over the years that kindness has been whittled down by the shadows he keeps at bay. He's grown more exhausted, but I suppose that happens to everyone in government.

His small dark eyes were the first thing that told me how gentle he was, but now they're dull and accented by crow's feet. I'm not sure when it happened. One of those little things like the river reshaping the shore. You don't notice it until it's already changed. It's strange to be with one of the men who raised me, knowing he's hardened, and not feeling like I've done the same.

Still, we pretend like things are exactly how they've always been. Things aren't supposed to change. That's why I'm here.

He shuffles some papers aside and pats his desk unrhythmically. "What can I do for you on this lovely Friday morning?"

I shift in the chair printed with daisies and dead leaves before mirroring him as he taps on his desk. "What can you tell me about the new family? The Jacksons?"

He leans back and rubs his jaw. "Well you don't need to be worried, if that's what you're here about."

"Maybe I'm not worried. Maybe I just want to know. Like, what if we're in danger and you're watching cat videos."

"Remind me to send you this really funny one I found," he begins.

"I already saw it, Chief. I've seen *all* the cat videos."

Chief Mun rocks forward, smiling. "Could you imagine if we let complete strangers into town? The chaos that would ensue? I would have to do *so* much work. And while it seems like I don't do anything, we aren't as incompetent as you like to think."

I glance at the piles of folders and thick stacks of paper on his desk detailing all sorts of minor crimes and missing people. Intentionally hidden beneath a few carefully balanced stacks is the same rotary phone on Winona's desk. I guess Chief doesn't like the reminder of who's really in charge any more than I like being ignored.

"I don't think you're incompetent, Chief." Quieter, I say, "I just don't like not knowing things."

"Welcome to the rest of the world." He chuckles. "Nobody knows everything all the time, Ash, not even you." I hear what almost seems to be a twinge of sadness in his voice. Is that regret in his brow? He looks away for a fraction of a second before correcting. "Listen—"

I scoot to the edge of my seat and point at him. "What's that look for?"

"What look?"

"I don't know, you had a look. Is there something you want to tell me?"

His smile returns, and he relaxes as best he can in his pressed uniform. "Ash, you know we don't tell you everything. You've never been in the loop of *everything* we do. The last few years, we've fallen into a good rhythm. We come to you when we need you, and you get to be a kid the rest of the time. Why is this the thing that's bothering you?"

I scoff. "Why would the town want to bring in more people when we orchestrate a *famine*," I say in air quotes, "every other decade for population control? None of this makes any—"

His gaze hardens. "Ash, we don't talk about that stuff. You know that."

I cross my arms and look to the side. "We aren't talking about anything."

He resigns with a sigh, his tone returning to its normal kindness. "Just trust me. Will you? There's nothing you need to worry about with the Jacksons. Just treat them like everybody else."

I scoff. "Then at least tell me what their abilities are. Winona told me I have to learn about them *the old-fashioned way*, but you could at least give me a briefing."

Chief Mun tilts his head. "None of the Jackson's have abilities, Ash. I thought you would've sensed that at least."

I blink rapidly and shoot out of the chair. "They don't have abilities?" I yell.

Chief holds his hands up. "Ash, come on. It's fine. As I told you, they aren't a threat. Can you understand that we have everything under control now?"

I gawk, my face warm. "How is that even possible? I thought the people from the other towns were just like us."

"I mean the towns are a *little* different than Veil Haven, but nothing major that the public needs to know. While it's uncommon, some people in Fox Falls, Leiton, Railston, and Bescour don't have abilities. Different gene pools and what not. But it really isn't something people need to know. Listen, you know what it's like to be different, how the people here talk. I'd imagine that boy could use a friend like you to navigate what's coming. Anyway, shouldn't you be at school right now?"

I feel like I'm hit by a truck. Why is he saying this groundbreaking news like it's common knowledge? Our entire lives we're told the other towns are just like Veil Haven, but now they're slightly different?

I clench my jaw and fail to understand why he isn't taking this seriously. Am I not saying this right? *There are strangers in town. They don't have abilities? The government seldom approves change. I didn't see them move in!*

"Why aren't you listening to me? Are my gut feelings ever wrong?"

Chief frowns as he walks around to meet me. He gently takes my hands. "I hear you, Ash. I understand how confusing and even scary this change is, but I hope you can find comfort knowing that everything is under control."

I sigh and my shoulders drop. But a new feeling snakes through me that makes my throat tight. "Aren't I old enough to be let in on what the director does? At one time I thought he was training me for... something more. I don't know." I hang my head.

Chief clenches his jaw. It isn't the first time I've asked. "You have to forgive us for not wanting to share the horrors of our work with a child." He laughs a little, but his somber undertone makes my heart restrict. "Come on, Ash... I know we've been telling you to be patient for years, but the director has a plan for everything, and you *are* part of that plan. And... the Jacksons are part of that plan, too."

He tilts his head as my gaze hardens. He pulls me into a hug, hoping to soothe the fire and fear out of me. "I understand you, Ash." He pauses, considering something, and holds me a little tighter. "It's okay to feel this way, but you need to calm down. You have to believe me when I say the director doesn't want to burden you with more responsibilities. You're only a kid once.

Don't rush that. And don't worry about the new family. Everything is under control."

I can't help but feel eased at the idea. I want to prod more but I sense our conversation is over. Even though it's my job to share secrets and hidden intentions with them, it isn't my place to pry them out of The Watchers.

"Try to have a good day. Okay?"

I sound deflated. "You too. Don't get too distracted by year-old cat videos."

"No promises." He laughs.

I leave his office feeling no better than when I woke up. The anxiety of missing something this strange gnaws at me.

I feel Detective Stevens staring at me from the snack table at the end of the room. He has a donut in one hand and a coffee in the other. He's a plain-faced blond man with a thin mustache and an average height. Everything about him is average. It's almost grating.

"Don't kids your age usually sleep in?"

"One of us has to break stereotypes." I scoff, grabbing a handful of donut holes on my way out the door. He looks around in awe but I'm gone before he can find the words to stop me.

I pause to appreciate the wind before climbing into my car.

I look toward the start of Dupont Drive as the noise of the world picks up.

Someone returns the family pictures they found at a thrift store to their rightful owners. Someone cups their hands and creates light. Someone is ignoring the poltergeist spelling out, I LOVE U, with their dirty clothes. Someone laughs so hard with their new friends they realize this is what life is about. Someone collects the crystals they charged last night. Someone is birdwatching with their dad.

I'm so close to the new family. I could go over there and introduce myself, go straight to the source. But would that be going against what the director has planned for me?

As my friends gather at school, I decide to meet them instead of the new family. It's like what Logan is always saying: All things in time.

CHAPTER 4
The Itch in Your Bones

Veil Haven High School could just as easily be an abandoned building. The school's name is in white block letters partially hidden behind a giant oak tree growing beside the entrance. Its brick foundation is strong enough to hold three stories but the school board is too nostalgic to do anything about its crumbling interior. In Veil Haven, things are the same as they've always been, no matter if they worsen over time.

When you walk through the main doors, you're welcomed by mossy floorboards, saplings growing under lockers, missing ceiling tiles with the sense that something is watching you, and the faint smell of sweetened rot.

This place has raised generations of Veil Haven Mothmen and those in power want to keep it as familiar as they remember it twenty, thirty, forty years ago.

The hallways are dimly lit and always overcrowded when the bell rings but at least the classrooms are flooded with natural light. Each teacher puts their own flair to their rooms but they're still stocked with well-worn wood tables, scribbled-in textbooks, failing holographic technology, and the overwhelming sense that nobody is actually learning anything.

I ignore the growing buzz of game day as I pace through the

halls, people throwing down our little M hand sign for support of our football team.

I never understood why we need a hand sign or how we landed on making our fingers vaguely form an M for Mothmen. It's just sticking your pointer finger and pinky toward the ground. Sort of like the "rock on" gesture but upside down. Though it *does* double as a way to ward off the evil eye, which is surprisingly useful in football.

When I meet Josie and Lydia in the courtyard, everyone is milling about, sharing stories and making plans for tonight's game.

The courtyard is a giant concrete pad spotted with greenery and metal tables framed by the sky above us. Most people make use of the steps outlining the space, some even lie down to catch a couple more minutes of sleep, but I'm far too wired to even consider it today. As I join my girls at the center of the courtyard, they read me like an open book.

"Ash, you look terrible," Lydia says. She looks me up and down. "And what is this?"

I study the frantic outfit I've assembled, assuming the worst, but it's not any worse than what I usually wear. It's my red flannel pajama pants and a yellow flannel shirt tied around the waist of a tie dye shirt. "I just threw something on." I shrug apologetically.

Lydia stifles a laugh. "It's an eye catcher, that's for sure."

Josie tells her to leave me alone with a smile. "Do you have somethin' on your mind?"

I rub my face and ignore the pimples I feel on the sides of my cheeks. "Yeah, but I don't think I can talk about it."

They steal glances with each other. They, along with everyone else, know I work with the government. The Watchers might have cameras and listening devices in every corner of Veil Haven, but I can provide a deeper look. I can home in on whoever I want wherever they go, even if they hide in the woods or scribble plans in the dark. But people hardly break the rules on purpose, and the director hasn't called me as often as he did when I was a child.

Still, my friends know that most of the things I see and especially the work I do can't be discussed without risk of endangering themselves.

So when I say that, it's reflex. But the more I think about it the more I wonder if that's even true. It's not like the new family is hiding. Their neighbors are already asking around. So before I know it, I'm telling my girls everything.

We lean in as I stage whisper, explaining how I didn't see anything while I was sleeping, how many there are, how they're almost unpacked, and what Winona and Chief told me—except for them not having abilities.

"What the heck?" Josie gawks. "How is that even possible? Like the portal downtown I guess. That's the only way visitin' teams come here. But even then."

"Wait, does that mean he's coming to our school?" Lydia wonders.

I shrug and tell them I don't know. It's a terrible thing to admit.

"I don't like the sound of you sayin' that," Josie says.

"Yeah, it's a first for me, too."

Lydia grins cooly. "Well... what's he look like?"

We playfully scorn her.

"He's big and tall, has really clear skin, his hair is in thick twists, he's got good bone structure—"

"Bone structure?" Lydia bursts out laughing.

"What? It's true." I pull on my cheeks. "They're round and cute. I don't know. How do you describe a person? I don't know anything about him. Winona literally told me to talk to him the *old-fashioned way*." I stick my tongue out.

"I'll talk to him, see what he's all about." Lydia smirks.

"Give the boy some space," Josie says, flashing her chipped-tooth grin. "If we're confused just imagine how he feels. In a completely new world? I can't imagine that." She folds her arms. "I don't want to."

I focus on the football boys at the other end of the courtyard, all of them in jeans, jerseys, and their letterman jackets. They're electrified for the game, even Hayden who I assumed would be dog tired after last night.

I tell my girls I'll be back and shuffle over to meet them.

Kane tracks me as I move across the courtyard, his sharp blue eyes sending daggers.

Kane and I have a complicated history. We used to be best friends, and unfortunately we're still neighbors. We did everything together. We basically grew up together, but after his uncle went missing, he blamed me, and that's when the rumors began.

It's not that a single kid made the town hate and fear me. That was the quiet undercurrent since I was born. *The Girl with Eyes Everywhere. Just another one of The Watchers' spies. She's barely human with all that power. No wonder she doesn't have any empathy.*

But Kane knew the things people thought about me, and he used his grief to fan the flames. Even though his conspiracies seemed to destroy what little positive reputation I had left, people don't really bring them up anymore. I guess it's just common knowledge now. But he still likes to hang it over my head.

He tucks his hands into his jacket, which makes him look thin as a rail. He has arrow-straight golden hair that rests at his shoulders. He looks extra pale whenever standing next to Hayden with his warm copper skin.

I untense my jaw as I shift my gaze to Logan, smiling as I join their group.

Kane still glares at me with that sharp, fake smile.

I roll my eyes, though it's hard to tell without pupils.

I'm greeted warmly by Logan and Hayden, which is all that matters. "Hey, guys, you excited for the game?"

"Yeah! We're gonna absolutely crush Fox Falls," Hayden promises. Then he makes some inside joke I'm not supposed to know about, and they burst into laughter.

Nearby groups smile at them, basking in the glory of the football stars. Everyone in the vicinity flashes the Mothmen hand sign for good measure.

I shift toward Hayden. "I'm glad to see you well-rested. You had quite the night."

His laugh tapers off. "What are you talking about?"

"Y'know, your night out."

He lowers his brow almost comically as he tries to piece together what I'm saying.

"At the Stoplight Motel?"

"You didn't." Logan gawks, disappointment trailing his surprise.

"Geez, Hayden." Kane pats him on the back. "You're really walking the line with Coach, huh?"

"No, I didn't," Hayden defends himself. "Ash, I have no idea what you're on about. Coach would kill me if I did that again."

My face drops. "But you got a text and there was that dead deer on the road."

"Ash." Hayden laughs. "What are you smoking?"

I look at him as the others laugh, Kane joking about what I would be like on drugs. Hayden is telling the truth. I can see him recalling his memories of last night.

They're completely different than my own.

"But I saw you," I say below the noise.

"Ash." He grips my shoulder. "I didn't leave my room last night. Check my outdoor cameras if you want. I promise I'm not messing with you."

"I believe you," I say distantly, catching Logan's worried glance. I release the tension in my shoulders and step away. "Sorry. Just ignore me. I hope you guys have a good game."

Kane jumps at the chance to say, "If only you could ignore us."

"Real creative, Kane." I flip him off as I leave and smile as Logan pushes him, telling him to leave me alone. Hayden breaks the tension with a joke, and they forget about our encounter entirely.

The bell rings before I can tell Josie and Lydia anything, though I'm not sure I'm capable of putting it into words. Noise rampages through my head.

Someone breaks a mirror. Someone watches a Bigfoot teaching their young how to safely cross the road. Someone pushes a half-eaten carcass to the curb with a hockey stick, cursing whatever cryptid left it there, and goes back to eating breakfast. Someone learns their great grandfather was an author. Someone tends to their front yard greenhouse.

Hayden didn't go out last night?

I feel stuck inside myself. The noise rises in my mind.

I don't dream. I don't make up scenarios. I only see what's real.

If Hayden didn't go out last night, what did I watch?

Because I know what I didn't see.

The Jacksons.

Before I know it the final bell cuts me out of my obsessive thoughts. I've been watching the new family all day and I'm astounded by what little I've learned. It seems like they really don't have any abilities. How terrible.

I can't quite shake the goosebumps surrounding this entire affair. I dreamed. I really, actually dreamed. And it was about Hayden of all people. But did I dream because the new family was moving in and it was an overwhelming experience for my subconscious? Or did something force me into a deeper layer of sleep so I wouldn't see them arrive? I sound crazy.

What's worse is that the only being I can think of who has that kind of power is the Forest Eye. But it can't reach me when I'm in town. And what would it gain from making me not see the Jacksons move in? Why would anyone want to hide that?

I guess the only way to find out is to go straight to the source. I need to meet this family. I don't care if Chief will be disappointed. I don't care if I mess up the director's secret plans. If they didn't want me to get involved, they should have told me the whole picture.

I ease through the hallways swarming with everyone excited for tonight's game. Most people leave as fast as they can, throwing down as many Mothmen hand signs as possible. Some people even sneak the use of their abilities in the excitement. A flash of light here, a flying kid there, some extra vine growth, some water ribbons from the water fountains, a couple of floating phones to capture the pregame hype, and so on.

I'm marching across the parking lot when Josie tackles me from behind. Lydia joins the hug-attack, too.

"To Paulette's!" Josie shouts.

My apologetic smile and half-raised shoulders speak for themselves.

Lydia wags her pink manicured finger. "Nuh-uh. Whatever it is, it can wait, girlie. Pregaming is sacred."

"But, well, uhm." We walk to my car as I try to put it into words. The jarring levels of noise make it hard to hear my own thoughts let alone speak them into being.

It's impossible to miss my car with the back window covered with stickers. From fandoms to stupid jokes, retailers across town, cute cryptid art, and nerd stuff, I can't help but keep my windows as cluttered as possible.

"It's like this…" I continue, following it with nothing.

Josie cups my shoulder. "Baby, what's wrong? You were pretty distant at lunch, too."

I sigh, and we all slide into my car. I close my eyes and grip the wheel, counting my breaths in an attempt to mediate the noise in my head.

I turn in my seat and look at them both. "I had a real dream. For the first time in my life. And it happened right as the new family moved into town. It was about Hayden doing something he didn't actually do."

After a breath of awe and silence, Lydia is the first to react. "Yeah I get those dreams, too."

"*Lydia!*" Josie scolds her.

"Sorry," Lydia says, still straight-faced.

"I'm not sure what to say, Ash," Josie admits, taking my hand. "That must be a really scary experience for you."

I swallow. "It's... something. And, on top of the mayor and Chief telling me to ignore my gut, I don't know, I just forgot about our dinner plans. I want to meet the new family *so* bad."

"What do you think you'll get out of it when you do?" Lydia's tone shifts in a way we've grown used to recognizing. She's playing the mouthpiece. She's leaning into her ability in an attempt to offer guidance. Some higher being is speaking to her. It's hard for her to put a name to any deity that contacts her and even harder to reach out to them, but that's what she and all other mouthpieces are in training for.

I clutch the headrest as I face her in the backseat. "What are your guides saying?" I look as desperate as I sound. Oracles like Logan aren't allowed to share what they see in the future, but mouthpieces are expected to offer guidance.

"Not much. But I did hear the tiniest voice telling me to tell you to stay away from them."

I rock my head back, blinking twice. "That's weird."

"It's always weird," she says. "But, I agree. And there's no better way to follow celestial advice than to follow our tradition and carbo-load before the game."

"Even though I don't like going against your gut feelins, and with this weird dream combo, I think trustin' Lydia's guides is the right choice. At least for tonight. The leadin' cause of death is ignorin' omens, after all."

"That *is* what they teach us," Lydia adds.

I rub my face and groan. "Do you know how hard it is to ignore this?"

"We don't expect you to ignore the things that are happenin', or the feelins you're experiencin'." Josie rubs my arm. "But maybe there's a perfect time to introduce yourself. Like when they're more settled in."

Her smile attempts to untangle the knots in my stomach. It doesn't make the unease go away, but it does take the edge off.

"Okay fine. You're right." I resign, turning on the car. "Everyone's right."

"You're right, too," Josie adds. "It's just about the timin'."

"You're starting to sound like Logan." Lydia laughs.

I turn up the radio as I drive out of the parking lot, catching the end of one of our favorite songs before an ad plays. Stuck in the stop-and-go traffic of highschoolers racing home on Friday, we're here for a little while.

Are you having night terrors while awake? Sleep paralysis without the sleep? Terrifying hallucinations beyond your comprehension? You're not losing your mind. You're being haunted by a devious, shapeshifting cryptid! Call us now if—

The Siren station always cuts their ads short, and when this one ends, their Top 10 Hits begin playing, and we sing on the way to our regular pregame spot.

Paulette's Diner is our favorite old gas station turned eatery. It's the only restaurant on the long stretch of road between downtown and the outlet mall. Surrounded by tall grass and sunflowers, the lights from the diner are visible a mile away.

In the valley of the fields, surrounded by periwinkle and maroon wildflowers, and of course the glowing sunflowers, it feels like you're in the heart of the world. Both the middle of nowhere and the center of it all. The mountains carve the skyline with their blue, rounded peaks, and you can see how they knead into the hillside of Veil Haven.

People don't even notice the abandoned history museum tucked on the final wooded hillside before the fields begin. Some ancient, wooded house as forgotten and untouched as whatever history it wanted to teach us. The past stays where it belongs, far more important matters always in our present.

You can see the farmlands of Rook Ranch from here. They grow everything up there and are actually the only civilians who work hand in hand with The Watchers—well, as much as anyone can work directly with the secret organization no one is allowed to mention. The Rooks have been feeding Veil Haven and providing us with everything we need for centuries. And when The Watchers declare famine, the Rooks listen.

As I park beside Paulette's overhang decorated with Edison bulbs and outdoor seating, we see our usual spot through the greasy fingerprinted window.

The conversations of a dozen people saturate the diner with a low hum as the grills steam with oil and butter. Paulette clicks her nails on the checkered counter and smiles at us passively as we walk in, running her sharp nails down her thick black braids. The rotating pie case glitches in place as we move to the side room of the diner.

"Do y'all think we'll win tonight?" Josie asks, sliding into our booth.

I'm pressed against the window as usual.

"Yeah," Lydia says without pause, staring at her phone. She's texting her boss about a late-night shift at the Foodie Mart next week.

"So confident." I laugh, trying to distract her. "This *is* Fox Falls, after all."

"I heard they've been practicin' extra hard just to beat us."

A breathy voice bubbles up in the back of Lydia's mind, some deity reaching out to her, saying only *Lydia...* before she sighs and puts her phone away in a huff. "Josie, don't you think they always do that?"

"It's always a good game, though," I tell her.

"You're gonna be the star of the show," Josie reaches for Lydia's hands.

This makes her smile, and she forgets about her future work commitments. "I guess it can't be helped."

Someone is teaching their granddaughter how to sew. Someone gives a stranger a bouquet of flowers. Someone falls in love with an old friend. Someone feels confident again.

A Cloud Person twirls their fingers through their stratus head as they're lost in a daydream. Someone is video calling their best friend's cat with their cat. Someone separates the ground with their ability and continues gardening.

Someone is dragging a young man to the shed at the back of their property. It's the first time he's going to kill, and in preparation, he has meticulously renovated his shed into a soundproof torture room.

The Watchers have always allowed human desires to play out. If they stepped in every time someone did something bad, then life would lose its luster. That's how the director described it anyway. But while it's easy for them, it's harder for me to ignore the sounds of torment on top of everything else on my plate.

I mindlessly pull out my phone and text Winona the man's name, mainly listening to what my girls are saying.

When Winona sees my texts she simply picks up the cream-colored rotary phone on her desk, speaks the name, and hangs up with a sigh before going back to watching her show.

The man will disappear within the hour, and the young man he kidnapped will be set free.

When Paulette walks to our table, I'm brought back to my present. She makes sure we're ordering our usuals and smiles when we agree. "I already got 'em cookin'." She eyes Lydia, resting her wrists on her hips. "You gonna do good on the field tonight?"

Lydia crosses her arms on the table, leaning close. "I'll dedicate my high kick to you, Paulette."

"Well, in that case, let me throw in an extra-large shake for the table, on me." She makes the Mothmen hand sign and winks before walking off.

We thank her and I smack Lydia's arm. "You always do that, you sweet tooth."

"Good," Josie whispers, "her free shakes are always the best. I don't know what she does to 'em."

"You're just jealous I get more with a smile than you." She sticks her nose up and I laugh her off.

When our burgers and fries arrive, we're in the middle of talking about the new family, agreeing there's a storm of rumors coming. Nobody has anything better to do than talk about what they don't understand.

Lydia pulls a bottle of sriracha from her purse and drowns her fries as I beg her to stop.

"Yeah, stop hoggin' it." Josie takes the bottle.

Lydia cocks her brow. "Ash, you're at least part Latina. You should learn to like this stuff."

"Maybe it's my mysterious upbringing and severe lack of culture." I laugh. "But your plate is swimming in it. You go through a bottle every week. How are your insides not torn to shreds?"

She just shrugs. "I can handle my spices. This Roman nose ain't for nothing."

"Stop—" we shriek.

The sun traces across the sky and nears the mountain ridges as we're happily stuffed. And before I know it, we're pulling up to my green craftsman.

The radio plays some ad in the background as the girls get out of the car. *Chupacabra got your tongue? Some nameless cryptid blockading your home? Poltergeist getting a little too frisky? We've all been there...*

"You guys head inside and get things ready. I have to... do something. I won't be long."

"Okay." Josie smiles. "The face paint is still in that kitchen drawer?"

I nod and they hurry inside with a skip. I just need a moment to myself.

I take a deep breath, and despite my best efforts to ground myself, my mind's eye focuses on Dupont Drive. The Jacksons are some of the only people in town who couldn't care less about the big game. Markus is sitting on the couch watching his sisters laugh and inch closer to the TV playing some game.

Markus is so still and so quiet that I swear I catch him thinking about what he would be doing if they hadn't moved. I swear, however impossible, that for a brief moment he's thinking about some vast never-ending body of dark blue water.

I quickly shake it away. That had to be a misunderstanding. The other towns are just like us—mountains, nothing but mountains. Josie's right. I should be using the noise of game day to distract myself instead of letting these strangers fill my mind.

I leave my car and head inside where Lydia has already begun painting Josie's face with swirling designs. And I know with the certainty that comes with every Friday, that this will be another perfect night.

CHAPTER 5
An Empty Future

Lydia slips into her cheer uniform and takes the diamond stud out of her nose as Josie and I finish applying our face paint. Lydia raids my freezer for some ice cream and I play keep away with her sriracha before she can use it. When I finally resign, she makes me take a bite and I almost spit it out.

Lydia checks her phone when it buzzes. "Okay, my mom is here."

Josie and I give her hugs and then playfully melt to the floor and couch as she leaves.

"Be careful on this darin' journey," Josie warns dramatically.

"Farewell, sister," I coo. "Perhaps we'll meet again after the war!"

Lydia leans against the doorframe as she laughs, holding her sides. "I'll literally see you two at the game. And, Ash, change out of your PJs."

I take her advice and change before Josie and I leave, sliding into my favorite green leggings and some print tee and flannel I find on my bedroom floor.

The mountains cast long shadows across the valley. The sun winks through the blue ridges as we drive. For a moment it seems like that spark of sunlight could set the world ablaze all over again.

Anything is possible if the Void is in the right mood. But second sunrises seldom happen.

Our face paint cracks as Josie and I shout to every song on the radio. By the time I squeeze into the student parking lot, it's already packed. One final ad plays before we park, and I cut the engine:

Have you been witnessing a horror you can't put into words? Are you paralyzed by the fear worming through your gut? Are you seeking answers but finding none? You aren't alone. You aren't alone. You aren't alone. You aren't—

We lock arms and move in wide, swinging steps toward the bottlenecked entrance to the field.

My head hums as hundreds of voices speak at once. Nothing can match the energy under these Friday night lights.

Our school colors are maroon and periwinkle. But no one has ever been able to actually pinpoint those colors on merch, so the crowd is every hue of red and purple.

Once we get through the main gate and walk down the asphalt hill, we see how packed the bleachers are.

"And here I thought we were early," Josie says. "Oh—" She spins one-eighty, clutching my arm as she blushes deeply.

When I follow her gaze, I find Josie's crush at the front corner of the stands.

Ford is a big boy with a big belly and a curly beard he's been trying to fill in since he was old enough to grow it. As Josie describes him, he has the most beautiful face, shining hazel eyes, and a laugh that makes you melt. But if you don't know him, you wouldn't know how funny he is.

Ford appears to be about as miserable as you'd expect an introvert who hates football to be. And Josie's surprise is valid. He never comes to the games. Taking a longer look, I realize a ghost is floating in circles around him. The ghost is about our age and looks like he's wearing a letterman jacket.

Ford is a ghost whisperer, so maybe he thought he could help this new ghost move on by reconnecting to his roots.

Ghosts have always been the piece of my ability that never quite made sense to me. The only people who know I can see ghosts are the director and Chief Mun. I never bothered to tell Winona, and she never cared to ask.

It's strange because while I can see everything in the present, seeing ghosts is an entirely different ability. Ford is a ghost whisperer. I am not. And no one is born with more than one ability. Yet, I can see and hear ghosts all the same.

The Forest Eye once suggested it was simply because I can see the present through the veil, too. Even though that always felt like half an answer, I just let it be. It's hard to press an ancient deity for answers it doesn't want to share.

As Ford's newest ghost friend shouts just as loud as the crowd, Ford crosses his arms tighter, his annoyance rooting deep. I don't think his plan is working.

"Do you want me to call him over?" I grin deviously.

"No!" Josie shrieks, turning back around and switching to my left side. She chuckles, knowing how silly she seems. "What's Ford doin' here?" She steals a glance at him, infatuated by his broad shoulders and big hands.

"I have no idea. But... I guess we'll give him his space. Maybe you can ask him about this later." I nudge her as we move closer to the field.

Josie and I latch on to the chain link fence in front of the stairs and lean over it as much as we can, shouting and waving to get Lydia's attention. She's in a group of women who don't look alike but who are dressed and made up to look exactly alike. She's one of the shortest girls in her squad, barely having to duck under someone's arm. She quickly jogs over to give us awkward hugs across the fence before heading back. We wish her good luck.

Veil Haven fills up both sides of the field bleachers since the only people from the other towns who can visit are the players and coaches. We've never sat on the opposing side, but some people prefer it. They like deafening the visiting team on the benches.

We hop onto the home side of the bleachers and attempt to avoid Ford's line of sight. Luckily, the crowd explodes as the players run onto the field led by our Mothman mascot.

Josie is relieved for the distraction, and we hurry deeper into the stands.

Our mascot is exactly what you'd expect a giant foam Mothman to look like: black wings connected to the arms trailing across the back, red glowing eyes, and foam talons for boots. He's wearing a football helmet that lets his fluffy antennae stick out and a signature maroon and periwinkle Veil Haven jersey.

The mascot does an amazing job doing flips and every crowd-hyping stunt in the handbook. His best trick is phasing through the costume and pretending like he's shown up underdressed before phasing back through. The crowd goes wild, especially the kids.

Finding a seat in the far-off student section would be difficult with everyone already standing shoulder to shoulder, but Shakira and her friends are in the lower middle rung saving space for us.

Josie and I move that way when I spot Chief sitting with his family.

Chief's sons see me and jump up, shouting my name. I wave up at them, matching their sweet excitement. Since they're half-Cloud Person, they only have wisps of clouds circling their faces, sometimes covering their eyes, steaming out of an ear, or hiding their mouth. The appearance of their half-cloud selves changes by day and mood. People who are born mixed have abilities while those who are full Plant or Cloud Person do not. Rather they have unique capabilities per their race.

Chief and Iliana see me in the shifting crowd, and Chief waves at me warmly. Iliana's clouded cumulus head curls softly above her shoulders, her arms crossed. She does not greet me.

The boys ask their dad if they can go see me, but Iliana tells them I have other plans.

And I do, but—

Well, I move on.

And just in time for the crowd to rise as the teams take position on the field.

We only have four teams to play because there are only four other towns. Veil Haven is in the center of the windless plane of Void and stars, and because of our proximity to the other towns, they come to us. It's easier. And we don't have to leave home. The other towns are Fox Falls, Leiton, Railston, and Bescour. Of all the teams, Fox Falls is our main rival.

Some speculate we could even go undefeated every season if it wasn't for them, but that's what makes the games so fun. Fox Falls are the orange and black Chupacabras, and despite knowing nothing about them other than they're good at football, we hate them all the same.

When I look at the people from Fox Falls, it feels like I hit a wall, that I'm being blocked. I've never been able to understand why or what it means, but I think the old mayor chalked it up to them being from across the Void and all the weird rules that follow.

I try not to overthink it, but the Jacksons give off a completely different vibe than any visiting team. Why would they be different?

Logan throws the ball long and Kane uses his telekinesis to pull it into his hands, making a first down at the thirty-yard line. The crowd goes wild. We aren't supposed to use our abilities in public, and I don't know if anything gets more public than this, but there's always exceptions to the rule. If it makes the games better and brings our town pride, you can toe that line.

Josie and Shakira go wild, the two most invested in the game among our mix-matched group. They jump and hug in unison and their long hair bounces wildly. When they aren't shouting creative insults at the other team, we're catching up. I haven't talked to Shakira in a while, so it's nice to hear about her time-traveling.

"My most recent jump was in the park and I saw this really sweet wedding." She tells me more about it between plays, and how her homework from her instructor at the training facility has all the time travelers pop in to visit this wedding. Sounds like it was some big event for the community.

"But anyways." Shakira bumps against me playfully. "I'm always in the past, never the future." She winks.

It's one thing to see the future the way Logan and other oracles do, or even to receive guidance from higher beings like Lydia, but physically going to the future could have more repercussions than even The Watchers could account for. In theory, at least.

I smirk. No wonder Logan likes her so much. Every time she looks at you it feels like you're the center of her world. Welcoming me to share her daring secrets of breaking time traveler rules gives me butterflies. I would never tell anyone she practices future jumps. It would only get her in trouble—or worse. And I don't think she's told anyone besides Logan.

The ball arcs downfield again, but before Logan is able to watch Kane secure the ball, I sense his vision devolving into shades of gray.

The boisterous crowd fades from his senses and are replaced by distant car alarms, crackling fires, and columns of black smoke across the valley. He watches the navy sky bleed to gray as his consciousness slides into the future.

Logan is a boy split by time, half here, half elsewhere, surrounded by friends and no one in the same breath. Our worlds are the same but the timing is off. Without warning he slips into the future, peeking through cracks in the timeline.

He stands in the center of the field alone. The bleachers are empty. His senses are dulled to the present while we remain in his periphery like ghosts.

The ground is dusted with snow and ash. Tire treads have pressed fresh marks across the partially destroyed field. The grass is burned, torn up, bullet casings scattered across it—everything that spells a horrible fight. But how could anyone openly use their abilities for violence? There was obviously backlash from The Watchers. Is that blood in the endzone?

He turns his attention to the sky, to the black pillars of smoke surrounding him. The smoke piles heaviest from downtown. Distant cries of panic travel toward him on a sharp winter breeze and a terrible recognition churns in his gut.

The validity of this future. The promise of it.

The future is always changing and ever-malleable, but some futures are more cemented. Logan can't control when or how far ahead his visions go. He isn't even sure when his visions will happen, but this isn't a simple glance. This is something else entirely.

And as he stands in the middle of that barren field, Veil Haven burning around him, a voice deep within him says, *Your future is empty.*

He's choked by the idea as he's breathing fast. But he blinks and his reality snaps back to the present. Our present.

The future snowmelt returns to the dried grass of early autumn and the crowd deafens him. The opposing players reset to their positions and the boys encircle him.

But he's looking around poised in panic, his eyes moving from the endzone to the unbothered navy sky to the rattling bleachers.

He's scanning the crowd for me and wondering if I saw it too. Even though he can't talk about the future, it's nice to know he's not always alone in his visions. I usually miss them, but this was something else.

As Hayden smacks Logan on the back, he sees Shakira instead. Her bright smile is hard to miss, the golden accents in her hair gleaming, her dark skin glowing in the floodlights. She doesn't notice him staring but it's enough for him. Logan shakes his head and refocuses on the play at hand, everything resuming pace.

"Huh," I say to no one, my shoulders going slack. Did he just see Veil Haven burning? Chaos like that doesn't happen here. It can't. My hairs stand on end the more I think of it, comparing it to my real-dream, to the new family, to Chief not hearing me out.

Josie grabs my arm as she jumps to celebrate another great play, but I'm thrown from my thoughts.

The bleachers shake and my head pounds with the noise. Every individual conversation roars in my mind. Every light and color blurs together, even when I close my eyes.

Someone is doodling on their homework. Someone hears their own voice calling to them from the woods. Someone is being protected by Beings of Light on the hiking trails. Someone on a date wonders who will buy the movie tickets; they're both girls and she's never done this before. Someone pauses in their hallway meeting a pair of red eyes in the dark. Someone is flying to the outermost reaches of the sky and disappears into the Void.

Josie registers my constipated look. I feel her thigh against mine as she slides close. She cups her hands over my ears to muffle the noise, and while it shouldn't, it helps. I study the sunflower ring in her hazel eyes. Her chipped-tooth smile grounds me.

"Is it better now?" she asks, her soft voice humming beneath the crowd.

"Yeah." I breathe, coming back to myself. "Thank you."

She removes her hands. "It's been a great game so far." She returns her attention to the field, and we watch the players trade places with the marching band and cheerleaders. Hayden winks at Lydia as they pass, and she rolls her eyes.

We watch as Lydia lifted to the top of the cheer pyramid. With two pumps and a high kick, she's launched spinning into the air. We wave frantically to get her attention, and she waves at us laughing.

But as the show continues, I can't help but focus on Logan. He's hunched over holding his head on the sideline bench. He tunes out the conversations around him as he tries to understand what he saw. Brows stitched together, he decides now isn't the time. He'll ask his oracle instructor later. But in the pit of his stomach he knows this wasn't meant for anyone else. This was meant for him.

It wasn't just the future of our town, it was his.

A cool breeze cuts into the valley reminding everyone that autumn is here, as though the football game didn't make it obvious enough. The clock ticks down, and nobody is certain we'll pull off the win. Fox Falls has the ball, and our boys are pushing them back as best they can, but they're inching dangerously close to the end zone. A touchdown this close to the end will secure their win. Everyone is at the edge of their seats hyperfocusing on what comes next.

But my focus shifts to someone standing by the goal line clutching the fence. It's Markus, the new kid. My chest tightens. I didn't realize he was coming to the game. I didn't think I would be so close to him so soon.

I stand up before the rest of the crowd rises with a deafening roar. We caught an interception. The electric joy of this many people at once is intoxicatingly warm. It sends shivers down my spine but I ground myself as I stare at Markus and how out of place he feels. My ears ring as my heart beats faster. I'm looking at someone I've never known—a stranger, a real true stranger. Is this what other people feel? This choking mystery?

I try to sound as sincere as possible as I tell the girls I have to go to the bathroom, but they're more lost in the game than focused on me.

Getting off the bleachers is easier this time with everyone glued to the field, but I have to push past people frozen in place at the concessions while they watch Logan throw the ball toward the end zone, Kane speeding after it. I slide and shoulder past them as Markus studies the players, Kane running closer to him. The tension in the crowd rises as the Chupacabras charge after him, but I can only focus on Markus and how close I am to somebody so strange.

I'm trying to figure out what I'm going to say when static fills my ears—my attention pulling me to the field. Kane moves across the five-yard line as the ball brushes his fingertips, but with a final stretch and his command over the ball, it nestles perfectly into his palm just as he crosses the endzone.

That's when the other players slam into him.

The world explodes with sound. I hear a harsh crunching in that dogpile as they collapse onto him. His head knocks against the other players before landing headfirst onto the ground, ball still in hand.

Everyone is celebrating the assured victory, but my knees buckle at the sight of it. I grip the fence as Kane holds down his vomit, the other players stumbling off him. He has his back to the crowd so nobody sees him, but I'm only feet away watching as he begs his shaking legs to steady. The world is spinning around him, his ears ringing like a bomb went off. It's impossible for him to open his eyes without wanting to vomit. Does he taste blood? The acid sting chars the back of his throat and he forces himself to stand before he retches.

The thundering celebrations blur our worlds in separate ways.

He stumbles in place, and when he opens his eyes, the stadium lights make starbursts over his vision. *Mind over matter,* he seethes, daring himself to take one wobbling step at a time. He lifts his shaking hand to the crowd and they burst with noise again. He winces and grinds his molars, forcing that smile. People are waving and cheering him on. How does no one else see this?

He moves slowly as he scans the crowd, but when he lands on me at the sideline fence unable to hide my concern, his gaze darkens. He would shake his head if the pain wasn't killing him.

He's still planning to play, he's going to muscle through it, and I want to yell *no*, the heat rising in my chest. He has a concussion. He needs to go to the hospital. Not injure himself more. But he's not going to let me get a word in edgewise.

"Don't," he tells me, too quiet for anyone else to hear.

I swear I catch the soft glance of the best friend I used to know. That kind boy who would chase me around our yards for hours, who would leave me coded messages in his bedroom window, who would sneak out to watch R-rated movies with me at night.

And when he says, "You owe me that much," my flooding emotions grow darker, the sharp flashes of betrayal cutting through his blue eyes: the loss of his uncle, the wave of rumors that destroyed my reputation, everything circling back to the two of us and the friendship we had.

The noise of the crowd pulses in our heads. "Don't tell anyone." He winces in the light, forcing himself to walk to the bench line, eyeing me from our distance. "Please."

I look away as he gains momentum in his stride, checking back on me just once before settling in with his team. And I nod, mouthing, "Fine."

Chills roll down my spine. Maybe I can convince him to see a doctor after the game. His friends pat him on the back as he grits through the pain, trying to celebrate like nothing's wrong. And it's working.

When Josie's gut reaction is to turn to me and celebrate she realizes I'm still not back from the bathroom, and I remember why I came down here in the first place. Markus. But he's already gone, walking back to his house, hoodie up, hands in his pocket.

I missed my chance. But I'm not letting it get away from me.

The excitement of the game has shifted, and I have to hide the worry-pit forming in my gut. Why would Kane look at me like that? I haven't thought of him as my best friend in years, not after the rumors he started about me in middle school. He's using it against me, and I've fallen for it. But something bigger has my attention, something far more important than whatever I may or may not owe Kane.

Before he gets too far away, I leave the riot of noise and chase after Markus.

CHAPTER 6
STRANGER IN A STRANGE LAND

It doesn't take me more than a couple of minutes to catch up with him. The cool air nips my ears and nose as I jog. I huff and catch my breath as I finally see him.

I'm surprised Markus would risk a nighttime walk. It's not like the cryptids would spare a newcomer. If anything he's an easy target.

As if asking for it, a cryptid manifests. It is a tall, lanky man holding an acoustic guitar with thick long hair and a voice that worms inside you so completely you forget who you are. The purple streetlight hides the not-man's handsome, hollow face, too-wide mouth, and dark eyes that aren't quite human. The night sounds, streetlight shadows, and warm road set the siren in his natural environment.

This cryptid has a name but not many can pronounce it. Something with an H and a Z. He strums his guitar and sings his enchanting melancholic folk tune.

Cryptids hunger in many ways, and not all of them desire flesh.

Markus pauses along the road as the song begins. His eyes glaze over as the cryptid's song slowly drives its mental claws into Markus' mind. If he listens long enough, if he's pulled into the siren's reach, he'll become another puppet to be toyed with. Another host to feed from.

But first Markus has to come closer... come closer... one step... at a time... But not before I—

"Ow." I rub my arm. I'm not sure why I tried to bodycheck him out of the trance, especially since it doesn't work. We're only a few yards away and Markus keeps moving forward. If the cryptid touches him, they'll be transported into the deep woods.

I have too much noise in my head for any siren to stake its claim on me, but Markus is my responsibility, even if we've never met. So, no time to waste.

I walk ahead of Markus, meeting the cryptid halfway, and glare at him, teeth clenched, white eyes wide, daring him to cross me.

The cryptid smirks, his mouth too large and stretched, his eyes hidden in his dark hair. He lowers his guitar and the night sounds still, leaving us in a deadly silence, as if even the woods are holding their breath.

The purple streetlight casts strange shadows across his face as he lifts his head, revealing his hypnotic eyes. His smile harbors way too many teeth.

The longer I stare at him I almost catch myself mesmerized... wondering how far that smile will reach. But I blink.

He winks and bows, though I'm not sure why. Have I bested him? Whatever the sentiment, I don't reciprocate it. And as he continues to bow, his entire form folds over on himself. He blips away—rematerializing deep within the woods, strumming his guitar to no one.

My shoulders ease as I rub my face, shaking off any nerves.

Markus falls out of the trance without a shred of awareness. He pauses when he sees me ahead of him, certain I was not there before.

"Uhm," is all he manages to say.

I spin around, the purple light illuminating us in the weeds along the road.

Markus is taller than I expected, well, taller than me. He has broad shoulders, a big body, and a distinct don't-bother-me aura. If I didn't know any better I would call him intimidating. But I've met far more intimidating figures than him.

For the sake of a new friendship, I decide not to mention the encounter.

"It's dangerous to walk alone at night, y'know," I say, brushing the short black hair from my eyes. I tug on my flannel to appear more presentable. "You're definitely new here."

Markus stares at me for a moment, still wondering where I came from. He shoves his hands deeper into his black hoodie pocket and scoffs. "How do you know I'm new?"

I swing my arms as I close the distance between us. "Small town. I know everything. You're obvious. Take your pick."

He grunts and continues walking, moving beneath the streetlight without pause.

I follow after him.

The roadside canopy blankets us from the milky stars. The far between streetlights seem to beg for another cryptid encounter. Hopefully I'm enough to keep them away.

"I'm Ash."

Markus lowers his hood, his neatly twisted hair bouncing a little as he does. The purple streetlight glows upon his dark skin. He has big, brown eyes, the smoothest complexion a teenager could dream of, and downturned lips. He eyes me skeptically and has yet to lower his raised brows.

"Markus," he says. "Is this one of those small towns where somebody moving in is the biggest news?"

"How'd you guess?" I tuck my hands inside my flannel sleeves. "I don't think anyone's ever moved to Veil Haven though. How'd you even get here?"

He looks at me funny, his nose scrunching as he squints. "A car, the road. Y'know, the usual? I was asleep by the time we got here. We've never lived in the mountains before."

I am trying to understand, but every word feels like a curveball and a gut punch. "That's weird… I thought the other towns were mountainous too."

His brows furrow as he tries to understand *me*. "I mean we were pretty close to the beach before this."

My chest tightens as the vague image of crashing waves pass through his mind—the blinding sun and sand between his toes, in his hair, under his nails. My gut knots. I have to be mistaken.

"The ocean?" I whisper carefully. The sound of it barely crosses my lips.

He hums in agreement and looks away like *I'm* crazy. "But it's whatever." He shrugs. "This is just a new place to explore before moving again." He sighs, annoyed by the concept. "You've lived here your whole life?"

I sway a little with each step, trying hard to shake this feeling. It's just a mistake. The ocean isn't real. Just me misunderstanding what's in his head. He's still too new for me anyway. "Yeah," I say, trying to keep this conversation alive. "Yeah, we all have."

"Weird. I wonder what that's like. But listen, I know people are infatuated with the new kid, wanting a taste of something different or whatever, but it's a waste of time. I'll be gone before things get interesting. I always am."

"I don't think you're moving again from the sounds of it. The mayor said they were bringing your family in as some initiative or something."

"You talked to the mayor?" He laughs. "God, what Podunk town am I in?"

"Well I work for her or through her. It doesn't matter. People in Veil Haven don't leave. Like, that's why the other teams come here for football and why we never go there. Are you from Fox Falls?"

Markus blinks twice as if I've spoken another language. He shakes his head as we continue down the road, watching as headlights curve around the bends. "I don't even know where to begin with that but uhm no, we moved from Surfside Beach."

I'm trying to keep pace with everything he says but *what*?

He feels the same way with me.

I'm pretty sure we're both speaking English. Like, I understand the words individually but they're not computing. "Is that a nickname for... Leiton... or Railston?" I watch his brows lower. "Bescour?"

"Are you high? What are you talking about?"

"No." I force a laugh, looking away. "It's just the mayor told me you came from Fox Falls, and I've never heard it called *Surfside Beach* before. Is that some sort of joke?"

He squints at me like I'm crazy, and I know I'm losing him. Whether they call it Fox Falls or not, that's the only explanation that makes sense.

I try to laugh off our tense silence. "You're just so different, Markus. This whole thing is foreign to me. I've been in the same classes with the same people my whole life. I know their parents. I know everyone. I don't know anything about you."

Markus smirks as I lead him through a shortcut to his neighborhood street, avoiding downtown and the lake.

"Everyone needs a healthy dose of mystery," he says, rolling his shoulders. "I guess I can be that for you, for the time being."

"Yeah." I huff, air quoting as I speak. "Until you *move away again*. I think you're stuck here, Markus. But at least you're stuck with me. I mean, someone's gotta keep you safe."

He laughs hard, looking down on my small frame. It's a good laugh, the genuine kind. The infectious kind. "Yeah, okay, Ash. You keep me safe."

My mind's eye searches our radius, scanning the dark and finding all the curious eyes shifting over us. I decide not to mention them. Ignorance is bliss and all that.

I shift my attention back to us and bring up Lydia's afterparty, trying to sell him on it. But he shoots me down, saying the party scene isn't really for him, and he promised his family he was just going for a walk.

I mention his new house and how it's been vacant for a while after the owner disappeared. He seems confused by that but jokes about me already knowing where he lives. That it must be really boring here if people think a new family is this interesting.

"Depends on your definition of boring. There's always something happening." I laugh. "That much I can guarantee."

As we approach his house, every window glows as his sisters run around inside playing tag unsupervised.

"You have to stick around long enough so I can learn more about you."

He laughs. "You're pretty forward."

We stand at the base of his yard where the steps cut into the hill leading to his porch. The Victorian is a beacon of light along their street as the rest of their neighbors are dark save for a few garage parties. The sound of celebration of another game won chimes through the trees, even from here, even without my ability. The final score is 30–27.

"You're the first person who's talked to me here," he says warmly, "the neighbors just stare at me. But I'm telling you it's a waste." He looks up at his new home. "Wherever we move we're always on the road again. So it's not worth it. Just ignore me like everyone else will."

"Ignoring people isn't really my thing."

He smirks, heading up. "Goodnight, Ash."

"Goodnight, Markus. I'll see you around." I watch him close the front door.

Maybe what I've been seeing really does align with what Winona and Chief said. They're just a normal family. But what about him mentioning the beach? No, it was just a misunderstanding. The ocean doesn't exist. The other towns are just like us.

I shake my head, but something catches my attention in the upstairs window.

Someone is standing in the master bedroom, staring at the street, at me. It makes my entire body shiver. They're just a dark shape, something not even my mind's eye can make out.

Markus' mother lies unmoving in bed, tubes and sensors hooked up to machines. This isn't her.

Markus is just now tackling his sisters in the living room.

No one else is in the house.

My body flushes with chills not because there's a cryptid is in their home but because there isn't. This isn't even a Shadow Person. I can see those cryptids. I can even see ghosts. But the figure I'm staring at gives me a headache.

My eyes water trying to understand it, my brain itching. Through my mind's eye there is nothing there at all. Not even the sense of a person. Yet here I am staring at the very real shape of someone shadowed by the night. And they are staring down at me.

For a moment the entire world slows to a hush. I try to understand what's happening—what I'm seeing, what I'm not. My ability promises no one is there, just a trick of the light. But I know what I'm seeing and I've felt this before.

It's the same discomfort as the Mysterious Mountain Lights.

My head pulses as I try to grasp what I'm seeing and not seeing. And as I stand under this now-towering house, the world tilting in my periphery, I watch as Markus passes through the front windows of the living room and heads upstairs.

My core temperature drops as the figure turns, pausing on me one last time before leaving the window.

I curse under my breath and step forward. Are they in danger? Should I go in there?

Markus doesn't seem to notice the dark figure.

I swallow and stare at the Victorian for a moment longer, hoping to catch another glimpse of that *thing*. Even with all my senses heightened, my mind's eye filling every room in the house, there's nothing.

My shoulders and chest are so tense I physically ache, the pit in my stomach growing. I never understood the feeling of facing the unknown, but it's horrifying. I refuse this feeling. I refuse the possibility that my eyes are playing tricks on me.

Something is going on with the Jacksons, and I'm going to find out what.

CHAPTER 7
Encounters Happen, Make Them Safe

I rap against the door with the same urgency I hope Markus will answer with. I see him sit upright in bed, brows stitched, but he hesitates. Which is why I audibly gasp when the door opens anyway.

A handsome, older black man with chiseled features and short, natural curls greets me with a curious smile. But I can't see him.

With my physical eyes, he's standing in front of me. But through my mind's eye I see nothing but an open door and an empty hallway. I step back, my throat tight. My eyes water a bit as I stare at him, though it's hard. It's like looking through binoculars with a lens blacked out. It's like looking at the Mysterious Mountain Lights.

The man smiles at me as though meeting an old friend. He shares Markus' dark skin tone but the likeness stops there. He has a slim face and nearly black eyes. He's a little taller than I am, which is saying something. The man has a towel over his shoulder as if he's been cleaning the dishes, his sleeves rolled up to his elbows. His work shirt revealing his toned physique.

"Hi, can I help you?"

It takes a moment to find my voice. "Who are you?"

The man laughs, though it's more of a low rumble and almost

ingenuine. "Well, young lady, you're on my porch. Don't you think I should be asking *you* that question?"

"I'm Ash. Who are you to Markus?"

His smile grows and I notice a dark shine in his eyes, as if we're playing some sort of lying game. "Oh, you're friends with Markus? I'm his stepdad. But you can call me Declan." He extends his hand for me to shake.

I almost don't touch him, my gut quivering as my mind's eye tries but fails to grasp on to him. And when I take his hand, nothing changes except the goosebumps rising across my body.

Warning bells shriek in my head as the world rises from my periphery like a flood.

Someone is being chased through the woods. Someone is holding their breath under their bed. A Plant Person tosses their long pothos vines over their shoulder and storms away from a heated discussion. Someone stubs their toes and in their anger-response, levitates all the metal objects in their kitchen. Someone is cornered. Someone is pulled under the surface of the Black River.

I can't see Declan with my ability. I'm blind to his existence unless he's standing right in front of me. I've never faced something so dangerous before.

Markus descends the stairs and the noise in my head becomes a hushed static, allowing me to rejoin the moment.

"Ash? Everything good?"

Someone goes outside and manifests lightning into their hands just to feel its power. A Cloud Person holds their breath, counts to ten, and their cumulonimbus head returns to a cumulus. Someone is having a sleepover. Someone digs up a missing person in their backyard after following clues left around their house by a ghost.

Someone is driving around with their friends screeching the lyrics to their favorite song when they slam on their breaks. Everyone falls silent as they stare at a woman veiled in white. Brown sludge drips from her face and hands, illuminated by the headlights. The driver hits the gas and runs her over as they all scream and tell him to drive faster.

I swallow the shake in my voice. "Oh, yeah. Sorry, I just thought it might be nice to swap numbers. In case you wanted to hang out later or if you needed anything." I eye Declan as he stands between the two of us like a guard, still smiling.

"You didn't tell me you made a friend," Declan says.

"Well, I mean, we just met," Markus half-mumbles.

"Yeah, we only just met." I can't take my eyes off him no matter how much my body is begging me to look anywhere else.

Markus shuffles beside his stepdad as we exchange numbers, and in this moment we share the awkwardness of Declan looming over us. To Markus, it must feel like a proud but nosy parent. But to me, I might as well be a deer, and Declan's gaze is the crosshairs.

"Okay, well, yeah," Markus says. "I guess I'll see you around."

"Yeah, Markus, have a good weekend."

"It was so nice to meet you," Declan says. "I'm sure we'll see each other again."

I nod, and he closes the door.

I stay on their porch for what feels like hours, but only seconds pass. I have to force myself to leave before they notice.

I avoid everyone.

I don't go to Lydia's party.

And as I walk back to my car, I hear a small pack of Night Crawlers hissing as they skitter closer to me on all fours.

Their lanky arms and legs make them look like deformed, fleshy spiders. The streetlights illuminate their moist, burn-victim flesh and the rows of razor-sharp teeth protruding from their tiny bulb heads.

I don't have time for this. I turn on my phone's flashlight and yell as I run at them. They're surprised by my sudden movements and scurry away quickly, hissing and clicking to each other.

With shaking hands, I drive home.

Sitting on my bed for a long time, the noise of Veil Haven washes over me.

Someone is falling, and falling, and falling. Someone is trapped in sleep paralysis watching a shadowy man crawl across their ceiling. Someone can't start their car. Someone walks into the lake.

Josie, Lydia, and Shakira are laughing at the afterparty. Hayden smacks Kane on the back. Kane seethes quietly, his head throbbing. Logan admires Shakira from afar, but he's distant too. Like me.

His vision.

My eyes widen. I pull my knees to my chest as I stare out my window. I already forgot about Logan's vision. Veil Haven burning. His private future.

But it can't come true. Not all future visions are real. They get replaced, or they shift and smooth over. And The Watchers would never allow our town to burn or be attacked or whatever that vision promised. They protect us. They keep us safe. That's why they're always watching.

But they let Declan Jackson into our home. The man I can't see. Do they know that?

Finally stomaching the idea of saying it out loud, I hold my phone to my ear and wait for Winona to answer. I don't give her the breath to say hello, and all the tension inside me comes screaming out.

"I can't see him! Winona, why can't I see him? I've never not been able to see someone before."

"Whoa, whoa, Ash, what are you talking about?"

Winona is lying on the couch watching a movie on the projector screen she's pulled down over the window overlooking the lake. The movie continues in the background. She doesn't pause it.

"Declan Jackson," I yell. "Why can't I see him? Do The Watchers know? I've never not been able to see someone before, I—"

Her brows raise but she sounds just as monotoned and exhausted as always. "Ash, calm down. Whatever it is, it's fine. There are no surprises on our end."

"You *knew*?" Warmth rises in my face.

Someone cuts their finger chopping vegetables. Someone drives into a parked car. Someone is bitten by their cat. Someone is pushed down the stairs. Someone shares a secret that isn't theirs. Someone faces a Skeletal Shifter with their young friends, all of them equipped with fire; this cryptid is mimicking their friend's cries, and they are going to get him back.

Winona pauses, not sure which will calm my nerves more: a lie, or her version of the truth. "I personally did not know, but it's not a big deal. Yes, it feels that way right now, but you know nothing slips by Director Capaldi. Everything is going according to plan."

"How can you say that to me right now?" My voice strains. "I want you to call him and tell him I wanna talk. I'm coming over right now."

"Ash, I don't want to see you." She sighs, shifting her attention back to the movie. "And I'm not calling the director. Just because you can't see Mr. Jackson doesn't mean he isn't being watched. I told you we're trying something new. You'll understand in time."

Before I can get in another word she hangs up.

I stare at the phone for a long time.

The static of the world pitches as if someone is about to speak. My eyes glance to my closet for a second, my chest growing tighter, but instead I turn to the sky. I don't even realize the tears brimming my lashes until I try to speak. Except I can't find the words. So I just stare at the rainbow stars in their milky avenue across the Void until the warmth in my face turns to fire, and the knot in my stomach hardens like lead.

How could they lie to me like this?

How could they bring in an outsider that I can't see? Why can't I see him? How is that possible?

I remember Director Capaldi telling me again and again how my ability works. That I can see everything. That nothing is kept secret from me. I can hear him so clearly. *"You can see it all, Ash. You're more important than you know."*

I wipe away the tears as I glare at the Void. "Why are they pushing me away?" I scream through the glass and clench my jaw, expecting some simple answer. But the stars don't fall and no voice whispers in the back of my mind.

Then the cosmic joke begins again. I know it well.

On the far mountain ridge, deep on the western peaks, an orb of light shimmers through the darkness. In my mind's eye, the mountains remain dark. I am half-blind once again. Maybe I always have been. A second light blooms. I glare. As if offended, they blink out of existence.

I grind my molars.

I can't call Chief because... well, because he's *with* Iliana.

I don't want to bother Lydia and Josie because I've already messed up our routine enough. Bailed on them. Given no explanation.

I don't want to bring this up to Logan because all I want to talk about with him is that vision—but we can't.

I stare at the black horizon cutting into the stars. This doesn't make any sense.

An idea snakes into my mind, but I shake it loose. Declan can't be associated with The Watchers. I can see The Watchers when they're in town. I can see Director Capaldi when he's standing in front of me. This is different. This is unknown.

And for me, unknown is dangerous.

I shove my face into my pillows and scream. How could Winona shut me down? How can they shut me out like this? I'm tired of pretending to "just be a kid," when I was never taught *how* to begin with. I don't want to lie around and wait and ignore and do nothing.

But...

I hear the director again, the phantom of my memories, and he cautions me to be good. Everyone in town knows what happens when I interfere. After all, I was born to watch. Not act.

I roll over and rub my face, the tension in my chest suffocating me. I keep going over that moment. A figure in the window. An open door. Declan standing there, my mind's eye seeing an empty hallway. How can he be invisible to me?

I repeat these questions but find no answers. Then somewhere along the passage of the night, despite it all, I fall asleep.

CHAPTER 8
THE KEEPERS OF THE COAST

As the world shifts to its night crew, the cryptids stir from the trees. They creep onto our streets and tap against windows doing anything to stir people from their homes. Death isn't certain in these hours, but it wouldn't be a surprise, either. It never is.

As I lie sleeping, visions of the town pass through my mind's eye.

The woods hold many secrets, and some are willing to pay any price to know them.

There isn't a set gathering place for the Keepers of the Coast outside their weird little castle, but you can always find them shifting around the woods. Their practices demand privacy and when you're inside you never know who's watching.

They gather deep enough in the woods so the prying eyes of town can't see them. Except for mine.

A couple dozen hooded figures in dark blue mud-stained cloaks hum ominously as they encircle their firelit obelisk shrine. Beneath the fire, dusted with rosemary, lavender, and wormwood lies the ceremonial obsidian dagger. It catches the firelight on its sharp, uneven edges like it has some strange heartbeat.

The Keepers of the Coast are not so much a secret than a terrible reality. They certainly aren't the only cult in town but they're the one no one likes to talk about.

Their cult was formed from some "ancient text" they "found" that mentions a world outside of Veil Haven. And in that world, there is an ocean—a vast body of water with unknown depths. The very opposite of our mountains.

This, of course, is in direct conflict to the truth we all know. The only things outside of Veil Haven are the Void and the four towns encircling ours. There is no ocean or other world, only the windless plane of Void and stars.

The Keepers of the Coast don't always gather for sacrifice. Most of their meetings are about contacting *previous* members. And while nothing has ever come from these meetings, they still gather. They still sacrifice. And I'm still forced to watch.

The cultists' humming intensifies as one of their members, dressed in a navy and gold robe smelling of mothballs and metallic gore, steps out of the circle and approaches the obelisk shrine.

None of the members know each other's names, but once you are chosen to sacrifice yourself, you must reveal who you are so they can guide you back from beyond the veil.

The man in the ceremonial robe removes the massive hood and faces the group; his pale, balding head glowing in the firelight.

"I am Harrison Isdale. I've worked at the automotive center for fourteen years. I was born with the ability to manipulate my bone matter. And I am willing to sacrifice my life for the pursuit of the truth. My beautiful wife Alora and my incredible daughter Nia do not know."

In a deep murmur the cult answers in unison, "They do not know so that you may know. Thank you for carrying our burden."

Harrison has spent a lifetime wondering. He has considered the balance of Veil Haven, how the dead come to life, and all the inconsistencies of our government's rule. He has decided that the reason why previous members haven't returned is because they were too weak of spirit and couldn't remember their purpose after death.

Harrison is certain he will be the one to return to his cult with the great truth of the ocean.

He turns to face the flaming obelisk and tries to memorize every second of this moment.

He takes the ceremonial dagger, tilts his head to the dark lilac sky, and with one swift motion slits his throat open like a smile.

I cannot look away.

Harrison falls to his knees. And in the fading twilight of his life, certain of his purpose, he collapses on the dirt and blood and finally rests.

Harrison Isdale is dead, and his daughter Nia turns passively in her sleep, feeling no supernatural difference between a world where her father is alive and a world where he is gone.

The surrounding cult members hum louder, raising their arms to the sky and chanting their nonsense language so loudly it echoes through the trees. Not even the cryptids want to deal with them. Not tonight, at least.

It has always been a simple ritual. Now they will remove the ceremonial cloak, dip their fingers in his blood, and mark his skin with meaningless symbols. The police will find him later but there will be no investigation.

All that for what? No secrets will be revealed, and now there's one more fatherless person in Veil Haven. It's not a club many are comfortable joining. But as I've understood it, being raised without parents is far easier than losing them.

This isn't where my night ends.

When one event is over, but I'm still asleep, my mind's eye has to fill the time with another interesting moment.

It begins to focus on a few kids sneaking out of a bedroom window. One of their friends is missing, and they think they know how to save him. But just as I begin to sink in, my perspective is whipped away and forcibly refocused at the tree line near the fields.

It's not uncommon for this to happen when I'm dreaming, especially if something more exciting happens, but this is different.

Something is *grabbing* my attention.

Vines and roots recede into the woods like bloodstained snakes, leaving something behind for me to witness in the tall grasses.

First the Forest Eye speaks to me at the abandoned carnival and now it's manipulating my attention while I sleep? The Forest Eye knows I can't run from it in my sleep, not before I witness what it has to say.

Written in blood and body parts is the simple yet poignant message: WE NEED TO TALK.

And I can't look away, can't ignore the gore of it.

My mind's eye zooms closer and closer to the bloodstained grass and still-bleeding limbs.

Who did they kill to leave me this message?

My sheets are hot and damp as I turn over in bed. I can't look away. I can't get away. The Forest Eye has grabbed my eye and is holding me here, forcing me to see its message like some dog who pooped in the house.

I inch closer and closer to the limbs and wet grass. It's making sure this moment sticks.

I turn and kick, and just before I'm about to wake up, I'm released like a sigh. My body eases as my mind's eye flickers back to the kids on a rescue mission.

Their flashlights burn through an abandoned cabin, everyone pointing at a trapdoor in the floorboards. The four of them look between each other. With shaking knees and brave spirits, they agree to venture deeper into the dark. Neither of us know what will happen, but we both know what needs to be done.

CHAPTER 9
MUSCLE MEMORY

By the morning, the Forest Eye's message has been dragged away by predators. The blood will be washed away by the next rain. No one will ever know what happened there.

Who did it kill to get my attention? *How* did it get my attention? I'm supposed to be safe here.

At the carnival I understood why it could speak to me. I was at the tree line. I was in the woods. But I'm home. In bed. Yes, tucked between the mountains in my holler, but it counts as town. It's always counted. Has the Forest Eye found some loophole? Was it because I was witnessing the cult in the woods?

The chills running down my neck don't cease, and my breath gets away from me.

Someone watches hair crawling out of their shower drain, and without pause they flick a lighter in front of a can of bug spray and the hair is singed away; they leave the bathroom rolling their eyes. A maple tree-headed Plant Person leaves a trail of red leaves behind them as they walk down their work corridor. Someone is using the diving pool at the training facility to track how long they can hold their breath. A Cloud Person watches vapor rise out of a deep cut on their leg while blood pools beneath them.

I clutch the covers close and take a deep breath. I count the seconds and then exhale.

Everything is fine.

Except that's the opposite of true.

A new family is in town. I didn't see them arrive. Logan had a vision of the town on fire. I can't see Declan. Winona and Chief are pushing me away. The director still won't reach out to me. And now this?

I didn't exactly leave on good terms with the Forest Eye some four years ago. But I made it clear when I left the Heart of the Woods that I was done.

I was eight when we officially met. This was before my girls and back when Kane and I were still friends. The Forest Eye raised me over the years as I visited it in secret. This was a separate affair from Director Capaldi and Chief raising me, though they overlapped.

I guess they all wanted their say in how I turned out. I guess I was more than willing to accept any family that wanted me.

The Forest Eye taught me how to control my omniscience. It loved me and protected me, but the cryptid god is possessive. And it hates humanity. Even though it acted like it loved me, it couldn't outplay its nature forever.

I kept our relationship a secret for years until eventually I told Chief. His concern snapped me out of its trance. Director Capaldi had always known, but he let me manage myself.

I was thirteen when I left. My fight with the Forest Eye was so bad I thought the cryptid god was going to reshape the mountains. People still talk about that week's string of cryptid attacks. But when I walked out of the woods, I never went back. From then on I focused on Director Capaldi and Chief Mun. They are the good in my life. If it weren't for Chief I don't know how I would've ended up.

I met Chief the month after I ran away and met the Forest Eye for the first time.

I can't remember why I wanted to run away, but I had a very hard time when I was little. I had no control over my ability,

Director Capaldi was pushing me too hard, tensions in town were rising against me, and the noise was so painful not even our best healers could help me.

So I ran as far from the noise as I could. And tucked deep and far within the mountains, I found the Forest Eye. It led me to its safe haven in the Wildwoods.

I was there for over a month.

The Forest Eye taught me how to quiet the noise in my head. It had eons of experience with its omnipotence, and it became my first real teacher. That initial month felt like years, and our connection was so real I was certain it had always been there, like we had known each other for lifetimes.

It showered me with silence and attention, and I thought that was love. It was bliss. But in the beginning even it agreed I should return home. I would come to visit it regularly for years to come. We were family, after all.

Only a few people called it a miracle when I returned unscathed. Everyone else glowered at my luck as though my survival was a direct afront to everyone who'd died in the woods. That's when the rumors began that I was some sort of cryptid.

Everybody thought I was dead but the director knew I was just throwing a tantrum. He expected me to come back completely fine. I'm not sure how he knew, but I chalked it up to his faith in me. It was nice to be believed in.

But when I returned, nobody was very happy about it. Except the chief of police.

When I came home covered in dirt and sweetrot, I was met by a short man with a kind face. I had seen him before, but we'd never officially met. The director assured me I didn't need to bother myself with in-town politics or any of the pawns that worked for The Watchers.

Usually, when Chief Mun was tasked with finding a missing kid, he wouldn't bother looking. He already knew the outcome.

But paired with the director's promise that I would survive, Chief knew when I was ready, I would simply come home. And he was right.

I stood on my porch and stared at the man in my house who slowly removed his wide brim hat. I quietly asked him if I was in trouble.

"No." Chief's dark eyes were reassuring. "Of course not. It's a miracle you're back."

"Are you sure he isn't mad?" I glanced over his shoulder at the cream-colored rotary phone I kept in the corner of my living room. "I can't see him, so you have to tell me if he's mad."

Chief's gaze softened, a soreness to his smile. "How about you take a nice, warm shower and when you're done, I'll make us dinner."

"You're the chief of police. Don't you have more important things to take care of?"

Chief Mun cupped my shoulder. "Ash, you *are* important."

I had been called important dozens of times by government officials and strange people in dark suits, but that was the first time I felt comforted by it.

It was the first time it felt genuinely kind.

I washed off the forest grime, and we had dinner together. To memory, it was the first dinner I shared with an adult that didn't feel like a chore or a meeting. We introduced ourselves and talked about nothing. It was the beginning of our friendship.

I've ignored the Forest Eye for four long years, but I know now it has its sight on me and the cryptid god isn't going to leave me alone. I have to shut down whatever conniving plan it's created. I can't allow it to manipulate me in my search for answers with Declan and everything else happening. I won't let it.

The Riverside Cemetery is the town's main burial place. Family graveyards and a few random tombstones are scattered across town and the woods, but this lush, grassy area is the place to be. Even though half the graves don't have anyone buried beneath them.

A pretty clear deer path leads to the back right of the cemetery along the Black River, leading to Offerings Dock. That's the only safe place you can be near the river besides the riverwalk downtown, and even that doesn't really count as close.

My destination is unmarked, not unlike the graves in the back of the cemetery. Any dates on these old tombstones have been long removed. No one is left to mourn whoever is buried there, anyway. Not even the ghosts remember.

The back left of Riverside is away from any of the bereaved who might wander the cemetery, and it gives me some space from the ghosts milling about, too. Not even the curious spirits want to follow me here.

I move slowly toward the tree line. The ghosts watch me at a distance, whispering to one another.

I try to steel my nerves with a little mantra. *I'm still in town. I'm still safe.* But it doesn't exactly inspire confidence. I cross my arms and wait.

I doubt the Forest Eye will teleport here to greet me. Speaking through the trees has always been its preferred method of communication anyway. Though I suppose now I can add dream manipulation to the list.

"I'm here," I address the trees. There's more bite to my tone than I expected, but I can't help the knotted tension in the center of my chest. It suffocates me. And even worse is that I already know the Forest Eye can see me. "You've grabbed my attention. What do you want?"

The woods become silent. Every creature flees or stills with fear.

A distinct pressure builds around my head as if my mind is gripped by an invisible palm, and the entire essence of the forest converges through me. The secondhand power is intoxicatingly dizzy and warm, but it's not as inviting as it was at the abandoned carnival.

The Forest Eye's voice echoes through my mind and permeates every inch of my body. Its stern parental tone sends goosebumps across my body.

"So this is what it takes for you to see me these days."

I clench my jaw and stare into the trees. "You aren't allowed to manipulate my dreams."

"How else was I supposed to get your attention? I'd say I've been more than fair with your freedom in town. We haven't spoken in years, and this is how you treat me? No, 'I love you,' or 'I've missed you'?" A soft breeze brushes my cheek. *"Won't you come home?"*

My face fills with heat. "I don't have a home with you anymore."

"Oh, you don't mean that," it coos.

"Do you know about the new family? About Declan Jackson?"

The breeze vanishes. *"Why don't you ask your precious director? Or has he turned his back on you?"*

I grind my molars and glare at the trees.

Whatever ghosts were in the area have all vanished. They're technically cryptids, which means they fall under the Forest Eye's domain. Not even the dead want to risk an encounter with the cryptid god.

"I don't need to be here. I don't *need* you anymore."

"But how else would you get your answer about the invisible man?"

My white eyes widen.

"Yes... so eager to know but without any patience to learn. I raised you better than this, Ash. Perhaps your strictly human lifestyle has burdened you worse than I imagined."

"I'm just fine."

"You used to be so happy. I never should've let you leave. Look at how they've hurt your precious heart."

The knot in my chest tightens as though I'm being cornered. Even the suggestion is a promise of what's to come. "What is happening to Veil Haven?"

"It isn't about the town, Ash. It's about what's happening to you. You're falling short. You need to come home so you can practice more."

"What?" I deadpan.

"You left so long ago, and now you're slipping. It's my fault, really. I should have made you come back years ago. Four years is too long."

My brows stitch together. "That isn't your decision. You only ever wanted to make sure The Watchers didn't have my kind of power. You don't care about my well-being or how much you hurt me."

"You're remembering this all wrong, Ash. I would never hurt you. I love you. I only ever try to help you."

I step back. "You're not even helping me now. You're not answering my questions. Was all of this just to convince me to go back with you? I have a life here." I motion to the town at my back. "My family is here."

"I'm your family."

"You lost the right to call yourself that when you tried to make me your mindless puppet. You hated that I was helping people. You hated Director Capaldi from the start."

The air dips cooler with every fast beat of my heart.

The Forest Eye's voice drops, too. *"And how is Anthony..."* It says his name with a dripping bitterness. *"Your pseudo father."*

The hairs on my neck stand on end. I've only heard his first name spoken aloud once. It's a privilege to know, and the Forest Eye *mocks it.*

"Even the chief of police is ignoring you," it continues. *"Your little family has turned its back on you and you've come to me willingly. You're desperate, you're lost, and you're scared."* Its voice shifts back to that soft, cooing parental love, *"But I can help you, Ash. I want to help. You know I'm the only one who can."*

My jaw is tight, and I'm half-poised to run.

"I want to see you again, dear. I miss the way things were. I can erase all your harshest memories. I can make you feel heard and seen. I can make you stronger. I can keep you safe."

I gawk at the trees, my anxiety turning to fear even as the warm breeze pushes against my back, easing me to step forward. I squeak out my final question, everything in my body begging me to run. "Why can't I see Declan?"

"It's hard to say really," the Forest Eye hums in my head.

Its presence is trying to soothe me, trying to calm my muscles, and that warm, comforting breeze nudges me toward the shadow of the trees.

"You're just not as powerful as you think."

The secondhand power is intoxicating me, and I feel as though I'm floating. Joyful memories of my youth rise to the surface of my mind while my heart fills. I step forward.

"You should stay away from that family until you're stronger. Until you've spent more time with me."

The sound of heavy rain suddenly permeates my mind, temporarily washing out the Forest Eye's voice and soothing energy. The hairs on my neck rise as a new voice—the Void—speaks to me with an urgency that snaps me out of it.

"The Forest Eye is lying to you, Ash. It's keeping the truth from you. It's true intentions are to—"

Then, the piercing noise of everything happening across the world tears through my mind. I shriek and fall to my knees, the breath punched out of my lungs. The pain moves down my legs like lightning. Everything at once. *Everything.*

Someone deciphers morse code from a woodpecker. Someone's car backfires. Someone is running out of an abandoned house with their friends, terrified of the living thing inside but collapsing on the grass in a fit of laughter, knowing they have enough evidence for their school project. Someone uses their fire manipulation to iron their clothes as they wear them. Someone's alarm doesn't turn off.

Someone is spray painting the outside of the abandoned history museum. A Cloud Person practices their lightning ability, summoning electricity to rove down their arms and dance between their palms. Someone pauses under flickering house lights.

I clutch my ears and gasp. I still feel the Forest Eye's demanding presence, and I know, in the whirlwind of my pain, that it is causing this. The Forest Eye is funneling this eruption of noise to drown out the Void, to prevent it from sharing the truth.

I ache as I stand, the noise beginning to settle to its normal levels, but my head is ringing, the corners of my vision blurring with spots. I gawk at the woods as my fear finally chokes me out.

I back away and break into a sprint, somehow shocked the Forest Eye has done this to me.

But before I can reach the first grave, a root bursts out of the ground and trips me. I turn back to see it coiling around my ankle. I kick the root with my free boot as I yank myself loose and sprint to my feet, running through the cemetery, dodging gravestones, and breathing so fast my vision darkens.

I have to use the mess of my mind's eye to navigate me to my car.

On the cemetery's asphalt, I catch my breath enough to make my head stop pounding. But as I fish my keys out of my pocket, I drop them.

I'm frozen in place. My chest rises and falls with the anticipation of that root coming for me.

Eyes wide, breathing hard, I stand against my car until the next thing I know I'm driving. I manage the noise of the town and decide not to go home. I just need to drive. I need to stay away from the trees.

I go in circles around West Veil Haven's industrial district until my hands finally stop shaking. Until I stop feeling the pressure of that root around my ankle. Until I finally digest what happened to me.

The Forest Eye knows something, and even it refuses to tell me the truth. And the Void. The Void was helping me, snapping me out of its trance. The Void saved me.

I don't know what the Forest Eye is capable of against the Void, but I know I've caught a glimpse of their eons-long rivalry.

I park in an abandoned lot and look at the dark green sky. I thank the Void. I ask them to answer me, but something cold at the base of my spine tells me the sky is empty.

CHAPTER 10
How Are You Still Using an iPod Shuffle?

I stay inside for the rest of the weekend. I even turned down Josie's invitation to go mudding with her. I don't say why.

I've never told my girls about the Forest Eye because I don't want them thinking of me any differently than they already do. Even though this isolation is like a festering wound.

I almost don't go to school, but something compels me to leave the house. Maybe it's all these rumors about Markus.

Markus is a cryptid pretending to be human. Markus is a government plant just like Ash. Markus has always been here, he's just been invisible. Markus is a voidwalker. Markus is a being from the Void. Markus is a freak, a weirdo, a loser. I heard Markus doesn't have an ability. I heard he has the worst ability we've ever seen. Markus is from Fox Falls. No, I heard he was from Railston. The mayor brought him here. It's all a hoax, Markus isn't real.

I dissociate most of the day, but sometime between classes as the hallways swell with tired students, I catch Markus frustrated at his new locker.

I watch Markus fail his lock combination for another minute before I approach him. You can't see it easily, but he's blushing with worry, wondering how many people are watching him, how they'll laugh at him later.

I listen to how he justifies his frustration in low mumbles, how the office's instructions must be wrong because he's tried the combination a dozen times and how can anyone understand something this old, and why wouldn't they just take his fingerprint for a biometric scan and—

"Could I help you with that?"

He clutches the lock and lowers his head in defeat. "Is it that obvious?" He tries again, this time forgetting to clear the lock.

"Well, you *have* been trying for five minutes now."

He turns around, ready to greet me with some snappy comeback, but he pauses as our eyes meet. I guess I didn't notice he never looked me in the eye before. I guess he didn't either. He steps aside as I take the lock.

"You twist it three times left to clear it and then twenty-three right, eighteen left, fifty-nine right." The lock pops in my hand, and I spin on my heel and give him the lock.

"Sorry," he breathes, shaking off his surprise. "I didn't think... Are you blind?"

I laugh. "I'm the opposite of blind."

"How?" he gawks.

"What?"

"You don't have irises or pupils. How can you see?"

"I just do." I shrug. "Plus I see with a lot more than *just* my eyes."

He studies the lock in his hand. "Wait, how'd you know my combination?"

I shrug. "I know lots of things. Except for you. Tell me, have you seen any strange dark figures walking around your house?"

He raises his brow. "Except for what I see in the mirror? No. You're so weird." He scoffs as he looks around. "Everything here is weird, and why is the school so decrepit?"

"It just has character," I defend with a smile.

He side-eyes me as he puts some books in his locker and

closes it, looking at my neon leggings and too-big leopard print overshirt. "Is this some kind of joke?"

I cock my head but he waves me off before joining the people migrating between classes.

"Markus—" I walk after him. The crowd parts around him, creating a wide berth for the both of us as everyone stares, new rumors spreading now that I've been seen with him.

"Seriously, how do you know my locker combination."

"I know just about everything."

He sighs. "Of course you do."

"I want to help you."

"Listen, about your stepdad. He doesn't have an ability, does he?"

Markus' brows twitch as though I've hit a bruise, but he tries to hide it under his more obvious confusion. "Oh, you mean if he has powers? No." He scoffs. "No one in my family does. Actually, I've been going on walks around my neighborhood, and it seems like *a lot* of powered people live here."

His wording is strange but I don't press. "Well we thought everyone was born with an ability. Even people from the other towns. So it's strange that you don't. And probably half the reason why people might be avoiding you. I would just ignore them."

"Yeah..." Markus looks down the hallway and sees someone flying above the crowd. Someone else manipulates the vines hanging from the ceiling and grabs him, entangling him midair. His group of friends laugh at him before helping him down.

Distantly, we hear them saying, "That's what you get for flying around."

"And your stepdad..." I continue, "is he always..."

"Yeah," he answers quickly. "Declan loves to find ways to embarrass me. I guess that's what dads are supposed to do." He pushes his hands into the pocket on his black hoodie, making it stretch across his wide chest. It seems like he's going to say something else, but he stops there.

I smile, trying to ease the conversation. "Listen, you were ten minutes late to your first class, and—"

"How do you—"

I tilt my head.

He clicks his tongue and let's me continue.

"Is making a new friend really that bad?"

He almost laughs. "You really want to be my friend that bad, huh?"

"Sure, why not. You need someone to show you around and I know Veil Haven better than anyone."

He pauses and glances at the people walking around us with shifting eyes. "You're still the only person who's talked to me here."

Markus' attention is quickly redirected to Val who waves at me as she walks past us, her goldenrod flowers in full bloom. They must not have Plant People where he's from.

"Be a little more obvious," I whisper.

He does a double take. "Did that person have a plant on their head?"

"She has a plant *for* a head, Markus." I laugh under my breath as the final bell condemns us to get to class. I backpedal into the crowd with a shrug and say, "Welcome to Veil Haven."

By the time the lunch bell rings, I find myself at my desk nearly alone in the classroom. I guess I zoned out again. Even with the sweet encounter with Markus, something still just feels off. Maybe it *is* me, after all.

The only person left besides the teacher is Ford. He seems irritated, and I'm sure this ghost is to blame.

This ghost looks about as young as us. He's a black boy with the same letterman as all the football players and is tall, toned, wearing glasses, and has a close-shaven head. He also seems pretty energetic and happy for a dead guy.

I sling my bag across my back and approach him. "Hey, Ford, what's up?"

He scoffs as he packs his bag. "You can't tell?"

For a moment, I almost forget no one knows I can see ghosts. I can hardly understand the ghost thing myself, but I've taken it in stride. Being the only omniscient person in our town's history has its drawbacks.

Knowing how Ford and other ghost whisperers have suffered over the years, I'm relieved the director kept this part of my ability to himself. The last thing I need is for ghosts to be bothering me too.

"A new ghost is haunting me."

"Haunting implies you're scared of me," the ghost says proudly. He teleports away and then reappears directly in front of me, shouting, *"Boo!"* He laughs and floats on his back encircling Ford.

I force myself not to react. "It's that bad, huh?"

"Yeah, Dante is gonna win the award for most annoying ghost ever."

"What an honor!" the dead sportsman says.

Ford rolls his eyes.

"Aw, come on, don't be like that, buddy. I'm just tryna have some fun!"

It looks like Ford is talking to no one. "You were supposed get your fill of fun at the game. *And* the afterparty."

"Oh, that's why we saw you at the game," I say, pretending like I didn't already put two and two together.

"Yeah." Ford throws on his backpack and together we move into the hallway. "I thought because he's wearing a letterman that maybe taking him to a game would satisfy him or bring back memories or even help him move on. But it only made him more... annoying. I even made an appearance at Lydia's." Ford tilts his head, rubbing his short beard. "Actually, you weren't there. Were you?"

"I had some work stuff come up last minute so I couldn't go," I tell him quickly.

"Ah."

I'm surprised how much Ford is even talking to me. He's usually so reserved. This ghost really has him amped up. "So, the ghost's name is Dante? And he's our age, like he died in high school?"

"I guess," Ford says. "The worst part is he just won't shut up. It's already bad enough that my brother is on JV and my family has been hounding me for years to join the football team, but now Dante is like the living embodiment of Mothmen pride." He sticks his elbows out and bumps into me but then apologizes profusely as if all his normal anxiety finally caught up with him. He rubs the back of his neck and looks away.

"Do you want to have lunch with us? Maybe you could ask Josie to help you with your ghost problems."

Ford and I pause. We're at the intersection of doors where one leads to the cafeteria and the others lead outside to the picnic table eating area. We would usually part ways here but I can see the gears turning in Ford's head.

"That's actually not a bad idea."

"I know." I laugh. "Come on."

I lead Ford outside where Josie and Lydia have already found their seats at our usual spot closest to the giant oak tree. Its colors are beautiful and vibrant this year, and its leaves sprinkle the grass like stars. The green sky makes the autumn mountains pop as they fold into the hills surrounding our school.

"Ooooh, another date with Josie," Dante coos as we approach.

Ford doesn't respond.

"Long time no see," Lydia grins, crossing her arms on the table. Her smirk turns devilish as she looks between Josie and Ford and then pulls me to sit next to her.

"Oh, I like this girl," Dante rubs his hands together while closely investigating each of us, waiting for drama to unfold.

Josie blushes and looks away wide eyed as Ford awkwardly sits beside her, trying not to be too close despite his large frame.

We're all quiet for a moment, but I break the silence before he decides to save himself and leave.

"Ford's being haunted by a new ghost, Josie. I suggested maybe you could help with that."

"Oh, yeah, sure, I would love to." She smiles at him, tries not to focus on how close they are or how she wants to slide closer, and then returns to opening her packed lunch.

"So how was your weekend, Ash?" Lydia turns to me, a brow raised, expecting a better explanation than whatever I sent in our groupchat.

"Oh, y'know..." I know she's going to prod me until I give her something exciting, and as Josie and Ford stare at me too, I decide to give in. "I met the new kid and his family."

Josie chokes on her sandwich. "What?"

"His name is Markus. Right?" Lydia asks.

"Markus Jackson, yeah. And his stepdad is Declan. And..." My throat closes in. "Markus is nice, but uhm, I don't think he knows what cryptids are."

Ford blows a raspberry. "What do you mean?"

"Well the night of the game he was walking around like nothing and he almost got *got,* and I had to save him. But he doesn't remember and when I mentioned cryptids he didn't seem to get it." I take a breath.

They gawk at me.

"You saved the new kid from a cryptid attack?" Ford asks.

"Yeah, one of those sirens."

"You saved him from a *siren*?" he asks again.

"Yeah." I laugh, brushing the hair out of my face. "I'm sorta glad he doesn't remember. He seems... well, I don't know how to put it."

"What else happened?" Lydia clutches my arm. I can tell she's taking mental notes to share with everyone she can.

"I don't think we should be spreading rumors," I tell her cautiously.

She leans back, disappointed. "It isn't a rumor if it's true, Ash."

"I need to tell you something." I look between Lydia and Josie. "And, Ford, you're part of this. I guess we're all part of this, but you can't say anything to anyone. It's been... well, I've been trying not to think about it all weekend but... Markus' stepdad, Declan, I..."

My throat is tense, and the knot in my stomach is so heavy I'm not sure if I can actually muster the will to tell them my biggest flaw—the most dangerous realization I could share about myself. But they're my best friends, and Ford is trustworthy and quiet.

I tell myself that their opinion of me won't change. Nothing will change.

I take a deep breath. "I can't see him."

They share looks between the three of them, untensing in their confusion.

I lean in to stage whisper and they follow me.

"I can't see Declan with my ability. Through my mind's eye, he doesn't exist."

Josie's eyes widen and she rubs the chills beneath her flannel.

Lydia leans back and waits for me to say more, her brows furrowed.

Ford's gaze shifts between us, trying to comprehend the gravity of it.

But Dante phases his head through the center of the picnic table and loudly asks, *"What does that mean?"*

Ford sighs and pinches the bridge of his nose. Then he realizes how it must look. "Sorry, I was... Dante said something stupid. Ignore me."

I cross my arms. "What's worse is I told Winona and she acted like it was no big deal."

Lydia scoffs, rolling her eyes. "Well that's the *mayor*. What did Chief Mun have to say?"

I look at my hands. "I haven't told him because he's been brushing me off lately too. I've talked to him about the new family already but he keeps assuring me everything is fine. But how can this be fine?"

"I mean, that's pretty scary," Josie finally says. "If you can't see someone, how can you make sure they're not dangerous?"

I reach across the table for her hand and squeeze it when she slides it into my palm. "It'll be okay. I've been assured everything is going according to plan. Despite not knowing the plan," I add, quieter. "But just because I can't see him doesn't mean he isn't being watched."

Ford looks around, visibly uncomfortable.

I let go of Josie's hand and tuck my hair behind my ear. "Sorry, Ford, I don't really talk about this kind of stuff. It's just... weird."

"Yeah, I get it." He pauses. "With my family, y'know, I'll overhear my parents talking about, uhm, *secrets* because of the farm and how we provide for Veil Haven, so, it isn't entirely unfamiliar to me."

"Well, we're friends," I assure him. "You don't have anything to worry about."

"But what about Markus?" Lydia asks.

"Markus is totally normal. Well, except he doesn't have an ability. None of the Jacksons do."

"No ability?" Josie exclaims.

Luckily we aren't near the other picnic tables. Though, the football table is the closest, and her noise gives Kane the perfect reason to glare at me.

I forgot about his stupid concussion and the stupid promise that I would keep it to myself. It's none of my business, despite the pain he's enduring. You'd think he would be nicer, even in a glance because of our exchange, but it seems like it's put me more into his central focus.

Great.

"Like I said, they're weird but not dangerous." *Except Declan.* The stray thought catches me off guard, and I clench my jaw.

The three of them talk a little more about the subject, Lydia tossing in the rumors she's collected throughout the day, but somewhere along the way, my mind's eye settles on Markus alone in the cafeteria.

Everyone is staring at him as he seems to sink deeper into his hoodie, probably wondering why he bothered coming here to begin with.

"Y'know what, he's had it rough all day. I think I'm gonna rescue him from the lunchroom and show him around the school."

"You sure it's a good idea?" Ford wonders.

I pause. The memory of the Forest Eye weaves to the forefront of my mind. The idea that the new family is safe, that the new family isn't the problem, that I'm the problem. But *that's* the lie. Isn't it?

"Yeah." I smile. "Actually, I think you'd like him, Ford. You're both kind of... reserved. You should talk to him." I wink at Josie and leave the two of them with Lydia.

Markus has awkwardly decided to sit by himself at a table nearest the door, except the people who normally sit there are staring at him from the lunch line. I meet him there before they can.

"Markus," I hum, standing over him.

"Oh, hi again." He shifts in place on the narrow seat.

"I was thinking now would be a great time to show you around the school."

He considers turning me down because he is pretty hungry. But while his bag lunch is appetizing, everyone staring at him makes his skin crawl so he takes his sandwich to go.

The cafeteria blooms with noise when we leave. I ignore it and soak in the silence of the empty halls.

"How have your classes been so far?"

"I thought you knew everything," he says between bites.

I nod. "You got me there. Boring, quiet, tense, lots of people giving you long looks."

"Wow, I was just joking but okay."

I suggest we start from the front of the building and work our way through his class schedule that way he knows the best paths to take.

He doesn't really say all that much between my rambling small talk, apologizing for the rumors and everyone's poor manners, but when I tell him about the cryptid in the ceiling he laughs at me.

"Ash, you can't prank me, I've heard it all. The secret swimming pool on the roof, a special key to make the elevator take you to a hideout in the basement, a walkway in the ceiling, the haunted theater."

"Well I don't know about any of that besides the haunted theater, but you definitely don't want to go *into* the ceiling. Though the cryptid is pretty nice. People usually throw food up there when they get bored in class. So if you see any Cheerios lying around, that's why. The ceiling cryptid is like this giant salamander thing, all black to blend into the dark up there, and it has several, uhm, orifices... but even though it's sweet, if you see it, you'll be delirious for about a week."

His head rocks back. "Well that's a new one."

"You really don't have cryptids where you're from?"

"You mean monsters?" He laughs. "Sure like Bigfoot and Mothman and Nessie, but nobody actually sees them."

"Oh, so you *are* familiar then. Well, they're a lot more active here from the sound of it."

"You say that like they're real."

"Of course they're real, Markus. Remind me to get you a copy of The Cryptid Handbook. Where did you say you came from again?"

"We moved from South Carolina, near the coast."

My head rings. I don't know how to react but my confusion and near-panic is plain to see.

"Yeah, it's about as bad as you imagine," he jokes.

"Just for the sake of it," I say quickly, remembering the ocean-memories I saw in him the night we met, "why don't you keep that to yourself... about where you came from. It's just we're only really familiar with Fox Falls, Leiton, Bescour, and Railston, so if you go around talking about *South Carolina*." I make air quotes. "...or *Surfside Beach*, the uh..."

How can I tell him that if he keeps talking about stuff outside of Veil Haven, he's going to be taken by The Watchers... without telling him about The Watchers?

"The rumors about you are going to get worse."

He squints, and after a little back and forth, somehow empathizing with my nerves, he agrees to keep his history to himself.

Before I can thank him, he continues, "Oh, and I thought you were joking earlier about the plant girl but I've seen a dozen of them, and people with smoke around their heads too. It just stays there. Like, they don't have heads?" He shudders. "It's pretty scary. I'm not gonna lie. Is it like a mutation? I know some powers can deform your body."

I furrow my brows. "Those are Plant People and Cloud People. They're normal and not mutated. A long time ago, people treated them more like cryptids than humans, so there can still be some prejudice against them. But they're normal people just like the rest of us."

"Oh," he says, suddenly self-conscious.

"It's okay, though." I smile. "You wouldn't have known. Nobody really hates anybody here. Maybe someone is jealous of another person's ability or something silly like that, but besides the occasional Plant Person remark from the older generation, everyone just accepts everyone else."

"Huh... well that's a first for me. You never know what you're gonna find in these small country towns, I guess."

I quirk my brow at him but don't say anything. We continue wandering the halls. I show him the student lounge, the auditorium, and the best bathrooms to use.

"So back to the ceiling thing, and the school in general." He motions to the mossy baseboards and vines hanging from holes above us. "How do people go to school here? I'm ninety-nine percent sure the roof is about to collapse on us." He laughs. "I thought some of the places *I've* been to had bad funding, but you guys are in the stone age. You literally go to school in an abandoned building. Your tech is almost nonexistent. And where's the school spirit? I don't even know what your mascot is."

"Aw it's a little old, but there's a lot of nostalgia to this place. I assure you it's completely safe. We're the Veil Haven Mothmen." I flash the M hand sign. "And I can show you our school spirit."

He seems to regret his request as soon as I smirk.

We push through some double doors and step into the giant, empty gymnasium. The dome lights flicker sporadically as dodgeballs levitate and soar across the court.

Markus freezes in place. "What is happening right now?"

"You asked me where the school spirit was. We have more than one, and right now they're playing dodgeball."

Markus looks at me and then back at the seemingly epic game, then back at me, and back at the self-moving balls. And when it finally dawns on him, he quickly leaves the gym and closes the door behind us with wide eyes and heavy breaths.

"Ghosts are real?" he yells, panicked.

"I thought you had ghosts where you're from?" I yell back, matching his tone.

"We do. I mean, I don't know. Not like that!"

"Playing dodgeball?"

"Existing at all!"

I have to stop myself from laughing. He's so shocked and confused, and all I can do is try not to smile as I shout back, "I thought it was a universal thing! Why wouldn't you have ghosts? Do the dead just stay dead?"

"Yes!"

We stare at each other for a moment, Markus catching his breath. I watch his tough guy façade completely melt, and finally, I laugh. I try to stifle it but have to clutch my sides before I fall over.

"Why are you laughing? There are dead people in there!"

I laugh harder. "There are dead people everywhere! You just can't see them."

"And you can?"

"Sorta, yeah," I confess, my laughter slowing down, "but don't tell them that. They only think ghost whisperers can see them. I'll have to introduce you to Ford. Oh, he's being haunted by this new ghost Dante. He's a riot. They make a good pair. Well, not really, Dante annoys Ford nonstop but—" I pause as he stares at me, mouth open, brows furrowed.

"This is normal for you?"

"Yeah." I shrug, stifling the last of my laughing fit.

"I was trying so hard not to freak out at the Lovecraftian nightmare that is Plant People but ghosts? *Ghosts?*" he stresses.

I clear my throat, the realization dawning on me. "I'm guessing this means you really haven't seen cryptids before. Even after the other night."

"The other night? I... Do I even want to know?"

"No." I shake my head. "But you're gonna have to if you want to survive."

"Survive?"

I rub my face and put my arm around his back, ushering him away from the gym. "I'm gonna give you some pamphlets and a guidebook that I want you and your sisters to read."

He considers this along with trying to rationalize ghosts, Plant People, my comments about the ceiling cryptid, and everything else he's seen so far, but all he can say is, "Uhh."

"I think it would be good to show you around town, too. Maybe I can introduce you to some of my friends while we're at it, help even everything out."

He swallows, trying to repair his façade. "Are your friends as weird as you?"

"Markus." I smile. "I can promise no one is as weird as me."

CHAPTER 11
THE CRYPTID HANDBOOK

When I park in front of Markus' house, I text him instead of walking up to his front door. I really don't want to have to not-see Declan right now. I want to stay focused on Markus.

The world hums softly as the year slows down with October, cruising smoothly toward the fated rest of winter.

Somehow Markus has become fast friends with Ford. He even played games at his house yesterday. Markus was telling me he enjoys how "normal" he is, and how his nerves about ghosts have settled a bit. I guess he can adapt quickly when he wants to. I'm honestly impressed.

He's going to start sitting with Josie, Lydia, and me at lunch, and that seems to be helping, too. Ford has agreed to continue to join us at our table, which I'm sure will be fun for everyone in the long run.

Logan even sat with us yesterday to get to know Markus better. Despite the rumors still in full swing, the decent people seem to be coming to terms with how normal Markus is, just like he's trying to become more familiar with his new home.

We still need to work on his cryptid sightings, though. The other night he texted me saying a bear was outside his window, and I had to convince him that Bigfoot was real. Today is going to be good for him.

The warm October afternoon is stirred by a cool, shifting breeze. The trees whistle as they dance. And the sky is the perfect shade of orange. Pumpkins line every doorstep, Halloween decorations dot the yards, and academia wardrobes are in full swing.

When Markus meets me at the bottom of his front yard, we hug, and I appreciate his burgundy sweatpants. He's still wearing his usual black hoodie.

I'm wearing a vintage blue and green track suit, or snowboarding suit, it's hard to tell what the initial purpose was. I leave the jacket open to reveal my black sports bra. I love feeling the autumn breeze on my stomach.

"Hey, so, why is the sky orange?" Markus asks me, a twinge of panic in his voice.

"Oh, I don't know. The Void just felt like it I guess."

He stares at me. I stare back. We say nothing else about it.

I grab a tote bag in my car and pull out a handful of pamphlets along with a fresh copy of *The Cryptid Handbook*, giving them to Markus. "I brought these."

"Oh, right, thanks."

Literally every household has a copy of this book. Though most of them are forgotten on some shelf, lost under the bed, stuffed in the back of the closet, or bent in an old bookbag. I suppose apathy is easier than saving yourself.

Markus flips through what I handed him and reads the titles of each old, waterlogged pamphlet I found on a town hall kiosk. He gives me a *look* between each title.

"Only You Can Prevent a Cryptid Attack. Encounters Happen, Make Them Safe. Ghost infestation? Know who to call. Discovering the Deep Woods: Where Not to Go. If you see something, say nothing. Disregarding Omens Is the Leading Cause of Death: How You Can Be Smarter." He lowers his arms and tsks me. "What is this stuff?"

I tap on the book grinning widely until he reads that too.

"*The Official Cryptid Handbook*: *The concise field guide to understanding and surviving the cryptids of Veil Haven.*" He scoffs, "Ash come on—"

I take the book and pry open the crisp pages, cracking the spine with pleasure. "Look, this is the book I grew up with. I got a brand-new copy for you and your sisters to read. It's important. The author, Ripley Taylor Peterson, was a genius, and super brave. I think he had an ability that prevented cryptids from wanting to kill him or something. He went everywhere in Veil Haven. The woods, the sewers, the abandoned places, people's homes. And he wrote this comprehensive guide to help everyone understand cryptids."

Markus raises his brow, looking at me flatly.

"And since you're new to our world, you need to study up. People die here all the time, or they go missing, which most times means the same thing. So..." I close the book and tap on the white and blue cover illustrated with three different cryptid heads looking to the right—a Skeletal Shifter, a Bigfoot, and a Being of Light.

He agrees and takes the tote with us as we begin our tour of the town.

We go down the hill from his neighborhood and pass the park before jogging across Main Street and walking the length of downtown, starting at the roadside shops. Markus remarks on how cute the area is, how nice the old brick buildings and brightly colored stores are. When we reach the end of the shops, I pause to show off our town hall.

I wave at Winona, who's looking at us through her giant circular window in the center of the dome. Markus has to squint to see someone up there, and he shakes his head laughing once he sees her. He waves too. Winona waves back.

We snake through the back of downtown where the stores face the river. I point out the *Jackalope Post*, our main news station and newspaper but he doesn't seem very interested in local business.

Markus stares at the smooth water. "You weren't kidding about the river being *black*."

"So long as you don't walk along the bank or go anywhere near it, the Black River is really nice." I smile. "Don't swim in it," I stress. "Tell your sisters that, too."

"Yeah, you got it."

As we come to the opposite end of downtown, we pause at the multi-bell clock tower. Wedged in the back, near the river stands the forty-foot-tall bell tower. The base is an awning of brick arches that support the black steel and copper pitched roof where twenty-five bells of varying size hang below the giant clock faces on each side of the tower. While it is clearly not at the top of the hour, we both hear the bells chime anyway.

Markus squints at it. "Wait, why is this thing ringing?"

"It rings whenever you notice it. Actually, it rings only for you. The people around the corner don't hear it at all. It's all in your head, Markus." I tap my temple.

"But that doesn't make any sense."

"Sure it does."

When the bells cease, we linger for a moment. I catch him reading the circular bronze plaque under the clock tower. It reads, *If you see something, say nothing,* and has our town sigil in the center—a celestial map of the five towns across the Void, connected like a constellation, and forming an eye with Veil Haven at the center.

I decide not to explain the symbol to him, half-hoping he already knows it. Instead, I look up at the bells, trying to work up the nerve.

"Can I ask you something?" I toss out.

"Sure." Markus shrugs.

"What's up with your stepdad?"

He huffs. "What do you want to know?"

Everything. "You're sure he doesn't have an ability?"

"I'm sure." He chuckles but he looks away. "Ash, the thing about my stepdad is—" He pauses, trying to find the right words. "Well I'll just say it. He isn't a good dad. After my mom's accident he was just gone. Working, he said. He was always working to support us." He sounds exhausted, like he's recited this speech dozens of times before, trying to believe it himself. "But I never knew what kind of work he did. We moved around because he couldn't hold any job for long, but he still supported us. Even if we had to live in shacks or trailers, we made it."

Leaves rustle onto the Black River without a sound.

Markus hangs his head low. He pushes tight fists deep within his hoodie pockets, and despite his large frame, he seems so small.

"I was only twelve, Ash. He left me to raise my sisters and take care of my mom on my own. Kyah was five when my mom became immobile. Jarissa was only two." He holds his breath, and I hang on his every word. "Just because he provided for us doesn't mean he's a good dad."

I swallow and stare at my turquoise boots. "I never had parents."

His lips tighten, but he doesn't say anything.

"I know most kids want their parents, wonder if they'll come back for them, wonder if they're alive or dead, but in Veil Haven..." My shoulders inch up, barely a shrug. "When people disappear they stay gone. The details don't matter."

My throat aches saying this aloud. I'm not sure why. "I never really think of them. I guess I didn't have the headspace to miss people who weren't here. I grew up without a family but I was never alone. None of us are. I was lucky enough to be raised by... the government." I eye him, my throat tense. "I know all about absentee fathers."

He holds my gaze so gently I'm sure we're speaking in a different, softer language. We settle in this strange feeling and silently agree that maybe for the first time we've finally met someone else who understands.

We move on, crossing the Lower Black River Bridge into West Veil Haven's Business Row. Every shop or restaurant that isn't downtown or in the shopping plaza on the other side of the fields will be found here.

Markus seems to vary between laughing and gawking at the various businesses.

I have to catch my breath from his jokes as we pass by The Strange and Unusual Oddities Thrift, Hair Cuts Not Throat Cuts Salon, Bank of Echoes, and Economy Exterminators. And when I point out the small brick building with a cardboard sign in its single window that reads, *WE DO THAT*, Markus and I nearly double over.

When we pass by the industrial district, I point out the two large buildings made of brick and concrete. "They might look like liminal spaces from the outside, but inside they're pretty high tech. These are the training facilities."

"Training... for your powers?" Markus smiles, deviously curious.

"Yep," I tell him as we watch a couple of people mosey in and out of the buildings. "The concrete building is for physical abilities and the brick building is for everything nonphysical. So like telepathy, oracles, memory manipulation, touching something and seeing the past, anything that happens inside the mind and stays there. The other one is reserved for anyone who has super strength, super speed, telekinesis, any kind of matter manipulation, so basically everything that happens outside of the body."

"Wow that's actually really progressive. Most powered people keep their abilities to themselves cause, well, you know. So it's really cool they allow you to openly work on bettering yourselves."

Half of me wants to prod him for more answers, but the other half of me knows better. I swallow the feeling. "Yeah, well, even though we aren't supposed to really use our abilities in public, it's still important that we hone them. So these buildings are like an outlet most times."

"Cool. So you train in the brick one?"

I smile but look away. "I would if there was anyone else with my ability who could teach me."

"Oh. Huh."

We keep walking. Between our small talk and my ramblings, I've also been reading off *The Cryptid Handbook*.

I tell him about the cryptid hierarchy. How we categorize cryptids from common to deities based on, you guessed it, how common they are, but also how powerful they are. I make sure he knows that the survival rate when encountering a rare or unique cryptid is very low, but that he would have an easier time with semi-common or common cryptids. I also explain the town's sentience and how certain buildings and landmarks are sentient because of the inherent magic of our world.

He looks me up and down, giving me that brow-raised look of, *You're actually crazy. Aren't you?*

We move up Church Row where Markus seems surprised by all the faiths. I can't understand why. Everyone in Veil Haven has a house of worship. No matter your religion or sect, there's a place for you.

Having them all crammed onto the same street has led to some interesting situations, which may or may not be hilarious depending on your perspective.

I tell Markus about the almost childish feud between the Christians and the Satanists. How each church raises the stakes a little higher with their retaliations.

"I heard the Satanic Church once spray-painted a pentacle around the entire Baptist Church just to piss them off. Or there was this time the Catholics put a bunch of firewood around base of the Satanic Church to be like symbolic or something, but the papa just took the firewood and had this epic community bonfire."

"What—" Markus grabs his sides, laughing. He's taken off his hoodie and tied it around his waist to reveal a printed tee from some anime I've never heard of. I love seeing him so comfortable. "How—I mean—" He raises his arms, motioning between all the churches. "*How* is this place real?"

I only smile and he fills the silence with laughter. I can't believe how good his laugh is.

When we cross the Upper Black River Bridge, we pass by town hall and pause at the sandy entrance to the lake.

Markus furrows his brows as he studies the glowing turquoise waters. I guess he didn't register the beauty of it before.

"You swim here?"

"Yeah, that floating yellow tube sanctions off the swimming area."

"It looks... I mean why is it *glowing*? I feel like I saw a radiation dump site that looked like this once."

"Radiation?" I scoff. "It's just the lake, Markus. It's sentient, technically a cryptid. It's in *The Cryptid Handbook*." I nod. He keeps giving me that *look*, and I cross my arms. "Our sunflowers glow, too, y'know." I shake my head and move on.

He stares at me slack jawed before catching up, casting long glances at the lake.

We walk briskly up the hill, past the police station and the Foodie Mart, and meander across the college campus for a little bit. I point out the hospital at the top of the mountain before we round down the road.

Markus points and laughs at a road sign that reads GORE, but before I can explain he sees the sheer rock wall dripping with dark, moist viscera. The part of the mountain which was shaved away to make the road bleeds with a deep red fleshy goop that sort of looks like what you'd expect a melted person to look like.

Markus pales and turns around. He shakes his head and walks back the way we came saying, "Nope," over and over again. I laugh after him, trying to explain, but he would rather not listen.

We decide to walk back to his house and get my car, our feet tired. Happily, we both agree to keep hanging out.

Our next major stop is the Abandoned Dam, one of the best places in town.

I tell him how the dam is our getaway because it's the only place in town that isn't secretly surveyed by the government. I'm not sure if he believes me.

The town looks the other way on anything that happens at the dam because that's how it's always been done. So people come here to openly use their abilities, something we aren't allowed to do anywhere else unless it's for work or training. Or helping win football games.

I park on the gravel patch beside the road and realize the other car here belongs to Shakira. With a quick check around town, I realize she isn't here. Not at this moment at least. She must be time traveling.

"Why do the deer on your deer crossing signs look so weird?"

"Those are Not-Deer signs," I tell him.

"If they're not deer, then what are they?"

"Yeah, they're Not-Deer."

He looks at me for a long time. "Am I having an aneurysm?"

"It's a cryptid." I laugh. "They look like deer but wrong. You'll get a cold tingle down your spine if you see one. You'll know."

Markus and I push through the grove that hides the clearing to the dam. The clearing is filled with knee-high bluegrass and clover patches. But the most obvious thing is the valley drop-off. You can't see the river from here, but what else would the dam be used for?

The dam is a concrete bridge long reclaimed by nature. Grass and moss cover the entire walking portion of it. The concrete wall that towers above the Black River is half deteriorated by weather and time, which exposed the twisting rebar within. The river has eaten away the base of the dam so it flows without interruption.

This great engineering feat has been cast away by the town but reclaimed by the people. Now this giant earthen walkway is ours.

I lift my arms and bask in the soft evening sun as we stand in the center of the dam, the river churning far beneath us. "This place feels like freedom. Doesn't it?"

Markus nods, taking it all in. "Yeah, this is a pretty cool spot." He leans against the waist-high concrete wall and crosses his arms, watching me, playfully cautious.

The thick swath of autumn leaves and the rolling mountains beyond the valley act as our backdrop.

"Veil Haven isn't so bad, you know," I tell him.

"But it *is* weird." He smiles. "Thank you for showing me around."

"Of course, Markus. I hope this place can feel more like a home to you. Despite how it feels sometimes, there are a lot of good people here. Sorry again about the rumors."

"Ah it's fine," Markus says, putting his hoodie on again. The cold air from the river whispers up the broken dam walls. "I've dealt with worse. Plus, I don't even care that people think I'm a spy or whatever. I just don't understand it." He chuckles. "People can say whatever they want. Doesn't mean it's true."

I think about the rumors Kane started about me in middle school. If Markus ever hears them, maybe he won't be swayed by them the way other people were. I swallow those sour memories.

He pulls his hair twists as he speaks, watching them bounce. "I've never seen so many powered people in one place before. Even if you don't use your powers, it really does seem like, normal. And everyone is okay with each other." He cuts his thoughts short, remembering that he promised not to talk about where he came from. He turns around and looks at the Black River. "So there's cryptids pretty much everywhere, huh?"

"Yeah," I say, standing beside him.

My mind's eye quickly snags on something across town, and I'm taken there, though Markus doesn't seem to notice.

It's a quiet moment, an assured quickness with everything they do. A black van marked with an eye like the setting sun between two mountains pulls up to the house of our school board president. He took the day off work to recoup from the flu.

In an instant his home is swarmed with people dressed head to toe in black armor, helmets hiding their identities even from me. Their existence has only ever been half-certain to me, and only when they operate in town. If I blinked I could miss The Watchers entirely.

The armed intruders surprise the man, his coffee cup shattering on the hardwood. There's little time for him to react, and even if he did, there wouldn't be anything for him to do.

The Watchers stick him with a syringe, and he's instantly knocked out, slugging to the floor. Like every other mission, the soldiers lift and carry their target out of the home without anyone knowing.

They toss him into their van. No one is nearby to notice, and if they were, they would simply deny seeing it. *If you see something, say nothing.*

As the van door closes, the school board president and The Watchers vanish from my mind's eye, blipping off the map.

A shiver runs down my spine.

Why would they take him? Higher officials aren't just taken for no reason. I didn't notice any wrongdoings or law breaking. He's only ever minded his business and tended to our school system in that vaguely unhelpful way.

Markus continues speaking and I'm drawn back into my present.

"I've really appreciated you showing me around, Ash. You didn't have to do this or give me all these weird reading materials, but you did." He shifts his feet. "I'll be honest, this place... scares me."

"Aw, Markus, it's okay," I say, sounding more distant than I intend. "The cryptids are really easy to get around if you just use your head. You and your sisters will be fine. And I'll keep you safe." I bump against him, trying to ground myself. "Give this place some time. It'll grow on you. And not in a weird, horrific way."

He stands up straight as he begins to roast me. "See, this is what I'm talking about. How can you just say—"

My mind's eye hyperfocuses behind us at the end of the dam, the world zooming in as I stand still. The hairs on my neck stand up as someone behind us manifests out of thin air.

Markus jumps and double takes the sudden person, sure his eyes are playing tricks on him.

But in a breath, my shoulders ease as I recognize the familiar presence of Shakira. I don't think I've ever been so on edge about her time traveling.

"Oh, that's just Shakira," I tell Markus, breathily, relieved it wasn't something more dangerous to deal with.

He's become closed off again and he quietly watches her.

Shakira checks her watch a little panicked. She stares at the golden time and date hologram hovering above her wrist and seems relieved, or at least satisfied enough, but it doesn't ease her discomfort. Finally, she notices us and waves a little, flipping her long braids over her shoulder before coming over.

With a quick, out-of-breath hug, she greets me and smiles patiently at Markus. "Hi, I'm Shakira."

Markus seems awestruck by her beauty, but I decide he's mainly confused as to where she came from since she just seemed to *appear*. Though, from what little he's talked about it, Markus seems to be familiar with abilities despite his lack of one.

"I'm Markus... hi."

"It's nice to meet you, Markus." Shakira's sweet as always, but she's distracted. I catch her hands shaking as she plays with her rings.

"You haven't really been around today, have you?" I say.

Shakira laughs nervously. I can see the worry in her dark eyes. "I was gone a lot longer than I expected." She moves her long, gold-accented braids out of her face again. "It was like I glitched... or somethin'. I don't know how to explain it. For a minute there, I wasn't sure I *could* come back. And now I'm back a lot later than I wanted to be."

I cock my head back. "Well that's weird. You haven't had trouble with that before. Have you?"

"No. And I have no idea why it happened. I mean..." She fidgets with the rings on her fingers and eyes Markus.

"He's the new kid," I tell her. "He has no concept of right or wrong."

"I'm literally right here," he deadpans.

"I just mean you don't know the rules here." I wave him off playfully.

He rolls his eyes, smirking.

Taking Shakira's hands, I let her anxiety speak for itself. "Did you go to the future again?"

"Yeah." She swallows. "I've been practicin' for a while now, and I never do anythin' or stay long, but it was different this time. I've never felt *stuck* before. I don't know. It was weird."

Logan's vision of Veil Haven burning snakes to the front of my mind. With wide eyes, I prod more. "Did you see anything?"

"No, nothin' weird. I only went ahead a couple of weeks, and I wasn't there for more than a few minutes, but it felt like bein' gut punched." She lets go of my hands to arch her shoulders, acting out the feeling. "I can still feel it now, like time itself was holdin' me there and rejectin' me all at once."

"You're a *time traveler*?" Markus gawks. I watch his walls come down as his wonder gets the better of him. "How does that work? I mean, how far can you go? Can you teleport too? Or is it just a stationary thing? Can you go anywhere or just in Veil Haven? What's it like?"

I stare at him as if I've spent my entire day with a completely different person. Of all the things I've shown him, time travel is what he's most excited about?

Shakira laughs, playing it up. "You're so sweet, oh my gosh." She touches his arm and looks back at me acting like a celebrity. "It's usually a lot of fun, and I would love to tell you more about it when I'm feelin' better." Her smile slips as she holds her arms and stares at the Black River. "This time though, it was pretty unsettlin'."

"Maybe you're just overworking yourself," I suggest, rubbing her arm. "You've been doing a lot of *secret* future jumping," I stress so Markus gets the message.

Markus puts his hands up. "I gotcha. And you can tell if I'm lying."

I almost laugh. "I'm gonna need to make you a PowerPoint for how our abilities work or something." I return to Shakira. "Maybe this is one of the reasons why they advise you against future visits. The strain of it, or the uncontrollable nature of the future. How the past is concrete but the future is always shifting, or whatever."

"Maybe you're right." She nods for a long moment before her gaze settles on mine. "Do you think Logan would talk to me about it?"

"I think Logan would talk to you about anything."

Her smile is so warm I understand why Logan stares at her whenever he gets the chance. Why most people do.

"Well, it was nice meetin' you, Markus. I'm a bit late for, well, everythin', so I better get goin'. We'll catch up, though."

I give her a hug goodbye, and we watch her speedwalk through the bluegrass, checking her watch again.

After a few minutes, half to give her space, half to let us digest all that, Markus and I return to my car.

I'm lost thinking about Shakira's experience. It's unnerving that she felt trapped and pushed out at the same time. She felt gut punched by the future? Does that mean something bad is coming? And what about Logan's vision?

But the town would already know if something was going to happen because of their employment of oracles and mouthpieces. Not to mention how time is always shifting. The future is confusing... I don't know.

"You good?" Markus asks me.

"Oh yeah, sorry, just lost in thought."

"Is *that* how your powers work?"

I smile and start the car. "Something like that."

CHAPTER 12
The Boy in the Black River

After I drop Markus off, avoiding his stepdad, and finally fall into bed, I realize how much energy that took out of me.

Markus is so interesting.

I'm glad he got to hang out with Ford yesterday, and that it seems like he's actually open to making friends. But why can't he find familiarity in Veil Haven? Isn't Fox Falls just like us? Aren't all the towns a near mirror image to ours?

As the fog horns hum through the valley, I finally let my mind rest. The giant, lanky Mist Walkers emerge from the haze, dipping in and out of the fog. They're one of the largest cryptids we have, but they're completely harmless, so long as they don't phase through you.

There's a kindness to the Mist Walkers, to their oblivion toward the town. I watch their impossibly long, foggy legs swing across the mountains, and as the night settles into the fog, I fall asleep.

There is a dead boy in the river. He does three things: exists, grants luck on college—sometimes high school—exams, and drowns you if you swim in the Black River. He lost his name and his identity when he killed himself. Legend has it that college was too much for him. It doesn't really matter now.

Right now, he stands at the bottom of the Black River waiting for a high school student to leave an offering and request something from him. Everyone knows that if you go to the back of the cemetery, avoid the tree line, and head to the lip of the river, you will find a short dock. The dock is decorated with half burnt candles and anything people assume a college kid or a cryptid would enjoy.

Yona Vann leans over this dark dock and scans the black water, their silky black hair hanging around their shoulders as they kneel. They hope the Boy will accept their offering rather than attempt to drown them.

Those who meet their fate with the Boy do not return, not even as ghosts. He consumes everything you are and feeds on it for eternity.

The Boy in the Black River homes in on your emotional state. He pinpoints your negativity. That's how he *gets* you. But Yona's new headphones and their mother's bracelet should be enough to satisfy him tonight.

The Boy's worn-down Converse are slick with the mud of the riverbed and his black hair waves passively in the current. He looks up, gauging what must be a blurred, impossibly dark image of Yona through the ebony water.

They want to say something so he doesn't waste any more time on the idea of drowning them. Yona's voice is like a hiccup and tears flood out of them.

"You know what it's like to be overwhelmed," they say to the river's face, to the dead boy far beneath it. Their muscles retract to counteract the tears as they speak against the sandpaper walls of their windpipe. "Everything is too much and it feels like I'm the only one who's falling apart."

The Black River's current appears to glitch and then stops altogether. The top half of a chalky face appears in its center. He is waterlogged from decades of death and only half resembles the human he used to be. The Boy, with bloodshot black eyes, stares at Yona with the base of his nose breathing into the river.

A chilled breeze runs over the water and pushes Yona's hair back like an omen. They blink. The wind stops. A silent tear like a runaway thought falls off their cheek.

"My brother is dead." Yona projects their voice. "Nobody paid attention to him. They pretended like he wasn't there. Maybe it was his ability. But it doesn't matter. He was real. And now he's gone forever." Yona catches their breath. "He was murdered but no one thinks so." Quieter, they say, "I think so."

The Boy doesn't blink, doesn't move closer. He stares at Yona emotionlessly in the stalled water.

"You didn't make it but now you're deathless. You live in this river like its shadow. You have seen so much more than me but..." They take a breath. "and..." They trail off, swallowing the lump in their throat. Yona considers which would be worse—finding the truth or being denied it again. "Do you know what happened to him?"

Like a bad TV monitor the image of the Boy skips in place before jumping forward. He shimmies across the river and lands mere feet from the dock.

Yona blinks, squinting to keep their tears and surprise at bay. The Boy's head remains half-submerged, his dark, angular eyes never departing from their gaze.

He isn't threatening them. They can feel it. It's the same way you know something is paranormal or if a person is harmful. It's in the air. In your gut. You have the taste of it between your teeth. You can touch those feelings. They're raw and thick. Like a river.

The Boy has abandoned the idea of drowning them. Maybe he knows who they are and what they're trying to prove.

Another gust carries off the river, and Yona can hear it whipping into their ears like a whisper.

His.

He doesn't have the answer to their question. He doesn't know. Instead, he tells them, *"Every problem has a solution, but answers can seldom be forced. Some truths take time."* And with the blessing of luck on top of Yona's natural luck manipulation, the Boy slowly sinks into the Black River as the current returns.

Yona's shoulders drop as they lose their breath. They shouldn't have expected much. They shouldn't have expected anything from a river spirit. Their brother was found in an abandoned factory, not the water.

Yona convinces themself that it can't be that simple. It's never that simple in Veil Haven.

I know Yona. Well, I know them in the way that I've had class with them once and watch them like I watch everyone else in town. They're two grades younger than me. I'm not sure I knew they had a brother. I certainly didn't see him die, or maybe I did. I usually push that stuff to the back of my mind. It's easier that way.

Still, I ache for Yona in this passing moment. It's never easy to lose part of your family.

If it weren't for their ability to manipulate chance, I would say they're pushing their luck being out here at night, even with the Boy's blessing. But Yona is in mourning, and mourners are capable of anything.

CHAPTER 13
PARADISE LOST

When I wake up, plans are being passed through town hall about renovations at the school. I almost don't believe it. The school board president was taken *yesterday,* and I haven't noticed anyone replace him. Still, as I watch the construction company prepare for the day, my stomach drops.

The sky is white today, not a cloud in sight, and the cool air dips around us as Logan and I stand on the front lawn of our school.

We watch workers cut down the giant oak tree by the entrance. The brick beneath the tree is darker, spared by the sun for decades. My heart trembles with every terrible crack of its heavy limbs. Its ancient branches collapse with whooshing cascades.

More workers are inside. People are scraping moss off the floorboards, ripping vines out from behind lockers, cautiously replacing our warm lights with hissing fluorescents.

Everything about this screams *wrong.* And I know I can only watch.

"Why would they do this?"

"Things are changing," Logan says.

We both think about his vision on the field. *Veil Haven burning.* We share a glance but don't say anything.

"I want to stop them," I say.

"You don't," he tells me.

As their chainsaws finally eat through the trunk of the grand oak, it collapses with a thud that echoes in our chests. We've only ever been able to see the big white letters spelling HIGH SCHOOL, but without the tree, the whole title is finally visible: VEIL HAVEN HIGH SCHOOL.

"Why is this happening? Who would do this?"

Logan raises his brow with a gentle answer, though he's surprised I don't already know. "Whoever runs the school."

My arm hairs stand on end.

"Like I said, things are changing."

Markus walks up to us with a bounce in his step. "I didn't even know there was a sign there before. Looks good this way."

I glare at him.

He clears his throat and avoids my white-eyed gaze.

"They shouldn't do this. That tree has always been there. The missing ceiling tiles and moss inside have *always* been there."

Markus tugs on his backpack straps. "I mean, a little change never hurts. Right?"

Logan watches me gawk but doesn't say anything, his attention quickly captured by Shakira passing us. He says goodbye before rushing to her side with a bright smile.

"You sure they're not dating?" Markus asks.

"I think Logan is waiting for everything to align."

"Must be hard knowing the future," Markus says. "You'd be expecting your entire life."

We turn back to the tree as they cut it into smaller pieces. "I loved that tree."

He looks at me like I'm crazy. "It's just a tree, Ash."

I sigh and step into the flow of people entering the school. Markus follows.

It would be dramatic to call it a warzone but the workers are tearing up every natural element of our school, disrupting all life, disturbing all our ghosts. The cryptid in the ceiling hums and hisses at those trying to install new ceiling tiles. My heart drops at the sound of its cries. We all went to school here. They should know better.

"This place is nasty," Markus says as we shoulder through the slow-moving people in awe of the renovations. "It's nice they're cleaning it up."

I scoff at him. "Markus, you're new here. There's a reason things don't change."

"What's the reason?"

I pause. "It's the way things have always been."

"That's not a very good reason," he says, clutching his bag straps again.

"*Things don't change.* It's basically our motto."

"Progress is important, Ash. This town feels like it's in the dark ages. Cleaning up the school doesn't make it different. It makes it better."

"I think that's subjective. They've destroyed the atmosphere, the vibe."

"And what a vibe it was."

His sarcasm hurts, but the bell rings before I can say anything, and we promise to see each other later. I turn the other way with a sigh. *Things don't need to change.*

The day moves slowly despite the swiftness of the renovations. It's unreal. And incredibly distracting. By the time everyone gets settled for lunch I'm packing my things and leaving. I watch Markus settle in with Josie, Lydia, and Ford. Dante hovers around them playfully. It's nice to see how comfortable everyone is, but right now, I'm at the end of my rope.

I need to meet the new school board president. Someone had to replace him. Director Capaldi wouldn't have sent in these orders himself. And I know the government wouldn't leave that position empty, especially with all these renovations happening.

When I arrive at town hall, it feels strange to stray from my usual path to Winona's office. The school board president resides on the first floor of the right wing of the building. Their secretary's desk is wedged into the wall beside a large wooden door at the end of a short hallway. The wall of windows makes this area of town hall almost seem inviting.

"Hi." The secretary, a young mousey man, smiles. "Can I help you?"

"Yeah, I'd like to meet the school board president. I want to talk to them about the changes being made at the high school."

"Ah, I'm sure he'd love to hear from you. His schedule is open now, so you can actually go right on in."

I cock my head and consider explaining to him that I know no one's in there, but something pulls me forward.

I slowly open the door and freeze when I see him. Or when I don't.

Declan is sitting at the wide mahogany desk and lifts his head as the door closes behind me. I swear I catch him smirk, a certain smugness before settling into being pleasantly surprised.

Alarms go off in my head, my body tensing as I'm half-blind to him. It's that brain itch I can't scratch. And something's off in his dark brown eyes. His strangely ingenuine smile is as white as power-washed marble. He can tell I'm tense.

I swallow my fast-beating heart as he stands. We meet each other in the middle of the room with a handshake. Touching him makes me nauseated, like reading a book in a car. Static motion sickness.

"Ashley." He smiles. "It's good to see you again. What are you doing here?"

"It's just Ash. I, uh, didn't know you were the school board president."

"Oh yeah, just got the position. Please." He motions to a seat in front of his desk as he leans against the table.

It almost hurts to look at him, half of me saying nothing is there. My eyes water a little and goosebumps ache beneath my flannel.

Declan leans poignantly. "Let me guess, you're here about the renovations. I assure you we're not changing anything essential. We're just giving your school a facelift."

"Right, and that's great in theory, but..." I hesitate as he raises his brow, still smiling. "You're new here. You don't need to change anything to make your mark or prove anything. Veil Haven is fine the way it is. The way it's always been."

"Ashley..." he begins.

"My full name is Ash."

He moves to the seat beside me. "Your anxiety is normal, and I appreciate you coming to me with your concerns. Change can be difficult at first, but I think you'll come to see how beneficial my ideas are. We're all trying to make the world a better place. Right?"

"Right... well, being that I actually go to the school, I can help provide better insight on our needs."

"I was hoping you'd say that," he says. "Winona was telling me how you help her and the chief of police with your gifts."

It's not that my ability is a secret, but the way he calls them *gifts* sets off alarm bells in my head. The energy between us is oppressive. My mind's eye is numb looking at the emptiness in front of me while my physical senses assure me that Declan is as real as I am. A headache forms swiftly and all my previous plans disappear with it.

"If I ever need anything, I'll come to you first. And please know my door is always open for you, *Ash*." He looks at me like I'm the only person in the world, and I am shrinking under his gaze. "Oh, and while I have you here..." He reclines in the chair. "I really would love to have you over for dinner sometime. It's nice to see Markus coming out of his shell. If his mother could entertain, I know she would have you over."

I speak in a daze as if from far away. "Sounds like a plan. I'd love to get to know your family better. He doesn't talk much about his mom..."

"She was in a car accident many years ago. She lost most of her motor controls and was left in a vegetative state, but she's still in there." His fists tighten as he looks down. "With all our technology, and all the power in Veil Haven, I know something can bring her back to us." He unfurls his fists with a sigh and smiles. "Sorry. I've had to defend our choice to keep her with us before. It's such a marvel that Veil Haven has free healthcare. Too bad there aren't healers. I guess that's rare everywhere."

My brows furrow. "How else would healthcare be?"

He laughs to himself but doesn't answer me.

I shuffle in the seat and feel compelled to fill the silence. "I understand. If there's a chance to save somebody, of course you'd take it. No matter how long the wait. The town takes care of us, all of us, even those of us who are... new."

He smiles thoughtfully before standing. "That's what I'm hoping for."

I rise with him, but he's still talking and quickly leading me to the door.

"I'll have Markus text you about dinner. I'm glad you stopped by, really I am, but don't forget to head back. We are in the middle of a school day."

"Right, well, I'll be seeing you."

"Always, right?" He winks.

I swallow hard and smile through my headache. I can't muster the words to say anything, instead chuckling at his poor joke before being ushered out. I'm so dizzy I nearly fall over, but the secretary doesn't seem to notice.

Someone is choking on their lunch. Someone melts their laptop with a candle. Someone drops a hammer and breaks their toe. Someone knocks over a bookshelf in the library. Someone is swallowed by a crack in the sidewalk. Someone being cornered by a nameless cryptid knows they're about to die.

My feet carry me quickly upstairs until I'm pushing through Winona's double doors.

She curses at my sudden appearance, jumping in place as she pauses her show.

I don't give her time to speak.

"Why is Declan the new school board president? Why would you allow someone like that to take office here?"

"Whoa, whoa, Ash, calm down." Her deep purple petunias stand on end. "Everything is going according to plan. This isn't a surprise to anyone who's supposed to know." Her flowers eye me as they settle gently to her chest.

I throw my hands up, yelling. "And why aren't I allowed to know?"

"Plenty of people don't know. We all have our part to play."

"He's destroying the school."

"He's *renovating* it." She scoffs, turning back to her show. "Don't get so pressed about a building, Ash."

"But things don't change here," I desperately remind her. "The government doesn't *allow* change."

"Maybe that's why we brought in a new perspective, huh?"

I straighten my back. "But—" My eyes flick to the rotary phone on her desk.

"Ash, I'm in the middle of something important. Shouldn't you be at school?"

My fists are heavy at my sides, but I leave without saying another word.

In my car, I consider driving to the station, but something tells me not to. Maybe it's how Chief is actually working, using his ability on some man who refuses to tell them the truth.

The man has killed someone and buried their body in the woods, one of the few places The Watchers have no jurisdiction or recording devices.

At one point, I would've been called in to help. I used to be more vigilant, or maybe I still am but I've just been distracted. I don't know where he buried the body, but I'm sure I could figure it out.

But Chief has decided to take on the affair himself. A couple of other officers had been interrogating the average-looking man, which is how they learned that their tip about his murder was correct.

They are in a small interrogation room where a metal desk and two chairs barely fit. Chief sits closest to the door, staring at this man with a tempered rage I haven't seen in years. He's frustrated and disgusted. They've been at it for hours, and now he's come to his final conclusion.

Chief Mun reaches across the table. The man, vaguely knowing the chief's ability, tries to pull away, but the table cuffs keep him in place. When Chief's hand touches the man's, a wave of energy pulses through him, and he tenses as if electricity were shooting through him. His eyes glaze over as Chief's power of suggestion worms through his mind and body. The chief's voice pulses through his mind, commanding him.

"You will tell us where you buried her."

And in a quaking breath, the man shares every detail of his victim's burial.

Chief's ability is as simple as that—manipulating through touch. Really makes things easy for police work. And despite my own discoveries, despite half of me yearning to run to him for an explanation, I leave him to his work.

On my way home, I text Josie and Lydia to meet at my house after school for our usual Thursday hang out. Until then, I simmer by myself, mulling over my options and slowly conceiving a plan.

I sit with my back pressed against my front door in the living room and try to breathe, attempting to accept Director Capaldi's grand plan. I struggle with it. I can't get past the fact that they aren't authorized to tell me his plan. I've never been excluded before, at least not when I asked.

Nothing needed to change. And now here I am, alone and confused.

I look to the corner of the ceiling where I know a secret camera is hidden, though it's nearly impossible to see with the naked eye. I can't bring myself to beg, so I look away.

I rub my face, count my breaths, and focus on this room to ground myself. No need for the noise in my head to get any louder than it is.

I've decorated my home nearly wall to wall with artwork, picture frames, fanart, and trinkets collected from various abandoned properties around town. The suncatchers in the windows overlay my maximalism décor with rainbow flecks of light. Though, besides the artistic mess of my home, my favorite spot is the stairs.

Every New Year, my friends and I paint a new step together. It's a tradition that unfortunately started with Kane, but Logan came over once and helped me paint over his parts. Now, several steps are layered with colorful paint that Josie and Lydia have added to every year we've been friends.

You can tell which areas are Lydia's because of the pink glitter, and Josie can't seem to help but add at least one sunflower on every step. None of us are good painters, but our sloppy lines and poorly blended colors make me grin.

When school ends and they finally arrive, Josie and Lydia instantly brighten my home, as it is theirs too, in a way. We've had countless sleepovers and endless evenings here.

We bump shoulders and laugh about nothing as we make mac and cheese together. But despite our fun, I still can't slide into the ease of our usual Thursday hangouts. I've called them here to ask them something, to ask for help. It's not something I'm particularly used to doing.

Halfway through eating at the kitchen table, Lydia cuts through our conversation. "Alright." She puts her fork down and raises a brow at me. "What is it?"

It's obvious I've been preoccupied, and I don't want to play dumb. "We need to do something about Declan."

Josie coughs down her mac and cheese. I should really stop surprising her halfway through eating. "What? What happened?"

"He's the one renovating the school," I stress, poking my table with authority. "They made *him* the new school board president."

"What happened to the old one?" Lydia asks.

"They took him." I shrug. "Though I have no idea why. He didn't do anything."

Lydia and Josie share a glance.

"Who in the world would let a stranger take charge of our schools?" I continue. "The man *I can't see* and they induct him into the government?"

"Well, at least the government doesn't do nothin'," Josie says. "Or at least they aren't supposed to."

"It's not that they're not supposed to. They're just lazy," Lydia corrects her. "Cops included. No offense, Ash."

"No, it's true." I nod. "But that's the way things are. Not this." I grimace, my mind's eye showing me the pristine white floors, the new fluorescent lighting, and how the ceiling cryptid howls to no one, trapped.

"Declan is ruining everything and being weird, and I'm supposed to do nothing? Winona is a jerk." I cross my arms. "And I don't know... I just don't want to see Chief. I feel like he wouldn't listen to me. Something about this whole situation is wrong, and... I need your help."

"With what?" Josie asks, taking another bite.

"We need to figure out who Declan is and what he's capable of. I can't *see* him," I stress, "so if he's planning something more than just the school renovations, we need to be prepared. Maybe if I find something, I can snap Winona and Chief back to their senses and they can kick them out of town. Or demote Declan at the very least."

Josie's eyes widen. "You want Markus to leave?"

"No." I look away. "He's fine. It's just Declan. Knowing that someone I can't see is just walking around Veil Haven is upsetting."

"Yeah, how can a person be a blind spot?" Lydia says, adding more sriracha to her mac.

"Exactly!" I lean closer to her. "So I was thinking maybe you could ask the higher powers to help us? Or point us in the right direction. Or tell us *anything* about Declan."

Lydia rubs her hands together deviously and nods, her mouth full of mac and cheese. "You know I love getting dirt on people."

I inch toward Josie. "And maybe if I got something of his, you could see into his past and we might learn more about him that way."

Josie watches me with her big, hazel eyes, cautious and sincere. "I don't know, Ash... I don't think lookin' into someone's past from another town is a good idea."

I lean back as the idea hits me. She's right. How could I have skimmed over the dangers of that?

We aren't supposed to know details about the other towns or the people from them. Our towns are separated across the Void for a reason. Them coming here to play football is like a treat, not a promise. Josie can't dig into Declan's history because of what it might reveal about Fox Falls. And we all know what happens to people who harbor forbidden information.

I feel a chill at the base of my spine for even suggesting it to her. "Good call, Josie. We don't have to do that. But I don't think there's anything wrong with asking for a little guidance." I look at Lydia.

She smirks back.

"I mean, I guess not," Josie says quietly.

Lydia's ability sort of works like a radio always scanning for open channels to sync into. Except there's only a couple of viable signals and she can't hold on to a frequency long enough to hear a full song. And the songs in this case are advice, messages, and omens. And the radio stations are vague ethereal beings from beyond the veil.

The reason people with this ability are called mouthpieces is because when they get good enough, they can actually translate messages from gods, spirit guides, deities, you name it.

Lydia and Josie and everyone in town have been training their abilities since they were in kindergarten. And although control over one's ability at this age varies, Lydia hasn't quite gotten the hang of being a mouthpiece. She more so just allows the messages to come through against her will. Though she tries to make it work when it's needed most.

Lydia closes her eyes, lifts her chin, and waits for some higher being to share any kind of insight about Declan. After a few minutes of meditation, a distant, wispy voice weaves through her mind like a delicate fog. But the message can't really permeate through Lydia's thoughts.

"Away..." it says distantly, the voice breaking apart and losing most of its message. *"Don't..."*

Lydia's brow creases as she tries to understand, tries to force it, tries to reach out and grasp on to this spectral presence. But the more she tries, the further the message recedes.

Lydia opens her eyes with a sigh and pushes away from the table, rubbing her eyes with her finger and thumb. "Sorry, Ash, signal's pretty choppy right now."

I try not to look disappointed as I reach for her hand, grateful for the attempt. "That's okay. We can keep trying later."

Josie leans forward, patting her hands on the table, relieved to move on. "Do we wanna watch a movie or something? Have a bonfire, get cozy?"

The world dims outside.

"Yes," Lydia prefaces, holding out her manicured nail, "but I do have the closing shift at the Foodie Mart, so I can't stay forever."

"Boo," I tease her. "Quit your job."

She laughs, running her fingers through her straightened hair. "You know my parents are still holding my car hostage until I can show that I'm *responsible enough*," she mocks with air quotes. "Whatever that means. That wreck wasn't even my fault!"

"Yeah, it was your phone's fault," Josie teases her.

"Well… I do have s'more supplies," I suggest.

Lydia jumps up. "I call holding the chocolate!"

We laugh.

"We aren't gonna stop you," I say. "Let me grab some blankets, and we'll get started."

"I'll get the fire ready," Josie hums, clasping her hands. "Oh, I love the fall."

As the sun slowly descends, the cloudless sky remains white, and a river of starlings canopies above us. The pattern-shifting birds make the Void look like static.

We wrap ourselves with blankets and huddle around Josie's impressive fire, chatting about everyday things. The sweetness of mundane Thursdays.

Watching the static, even now I can't help but feel an emptiness up there, as if the Void itself is locked out of the sky. Or at the very least, unable to communicate with me. Trapped behind the glass.

"Josie, have you met up with Miss Ava lately?"

"No." Josie half-laughs. "But I'll probably visit her soon. She secretly likes the harvest help. My sweet neighbor." She hums, as if reminding us of the elderly woman she fawns over regularly. "She has the best garden in her front yard. Oh, I bet she's preparin' her greenhouse. But why do you ask?"

The fire pops as the wood shifts.

"No real reason. I guess I thought of her because she's a mouthpiece, too."

"She's the one who communicates with the Void," Lydia tells us. "As far as mouthpieces go, she's a legend. She's visited our trainings a couple of times but she seems pretty reserved. Maybe one day, I'll be as powerful as her." Lydia pushes her well-crafted s'more into her mouth and continues talking. "But that'll take *a lot* of work, and I have other things to focus on right now."

Josie laughs as she unrolls her flannel sleeves. "Like what? Failin' math again?"

"Ah-ah." She wags her finger. "Ash is helping me pass this time."

"I helped you last time, too," I remind her, "and you still failed!"

Lydia rolls her eyes and turns her back to me. I try to get her to turn around but my marshmallow falls into the fire. Josie attempts to rescue it but it's full of ashes now.

"That's me graduating on time," Lydia jokes.

We erupt with laughter.

"Best I can do is literally give you the finals answers for you to memorize."

"Deal!"

"Y'all are so wrong," Josie teases between chewy bites. "But honestly, we need a miracle to keep you from summer school this year."

"Any advice?" Lydia shouts to the sky. She stands and opens her arms widely, the blanket draping around her as she tilts her head to the rainbow stars twinkling through the dusk-gray sky.

We pause in reverence, but after a minute, she gives up and plops back to the cushioned seat. "Nothing."

"Nothing *yet*," I say. "We have time to figure this out."

"What's Logan always saying?" Lydia wonders. "All things in time? Yeah, my teacher is always preaching patience, but why can't I just receive when I ask?"

"Thanks for always raisin' expectations, Lydia." Josie pokes her.

We cozy up around the fire as the world turns dark, and we begin telling scary stories.

I've always made up the most exaggerated tales, which pale in comparison to the passed-down-horrors from Josie's youth in the mountains and Lydia's true-stories from our high school's past. Being a poor storyteller is another tradition I'm happy to lean into. I could listen to them tell the same stories over and over, ooh-ing and gasping on cue.

Despite the building dread around the idea of my usefulness to The Watchers, my place in the world, and my control over my ability, Josie and Lydia make it all wash away.

By the time Lydia reminds Josie that she has to start her shift, the fire still burns brightly. Lydia promises me that she'll keep reaching out and see if anyone beyond the veil has anything to say about Declan. It's only seven but these autumn sunsets make the night feel endless.

After Josie and Lydia have left, I return to the fire, trying to hold on to the receding comfort they bring me. I study the way the fire chars the wood and makes it glow, how the sparks fly off to join the stars. But my head whips to Kane's house when I hear his screen door slam shut.

The back porch light illuminates Kane's long golden hair as he stands on his deck, his hands tucked into his letterman jacket. He looks at the faraway trees for a moment before his gaze lands on me.

I could see that look in the dark, a mile away, behind closed doors. One of the worst parts of my omniscience is being unable to escape my once-best friend and how much he hates me now.

Kane descends his porch steps with overzealous bounces, his blue eyes locked on me. Without saying a word he meets me at my campfire.

I glare back, holding the blanket closer to my body. "Remind me again why I'm keeping your brain damage a secret?"

He rests his hand on the chair Josie was just sitting in, his hollow features appearing extra sharp in the firelight. "First, it isn't your secret to know. And second, you only agreed to it because deep down..." He leans forward, smirking. "You know what you did was wrong."

I try not to scowl. "Helping an old friend isn't an admission of guilt. But keep prodding me, Kane, and I'll tell your coach the truth. Then you'll be nothing more than the used-to-be star player benched for his final season."

His smirk falls.

"You should try being nicer to the person keeping your secrets."

He straightens his back but his shoulders fall slack. "You wouldn't burn me twice." And there's that look again, that passing *humanity* in his eyes.

For a second my heart pounds. For a *second* my guise falls.

His sharp gaze returns, saying, *checkmate.* "Maybe you *are* human after all." He turns to walk away.

But I stand up, throwing my blanket off as heat flushes my cheeks. "You really don't think I'll do it."

He stops, looking ahead of him where the Plant Boys are waiting to pick him up in their red lifted truck. "Of course I think you'll ruin the entire town's fun. You did it before." He looks back at me. "You'll do whatever you want, Ash. You always do."

"Your uncle was a criminal," I hiss, stepping forward.

"So you do know what this is about," he huffs, his eyes going dark. "Good."

"I don't owe you anything," I shout as he walks away.

"Sure you do," he says softly, only my mind's eye picking it up.

I stand here for a while, feeling like a fool and not knowing where my anger should go. *It's just one more thing,* I keep telling myself. *It's just one more thing in the noise.* I stir the logs as I return to the fire. I stare up at the quiet sky for a long time, my head a whirl with the usual night noises.

Kane and the Plant Boys meet up with Hayden at the Stoplight Motel. I wonder back to that first dream I had—my first real dream. I repeat my visits with Winona and Chief and their indifference burns me. Declan's invisibility scares me. His placement in the government feels like a warning. And Logan's burning vision on the field still stalks the creases of my mind like a predator waiting to strike.

I see Logan in his bedroom playing video games as he leans against his bed. Nothing is different. Nothing has changed.

Except the sky is empty, the Forest Eye wants me back, the Jacksons are cemented into the inner workings of our home, The Watchers seem to be working in tandem with Declan, and I'm supposed to be patient.

I hope Lydia learns something tonight. I need somewhere to start, something to confirm my unease. Something to prove to them that I'm worth listening to. That I'm still strong enough to help Veil Haven.

The Forest Eye lied to me about that. It lied to me and I can figure this out on my own.

CHAPTER 14
THE BODY

In the twilight before I fully wake, the world is draped in silence. I lay in my pocket of warmth, feeling more refreshed than ever. My usual exhaustion is behind me, and I feel whole.

Half-awake, half-sleeping, I wonder if the world will wake with me, noticing that the silence is heavier than usual, longer than usual.

I recall my nightly visions about some girl named Jeanie painting her room black, how she smeared the paint across her face and stained her pillowcase.

The more I come into my body, the more I realize how tense I am, how tight my shoulders are. My hands are balled into fists, my jaw is locked, my breathing is shallow and quick.

When I open my eyes I'm thrown into my body. The riot of noise and color and movement from the world overwhelms me with a shriek. My ears are ringing. My head *aches*. Why is my heart beating so fast?

My mind's eye snaps to the police station without warning and my senses readjusting. I sit up and rub my chest as it tightens.

Hayden is in the waiting room crying into his hands. He's wearing mud-stained pajamas and shaking under a thin, fleece blanket. He's pale and damp with cold sweats and wondering how much more he has left in him. How much longer he can cry like this.

My heart is a lump in my throat. What happened? Why don't I know what happened?

If he's at the station that means he found a body, someone who died, and if he's crying—

I throw off my covers and sit on the edge of my bed.

Almost everyone in the station is anticipating what comes next. But what comes next?

It's like an electric current is running through the officers as they shuffle through documents and camera footage trying to solve or confirm whatever happened.

Chief looks ill as he mulls over a dozen questions at his desk. He grabs his head, overwhelmed with grief. He thinks about how this could've happened, how he will have to tell *her* parents. He feels terrible for Hayden. He feels even worse for me.

I pull my mind's eye from the station and focus on the creases of my floorboards. The only thing I hear is the beat of my heart.

Next thing I know, I'm grabbing my keys and walking out the front door. The cold air bites my exposed arms. My hands shake as I grip the wheel and head to the station.

Nothing happened last night. But now Hayden is having panic attacks and replaying the moment he found—

No. I don't want to see it. Nothing happened.

It hurts to breathe and swallow, and the heat rising through me stings my eyes.

I break every traffic law as I lose myself in distractions. *Someone is making cinnamon rolls. The ghosts are preparing for another endless shift at the Bread Barrel. Someone burns their breakfast. Someone is making a deal with a Mothman behind the Danny's. Someone is being protected by Beings of Light as they jog on hiking trails. A Cloud Person's cat is batting at their wispy cirrus head. Someone is pulling themselves from the packed earth and coughs up earthworms, gasping for breath. A Plant Person with a head of coneflowers brushes their soft petals in the mirror. Someone is kissing their loved one awake.*

I stare at the mossy building as I turn off my car. My stomach flips. A voice in the back of my head tells me, *She's dead.*

I don't remember leaving my car or pushing through the station doors, but now I'm kneeling in front of Hayden, my hand on his mud-caked knee.

He meets my gaze with what little energy he has left. His eyes are red from hours of crying. *Hours.*

Neither of us say anything. He swallows sharp, wet breaths and buries into his hands again. His heaving cries set off alarms in my head as goosebumps cover my body.

I stand, numb. The world is completely silent.

I see myself through my mind's eye as I walk deeper into the station. I don't register the faces staring at me. I try not to observe their surprise or pity or disdain. I hear them whisper they're doing this for *me.* They talk about how unconventional this pointless work is.

It's so she doesn't go ballistic, someone whispers.

We all know why, someone else says.

I move to the side hallway toward the morgue, but I'm stopped before I can reach those metal doors.

Chief grabs my arm and stands in front of me. He's talking to me but I barely hear him.

I shake my head, the silence of the world pressing on my ears.

He refuses to move. I refuse to make him.

My mind's eye floats through the doors, to the table. I pull back. My knees are shaking.

Chief tries to get my attention. My vision blurs as I look at him. I can't hear him.

I sound like a distant echo. "I need to see." My throat burns. "I need to see."

"Ash," he cautions, "you don't."

I shake my head, tears finally spilling. "Let me."

His arms fall slack as I move around him.

I enter the morgue. It's somehow both sterile and disgusting. The reek of chemicals stains the air. It's a large, white and metal room, like the ones you see in those police procedural shows. I don't think I've ever been in here. I've never needed to be.

The coroner is a large, tired man in a lab coat, and he's surprised to see me. But his nerves settle when Chief follows me in. The two men stare at each other. I only stare at the table in the middle of the room. The white sheet covering *her* body.

Suddenly, I'm next to the table. Chief's hand is on my back. The coroner is on the other side. He studies me. Chief nods. He pulls the sheet back.

I know her instantly.

My core temperature drops. My stomach drops. I'm—

The world vanishes from my periphery.

I never knew there was so much noise in the silence.

I don't blink. I don't breathe. I don't feel my heart beating.

I don't sense hers either, but I do feel the bugs worming inside her gut.

She's caked in mud. Her jaw is scraped. Her brown hair is twisted with dirt and leaves. She's so pale. So pale. The blood has pooled to one side of her face making it discolored and bloated. I see no injuries, no missing parts. She's whole and still and the stench...

This isn't her. It-it can't be.

Chief catches me as my knees buckle. Shaking. Unable to look away.

"Lydia! Lydia!"

The coroner covers her again. Chief removes me from the room as I scream. My sobs boom through the station as he holds me in the hallway. I sink into him. My vision spins. My body isn't my own. My mind escapes me.

Someone burns their tongue. Someone breaks their arm. Someone finds their dog at the end of their yard. Someone hits the person they love. Someone is screaming. Someone is paralyzed.

None of this is real. It can't be. But as I search for sign of her across town... I know.

Deep within me, I know.

Dante is phasing his hand through Ford's face. Ford starts listing causes of death to scare him away. Josie finds a parking spot at school. Logan smiles at Shakira. Shakira smiles back. Kane hot boxes his car before class. Markus kisses his sisters' foreheads and wishes them a good day at school. Hayden is hyperventilating.

I can't stop sobbing. Screaming. Demanding answers. *How, how, how.*

They were supposed to protect her.

They were supposed to protect me.

I was supposed to protect her.

The heat inside me burns my chest and makes my head pound. I feel myself shouting her name again and again but I don't hear it.

Chief holds me in the hallway outside the morgue, trying to keep me steady, trying to help me catch my breath. But I'm pounding his chest and he's surprised by my anger, my vitriol.

She can't be dead. Why is she dead? Why didn't I see it? People lose people all the time, every day, but not me. Never me. This isn't supposed to happen.

I stare at the morgue, my mind's eye taking me through the doors. My best friend is on that table. Lydia is dead. My stomach is full of molten lead and I'm certain I'm going to vomit on Chief's shoes. I push away from him and lean against the cool walls, trying to soothe my headache.

Then, I remember the last thing I asked her to do. My face is damp, my lips still quiver, but slowly, my features harden. I stare at nothing.

"He killed her."

Chief's brows furrow as he steps closer, studying me for a moment. "No one killed her, Ash."

I push myself off the wall and get in his face, counting the reasons on my fingers. "Cryptids don't leave bodies lying around for someone to find. She's a mouthpiece. She gets omens when she's in danger. She's only eighteen. And I asked her—" I tremble, losing my voice. I suddenly become aware of the possibility that this could be true. That whatever her guides told her was dangerous enough for her to be...

But no, The Watchers don't kill people. I should tell Chief what I asked of her.

I don't.

"For the first time—no, *third* time in my life—I didn't see something and now she's *dead*. How can you explain that?" My voice cracks.

I don't care if the entire station hears us. I don't care if the entire town knows. I'm begging him for an answer. He has to know something. He *has* to.

"Ash," he says softly, "there aren't any signs of attack, no foul play. She had an aneurysm."

"No." I shake my head. "*No.*"

"She passed away without pain. It happened so fast, Ash. And she fell down the hill. She rolled into the mudflats. But she was already gone. I'm so sorry, Ash." He hangs his head. "She died of natural causes."

"Nothing about this is natural." *I told her to learn about Declan.* I can't will myself to say it. The room spins. I stagger back, shaking my head. "So you're not going to investigate?"

"We already have our answer." It's painful to see him so desperate to aid me, but he's still not listening. Lydia couldn't have died of natural causes. Something *happened*. Her guides would've told her about an aneurysm. They would've warned her about anything.

When I don't respond, he fills the silence. "It was an aneurysm, Ash. Same thing happened to that poor homeless kid. It's just something that happens."

I can't understand what he's saying to me. "Who?" The world pounds at the back of my mind, demanding to be let in.

"Mohe Vann. No one really noticed him. Something about his ability. Look, it doesn't matter."

Sirens go off in my head. *Vann.* Why is that name familiar?

He looks me in the eye, holds my arms tighter, and gently moves his thumbs to comfort me. "It's never easy when a young person dies."

Something inside me snaps, and I hear myself before I realize what I'm saying. "Only easy when they disappear."

We're both surprised by my tone. The rage. The defiance. And something in his dark eyes shifts, like a wall going up.

Chief brushes the damp hair out of my eyes and hugs me so tightly I wonder if it could mend me. He tells me to take deep breaths, and I do, *despite, despite, despite.* He pets the back of my hair as I soak his uniform. I hear him whispering.

"Know you'll survive this, Ash. You will get through. This sadness will not break you."

It's almost comforting somehow. I can't explain why. But I don't think I'll ever feel whole again. I can't be myself without her. Without her—

I lean my head against his chest again, catching my breath. "What's wrong with me?"

His shoulders drop. "You *cannot* expect yourself to function a hundred percent of the time." He kisses the top of my head. "You're only a kid, Ash. You're not supposed to have all the answers."

And just like that, I fall apart.

CHAPTER 15
BITING YOUR TONGUE ALL THE WAY THROUGH

I'm leaning against Hayden. We don't speak. There's nothing to say.

Chief is standing over us and telling us his plan. He's going to drive us home and we are going to rest. I ask if he can leave us both at my house. Hayden nods. Neither of us want to be alone.

And so we're dropped off. Chief lingers in my living room. Hayden and I fall onto separate couches staring at nothing. Chief tells us he's sorry again, tries to explain grief and how what we're feeling is normal. He's not very good at this.

"Please go."

He lowers his head and nods. Guilty.

The silence between Hayden and me is enough to paralyze. We cry intermittently without speaking. I say something about school, how nobody knows. He hurries to the bathroom and vomits in the toilet. I shrink on the couch, holding my knees under my chin.

Everyone is at school like the world hasn't changed forever.

Lydia's parents get ready for work unaware that their daughter is gone. Don't they know she didn't come home last night? *Did* she go home last night?

My gut curls at the thought that somehow I'm responsible.

The room spins and heat roars through me again. I sprint upstairs and hurl into the toilet.

I stare at my phone for a long time. Josie texted the groupchat asking us where we are. I watch her in the courtyard talking about the game tonight with Shakira.

I sob into my hand, pinching my eyes so hard I see spots. The side of my bathtub is so cold.

My fingers shake as I dial her number.

"Hello?" Josie chimes. The noise from the courtyard bleeds into the call. She plugs her ear and asks if I'm there. She wonders what I have to say. What do I have to say?

My voice shakes so much more than I expected. I wanted to hide it. I sound terrible. "Come to my house."

Josie's chest tightens. "Ash? What's wrong? I can't hear you."

"Leave school. Come here. Please."

"Are you okay?"

My voice bubbles up and I sob instantly. "No. Please come over."

"Okay, okay." Josie leaves the courtyard in a rush, giving Shakira a vague explanation. "I'm coming."

I throw my head back and hang up, holding my breath. My tears leave me cold.

I'm not strong enough to stand but I have to be there for Hayden. I have to be there for Josie. I have to tell her what happened. But what happened?

As Josie runs through the halls back to her car, she passes Logan without knowing it. He calls out for her, but when she doesn't answer, a pit forms in his gut, and he chases after her.

When Josie finally realizes Logan is jogging up behind her, they're at her car. There's a small exchange. Both of them worried. And Josie agrees to let Logan come with her.

I don't know if this is better or worse. Having to face them both. I get sick at the idea.

I collect myself, still shaking, and I tell Hayden minutes before they arrive.

He tries to steel himself but as soon as they come through the door, and see us wet-faced, our minute-long façade slips.

The realization dawns on Josie almost immediately. Something's supernatural about it. Something we can only communicate because of our shared girlhood.

Her brows smooth into a single expression of horror.

My thin, dark blue hoodie is drenched in tears and sweat. My hair sticks to my cheeks and neck. "I don't know how to say it."

Josie walks up and holds me, unspeaking, unblinking. She looks at Hayden but he turns away with shaking lips.

Logan is standing in my doorway watching the scene unfold.

Hayden wants to walk over and hug his friend, be held by him, to hold anyone, but he isn't certain his legs can hold him, let alone carry him to the front door.

Logan knows he's dressed in my clothes. In any other circumstance they would judge his out-of-character outfit. An XXL gray petting zoo print tee and star-covered sweatpants.

"I can't say it," I admit. "It's too terrible to say."

Hayden cups his mouth, bracing for the blow.

Logan looks like a ghost as he walks over to Hayden, trying to make sense of what's happened. Trying to map it out in his mind as he disregards even the most obvious conclusions.

Josie's nails dig into my wrists as she watches my mouth part.

"Hayden found Lydia."

Josie collapses, screaming. She clutches her chest, holds her face, and cries out.

Nothing else in the world is happening.

I fall beside her.

I don't know how Logan reacts. I don't know what Hayden does. I can only stare at Josie as she sobs. I take her against my chest. I get tangled in her long hair. She hugs me too tightly but I don't mind the pain. I don't know how to soothe her, so I hold her, knowing it isn't enough.

She shakes her head. "No, no, no, no."

I can't speak.

She begs me to say what happened.

The truth has me in a vise grip. It splits me down the middle. My gaze settles on my painted stairs. On a set of Lydia's pink-painted hands. On all the glitter thrown between the years. I hear her there. I see the phantom of our happiness. And just as I think I'm going to vomit, I hear Logan and Hayden.

"What happened?" Logan breathes, his face pale.

Hayden squints. "You-you don't know? I thought you were just being polite."

"No," Logan says quickly. Too quickly. He stares down at me, his blue eyes wide. Confused. Terrified. "No, Lydia isn't supposed to... she doesn't... she..."

I stay on the floor with Josie, but my mouth dries out. I know that look. I know that feeling, too. Logan didn't see this either.

The day goes on in a blur.

Someone can't make their eyes stop glowing. Someone meets with a flaming skeleton in the woods. A Plant Person with cattails for a head sits along the shoreline of the lake, crying. Someone is kicked out of the training facility. Someone is choking. Someone punches their wall and breaks their hand.

Chief Mun drives to Lydia's house. Her mom opens the door. I'm sick watching him take his hat off. "Lydia was found dead early this morning."

Mrs. Boswell laughs at him. He stands there and lets his somberness speak for itself. Her smile fades quickly, and she collapses without speaking, without crying. He helps her to the couch, explaining what little he knows and how a friend found her, how her identity has been confirmed.

She asks if it was me or Hayden but he doesn't answer as his heart sinks. Chief explains that another officer is reaching out to her husband, and he'll be home soon.

When Mrs. Boswell finally breaks, it happens all at once. Her face shifts in the way only a mother's can.

The same question plagues her just as it plagues me and everyone who knows. *What happened to Lydia?*

We're sitting on my two couches when I tell them.

"I don't know what happened." They stare at me. I can't stand it. "I-I-oh god." I break. "Oh, Lydia. *Lydia.*" I hyperventilate her name. I can't do this. I can't—

Josie rubs my back, guides my head between my knees, and teaches me how to breathe again. My skull pounds, grief suffocating me. My chest feels full of daggers that pinch and cut me with every word, every breath, every thought of her.

"I didn't see anything. I didn't know. You found her," I say to Hayden, "and I didn't even see *that.*" My hands shake. I cover my face and sob, screaming between breaths. Josie cries beside me quietly. Logan and Hayden do the same. All of us are lost.

"If I had seen her, if I was awake, I could've saved her. Chief says it was natural. He says she died of an aneurysm. Did he tell you?" I ask Hayden.

Hayden nods.

"An aneurysm?" Josie echoes.

Logan rubs his temples. He mutters to himself, "The future changes all the time but this is different than... It's just so different."

"With everything I'm capable of I could've saved her."

"You don't know that," Josie tells me. "You can't put that on yourself." She's distant. She's pushing through. She's trying to be strong. That's what people do in these situations, isn't it?

"I feel like I'm losing my mind." I stare at my hands again, watching how much they shake. "Do you know how many times I've watched people die? Watched them struggle for breath? Fight for their lives? Scream, kick, claw at the ground, break nails, chip teeth, cry, cry, cry." I lose my breath. "And I didn't see it happen to her?" My anger is interchangeable with my grief. Or maybe this grief *is* rage.

Josie scoots closer, but she wants to turn away. She can't imagine all I've seen. She doesn't want to, but I know she's caught between wanting to help me and tending to herself. And I am guilty that I want her help.

And I want Lydia. And I want this to go away. And I want this to make sense. I want the director. I want to run away from this. I want to wake up.

Then, something dawns on me. My tears dry. "I've seen everyone but her." I sound distant, anger rumbling in the back of my throat. "*Everyone* but her."

Josie stares at me, her brows low. What does she see in my blank white eyes?

"You know what I asked her to do," I say, my face contorting as I return to my original train of thought at the station. "She must've learned something. Don't you think?"

"What are you talking about?" Hayden asks us, leaning closer.

But before I can answer, Josie stands up, her fists tight with worry. "Nothing. Nothing happened. Chief Mun said it was natural causes." She looks at Hayden and Logan, her teary eyes begging them to understand.

Hayden buries his head again, any deeper meanings passing over him. Josie sits beside him and they hug each other, realizing they both share the same depth of love for her. Realizing how intimately they know Lydia. Knowing that they'll never know more about her after today.

But Logan looks at me.

I see something in his gentle eyes, like he's fit together two puzzle pieces. He recognizes my anger and he isn't surprised by it. He's worried. Not for himself, not for Veil Haven, but for me.

I asked Lydia to learn about the one man I can't see, and now she's dead. I've been worried about the new family since they arrived. I went to them about Declan, but they won't listen to me. They say I'm not supposed to know.

The Forest Eye told me it was because I'm not strong enough. The Void warned me the Forest Eye was lying. But was it lying about my ability or how dangerous the Jacksons are?

"I saw you on the field last Friday," I tell Logan.

His eyes widen, the hairs on his neck rising. He swallows. "This isn't that."

Veil Haven burning.

"It might as well be."

CHAPTER 16
YOUR BODY IS A BURNING HOUSE

At school, news begins to spread that somebody is dead. People with empathetic abilities add validity to the feeling. Someone connected the dots between the absences at school and how quickly Josie left. They understand Hayden probably found a body. The most popular rumor is that it was me. They are not kind.

The rumors branch off from there with more false theories. Anyone who is absent could be the victim. Anyone but Lydia.

When the announcement is made at school over the intercoms, everyone is surprised. Shakira leaves and comes over right away. Markus and Ford plan to arrive later, not sure how to handle the news.

People agree it's strange there's an announcement at all, but when it continues, it begins to make sense. The game is still scheduled to happen. They're going to hold a small vigil at the game to honor her, one of their best cheerleaders.

When I share the news with everyone in my living room, they're in shock. Logan can hardly believe it. Hayden begins panicking. Josie tries to soothe him.

Logan checks his phone but hasn't received any messages from his coach. "What are they thinking?" he grimaces. "None of us are going to play." We watch as our quarterback, *Veil Haven's golden boy*, marches furiously to the back deck.

He drills his coach as soon as he picks up, trying to make him realize how insensitive this is. I've never seen him yell like this before. He's trying to make Coach Strongman understand the position he's putting them in, but Strongman doesn't care.

"This happens, Logan," he says.

"Find new players tonight. We aren't coming."

Next, Logan calls his teammates one by one and tells them not to play. A little less than half agree to sit out, but Kane seems to be driving the opposition. Logan's features contort as he tries to make sense of it. "What is wrong with you, Kane?"

"Am I the only one who isn't captivated by another person dying?"

Logan's lost for words, his anger boiling down, his voice soft and low. "This is Lydia. She's our friend."

"No, she's *your* friend. But... is she? Why *do* you care? It's not like you hung out with her. She was just a cheerleader."

"Some of us have empathy, Kane."

"Well, some of us know better." He hangs up.

Logan puts his phone on the railing and stares across my yard, lost for words.

The midday sun is so soft. The world feels warped by the chill.

I watch him through the sliding glass doors before meeting him outside. Logan and I don't say anything for a long time. We only stare at the golden and deep red leaves cradling the long stretch of my grassy backyard.

Logan's voice cracks. I've never seen him so emotional.

"I swear I didn't see this, Ash." He's begging me to forgive him. "I... I don't know what happened. How could this have happened when..." He's so frustrated he has to pause to collect himself. "I was *so* certain that..." He looks away, his jaw tight. He slams his hands on the railing before burying his face in his arms to hide his tears. "She was always alive in the future, Ash. I don't know what's happening."

I stare at him in shock. The mess of the world seems to race at me like a wind tunnel.

"Can the future be changed like that?"

He picks his head up, not bothering to wipe his eyes. His voice is softer now but still broken. "Yes, of course it can. I just never thought..." He runs his fingers through his hair. "I wish I could say more but I... this feels so out of control."

Without warning, I hug him. He lays his arms across my shoulders and we catch our breaths. Neither of us close our eyes.

What can I say? What can he say? In a world where laws and secrets have us by the throat, our shared silence needs to be enough. And for now, it is.

As evening rolls around, Ford, Markus, and Shakira arrive. We decide to have a bonfire in Lydia's honor. Hopefully it'll be enough to distract us from the game, from everything. But my god this is hard.

We're all somber, lost, and exhausted. Josie tries to make small talk with Ford but she breaks down in front of him instead. Ford holds her gently with one arm.

It's cold enough to see our breaths as we huddle around the fire with blankets. The stars burn above us in a black sky. It's been so long since the night has been black. The Void must be mourning with us.

They're still up there watching, then. Maybe I'm just making up that hollowness above me. Maybe I'm... I don't know. Maybe I'm just tired and scared, and the world has become unfamiliar, and I can't cope.

Maybe what Chief told me is true. I'm just a kid who doesn't have to know all the answers. But that's a terrible conclusion.

By the time the football game begins, most of the town is there since they heard one of the cheerleaders died. No one close to

Lydia attends the quick candlelit vigil. Half of the crowd doesn't understand why they're holding a vigil for her at all. Some of the people mourn and hold space for her loss. Others are a mixed bag. Some are even offended by the vigil.

There's an undercurrent there, too. The girl who died was one of *my* friends. It's like they're waiting for me to have some sort of outburst. Why are they afraid of me? Why are they thinking of me at all? What do they expect me to do?

We don't care that the game is dedicated to her. Or how the people hum a couple of sad songs, give a lame speech, or hold out the Mothmen's hand symbol as if being a cheerleader was the only thing that defined her.

This is how Veil Haven grieves. Quickly.

Instead, Josie, Shakira, Logan, Hayden, Ford, Markus, and I huddle around our bonfire. They try to make each other laugh. Even Josie tries to cheer herself up. It's gentle how much love we share between us. But I can't stop knowing how Lydia was just sitting beside me last night. She was *here*, and now she never will be again.

My mind's eye takes me to the biggest noise generator in town. Kane is talking to someone he half-knows before taking the field.

"You really think her friends don't have it coming?"

"Who?" they wonder.

"Ash." He nearly growls my name.

"You think Ash had something to do with Lydia's death?"

Kane doesn't say anything. He just raises his brows and turns away.

My molars grind, knowing this is how his rumors begin.

Kane's concussion continues to pain him, and it seems to be magnifying his hatred of me. I haven't heard my name come out of his mouth this much in years. Before, he would just ignore me or pretend to be embarrassed for me. Now that I saw him at his lowest, he's obsessed with bringing me down with him.

Before my rage can undo me, I notice Shakira staring at me with intent.

She's waiting for a good moment to bring something up to me. And when our eyes lock, she makes sure I see her leave her phone on her chair before she gets up and moves away from the fire. I follow her gesture with a knot in my stomach. Whatever it is, she doesn't want any outside ears.

Together, we walk deeper into the darkness of my yard. She feels safe with me. I guess my friends always do.

As if on cue, I notice a Not-Deer at the end of my yard half-hidden by the low branches. You can always tell when something's not a deer. Crooked limbs, unhinged jaw, maggots in the eyes, gnarled antlers. Hungry things.

I step in the direction of the faraway cryptid, making sure it sees me staring it down. And just like every cryptid that's dared to cross me, it turns and leaves.

Shakira watches me but says nothing.

I step back to her and ground myself. The air is cold, even under my joggers and sweatshirt. Shakira rubs her arms as we stand barely able to see each other in the quarter moon light.

She clenches her jaw. Her fingers run the length of her hair. "Y'know how Logan has been sayin' that things are changin'? And... now this... and when I couldn't come back from the future... Ash, I'm afraid somethin' bad is comin'. But I think I can figure it out. I think I can prepare us."

I stiffen. How could her thoughts align so well with mine? I feel so seen. Does she know my ability hasn't been working? Does she know more about Logan's vision of Veil Haven burning?

"I have this idea that if I could go to the future and scope out what's happenin'," she continues, "maybe things don't have to change. Maybe if we know what's comin', we can make sure the bad stuff doesn't happen. Is that crazy?"

I push my hair back slowly and hold my head, zoning out. "No, you're not crazy. I've felt the exact same way."

She puts her hands out and I grab them, feeling her many rings. "I know we aren't the closest, but I feel like I can tell you anythin', y'know?"

I nod. She smiles, and I feel like I might cry.

She squeezes my hands, knowing. "Logan keeps sayin' this wasn't supposed to happen, and it makes me sick. He seems so lost. And you're... and I'm... Somethin' is happenin' to our home, Ash." She pauses, a noble air about her.

"I know. I've felt it since Markus' family moved in. Nothing has made sense since then. It feels like I'm losing my mind."

She takes a steady breath. "If I go to the future, to whatever version is laid out right now, I could see what's happenin'. I could figure out what's comin'. And then maybe we could work together to stop it. Because everythin' feels so wrong right now, but... this is dangerous, and the last time I went to the future it felt like... well, you know. But I can't shake the idea like I'm supposed to do somethin'. And I wanted to ask you if you think I should do this."

I look back at the fire, our friends' dark outlines shifting around the golden flames. Something heavy moves through my chest as I think about Logan's vision of Veil Haven burning and how my ability has failed me. I think about Winona and Chief shutting me down. I think about the Forest Eye reaching out and the director ignoring me. I contemplate how capable I am on my own.

Director Capaldi won't talk to me. I know that. He *let* Lydia die. He must have. I don't care what they say. This isn't natural. Not when I asked her to help me with Declan. Not when I wanted to know more despite direct orders to let it go.

Shakira waits for my answer, as if whatever I tell her will define what happens next. If I say no, she won't go to the future. If I say no, I'll never be prepared for what comes next. I can't see the future. I hardly know the present. And I can't stand not knowing. I can't risk it anymore. What if someone else dies? What if this is all preventable?

160

"I think you should try."

She leans forward, and despite the foreign motion, I rest my forehead against hers. It feels right. Nothing else needs to be said.

We stand here for a moment in the hum of the night sounds mixed with the distant laughter of our friends, and I breathe steadily for the first time all day. When we return, we act as though nothing has happened. We know the weight of this secret.

Shakira tucks her phone into her pocket and forgets about the plan altogether. After all, you never know who's watching.

CHAPTER 17
MYRAH AND THE CRYPTID OF VAPOR AND FLESH

Even though I was taught and told to help the people of Veil Haven, I lost the desire to go out and save them a long time ago.

You can't save someone unless they want to be saved. You can't help someone who's in the maw of a beast. If you try to help, you'll get yourself killed. This the undercurrent of our world.

Most people don't know bad things are happening to their loved ones until it's too late. But if they hear their cries in time, of course they'll help. Despite the numbing apathy of another life lost, people in Veil Haven are here for each other. I've never felt their community, but I've seen it.

Every once in a while, people will still come to me and accuse me of letting their loved one die. I've heard every variation of, "All they needed was someone to call an ambulance, but they were alone, and they died alone. But you're always watching. And because you did nothing, their death is on your hands."

It's just another thing I've gone numb to. I can't do it all. I can barely keep the noise in my head from hurting me. But now that Lydia is gone... I can't help but wonder if those people were right. If they've always been right.

The first and last time I tried to save someone I was six.

If I said I remembered things like the day of the month, what Myrah was doing before she got stood up on her blind date, or why I focused on her to begin with, I would be lying. What caught my attention was when she fumbled her keys in the restaurant parking lot. She pushed back her blonde curls and said something like, "This just isn't my night."

And she was right, of course. The night doesn't belong to us. It belongs to them.

I've watched countless kidnappings by man and monster alike, but when the Cryptid of Vapor and Flesh charged at her from the shadows of streetlights, when it grabbed her so hard she didn't have time to scream, I sat upright in bed and watched the entire event unfold.

The forest was an uproar of hunger but the other beasts knew this kill was already claimed. Myrah gagged being so close to the cryptid's stench of chlorine and rot. When the Cryptid of Vapor and Flesh laughed at her, it sounded like a pool drain gurgling viscous liquid.

Eventually, Myrah and the cryptid arrived at an abandoned house. The structure had long since been claimed by humans, the roof half-collapsed, the walls partly eaten by rainwater and mildew. Even the floorboards were slanted with rot. The black-wood cabin only had four rooms, a giant cross of wood dissecting the floorplan. It had become the killing grounds for this cryptid. Bone fragments and dried blood stained every room.

This house, like most abandoned places in Veil Haven, was not that far from town. But still, no one would hear her and no one would save her if they did.

The cryptid threw Myrah into the small house like a ragdoll. Mud-stained and bruised from being dragged through the woods, she crouched into the corner below an open window and stayed there.

The Cryptid of Vapor and Flesh had never adopted a name other than that, nor did it want one. It was content without any human identity or pronouns. The townsfolk hardly knew about the cryptid or its tendencies, but still, Myrah could tell from the base of her spine that as soon as she tried to leave that cabin the hunt would begin.

The cryptid eclipsed the rooms, having to crouch and duck just to fit its tall frame inside, which made it appear that much larger. The chlorine curled in the back of her throat and burned her, made her eyes water, her stomach churn. But still, she did not move.

While they both waited for action, the cryptid crept between doorways to scare her. It would wrap its long, pale boney fingers around doorframes expecting Myrah to be inspired to run.

She was not. Things went on like this all night.

The auburn sun rose slowly over the mountains, and still Myrah was frozen in fear and frost. Her hyperventilation formed a cloud of breath around her. She flinched any time she felt it draw near, the chlorine gagging her, but the cryptid would recede with a steaming hiss.

Despite her hope the police would save her, I knew they were not coming. They always ignore missing person reports since they have too many to keep track of, and the search is always more dangerous than what the find yields.

No one saves the missing. It's better that way.

I've watched this town live and decay knowing that at some point I will watch a third of our population die. I am a narrator, a watcher, and I don't have a role in their stories.

Myrah wasn't special, but maybe that was the point. So many of them weren't, still aren't, and never will be, but does that mean they should have to die? Did that mean I couldn't do something with the power I was given?

I could feel myself in the reflection of her eyes miles away in the comfort of my bed. We were both unmoving, waiting, watching. Maybe her stillness or her prayers or how she urged someone, anyone to do something led my feet to the floor.

I didn't remember how I got out there but once I stood in the crooked shadow of the dilapidated cabin, I knew this was it. I was only a few yards away from Myrah, who still cowered and prayed and shielded her eyes.

The cryptid was there too, ten feet tall, hunched, and gray skinned. It stood at the back window staring into the trees as if having profound thoughts about its circumstances.

It was easy to tell it wasn't human, or if it once was, it certainly wasn't anymore. Its skin was stretched thin and burned by vapor and mist, the opaque air curling from various patches.

It didn't *not* have a face but rather the waterlogged blueprint of what a face might look like. Its eye sockets were sunken and dark. It had rows of razor-sharp teeth that curled high into its cheekbones—forever grinning. Its jaw was detached but hanging by taut strands of flesh as vapor curled between its sharpened smile like an evaporated candle wick. What once might have been soft palms and gentle fingers were now bone-ashen claws, pointed at the ends, and lacking a left ring finger.

The Cryptid of Vapor and Flesh ignored Myrah who was paralyzed in fear two rooms away. And it ignored me, too.

I made note of any loose branches, dried leaves, or particularly ruined floorboards as I crept forward. The house reeked of mold and rot from years of feasting and never swallowing every piece of meat.

Myrah had spent the night debating whether she should give up or keep praying for a miracle. Many people speak to gods here, but in these cases, it only matters if they show up, which they rarely do.

Instead, Myrah was met by a six-year-old girl with blank white eyes.

When she registered me, she was caught between confusion and horror.

Regardless, I extended my hand, assuring her that the cryptid hadn't moved and we needed to stay quiet.

Myrah's bloodshot eyes locked on to me as she frantically shook her head no.

I nodded in response, waving for her to follow me out.

Nobody is perfect at making decisions when swallowed by fear, but in a stroke of luck Myrah inched toward me. And as fate would have it the floorboard split under her.

The panic was overwhelming—chilling, sour, and deafening. The cryptid eclipsed us instantly, careening its smooth head into the room with that unhinged smile. It smelled of rancid chlorine and decay, its vapor curling without wind.

Seeing rare cryptids in the periphery of my mind's eye was one thing but experiencing them in person was far worse.

I wanted to tell Myrah to run, but before I could part my lips, the cryptid slammed me into the wall, knocking the breath out of my small body. It pinned me there, hot vapor wafting over my clothes as it smelled me through its cavernous mouth. It traced my arm with a boney finger and cut me there. I hissed in pain, and it matched my sound, mocking me.

Myrah crouched under us screaming. I wanted her to run so badly but she wasn't moving.

The cryptid licked my blood from its finger and hummed with interest.

When I told Myrah to run, she listened, stumbling quickly out of the rotten house and into the morning sunlight.

The Cryptid of Vapor and Flesh cocked its head and tsked me pitifully. I fell to the floor faster than I realized it had let me go.

As it chased Myrah, it deformed into smoke and sopping flesh. One of those terribly unique sounds you can't forget.

She ran until her lungs and legs were burning, but it was never going to be enough. I think we both knew that.

The steaming cryptid clutched her throat like a soda can and her spine popped in an instant. It dragged her back to the cabin slowly.

It cornered me with Myrah as its shield. She was twitching more than she was moving. Her eyes were glassy as she gasped passively for air. When I flinched, the cryptid cackled, sounding like boiling water putting out its own flame.

In your final moments, or a moment of near-death, you experience an elevation of the senses as a last-ditch effort to survive. A voice comes to you in those moments. It doesn't matter where it comes from, but when it speaks, you listen.

Myrah had accepted that she was going to die with what little oxygen was still feeding her brain. But a feeling deep in my gut told me I was going to be spared despite every intention this monster had to kill me.

The cryptid's jaw didn't move as it spoke, vapor curling through rows of sharp, jagged teeth. *"I know what you are, child."*

Myrah's shoulders fell limp, her heart finally slowing.

"You were made to watch."

Its vapor was so hot I was sure it was burning me. The chlorine seared my throat.

I met its sunken blackhole eyes and waited.

Its gurgling voice smirked. *"Watching is your place... and this is mine."*

Its fingers broke through Myrah's chest in an explosion of red mist. Half of her in my hair, on my lips, in my ears. The cryptid laughed like a burst steampipe, and I froze, watching its teeth carve holes in her neck, her shoulder, her breast. Bit by bit it was swallowing her without pause.

In its hunger I slipped away, and it let me, laughing like a slurping pool drain as I ran.

"You will never save them, child." It wasn't speaking louder than a hush between bites, somehow knowing I would hear it anyway. *"You are one of—"*

The Cryptid of Vapor and Flesh was cut short as a root speared through its chest. Looking down at its wound, still gripping Myrah, the cryptid clutched the living root, surprised. "After all I've done for you?" I wasn't sure who it was talking to.

The earth did not shake when it split open. The trees and forest floor simply shifted apart and opened a cavernous hole beneath the cabin. It fell into the ground with an almost silent *whoosh* as if the cabin too was surprised by the sudden loss of foundation. The roots in the earth moved like hungry vipers.

The Cryptid of Vapor and Flesh hissed and roared and cursed as it tried to deform and escape, but hundreds of roots had speared it and Myrah. Vapor curled from every puncture as the cryptid writhed to break free, hissing threats until it couldn't move at all, until it never spoke again.

The attack only stopped when both bodies were more root than form. And as I stood there and watched, my mind's eye lowering me into that hole, I saw one of the most dangerous cryptids in Veil Haven become nothing more than food for the earth.

As quickly as the cabin was devoured, the ground resealed itself. Leaving no trace that a structure had ever been there. The cryptid was gone and so was Myrah.

In my panic, the rest of Veil Haven melted away. I heard nothing but my thoughts for the first time in my life. It was horrible. Then a noise I had never known broke through the silence, and I realized something was watching me. Something ubiquitous.

A feeling rose in me that wasn't the promise of death but rather an overwhelming change I was not ready to face. So despite a voice asking me to stay, I ran.

It took me a long time to scrub off Myrah's blood, skin, and bone dust, but when I was done and dressed, I realized someone was in my house. I crept down the stairs and paused, clutching the banister with teary eyes, my trauma bubbling over.

Director Capaldi stood in my living room—tall, wide, and imposing. He always wore a pressed black suit and preferred to keep his hands tucked into his pockets. His frown made his small mouth look smaller, and he didn't seem to care that his receding hairline pushed to the top of his head. He watched me with those low, dark eyes.

I was hyperventilating by the time he finally raised his arms and invited me into a hug. I ran into him, his protruding belly soft against my face. The smell of cigars wafted around me but I preferred it to the metallic gore.

We stood there for a while, and he pet me as my shaking sobs soaked through his clothes. I don't know what he saw or how but I assumed he knew everything. He was the director, after all.

He tapped under my chin, and I craned my neck to look at him. I saw pity in his eyes, and he sighed, finally crouching to meet my gaze. His thick fingers wiped my tears.

He patted down my wild hair and tucked it behind my ears before finally speaking. "You're okay," he soothed, though it doubled as a command. "You're okay."

I was never sure what came first—Director Capaldi or mobster movies—but I was certain they sounded exactly the same.

I nodded and held back tears, wiping my nose against my arm.

He sighed again and shook his head. "This is what happens when you take action without direction, Ash. You get hurt." He held my cheek, dwarfing my face in his large palm. "You can't do that, Ash. You can't save them."

"I tried." My voice shook. I felt so small.

"And look what happened."

My lips quivered as my hairs stood on end. He pulled me into a hug again, and I sank into him.

"You could've died, Ash. What would I do without you? You have to think." He held me tighter. "It was stupid and you can't do it again."

"I won't."

"And why?"

"Because I just make things worse."

"That's right, baby," he soothed me. "Let me worry about this stuff. That's what I do. I'm here to protect you."

My eyes burned. "I just wanted to help."

"You help *me*. Understand? You help me and *I* help them. You know that's how we do things."

"I'm sorry."

He looked at me, the tops of his dark eyes always half hidden beneath his lids, and he smirked. "It's okay, sweetie. Just don't do it again."

I could sense him wrestling with disappointment and worry and love. I couldn't risk my life for someone else when Director Capaldi always had it figured out.

I asked him if he was going to stay, and he told me no.

When he vanished from my mind's eye, going back to wherever he and The Watchers operate, I was left in an absence that felt like punishment. I disappointed him. I didn't save Myrah. I took a risk when I shouldn't have. And I wasn't going to make that mistake again. So I didn't.

That was the first and last time I interfered with the missing. Myrah's death wasn't my fault or my responsibility any more than all the others. People in this town have the luxury of looking away. They can find your keys in the parking lot during their smoke break, know what happened to you, and continue cooking for the rest of the night. But I am made to watch what comes next. And I know I will never be able to save them.

CHAPTER 18
A Black Bedroom

A chickadee whispers at my bedroom window, nestled somewhere sweetly between the branches serenading a new sunrise. It seems like only one bird is daring to speak in all of Veil Haven, and here it is singing just for me.

It is unseasonably cold today, the frost threatening every garden with the promise of snow on the way. Everyone feels the shift of a world in mourning.

I didn't sleep last night, not really.

I haven't thought about Myrah in a long time. I forgot how hard it was to watch Director Capaldi leave after that.

I stare at my closet.

Wrapped in now too-small clothes and shoved in the back of my closet is a cream-colored rotary phone. It's my only line to the director.

Last I heard his voice we were fighting. I did everything he asked yet he never wanted to see me. So when he threatened to take Logan after a stupid mistake, and after he promised to leave him alone, I was so tired and angry I tore the phone out of my wall.

He speaks to me now through Winona and Chief. But I'm wondering if I should finally call him myself. I could ask him what happened, hear his voice, know he's aware of my pain. But I don't want to hear how disappointed he is in me. And I don't want him to talk about how my ability isn't working.

I turn over in bed and try not to cry as my mind's eye slips away from me.

Someone listens to the message on their answering machine from 3 a.m. The man on the line breathes heavily and slowly. "I saw your house. I stopped. I peeked through the windows. Seems nice. Like a place I'd want to live. Maybe I can take it from you. Take it off your hands."

They scoff at the offer and delete the message. "Stupid realtors." They continue cleaning their house.

Someone sees a cryptid in their bathtub—some dark thing in the shape of a naked girl clutching her knees to her chest. The cryptid stares at them, waiting, but the person only rolls their eyes and barks, "Leave!" The cryptid does. Now they can poop in peace.

Someone walks to the edge of the Offerings Dock. They haven't slept in weeks. They haven't felt like themselves in years. The Black River has stopped and the Boy emerges from the center. Watching. They have a short dialogue as the Boy feeds off their desperation and depression. This man is ready to die, and he wants to be sure he won't come back.

"What will death feel like?" he asks.

Through a swift breeze, the Boy answers. "Not everything feels like something else."

And in a gesture of relief, the man walks off the short dock and disappears beneath the river's surface.

A van blinks into existence as my mind's eye fixates on the scene. The side of the black van is marked with an eye like the setting sun between two mountains. Soldiers spill out dressed head to toe in black armor. Their shoulders are marked with the same symbol.

The unit quickly and precisely secures the perimeter of the small, one-bedroom house. Their movements are almost robotic as they move silently into the home. No lock can keep them out.

The sleeping couple does not hear them. They are lovingly entangled, completely unaware. And when The Watchers inject some serum into their necks, their sleep becomes even deeper.

The soldiers uncouple the woman from her partner and roll her out of bed. They carry her back to the van, close the doors, and blink out of existence.

I sit up, confused.

I can always tell when someone breaks the law as my mind's eye usually focuses on the act. But this woman, what was her name, Sarah? What did she do that would warrant being taken?

Cryptid attacks are common, but The Watchers don't take people unless they have a reason.

The same thing happened when they took the school board president. It's strange.

What is the director doing?

If I was supposed to know, I would know. I sigh and wrestle with the idea of getting out of bed.

By mid-afternoon, I make it to the couch, a bagel with cream cheese in hand.

I've ignored the condolences streaming to my phone all day. Josie and Hayden and anyone who knew Lydia are also being flooded with apologies. Even the cheerleaders, despite how much they feuded with her.

I curl up on the couch and don't move. I ignore my empty stomach. I ignore my bladder. I ignore my dry throat. The only thing I can't ignore is the world pulling me under again and again.

A young woman watches the trees through her window. She smiles as the starlings settle onto the branches. She listens to their cacophonous song. She walks into her yard, stands in the noise, and with a single clap, she forces all the black-bodied birds into a silent explosion. They evacuate into the sky with a daunting silence. The woman smiles. She remembers the first time her dad showed her this trick, and how even though he's been gone for years, she still finds him everywhere.

Josie cuddles on the couch surrounded by her family. Her sisters and mother are so kind to her. Even her stoic stepdad is gentle. I can't help but yearn for that kind of love.

Logan considers taking notes about something but decides against it, feeling strange and raw and alone.

Ford is playing games and ignoring Dante as he makes spooky ghost noises and laughs at himself.

Shakira parks outside the abandoned dam.

Kane is breathing fast as he clutches his head, standing in the middle of random objects scattered across his bedroom floor. He's pushing his telekinesis to its limit with his concussion. He wonders if he'll even be able to move a football soon, but he grits his teeth and forces himself to try again.

Kyah and Jarissa take turns sitting in Markus' lap as he brushes and twists their hair.

Hayden is crying nonstop.

I'm crying nonstop.

The world goes on and on and on.

I try to breathe deeply but my god it's hard.

It takes a long time for me to ground myself, and when I do my fingers still shake. I don't have time to panic. I'm supposed to help this town. I'm supposed to keep my friends safe. And if I can't do that, what am I good for?

As the day passes, I use what little control I have of my ability to continuously pull myself away from the morgue... from *her*. When that begins to slip, I intentionally focus on Josie as she attempts any semblance of a routine to keep her mind off everything.

She is delivering the preserves her mom made to her nearest neighbor, the old woman she affectionately calls Miss Ava.

Ava has a little slice of the mountains all to herself, and Josie's mom worries she gets lonely in her age. But from what I can tell,

Miss Ava is comfortable alone with her gardens, yoga, and crafts. Though she does appreciate Josie's visits.

I've watched Miss Ava like I've watched everyone. She's a beautiful old woman with toned arms after years of working outside, and her long silver hair wraps around her like a shawl.

She's a mouthpiece, like Lydia, except Ava is one of the only people who communicates and receives messages solely from the Void. I think only one or two other people can do that. I always thought it was nice that the Void has someone else to talk to, maybe even more clearly than me.

Despite her comfort with being alone, Ava has a deep longing she's never been able to place. She's talked to Josie about it over the years as though something was taken from her.

Josie offered to help Ava with her memory once, wanting to dive into her past, but Miss Ava told her sternly that some things are better left forgotten.

That flipped a switch in Josie, and the next day she signed up to be an intern with the Paranormal Relations Department. She wanted to use her ability to help bring people peace, even if those people were already dead.

Then she was assigned to work with Ford. And as Josie says, without Ava, she might've never really had the chance to notice Ford. For that, Josie is deeply grateful, and part of why she enjoys her neighbor so fondly.

As the sun sets, Josie arrives with the preserves, and Miss Ava invites her to stay and help her bake.

The sting of jealousy makes me shrink away from the scene. But before I leave entirely, I hear Ava admit that the Void told her Josie was coming and would need a loving distraction.

I sit up with a sigh, hyper-relieved that the Void has reached out to her, to *someone*. So they *are* still up there, they *can* communicate. But does that mean the Void is ignoring me? Is the Forest Eye somehow blocking out the Void? Or maybe Ava is just lying. I can't tell.

Before I can sink deeper, my mind's eye pulls me to Kane. It feels like a punishment. I can't catch a break.

The sun has set and he's already high at a bonfire. It's only Saturday but the rumors about Lydia's death are as vicious as a wildfire. I guess it's easy to make fun of someone seemingly untouchable.

These are Kane's people. That's for sure.

Almost everyone at this small party is cruel to her or me—the omniscient girl who let her best friend die. I must've been involved in her death. And I actually know what happened, but I won't tell anyone, not even her mother.

Kane seems to be impressed with his work.

My face is hot as I hear the worst rumor yet—the one coming directly from Kane's mouth.

Apparently, I killed Lydia and covered it up like I always do. And I am, once again, the sole reason why people go missing in this town.

Kane grows crueler and more obsessed with me by the day. I've lost my reason to keep his stupid secret.

I throw off my blanket and grab my phone to text the football coach. My face burning, my heart pounding in my ears.

Kane has a concussion, I text anonymously. I know everyone's number but they don't know mine. *He's been lying to everyone so he can keep playing but his injury is getting worse.*

I watch the plump, balding man read my message in front of his TV. He squints at his phone and considers asking who texted him but decides against it. He leans into his La-Z-Boy and considers if this is true.

My head buzzes as my hands shake, but I smile. *That felt good.* Except my heart is still racing, and I don't feel any better.

I decide to roll onto the floor to give myself a little change of scenery. But it doesn't help.

Someone breaks their toe running down their stairs. Someone leaves their PlayStation at the Offerings Dock and asks the Boy for luck on their dissertation.

I wish I knew why The Watchers kidnapped that man. I wish Director Capaldi would reach out. I wish I was brave enough to connect the rotary phone myself. I wish Chief would listen to me.

Someone turns on a movie and the opening title scrawl says, "This film is about you." It stays for an uncomfortably long time before the camera slowly closes in on their house.

I grab my hair and yell as my mind's eye floats toward the morgue again. I open the floodgates to fight away the sight of her.

Someone sees a human face outside their second-story window. Someone gets a notification that reads, "You don't have much time left." Someone hears their mother's voice calling them to the kitchen—and their mother's voice down the hall warning them not to listen to it.

Chief is wrong. He has to be. She can't be dead for no reason. There *has* to be a reason. There's meaning behind everything in Veil Haven. Lydia can't be the exception. So if the police won't investigate, I will.

I send my mind's eye to the Foodie Mart. Chief said they didn't need to investigate because the autopsy showed natural causes, but I am certain they've missed something.

I review Lydia's time logs, listen to her coworkers talk about what they know, how she was working late, closing by herself, that she was alone for probably an hour. I try to create a timeline of what could've happened.

That manager has left her to close alone a few times before but it doesn't make sense now. Leaving a young girl alone at night? Her coworkers are numb and nervous as they go back and forth on theories and rumors. They wonder if someone killed her but decide against it. Everyone knows the night belongs to the cryptids and she should've just gotten a ride home instead of trying to cut through the mudflats.

The Foodie Mart is one of the few stores in Veil Haven that operates at night. However, since it's wedged between the police station and the college campus, backing against the mudflats, which leads to the richest neighborhood in town, everyone assumed it was perfectly safe.

I review the camera footage from that night, my mind's eye searching the seemingly endless liminal back rooms and their recording equipment in their camera room. It's customary for the police to wipe any security tapes used for an investigation and return them blank. It's to cover up any evidence from prying eyes or whatever excuse the police come up with. So I will be able to see what the police refuse to review.

But when my mind's eye goes over the recordings from the night she died—even the entire day, I find them completely blank. Wiped. Empty. Full of static.

My core temperature drops, and I sit upright. I stare across the living room blankly. My vision is overlaid with the static of missing time.

He *did* investigate.

Chief lied to me.

Goosebumps wash over my body.

I stare at the corner of my ceiling, homing in on the microscopic camera watching me.

What's there to hide? This is *my* Lydia. *My* best friend. Why has she become another secret on a list I'm not sure has an ending?

Chief lied to my face. Held me there. Ignored me.

I can't put words to this feeling.

Director Capaldi refuses to acknowledge me. Winona pushes me out. None of them believe that Declan is dangerous. That something isn't right about the new family. And they *lie* to me?

A Skeletal Shifter echoes a loved one's voice to trick someone deeper into the woods. Someone cracks off their front tooth. Someone pulls a hangnail and their finger bleeds. Someone's dog is being eaten by a chupacabra.

What happened at the Foodie Mart when Lydia was alone? What are they hiding from me? The government knows what happened to Lydia. They have to. And they're keeping me in the dark. *Me.*

Someone breaks their boyfriend's windshield with a baseball bat. A Mothman attacks someone's car, causing them to veer off the road. Someone kicks their child out of the house. Logan throws his controller and holds his head, frustrated at something outside his game. Someone is shaving their hair as their mental state spirals. Hayden is crying again. A Shadow Person appears in my kitchen.

Instantly, the cryptid's dread consumes me and I am frozen, too afraid to even look behind me. It amplifies my grief, my panic, and my anger.

My emotions swell and choke me the closer the Shadow Person comes. The vaguely humanoid figure watches me with its white glowing eyes. Its infectious fear makes me move away from it, and for some reason I'm certain it will kill me. That it'll take a knife from the kitchen and—

But I know better. I know Shadow People are only tangible if you believe they are. They can only hurt you if you think they can. Their only power is their fear and dread. And they have caught the wrong person at the wrong time.

I'm sure it plans to feed off me for weeks until I finally de-volve into paranoia, pain, panic, and off myself. But not me. Never *me.*

My body trembles as I bare my teeth look at the cryptid. I curse at it to leave. "You can't feed off this!" I stand. "This is *my* pain, not yours!"

I dare to step closer to the shadow despite the dread. It's as thick as fog, as toxic as methane.

Despite my attempt to scare it away, the Shadow Person grows in size until it's towering over me, hunching beneath my ceiling.

I'm shaking, but my rage blinds me, and in an instant I'm screaming, "Unless you want me to call the Forest Eye, *get out!*"

And in an instant the Shadow Person blips across town, taking all its negativity with it.

I slump onto the couch, catching my breath and keeping my eyes on the kitchen doorway. I hold my chest. I can't believe that just happened. I can't believe I just used the Forest Eye's name to save myself.

I pull my greasy hair back and bring my knees under my chin. My house has never felt so empty.

The government doesn't trust me. The cryptids are forgetting their place. I'm losing control. And my best friend is gone.

What was so important about that night that I had to watch anything other than her?

I rack my brain as I settle down and slowly, slowly, I remember.

It was some pointless vision about someone I don't know doing something as simple as painting their bedroom black.

But wait.

I uncurl, chills racking my body.

Jeanie's room isn't black. It's the same violet it's always been.

Why didn't I notice that before?

But I *remember* her painting her room. How panicked she was to catch the drips racing down her wall. How she brushed her palm against her cheek and accidentally stained her pillow when she fell asleep. How could that not be real?

I scramble for my phone and call her, a complete stranger. We haven't even had classes together.

And with whatever luck I have left, she answers.

"Hello?" Jeanie readjusts her septum ring, curious about the unknown number.

"Did you paint your bedroom recently?"

"What? Who is this?"

"Did you paint your bedroom black?" I press.

She tries to understand what's happening, but I'm panicking, and she doesn't have the patience for this. "I think you have the wrong number. I've never painted my room in my life. And my mom would never let me paint it black. Anyways, sorry." She hangs up.

The phone is heavy in my hand.

I've seen every disgusting thing this town has to offer. Every death. Every instance of torture, torment, and abuse. How families and friends fall apart. I've seen every bad day. But the one death that matters the most... I dream of fiction.

The Cryptid of Vapor and Flesh comes to the front of my mind. I swear the stench of chlorine and rot comes with it. I see Myrah twitching half-conscious in front of me and her chest exploding in my face.

You were made to watch.

I clutch the couch cushion as my head pounds. This isn't a coincidence. This wasn't my subconscious sparing me.

If you were supposed to know, you'd know.

Something is making me dream.

Something didn't want me to watch Lydia die.

CHAPTER 19
EVERYTHING I'VE HIDDEN FROM THE WORLD

The sliding glass door catches on its track as I race out of my kitchen and off my back deck. The air is humid despite the chill, and I can't help but cry as I run to the woods at the end of my yard.

Shrouded by the hissing autumn trees, I shake as my breath draws thin and the world closes in—roaring, screaming, pounding. My nails bite my palms as I scream at the trees, at the Forest Eye who is sure to be watching me.

"If you ever loved me, you would've saved her!"

There is no reply.

"This shouldn't be happening!" I scream until my throat feels cut. I know my neighbors won't care. If anything, they'll think I'm just a Skeletal Shifter.

The world taps against my inner skull, begging me to bear witness, but I refuse. I don't *want* to. I don't want *this*.

I grab my head and cringe. The pain of my ability makes me rigid, and I catch myself wanting the Forest Eye to help—remembering the nostalgia of the Wildwoods, my quiet, soothing home. But I grind my teeth and audibly grunt, chasing the memories away.

Somehow it works. The world is swallowed into the pits of my periphery. But it isn't my doing.

Some creatures are capable of amassing a depth of silence so quiet that the lack of noise feels like an entity itself. This, of course, means that the ancient cryptid known only as Mr. Boogle has appeared behind me.

I don't know why we call him that.

The leaves slip under my feet as I spin around to face him.

Mr. Boogle is not a Shadow Person, though glimpsing at him might convince you he is. His only defining features are his red pinprick eyes and his two tentacle-like arms he can lengthen at will.

Although he can shrink and morph to fit any shape, his natural form is long and narrow. He hides behind tall, thin structures or lurks along the ground like a shadow.

Mr. Boogle is not made of shadows but from a toxic darkness that I can only describe as a pocket dimension—his stomach. The entirety of him is one massive gateway. I've never known anyone to return after being taken by him.

His lore suggests he can bestow knowledge because of his immortality, that he has a sort of omniscience, but I've never seen it in action.

In the gray shadows of the moon, Mr. Boogle peeks around a loblolly pine, lanky and hyper-black. His red dot eyes lock on to me and I freeze.

But I'm not afraid.

I wait for him to decide his purpose. He doesn't indicate what he wants. Though, at the core of every cryptid lies hunger. Defining that hunger is where appetites get interesting.

In this suffocating silence, I find clarity in my rage. Fists tight, hair across my face, I stare back at him.

Mr. Boogle stands a few feet above me and only a few feet away. His two tentacle arms slither slowly across the leaves like shadows. The silence pulses, but neither of us blink.

I bare my teeth as the moon glints off my white eyes. "Do you know what happened to the last cryptid who touched me?"

Mr. Boogle pauses. He slinks out from the tree to reveal more of his slender two-dimensional body, his jagged shadowy head.

I step closer. "I am *not* in the mood, Mr. Boogle."

"Take my hand..." His voice is soothing, low, and warped with the thickest mountain accent I've ever heard.

My façade falls. "What?" I deadpan. I've never heard him speak before.

"Take my hand..." He might be naturally unnerving but his tone is calm, even kind.

Am I hearing him in my head, or is he speaking out loud? My ears hum. I take a step back watching wide-eyed as his slithering void-black arms move toward my chest.

"Take my hand..." His small, red circular eyes bore a hole in me. My neck hairs stand up.

"No," I stutter.

"Take my hand... I will show you..."

I move further back, but his rounded, handless arms keep stretching toward me. "Show me what, Mr. Boogle?" I raise my arms in defense and gasp when I bump into a tree.

"Everything," he hums.

Then the world drops from my periphery. But it isn't my doing, and it isn't because of Mr. Boogle either. In an instant, we both know the Forest Eye is watching us. It won't manifest, but we can feel its unyielding presence in every tree, leaf, sprout, bug, and animal around us.

The woods seem to bend over us, and Mr. Boogle retracts his arms.

Even though he has no face or features besides those unblinking glowing red eyes, I sense fear from the cryptid. Like he's been caught doing something he knows he isn't supposed to do.

A new kind of fear sinks into me, too, clarifying my senses. What was I thinking provoking the Forest Eye? What am I doing in the woods at night?

I stare at Mr. Boogle who has kept his glowing gaze set on me.

"Run."

It's almost impossible to make sense of it, but I feel the Forest Eye bearing down on Mr. Boogle. All the pressure and pain it can punish him with, it does, and as soon as I hear Mr. Boogle's piercing unearthly scream, I take off running just as he asked me to.

In my mind's eye I see the void-like creature's smooth, slim body stretch out in spikes as if physically embodying his screams. I begin to cry at the sound of it. The muscle memory of that kind of pain knots my stomach.

I slip on wet leaves in my yard as I scramble back to the light-haven of my house. With heavy breaths and a cramp in my side, I close my glass doors and draw the blinds. But I can still hear him screaming. In my mind's eye, I might as well still be standing in the woods, and even though every ounce of me is begging to turn away, I force myself to look closer, hear deeper.

Despite my pounding heart and heaving breaths, I hear something from this torturous encounter.

I hear the Forest Eye.

"You dare go against my will? You would show her all she isn't ready to see? After I explicitly commanded you not to?"

"She deserves to know!" Mr. Boogle screams between the pain. *"You are a cruel master, but you are not mine. Don't forget you didn't create me, Forest. I am beyond your domain."*

"Then leave!" the Forest Eye booms. *"Abandon this place or I will destroy you in ways you never thought possible. I will wound you so badly you'll pray to your old god."*

And with a final piercing scream, Mr. Boogle blips out of existence.

Where did he go? I scour the edges of the world for him but he's nowhere. He *left*. Is he a voidwalker? Or did the Forest Eye physically banish him? What was he trying to show me?

I move backwards until I'm gripping my couch for support, staring wide-eyed at my kitchen doors, my mind's eye still out there in those woods.

I hear the Forest Eye register my ethereal presence. *"Ash?"*

But I pull out of there so quickly I make myself dizzy. The room shakes. I've never felt this way before.

I take out my phone and text Josie, asking her if she can come over and spend the night. I don't know why I expect her to respond. I see her tucked in bed, asleep with her phone in hand.

I ease down the back of my couch and sit there, holding my knees to my chest. I need to stay here. I need to keep my mind's eye with me. But the more I try to, the more I feel it flaring across town, reaching out to witness everything.

The only thing powerful enough to manipulate my dreams is the Forest Eye. Declan doesn't have an ability. The Watchers have never had that kind of technology. And it wouldn't be the first time, recently, that the Forest Eye has grabbed my attention while I'm asleep.

How is that possible? How is that fair? I never got answers.

I hold my legs tighter, resting my face on my knees.

Distantly, I wonder if Director Capaldi is watching me. I wonder if he understands what I'm going through. He's always been at odds with the Forest Eye. Would he know some way to help me? Would he have built something to hold off the cryptid god?

I look up and rub my face, waiting for him to knock on my door, for him to call Winona or Chief, for him to make some remark on my situation. I want him to help me. Can't he see I need his help?

If the Forest Eye didn't want me to watch Lydia die, and if it doesn't want me to know what happened, what am I supposed to do? If a god is against me, do I even have a chance?

My mind's eye yearns to spread across the town like a fog, but I need to stay away from the tree line. I have no idea how this evolution of its power works, but for tonight, I just need to focus on something in town.

And as if on command, I notice Ford and Dante wandering the halls of our high school.

Sometimes working for the town's Event Services means working late setting up or taking down random audio and light equipment. Which is exactly what Ford is doing now. The renovated halls of our school are foreign now, everything sterile and clean, lacking any sign of decay or overgrowth.

Dante hovers lazily on his back as Ford wheels a noisy cart stacked with giant speakers and bundles of neatly wrapped wires.

"How can you work in this silence?" Dante asks.

"It's hard to imagine doing anything in silence with you around." Ford sighs.

"You know, I probably went here," Dante says, tucking his arms behind his head, *"I probably walked exactly where you're walking now."*

"Probably?" Ford scoffs. "There's only one high school. It's not like you got that varsity jacket anywhere else. Who wears a letterman when they're killed?"

"Hey!" Dante floats upright, pulling on his jacket. *"There's style to this."*

"If you say so." The library catches Ford's attention and he pauses as an idea forms. "If you were on the football team, you'd be pretty easy to find in the yearbook."

Dante floats to block Ford's sight of the doors. *"Your sudden interest in me is flattering, but you shouldn't stay here for too long at night."*

"Why?" Ford smirks and walks through him. "You afraid of ghosts?"

The library is always unlocked. Everyone is welcome to take a chance in the large musty maze of untouched books if they want. The room is potent with the scent of old books, stale strawberry gum, and the faint metallic whisper of dried blood. The lights flicker on with Ford's movement and shut off the further he moves to the back of the library, only lighting where he stands. So long as he doesn't look at the figures moving in the shadows he'll be fine.

Dante, on the other hand, has forgotten this rule and shivers at the horrific beasts that stalk them, bound never to cross into the light. They're hollow, hunched, and hungry. Dante watches the musty cryptids swarming the darkness as they snap and claw at him.

He screams and kicks away, floating backflips through the shelves. Ford hisses at him to stop as the sudden noise gives him goosebumps.

"Did you seriously forget cryptids can see ghosts? You're all the same now. They can mess with you as much as they can mess with me. To some extent at least." He scans book spines.

Dante's head and shoulders phase through a shelf as he follows Ford wide-eyed. *"No I did* not *know that."* He looks around him and pretends to clutch on to Ford. *"Are you sure this is a good idea?"*

"Just stop messing with them," Ford says, grabbing an armful of old yearbooks. He shivers as Dante phases through him. Ford waves him away but nothing happens. He sighs and moves to the nearest table.

The yearbooks are half-paper, half-electronic. The dates and pictures are made of copper-brown screens that are powered by shadows. They couldn't be solar powered because books don't do well in the sun, obviously. But where the logic makes sense, the technology fails.

Shadow-powered tech isn't nearly as strong as its counterpart, which is why you'll only see it in yearbooks and those plastic keychains with your name on them.

All photography printed with shadow tech eventually fades, and the dates of the yearbooks are also nearly impossible to read. But hey, they have to do something to make you feel good about spending eighty dollars on a book filled with memories of people you half-like.

Ford sets the yearbooks down with a slap. The lights around the table illuminate him and the yearbooks dating back dozens of generations.

"How old do you think I am?" Dante gawks. He hunches his back and pretends to hobble around with a cane, sputtering off stereotypical elderly phrases.

Ford ignores him. "We have no idea how old you are because you won't tell me and refuse to remember anything. But historically, ghosts are old. Older than this, but whatever. Do you want to help me find your graduating class or no?"

Dante blows a raspberry. *"You just want to get rid of me. How could you get rid of family?"*

"I don't need any more family hovering over me, thanks."

Dante floats off the table, his shoulders low. *"Geez, buddy. You don't have to be so harsh."*

"I'll let you know if I find you," he says and then mumbles, "and knowing you, you're probably cheesing like a moron."

Dante laughs as he floats away to distract himself, deliberately ignoring the wide-eyed library cryptids.

After almost half an hour, Ford finally finds a Dante that perfectly matches the ghost. Glasses on, smiling wide, shaven head.

"I think I found you," he calls out. "Dante Williams. Does that ring any bells?"

Dante is deep in the fantasy section reading cheesy novel titles to himself and laughing.

"*Dante,*" Ford drones.

Dante teleports behind him and Ford jumps in place. *"Ha! Scared ya!"*

Ford looks at him dead in the eyes and says, "Dante Williams."

Dante's expression softens as the name settles into him. Familiar. Home-like. *Him.* He looks over the page and traces the image. The electronic pulse makes the image clearer momentarily before his hand phases through the book and he pulls away.

An airy breath escapes him. *"Wow."*

"Look at that." Ford slaps the book page. "I actually found you. I wasn't sure if there would be books old enough but here we are."

"It says I'm on other pages, too. Go look at them."

Ford flips until he lands on the marked pages. Most of them are from football games but one of the pictures shows Dante smiling with his arm around a girl. They're standing under a banner that reads, "Congratulations, Mayor Freeman!" She's significantly smaller than him, round-faced, and smiling brightly. Her straightened black hair catches the camera's flash.

But as Dante studies the page, he frowns. He doesn't remember her.

Ford turns to the final marked page with a giant picture of Dante and the same woman. They're clutching each other on a stage donned in royal crowns and capes.

Dante does a backflip when he sees it, chasing away that strange longing. *"Woo-hoo! Prom King! Now* that's *the way to go out. In true style. Royalty!"*

Ford rubs his face. "I guess some mysteries are better left unsolved."

Dante and the young woman stand in the gym decorated with balloons, glitter, and glow sticks. They're dressed to the nines and smiling widely with glamorous crowns as he pulls her close. But Dante doesn't remember this either. He doesn't remember anything about his life.

Ford is surprised by the knot forming in his gut. If Dante is the same age in these pictures he must've died soon after these were taken.

"Do you recognize her?" Ford checks the electronic date on the cover that reads, *Nineteen Years Ago*. "Whoa. You only died nineteen years ago? That's really impressive, Dante. It usually takes lifetimes for the dead to manifest."

Dante stops his celebration to study the picture. His smile drops the more he looks at his old life and all the things he can't relate to.

"I wonder what brought you back," Ford wonders. He reads the names under the picture, "Dante Williams and Althea Freeman. Huh."

Dante remains silent, taking in every detail of the photo. How they smile, how her plump cheeks make her eyes squint, how his hand rests on her hip, the faint outline of lipstick across his cheek. Ford's question echoes in his head: *Do you recognize her?*

When Dante finally answers, his unusually quiet voice falls on deaf ears. *"No, I don't."*

"We're one step closer to figuring you out," Ford smiles, taking pictures of the yearbook. "Maybe Josie can help us out after all."

"Josie, right…"

Ghosts usually retain some memories of their life, and they usually regain more when they're shown evidence of it. Dante has learned that from other ghosts at least. So why doesn't he remember anything?

Ford puts the books back where he found them. When he returns he finally registers Dante's thousand-yard stare.

Ford clears his throat. "Listen, we'll get your memories back. That's my job. Literally. Josie and I help ghosts move on all the time. Remember?"

"What if I don't want to move on?" Dante looks at him, shoulders low, feet almost touching the floor. *"What if I like being a ghost?"*

Ford studies him with tight lips. It isn't the first time he's heard this from a ghost. He knows how time corrupts the dead, and he knows Dante needs to move on eventually, but the heartbreak in his eyes makes Ford reconsider his approach. Dante is brand new, and he has plenty of time before death starts to change him.

"We don't have to tell you how you died if we find out."

Dante raises his brow, leaning away. *"You don't?"*

"Josie's whole thing is touching something and seeing the past. It isn't always death, just when she touches an anchor. But since Halloween is coming up and ghosts become tangible... maybe she can touch you. Maybe she can relive your football glory days or something."

"Really? That would be awesome!"

As they leave the library, the conglomeration of cryptids nip at his ankles. Ford knows it's best not to run and instead stay in the slow-moving lights. So when the doors close, he untenses and sighs in relief. They both watch the lights flicker off and see the vague shapes clawing at the door, crying out with an uproar of frustration.

Ford and Dante eye each other and move on.

"I guess we could *try something on Halloween,"* Dante says distantly, rubbing his close-shaven head.

"Yeah, I don't know if anything will happen or if it's even possible, but it's worth a shot, I guess."

The cart rattles as they leave the school and walk to Ford's weirdly small truck parked outside. His parents gave him this car for his sixteenth birthday. Ford wanted a sedan, but his parents wanted him to have a truck, so they surprised him with this compromise.

Ford loads the speakers and wires into his truck bed, preparing to return them to town hall.

"That woman... Althea Freeman. I-I want to know her again."

Ford eyes him as he balances the cart in his truck bed. "We'll figure something out. Maybe Ash can help, too."

Dante smiles as he phases through the truck door while Ford buckles in. *"You promise?"*

"I mean we can try."

"Alright then," Dante fidgets in his seat.

Ford has never met a ghost like Dante. They're usually sad, desperate, or angry. And besides annoying him nonstop, keeping him awake all hours of the night, jump scaring him, making random animal noises, laughing at his own bad jokes, and using his electromagnetic abilities to mess with his games, Dante possesses a real depth he didn't notice before.

He's scared. He doesn't want to move on, but he doesn't have anything to keep him here either. No death anchor, no memories at all. It's even more strange that after being shown pictures of his old life, he still remembers nothing. And to manifest only nineteen years after his death? Ford isn't sure he's heard of a ghost like Dante.

"Yeah, Dante, we'll figure you out," Ford promises. "That's what friends are for. Right?"

Dante smiles warmly, hearing him call them friends for the first time. *"Right."*

CHAPTER 20
THE RIGHTEOUS WRATH OF AN HONORABLE MAN

Josie and I stand in front of the windows overlooking the court-yard. We stare at the groups outside.

They smile and laugh like nothing's different. No new undercurrent. No real loss. I guess that's the one thing that hasn't changed.

The new fluorescent lights buzz above us with sharp unwelcoming light. The renovations are still underway, but they've finished most of the work.

How can everything change in a weekend?

Markus is standing with Ford, both of them trying to find the best way to carry a conversation, knowing what's happened.

Josie grabs my hand, and I make my mind's eye look anywhere but here.

A disembodied, floating face lives in someone's closet. The cryptid isn't too horrifying if you don't look at it long. Every time the woman opens her closet doors, the face begs her to wear a specific jacket. The woman doesn't understand why. But now that the weather has changed, the woman finally decides to grab the jacket in question. The cryptid gasps, yelling, "Slaaaay!"

A Being of Light chases someone's dog playfully through their yard. A shapeshifting cryptid has taken the form of someone's husband. A pack of Black Dogs run together in the deep woods. The ceiling cryptid's moans can be heard in all the quiet places in the school. The auditorium ghosts float in the rafters, trying to soothe it.

Someone is giving sandwiches to the homeless. Someone is popping a pimple the wrong way. Someone crunches all the best leaves on their walk. Someone feeds a stray cat. A dozen people sneeze.

I see Lydia's locker in the back of my mind. Her memorial has been growing and now consists of a pile of flowers, handwritten cards, unlit candles, herb bundles, a set of drachmas, a bottle of sriracha, a pink scrunchie she let someone borrow, and her pom-poms.

The white vinyl floor sways beneath me.

We stand here and stare at the courtyard, saying nothing. We don't hug. It'll only make us cry. We're exhausted from a weekend of... what do you even call it? Mourning? That sounds too simple.

People eye us as they pass. Some whisper, and some offer condolences. We nod, forcing small smiles, but still don't speak.

The more I think of Lydia the more I hold my breath to stop the flood. The last thing I need is for these people to see me cry. The rumors about what happened have already reached a fever pitch.

I guess they didn't think I would come back to school so soon. I wasn't sure either, but Josie thinks a routine could be good, and we're in this together.

I hate it, though. Being here makes my skin crawl, makes the noise worse, and I want nothing more than to run away.

I take note that Hayden isn't here. He's still in bed facing his wall, crying intermittently. He hasn't eaten as the piles of plates and cups of water stack on his desk. His parents are good people. Hayden is not taking this well. None of us are.

As the bell rings, and everyone moves in sync, I'm startled by the uptick of noise.

Before we part, Josie and I agree to see each other at lunch.

I walk through the newly renovated halls, and notice everyone's eyes gravitating to me.

I have bags under my eyes, my acne is worse, and my hair is greasy. They all see the state I'm in and make assumptions on what my appearance means. Some are kind. Others aren't.

I stop at my locker, just to catch my breath.

The lights are blinding, the floors are too sterile, the ceiling tiles are new and white. Our ceiling cryptid is basically suffocating being so enclosed. It swarms and hisses looking for a way to lash out, but it can't. A caged, cornered beast.

I lean inside my locker to catch my breath when someone taps me on the shoulder.

It's Yona Vann, a sophomore theater kid. We had a class together a while ago but haven't spoken since. "Ash, I'm—" Yona pauses as I turn around. I forgot how startling my white eyes can be.

Yona tucks their long black hair behind an ear. Their skin is darker than mine but still golden, and they have high cheek bones and soft, rounded features. I remember they had just come out as nonbinary when we were in theater together. We had a little class party to celebrate.

"Well maybe this is weird," Yona begins, "since we don't really know each other, but I wanted to say I'm sorry this happened. My heart breaks for Lydia." Yona swallows and clutches their deer antler necklace. "I lost my brother recently and... I wanted to let you know that I'm here for you if you need me."

My brows furrow as I piece together what they're saying, and why it sounds so familiar.

"I didn't know you had a brother." I sound distant. "I'm... sorry."

"Most people forgot about him. It was sort of his ability. He used to say that he was one big blind spot. It made life hard and maybe because of my ability, my luck, I was able to remember him... even when our parents couldn't. His name was Mohe." Yona's brown eyes water as they hold back tears, trying to smile through it.

But then it hits me. A blind spot. I step back, gawking, stammering a little. "Your brother, he died of an aneurysm. Just like Lydia. And-and you went to the Offerings Dock that night with the fog." I push my hair back in awe. "You don't think it was natural causes."

Yona looks away, rubbing their arm, but I reach out, and they meet my eyes.

"I believe you." I lower my gaze and try to remember any detail about their brother, even what he looked like. But I can't. "How old was he?"

"He was twenty-seven." As though Yona knows what I'm getting at, they take out their phone and show me their lock screen. The young man appears a bit sickly but looks exactly how you'd expect Yona's brother to look. Is this who Chief was referring to? *That poor homeless kid.* A blind spot. Another man I've never seen before. Just like Declan.

I draw Yona nearer and whisper, "I don't think Lydia died of an aneurysm either. Did you ever find anything about your brother?"

"I—" Yona's brows quirk. "No, it's too dangerous to ask questions like that. The police gave their report."

And just like that, I'm snapped out of my trance. "Right." I straighten my back and step away. *If you were supposed to know, you'd know.*

"But maybe we could hang out some time," Yona says, a little louder for any passersby or recording devices. They clear their throat. "And, Ash, I wanted to say, me and my friends don't believe any of the rumors about you or Lydia. Plenty of people don't. Just..." They touch my arm. "Just know you have people on your side."

I blink at them, but before I can even open my mouth to respond, Kane spots me down the hall and makes a beeline toward me.

My stomach twists, though I don't know why. Caught off

guard maybe. Oh wait, I told Coach Strongman about his concussion. Whoops. But did they talk about it already?

"I'm sorry, Yona, I have to go. But, thank you. We should definitely hang out some time." I don't wait for a reply as I slip into the crowd. My head pounds. I don't want to deal with Kane right now.

I never saw Mohe, and now I know he died the same way Lydia did. Apparently. So does that mean Declan *does* have an ability? Can someone's ability *be* a blind spot? But other people recognize Declan, which seems the opposite for Mohe. Maybe Declan just got trained better in Fox Falls.

I push my hair back again and ignore the pimples lining my face.

None of this makes sense.

Who else am I missing? Declan might be new, but Yona's brother was living in Veil Haven for twenty-seven years, and I never noticed him once.

The hallway sways in front of me. I swear I'm leaning to one side, and I wince again as the noise pounds against my temples.

Someone wishes they had better friends. Someone wishes they had friends at all. Someone wishes they had food. Someone is moving ceiling tiles to help the cryptid. A cactus-headed Plant Person accidentally pricks someone in the hallway. Someone writes a wish on the bathroom wall. Someone drops their books. Someone believes a rumor. Dozens of people slam their lockers. Shoes squeak on the new floors. Everyone is talking. Everyone is talking!

Chief lied to me about investigating Lydia's death. And if I can see everything, and The Watchers know everything, why didn't anyone tell me about Mohe? What else are they hiding from me? What is the *Forest Eye* hiding from me? Is everyone working against me?

I dodge into the base of a stairwell and drop my bag, pressing my back against the cool wall under the stairs. I catch my breath out of sight and stare at the landing above me.

Will I ever know peace again? Maybe I never knew it to begin with.

Kane has been thinking about me too much lately. I liked it better when he just glared from a distance. God forbid it isn't enough that we're neighbors or I see him twenty-four-seven. Now his twisted mind is hyper fixating on me like my mere existence threatens his.

Oh right, and I told his coach he's unfit to play.

Kane saunters under the steps smirking. He wears his letterman with a little too much pride despite its oversized nature making him look like a wet blond rat.

"I don't understand how they let things like you come to school." His cigarette breath builds between us as he steps closer. "I know you told Coach. And we both know how he reacted."

Did they already talk? Did I really miss that?

He sees my surprise and leans back with a victorious sort of grin.

I glare at him, heat quickly filling my cheeks.

"You really missed that, huh? I guess some of those rumors are true after all." He leans closer. "You're losing your grip, Ash."

I scoff. "You're one to talk."

"Well, Coach and I talked, and I'll fill you in here, he doesn't actually care." He claps his hands and rocks on his heels. "Can you believe that? Says I might as well finish out my senior season. You tried to ruin me, and it still didn't stick. I mean, you really *are* losing your stuff, aren't you?" His blue eyes harden with his final remark.

I sneer, my fists tight. "You're a monster."

"No, no." He laughs dryly. "Between the two of us—and the town agrees with me—*you're* the monster. It doesn't matter how many people you trick. I've seen you."

The noise shrieks. The world overlaps with my vision of Kane and the stairwell.

Someone stares at the Shadow Person in their closet. Someone runs through a junkyard being chased by a tooth-covered cryptid. Someone learns the abandoned carnival is closed. Someone is banging on their attic door begging and screaming to be let out. Someone snaps their hair tie. Someone hits their partner. Someone rearends a car.

I step forward slowly. "Then you should stop prodding me."

He tsks playfully at my rage. "You wouldn't want to ruin your reputation."

"Last I checked, you already did that. Years ago. What do I have left to lose?"

"Too bad I don't have another uncle. We could really raise the stakes."

In a single sweep, every present moment of rage and spite floods my mind's eye, and I burn. I feel my heart pounding between my teeth. My molars ache. And every fiber of my being wants to *do something* to him.

He smirks and swallows the lump in his throat. "See that right there. That's the monster."

"I didn't do shit to your uncle."

His façade drops. "I'm the only person you will never convince. I've lived your consequences for years. You don't care what that does to a person. And I'm glad Lydia is gone. Because maybe now you'll understand what it feels like to lose someone."

I don't even know what to say. A million things twist across my face as my mouth tries to form the words, and despite everything I want to say, I can only muster one thing. "Leave her out of this."

He has the audacity to laugh at me.

I snatch my bag and push past him. "Get out of my face, Kane."

He lifts his arms and calls out to me as I leave. "The best and worst part about all of this is that we'll never be able to escape each other. You've made sure of that."

"Don't flatter yourself."

I sit in class, but the people around me feel strange. Between the rumors and the grief, it's hard to tell who falls into which category.

When I hear people utter her name, chills roll down my spine. People whisper that she was eaten by a cryptid, or that some freak who likes young women killed her, or she rejected the wrong guy, or she was texting and driving again, or, or, or—

The worst one suggests I put a hit on her. That I killed her. Because after all, I'm a monster without empathy, so it makes sense I just snapped. They've always thought of me like a cryptid in human flesh. But how can anyone believe I could kill someone? Let alone my best friend.

I couldn't have imagined how many people would use her death for attention. The cheer squad is milking it as expected, but the people who barely knew her and the boys who hooked up with her once are the most offensive.

My fingers shake as I place my pencil down, my mind's eye carrying me through the school. One boy tried hooking up with her last year at one of her parties, but she rejected him. I remember how upset she was, someone doing that to her in her own home. And he's telling his friends in the locker room that Lydia couldn't resist him. That she was almost annoying. That he'll miss her mouth most of all.

Two girls skip the last half of class to talk about Lydia in the bathroom.

"I mean, it's sad that she's dead and everything, but she was like so rude so who really cares."

"She was literally so stupid," the other says. "Our math classes would go *so* slow because of her."

I cover my face as the noise builds like pinpricks across my body. My ears ring.

During their free period in the student lounge, someone tries masquerading a naked picture of his ex as Lydia, garnering awe and pity from his boys. Someone else joins, convincing people Lydia gave him herpes. And Kane continues adding to the fire.

He dramatically throws himself on the couch, his long blond hair shifting across his gaunt, pale face. He tells the others with a sigh that he's not surprised she's dead. "Between her serial dating and rabid hookups, it was only a matter of time."

The static in my periphery drowns me. I cover my ears, pinch my eyes, and shake my head, but the noise and heat remain. Every horrible thing they say about Lydia. Every utterance of her name roaring through my mind. *Lydia, Lydia, Lydia!*

"Shut up!" My chair skirts across the floor as I stand.

The teacher stops. The class stares at me. And I stare back, surprised.

With heavy breaths I grab my bag and leave.

Our teacher sounds defeated as he says something about class almost being over anyway. But there's only one thing on my mind as I march to the student lounge.

I stand in the threshold of the room and glare at Kane sprawled across the couch surrounded by other guys.

He grimaces. "What do you want?"

"Stop talking about her!" I'm surprised by the bite in my voice, how steady I am despite my shaking knees. "She's not just some *body,* and she wasn't your friend. You didn't treat her right then, and you're not allowed to talk about her now."

Everyone looks between us in shock, but Kane only scoffs and rises to meet me.

I recognize the amplified noise of people leaving class, but I don't hear anything besides us.

"I'm not afraid of you, Ash." He sneers. "You don't control me. You have nothing over me."

"God forbid you recognize right from wrong. Lydia isn't here to defend herself."

He leans into my face since he's taller than me, his cigarette breath choking me again. "There's nothing to defend." He smiles back at his boys, and they gawk, some of them genuinely afraid.

My molars grind. "Don't look at them," I bark, poking his chest. "Look at me. You're going to stop talking about Lydia."

"I'm not."

My eyes narrow. Darkness pulses at the edge of my vision. The static hums with the pulse of my heart.

I hardly hear myself speak, my mind's eye deathly quiet. "You forget what I know, Kane. You forget what I'm capable of."

His jaw clenches, his eyes darting to the crowd building behind us in the hallway.

My attention breaks as I recognize everyone watching us, whispering, recording. The static in my ears malforms into a piercing headache, and I flinch.

"I'm asking you to stop, Kane. No one should talk about the dead like that."

I watch him weigh the decision to speak as he runs his tongue along his teeth. He's aware of his audience now and it's feeding his ego.

"And that's all she'll ever be," he says. "Just another dead girl."

I split from my body as the world shifts around me. My mind's eye tilts to one side as it moves above Veil Haven. I see the town perfectly from the western mountains. It's airy up here despite the heat raging through me. Everything is quiet.

I can't account for these lost seconds, but when I come back to my body, I've grabbed his shirt and I'm grinning, almost snarling. I whisper so quietly I can barely hear myself over the rush in my ears.

"Do you think you're safe, Kane? Push me again. I didn't take your uncle to torment you, so just imagine what's possible when I try."

We both step back. From the look of him, his fear and surprise, I know he heard me.

I spin on my heel and push through the crowd. No one wants to be near me. I feel untouchable. And as the heat curls through me like some stalking cryptid, a voice deep within me whispers, *Let them be afraid.*

CHAPTER 21
THE ROTARY PHONE

I sit in my car in some abandoned lot in West Veil Haven and scream. I pound my fists against the wheel as hot tears burn down my face. I scream until my throat and lungs beg me to stop, and then I scream more.

Someone hears their name called around the back of a building. Someone is tormented by a cryptid that has shapeshifted into the person they killed in an accident. Someone cuts off their finger. Someone finds rows and rows of energy drinks behind their walls in a home renovation. Someone is planning their wedding. Someone steps on glass. Someone being stalked by a Shadow Person finally spins around and shouts, "Will you stop!" and to their surprise watches the cryptid leave.

The sky is just as heavy as I am. Black clouds waiting to burst, cold wind cutting through the valley like a hiss.

I've never felt this way before. I've had the town against me, but it's so much worse with Lydia at the center of it.

The video of me and Kane circulates like wildfire. People are especially curious about what I said to him that made him so pale.

Kane chooses not to repeat what I said, stoking the flames of my inevitable downfall.

Markus hears all of this and becomes curious. Too curious. I wish someone would stop him. I wish I could stop him. But I don't bother to try. In this town, it's only a matter of time until you hear all about the "horrible" things I've done.

He asks around, listens to the hushed past, and tries to weed out the truth from the lies. But so much of it bleeds together. People tell him bits and pieces of my history with Kane, and soon, a story forms.

They were never fond of me, *the Girl with Eyes Everywhere*. I've always made people nervous—still do. Everything was fine before I was born, but then there was a child living among them had the same ability as The Watchers.

I was their prize, their little spy, the director's favorite, and everyone knew it. A child who can see you at all times, hear your thoughts if she focuses enough, be with you even without the cameras. It was their nightmare.

But I was only dangerous to anyone who broke the rules or thought against The Watchers. Anyone who is against them is against all of us. Those kinds of people want to do us harm, cause chaos, ruin the balance of our society. The Watchers are our law and order. They keep us safe. And I keep us safe.

This is where Markus learns about Kane's part in my downfall. It was his uncle. The previous coach to the football team. His idol. Everyone loved him. He was the best coach Veil Haven had ever seen. He was everyone's friend and a pillar of the community. But he had alarming ideas.

He thought if people banded together they could stop The Watchers, do something about them. He acted as if The Watchers were our punishing overlords. And for that, he was dangerous.

I warned Kane about him, but he already believed what his uncle thought about The Watchers. He told me his uncle was secretly gathering people slowly to *do* something.

So I told Director Capaldi.

He sent The Watchers.

And Kane's uncle went missing.

We were twelve.

Everyone knows what it means when someone goes missing. It isn't talked about. But Kane connected the dots and pointed his finger at me.

The anger-fueled heartbroken claims of a child who just experienced his first loss is far more believable than a child people already mistrusted. But they didn't understand what his uncle was planning, what he wanted to do, how much it would harm Veil Haven.

When Markus hears the stories of my past, I think his opinion of me shifts. It took me a long time to get friends after the first rumors spread, and now everything is circling again. I already lost Lydia. I don't want to lose anyone else.

My heart beats faster the more that video of me circulates. Everyone has an opinion.

I remember how helpless I was in middle school, how the world turned against me, how I ran to the Forest Eye, how I want to run now—but no.

The pleather steering wheel squeaks under my grip.

I can't go there anymore. I won't. I don't need the Forest Eye.

But this pressure building in my chest sets me on edge, makes my head ring, makes the world drown me like when I was a child.

I am not a child. I am not a monster. I am a human being. I am in mourning. I am burning and the world is spinning, and I know someone knows what happened to Lydia.

I'm tired of the distractions. I'm tired of waiting for the answer to find me. I'm tired of being the good girl the government raised me to be.

If you were supposed to know, you would know.

I pound my fists and chase the thought away, my ears pulsing with static.

I'm supposed to know everything. They raised me to believe that.

I'm *the Girl with Eyes Everywhere*. That stupid nickname always whispered like a curse.

If I wasn't supposed to know, why did The Watchers raise me? If I wasn't supposed to know, why do I work for them? If I wasn't supposed to know—supposed to turn in Kane's uncle, supposed to keep the town safe—why is my reputation ruined? Why does half the town hate me? Why am I being lied to? What has all this been for?

I crank my car and tear through town until I stop hard in my driveway.

The fog horns wail their sickly cry as the storm-laden clouds creep down the mountains. The autumn leaves appear to glow.

I'm tired of biting my tongue and doing what I'm told.

If I was supposed to know—I'm going to find out. I'm going to *make* him tell me.

I bolt to my bedroom, throw my closet open, and dig in the back until I clutch the bundle of clothes. The rotary phone spills out of its wrappings with a metallic *ting,* and I glare at it, fists tight.

Nothing is sinister about the rotary phone, but some things need context.

When I was a child, the director gave me a rotary phone, one of those old timey cream-colored ones with a coiled cord and a dial with the phone receiver resting on top.

Director Capaldi and The Watchers are the only people in Veil Haven I can't see. They move, serve, and exist in a space that my mind's eye cannot grasp. The Watchers, his soldiers, hide their identities under black armor and helmets with face shields. I can't see through them. I can't see into their vans marked with an eye like the setting sun. But even though I could see the director when he stood in front of me, he is shrouded in even more mystery than The Watchers he commands.

A chilling energy hangs around him like an autumn fog, like the one building outside right now.

Director Capaldi would loom over me when we met, tall with a protruding gut. He treated me more like a soldier than his child. He expected me to follow his every order and provide intel when he asked.

I did everything I could to cut through the noise and give him what he wanted, but I was only a child. I was lonely and confused, drowning in a world that was deafening. Still, I tried to appease him.

Before Chief Mun, he was the only father figure I had. He was my everything. I was obsessed with him.

One day, The Watchers came into my house without knocking or speaking and set up this rotary phone in the corner of my living room. They nodded as they left and disappeared into their van. Then the phone rang for the first time.

I eagerly picked up, not sure who would be on the other side.

"Hello, Ash," Director Capaldi said. His low raspy voice always reminded me of mobster movies. It was impossible to misplace. "This is a line directly from you to me. If anything important happens that I need to know about, you call me right away. Understand?"

I was seven at the time. "Yes, Director, I understand." And I did. Except we both had our own definitions of *important*.

I learned early that my words either had so much weight they changed lives or no weight at all.

I would tell him about my day, how mean the other kids were, and what their parents said about me over dinner. I would call to ask him questions about what good behavior looked like and why it was alright for kids to use their abilities but not adults. And whether I should listen to the voice calling for me into the woods. But Director Capaldi didn't care about my evening calls.

Of course sometimes he would take my whining with some weight, take action, and make people disappear. But for the most part he would only sigh and scorn me, reminding me not to bother him with things that didn't matter.

Because of my daily calls, they introduced the Static Man. I always imagined him as a tall, slender man in a dark suit. Maybe he had a pleasant face or a face full of colorful static, but none of it was true. He didn't have a body or a face. He was the voice that lived inside the rotary phone—the director's digital secretary.

Instead of hearing the director I got the Static Man.

I became so used to this that I would simply start by asking, "Is the director there?" and waiting for the disembodied voice to speak through the hissing static of the receiver.

Every time I called, the Static Man would give the same answer. *"The director is not available."*

The first time it happened, I freaked out and asked a hundred questions until my panic finally put me through to Director Capaldi. He explained he was a busy man and that I would have to talk to his assistant first. They would decipher whether what I had to say was important enough for his time, and if not, it would be catalogued for later review.

I still called a lot at first, waiting for the almost-human automated voice to hum through the static, but the Static Man would only ever answer me with, *"The director is not available,"* and then hang up.

It happened enough that eventually I stopped calling altogether. Maybe that was Director Capaldi's plan.

The last time I talked to him, I was angry and desperate and fourteen.

Logan was basically my only friend at the time, and at some point earlier in the week he started sharing his ability training with me. He would tell me how his teacher was helping him, the types of visions he was seeing, and he even tried to help me get a better grip of my omniscience.

But no future seer is allowed to share what they see. And for that, despite my connection with The Watchers, I woke up in a cold sweat as masked soldiers surrounded Logan's house.

I raced downstairs, panicking. When I called Director Capaldi he answered right away.

"Are you crazy? What are you doing? You can't do this! You can't take Logan away from me. He didn't do anything vicious."

"He broke the law, Ash. You should know better. And you should've told me."

I imagined him leaning back at his desk. His voice was too relaxed. But I could tell he was upset with how I spoke to him.

Between my tears and my anger, I begged him to call it off. I reminded him that Logan was my best friend. I repeated all I had done for him without question. And I reminded him what it cost me.

"I thought you loved me," I told him, finally.

And he paused. The Watchers surrounding Logan's house didn't move. Then the director sighed. "Fine." And he hung up.

Just like that.

I had poured my heart out, and even though he gave me exactly what I asked for, it wasn't enough. He never even said *I love you*. And why did I have to beg him to begin with?

He greeted me with the same indifference I had felt for years, and in the hum of the dial tone I finally snapped. I ripped the phone from my wall, took it upstairs, and buried it in my closet. Maybe I should've been grateful that he spared Logan, but in the moment, all I wanted to do was scream.

It felt like he forgot about me and the people I cared about, so I would forget him.

Thunder rolls through the valley like a cryptid stalking prey it and pulls me from the past.

I untense my jaw and lift the phone from the floor.

It's heavier than I remember.

The wind knocks against my house as the storm's momentum builds. The world outside my windows grows darker by the minute.

After I plug the rotary phone into the corner of my living room, I stare at it a few feet back. My heart feels like an animal taking shelter in my throat.

I haven't spoken to the director in years. What will he think of me? Will he be mad I unplugged the phone? Will he be happy to hear from me? What if he blames me? What if he knows my ability hasn't been working, and he can't do anything because he hasn't done anything because all of this is my fault and I'm useless and—

My gut twists and I stop, taking a deep breath. I'm better than this. I flex my hands.

He's still my dad. Even if we haven't spoken in years. Even though it hurts. Even though we aren't blood related. He's my dad. I know he'll listen. He has to.

A thunderclap shakes me from my trance and I pick up the handset.

The nostalgic static in the receiver tickles me and sends chills down my spine. I haven't heard this noise in so long. It doesn't compare to any phone or radio or TV. It sounds like the hiss of shooting stars and fireworks and sheets of rain.

My shaking hands are clammy. "Hello? I need to speak to Director Capaldi."

The noise changes pitch as if someone were wading through the static, physically pushing aside all the noise. And finally, the long-forgotten voice of the Static Man splits through the receiver.

"Director Capaldi is no longer here."

The room spins. My mouth dries out. "What did you say?"

"Director Capaldi is no longer available." His voice is just as I remember, formal and calm, but it's somehow more familiar.

I don't have the energy to figure that out. I can barely catch my breath. Something is wrong. The Static Man *always* said the same thing. Always. *The director is not available,* not this.

"What do you mean he's not here?"

"He's no longer here," he says, the static intensifying and lingering on the word *here.*

My core temperature drops. The world shifts off-kilter.

I know what that means.

I fall onto the couch, my hands shaking. The Static Man has to be wrong. My fear slips out like a whisper.

"He's *dead?*"

When I'm met with no reply, I push the receiver closer to my lips, panicking. "What happened to Director Capaldi?"

Static.

"Hello?"

The Static Man chirps back a greeting, sounding as calm and elegant as before.

"Where's Director Capaldi?" I shout.

The storm shakes my house. The thunder is deafening and my lights flicker just before the Static Man answers.

"He's no longer with us."

I crash the phone into the receiver. The room is still spinning. My breaths are quick and shallow. My mind's eye slips away and the world grows so large and loud that I feel like a bug pinned to a board—everyone looking down at me, talking over me, forgetting about me.

I stare at the camera hidden in the corner of the ceiling, and the next thing I know I'm unplugging the phone and throwing a blanket over it.

I refuse to understand what this means. I don't want to. It's not possible. It can't be true. It has to be some misunderstanding.

I can't catch my breath and my vision begins to darken around the edges.

What else could *no longer with us* mean besides being dead?

I scan Veil Haven for any sign of him or The Watchers but there's no one. Except that's normal. Instead, I hyperfocus on Chief.

He's at home watching TV with his family as the storm rages outside. His boys cuddle on either side of him. Iliana rests in the loveseat beside the couch.

My passing thoughts say it would be wrong of me to disturb him, but the rest of me is screaming, *I don't care!*

He doesn't hear his phone at first, the rain and thunder too loud.

Lightning cuts the air.

My vision blurs as the world goes full tilt. I'm pacing around the living room calling him again, waiting, begging.

Chief shuffles into the kitchen when he sees me calling. I don't give him the breath to say hello when he answers.

"Did you know?" I shout, my voice cracking.

I'm mortified. I'm trying to convince myself the Static Man didn't just confess that Director Capaldi is dead, that someone else I love is gone, that everyone has been lying to me, that I'm the last one to know.

Chief's heart skips at the sound of my anguish. "Ash? What's wrong?"

"Did you know about him?"

"Who? Ash, slow down you're not making sense."

"The director," I hiss quietly.

Chief pales, his back arrow-straight.

Thunder shakes both our houses. Rain blinds the world in sheets of white.

After a long pause, trying to understand how I've come to this conclusion, he rolls his shoulders.

I'm too dizzy to know what's happening inside his head, but as he steadies himself on his kitchen tile he sounds scripted and professional.

"You know we can't talk about—"

"Andrew." My voice strains. "Please. It's me. Something is happening, and I don't understand. I'm scared." Tears hang on my lashes.

If the director is dead, who is protecting Veil Haven? Who is leading The Watchers?

Chief Mun reverts back to the kind, coddling father we both so desperately want him to be. But I hear a hollowness in his voice. He's distant. "You don't need to worry about anything, Ash."

Lightning charges across the sky. It turns the rain into sheets of light.

"Why did you erase the tapes?"

He pauses. There's a fight in him, some desire to tell me one thing before settling on another. He hangs his head and pinches his eyes, trying to hide the heartbreak in his voice. "It's protocol, Ash. You know that."

"Why are you lying to me? *Me?*" I stress.

The rain pulses outside like a strange heartbeat. Lightning flashes in morse code. Thunder chases after it. My dizziness does not retreat.

"Do you need me to come over?"

Iliana's cloud head darkens from the other room.

For a moment, my gut clenching, I almost say yes. Of course I want to see him, want to hug him, and believe everything is okay. But I know it isn't. And I know he won't tell me the truth.

"No."

"Are you sure?"

I hang up and fall backwards on the couch.

For some reason the room stops spinning.

Veil Haven isn't changing. It's already changed.

Lydia is gone. Chief is lying to me. Director Capaldi is missing, dead, *no longer with us.*

Why didn't I know from the start?

I feel cold, but my hands have stopped shaking.

How can Veil Haven be safe without Director Capaldi—the man who raised me?

But if the director is gone, who is making Chief lie to me? The Watchers have been operating like normal.

Actually, no, they haven't. They've been taking innocent

people. They took the school board president for no reason. They took that woman, Sarah, from her bed without reason. They let outsiders in. They let Declan change the school.

And more than anything Lydia is dead. My best friend, my family. She's dead and they're lying to me about it. *Did the director die the same way Lydia did? The same way Mohe did?*

My nails dig into the couch. My molars grind. Tears build but I can't cry. I can't root out this ache in my chest.

I jump to my feet and tear the blanket off the rotary phone. Heat blooms from my chest as my vision narrows, and before I know it I'm screaming, "*Why can't I see anything!*" until I'm dizzy.

I kick the couch, the wall. I throw my fists anywhere I can. I thrash around my living room like an animal, my hair flailing wildly. The thunder yells with me.

I tear the rotary phone from the wall, raise it above my head, and slam it down.

It isn't satisfying.

It doesn't break into a million pieces. It doesn't even crack. It just unhooks itself.

I stand over it and pant, glaring at the phone and everything it stands for.

The rain is slowing. When the thunder roars again, it sounds further down the valley. But in the silence between the storm and my breaths, I hear the static in the receiver... despite it being unplugged.

The Static Man creeps through the noise with nothing more than a quick breath, a whisper, a warning. *"Don't call again, Ash."*

I stare at the phone, the static filling my ears.

"Veil Haven is changing."

CHAPTER 22
THE LIFE AND DEATH OF KIMI KINGFISHER

I press my head against my bedroom window, my knees to my chest. Could Director Capaldi really be dead? Would I really not have felt a difference if he died?

No... It isn't possible. There's no reason to believe—

Don't call again, Ash. Veil Haven is changing.

I consider calling Logan but I'm sick to my stomach. The last thing I want to do is talk.

I buried the rotary phone again. Maybe the Static Man never let my call go through and The Watchers don't know what I know.

If Director Capaldi really is gone, even though he can't be, who is leading them?

Stray thoughts come and go.

Wasn't I supposed to... Wasn't the director training me for...

I don't let the idea fully form.

The window is cool against my forehead. My backyard blurs as tears swamp my face.

I don't want to be here. I want everything to make sense. I want to see the director.

I close my eyes and hold my breath. I'm not going anywhere.

I need a distraction. I need this to make sense. I need to rest. I need the director.

The pit in my stomach curls with nausea and I half-turn about to sprint to the bathroom before holding it down. I return to the window, staring at the west mountain ridge and all the clouds that rise post-storm.

It's ethereal out there. A fresh world after havoc. Cleansed. Renewed. If only.

I hug my knees closer as my mind's eye wanders without my permission. The world never stops. It never yields to me. It never slows or quiets or rests. I just want to rest.

I see a house in the mountains, worn with decades of abandon. It is a common destination for ghost enthusiasts and curious kids, but the ghost who inhabits it has been bothered one too many times. The last group who ventured here returned with glass shards in their elbows and nail marks down their backs. Concerned parents have complained enough that the town has to do something. Which is why they've sent their best interns.

Ford and Josie arrive on the muddy gravel driveway as he explains what he wants to do for Dante on Halloween. Josie heartily agrees. Any chance to be with him, especially to help him.

Ford parks on the washed-away gravel patch beside the house, Josie's favorite song humming under the engine. "You ready?"

"Always." Josie smiles.

The heavy air is cooling fast as fog rises around them. It creeps down the mountain and hangs between the pines and tulip trees, welcoming any Mist Walkers who wish to strut through our world.

Josie and Ford take in the size and decay of the old home. The saltbox is made of blackened panels long exposed to the elements. The charred corners and caved-in roof spell a fire or two over the years.

"Let's get this over with," Ford says.

He hikes his large frame through the threshold and the floorboards creak under him. He offers his hand to Josie. Josie blushes and slides her small hand into his palm, despite not needing the help.

They pause, chests close, breaths caught in their throats, hazel eyes shining. But Ford shuffles back and their hands slip apart.

"No Dante today?" she asks, fiddling with her long brown hair.

Ford scratches his beard as he looks around. "As chatty as he is, he doesn't seem to like other ghosts."

They survey what they're working with inside, but the dilapidated furniture disrupts their thoughts with the choking smell of mothballs and mold.

Ford's chest fills with weightlessness as he senses the spirit upstairs. He clears his throat and walks to the steps. "Let's check up here for the death anchor. I'm surprised it hasn't been taken after all these years."

A ghost can be tethered to anything that was once sentimental to them. Josie's ability to touch an object and see the past isn't specifically for death anchors, but they're imbued with enough energy that she is often pulled toward them rather than the otherwise dull ache she feels for everything else.

When the sound of a creaking tree echoes through the house, Ford grabs Josie's wrist and moves in front of her, expecting the worst.

It's hard to tell what kind of ghost they're dealing with whenever they're sent out. How could they forget the time a ghost nearly took Ford's head off with a levitating desk? One might assume interns would never be in any real danger but the opposite is true. Why would the town want their paid employees getting hurt?

A soft, feminine voice tries to manifest through the creaking noise but it breaks apart. *"This isn't real. This..."*

Ghosts are either silent to those who can't see the dead or will seep through the veil with creaks, breaths, or screams. This one sounds weak from years of self-torment and confusion. She's been a ghost for too long and she's deteriorating, losing her grip, her patience, and her mind.

Ford leads Josie to the second floor where they're met with a long hallway comprised of three doors and three large windows letting in the late afternoon light.

The fog shields them from a swath of predators, and they don't notice the hollow eyes of a Skeletal Shifter in the woods below. The towering cryptid of bone and decay pauses to study the house—its elk antlers speaking to the last corpse it devoured. And after some consideration, the cryptid stalks higher up the mountain.

Ford and Josie step onto the moldy half-sunken floor. The weightless feeling in Ford's chest intensifies. They're getting closer.

"Watch your step," Josie warns. When Ford doesn't respond she asks, "Was the sound hostile?"

"Not really."

"Male or female?"

"Female."

They inch to the first doorway when the high-pitched creaking returns. It's louder this time, causing goosebumps to creep up their arms and down their backs.

"All of it. A lie. Veiled."

"I'm gonna check for the death anchor," she says, turning into the first bedroom. Josie investigates around the two children's beds half burned and filled with mildew, hoping the energy is strong enough to guide her to its location.

Ford sets his gaze down the hall and waits for the ghost to appear.

"Shouldn't be this way. Not safe." Her voice is hoarse, on the verge of tears, and her panicked breaths fill the pauses between her words. *"This place... This place, this place."* She's weeping now. *"How don't you see it?"*

Ford catches a glimmer at the end of the hall as an orb of light manifests and expands like a puddle of illumination. Slowly, it fills into the vague shape of a human, and then it solidifies.

Only the top half of the ghost appears, a transparent girl maybe middle school age. She's small in frame but lean and her long black hair spills over a colorful hoodie. Her golden-brown skin glows as she stares emptily out the broken windows.

Without finding anything in the first room, Josie cautiously watches Ford, connecting the dots as his gaze locks on to something she cannot see. But she has a job to do, and she can't pause now.

"They never knew," the ghost creaks. *"They..."* Her eyes dart to Josie as she sneaks to the next doorway.

Ford's breath catches in his throat and he steps forward to distract the ghost. "I can see you." There's a dip in the air. "I can hear you, too."

The ghost's foggy eyes lock on to Ford.

"You don't know what happened but—"

"I learned the truth," she shrieks, her eyes wide. *"This place. I found the lie."*

"The lie?" Ford echoes. The weightlessness in his chest hardens the more agitated the spirit becomes. He watches Josie disappear into the next room, and his shoulders ease.

There's more to this room than the last. A full-sized bed, a rusted nightstand, a dresser peeling apart, and a sun-bleached photo on the wall.

Josie walks around, mindful of the protruding nails and missing floorboards, until she stands in front of the photo. It's a family portrait—two dads, two young boys, and a young teenage girl. They look happy, even with the color drained from their faces.

"What lie?" Ford asks the girl. Ghosts either love sharing or want to hide, and since this one has already shown her face, Ford has a feeling she wants to talk.

She dares to move closer to him as she pats her chest, her voice mimicking the hissing wind. *"Ours."*

"If you have something to say, you can tell me. I'm the only one who can hear you."

The ghost tilts her head at Ford, fear creasing her brow. *"But they can hear you."*

Ford tenses, his eyes wide, and wonders why he agreed to come.

After checking the nightstand and finding only dust and dead moths, Josie moves to the dresser. When she opens the top drawer her vision buckles as butterflies fill her gut and she rocks forward, lured by the potent energy.

It's here—somewhere.

Her pulsing fingertips urge her to find the source. She opens every drawer but finds nothing. And still, the energy remains the same. She checks the whole dresser again as her body shakes, swarmed with pinpricks. She's so close—and like a magnet finding metal, she *needs* to touch the death anchor.

The ghost manifests the closer she floats to Ford. Her legs form with pajama pants and her once-glowing skin now fills in with translucency. She looks tired and afraid. *"No one can help us."* The floorboards creak under her as she stands within arm's length of Ford. *"This place is veiled with lies. Look closer and you'll see them. But please be careful! The edge is fake,"* the ghost says with wide-eyed urgency.

Ford wonders why ghosts have to be so cryptic.

Josie moves the dresser to search the back and finds a hole in the top corner. The wood scratches her arm as she gropes through cobwebs, searching for the object. When her fingers brush something boxy, her skin crawls with relief. Sighing, she pries her nails around the object and it pops into her hand.

Josie pulls out her prize as the energy flows freely through her body, and she's dizzied with ecstasy.

The death anchor is a small, black, leather-bound journal. It feels ancient and the inside cover is inscribed with the name Kimi Kingfisher.

Josie carefully opens the delicate book and flips to the last entry. The half-cursive handwriting is sloppy, slanted, and hard to read, but she gets by.

Ever since I returned from the edge of the world I've been watched. I know I have. I feel their eyes on me every hour of the day. Even in my dreams. I'm not safe here. I don't think any of us are safe here. I tried convincing my dads to leave in the most discreet way, but they don't get it. I can't tell them what I saw and put them in danger. I hate this town for keeping secrets, but I hate it even more for not keeping them well enough. I found it. I know their terrible secret. I know why we don't go to the edge of the woods. I'm worried they'll kill me. I'm worried they'll kill my family. But I don't know what to do. Should I leave?

Josie shakes when she realizes who Kimi is talking about. She doesn't dare think their name.

Josie runs her fingers over the pages and connects with every ancient pen stroke until she feels pulled into the past. Her body goes stiff and her eyes glaze over as she sinks into the memories Kimi left behind.

Every time Kimi held this journal, every time she wrote in it, her emotions became imbued in these entries. Josie exhales deeply and goes numb as she's transported through the shimmering dark into the past. And when she opens her eyes she's anchored in the body of the soon-to-be dead girl, Kimi.

The house isn't rundown or wet. It's a perfect home tended to and cared for. It smells like rosemary from dinner and cinnamon candles. It's midnight, and the rest of her family is sleeping. But Kimi is sitting upright in bed staring at the waning moon. She is anxiously lost in thought, twisting her long black hair.

"Nothing will happen at home. My family is here. They won't hurt us. They won't hurt them. Only me." She must only be thirteen.

Kimi lets out a shaky breath and buries her head in her hands, weeping in a moon beam on her bed. "If they hid it better, I never would've found it. Why did I have to follow that stupid path?" She slams her fist onto the bed. "This stupid town. This stupid name. Everything's so obvious and I'm being punished for it." She devolves into sobs. "I don't wanna die."

Josie focuses harder, trying to shift deeper into this memory. She doesn't often look for older memories, but something about Kimi makes her curious. Her gut tells her what happened before is more important than what comes next.

Josie grounds herself in Kimi's body, thinking, "You say you followed a path. Show me that." And in an instant, Josie is sent further into the past.

An abandoned asphalt road crumbles at the edges. The road has collapsed over a ravine where a bridge must have been at one point.

Kimi looks up and is terrified by the blue sky.

Kimi, and through extension, Josie, stands on the far end of the road opposite of the ravine. Josie feels like Kimi is further in the woods than she's ever been.

She walks toward a metal gate in the middle of the road and finds several reflective warning signs that read:

DANGER.
BRIDGE OUT.
ROAD CLOSED.
DEAD END.

Next, Kimi is sprinting away from the gate. She runs straight for the ravine but doesn't slow, doesn't speed up. As Josie anticipates her jump and fall, she's shocked to find Kimi stomping over it. The image of the ravine shimmers with each step. She isn't flying, she isn't floating, this isn't her ability. The cliff is a mirage.

Kimi runs through the woods until she phases through a rippling wall that seems to change nothing. The woods still surround her. But now the sky is violet, not blue.

Josie jolts out of the deeper memory in shock by a creak in the floorboards. This is the moment of Kimi's death, and Josie must bear witness for entering the past through an anchor.

Kimi gasps, jumping upright in bed. She presses her sweaty palms to the comforter and stares at a figure dressed in black armor. The symbol on their shoulders of an eye like the setting sun seems to glow in the darkness.

"Please," Kimi begs. But The Watcher grabs her anyway.

She scrambles, but her covers restrain her. The Watcher moves with precision and ease. They spin her around, press her onto the mattress, and pull a thin metal wire around her neck. Kimi sputters in panic as blood spills onto her collarbone and—

Josie's vision is replaced by shimmering darkness before she is flung back into her body, gasping and looking around wildly. She rubs her neck, frozen in place, and drops the journal like it's burned her. She stares at the black book, her face smoothing with horror.

After a long minute of catching her breath, she remembers why she's here in the first place. She picks up the journal like it's a bomb that could go off at any moment. Josie used the last of its energy, but she doesn't want to take any chances. She doesn't want to go back there.

Hearing Ford in the hallway is enough to ground her, so she heads out.

I, on the other hand, am completely shocked. I've tucked myself into bed, but now I'm upright looking around trying to make sense of this.

The Watchers don't kill people. They only make them disappear.

Josie peeks around the doorframe and studies Ford as he leans away from something very near to him. His eyes dart to her, and when Josie flashes the journal, Ford responds with a tight, toothy grin.

"We'll help you move on," he tells Kimi. "Everything can make sense again. You can be at peace."

Josie steps into the hallway, journal in hand.

Cold, dense air sinks around their ankles as Kimi turns to Josie. *"Hide it,"* she begs. *"Don't let them find it. Don't let them know you know."*

"Kimi," Josie swallows, not hearing her, "a... stranger broke into your house and choked you with a wire. You died and your secrets stayed with you." Josie shakes with a chill as Kimi gently cups her cheek.

"I'm so sorry." Light consumes Kimi's face and moves down her spine until she contorts and condenses into a ball of light. She fades slowly as Ford hears one final message. *"You will never be safe here. You have to leave."*

When Kimi finally passes through the veil, the chilling weightlessness in Ford's chest leaves with her. But her final message stays with him. He swallows sharply and turns his attention to Josie.

She stares at the leatherbound journal as Ford rests his large hands on hers, careful not to bother the book. The only thing that cuts through Josie's paranoia is the thought that Ford's hazel eyes are so green today. She wants to press herself against his chest and feel the weight of his arms around her, but she blushes and looks away, focusing on the warmth of his hands instead.

"Are you okay?" he asks. "You look more pale than usual."

She forces herself to laugh. "Yeah, I uhm, it's just hard." She frowns, begging herself not to cry.

"Yeah." This ghost was so different. Why would she tell him or anyone to leave? Leave and go where?

"What did she say after I told her?" Josie asks, her throat closing.

Ford considers telling her, but it feels wrong to even utter it. "Nothing. She was grateful for the help."

Josie looks at the journal and wants to tell him everything, but a much louder part of her screams, *No!* Kimi's secrets should've died with her. They should've left with her. But now they're in Josie's gentle hands.

"Anything good in there?" Ford asks, eyeing the journal.

"No," she says a little too quickly. "I mean, it's hard to read and really old so, no."

"Well whatever happened to her can't happen to you." His hands tighten on hers. "It was just a vision."

They stand awkwardly and feel as though something more should happen, a hug, a nudge, but it doesn't.

Josie frowns. "I'm glad she's moved on. She'll be happier now."

"Yeah," Ford says as they descend the stairs.

"Do you mind not tellin' anyone about this journal? I want... I don't know, I want to keep it."

He eyes her as she jumps off the broken stoop. "Sure."

They approach his car in silence, leaving the no-longer-haunted house and plan how to tell their supervisor that the ghost has been dealt with. They'll write their reports together, and neither of them will mention the journal or Kimi's desperate pleas. They decide it's best to keep their promise to the dead.

I stare at the bundle of clothes in the back of my closet as my head swims. My mind's eye quickly traces the far reaches of town, even in the Wildwoods, but nothing's out there except trees and an abrupt stop. The Void is the sky and the border of Veil Haven and what lies beyond it. Nothing else is out there. Nothing.

I've never seen The Watchers kill anyone. They don't. Why would they? What would they have to gain from a dead body? And they certainly don't leave evidence. Maybe that was just someone dressed up as a Watcher who broke in and killed her.

My shoulders and jaw relax at the idea. Yeah, that makes sense. The Watchers work in a team. There's always multiple soldiers, and they never kill people. They just take them. The Watchers didn't kill Kimi and she didn't leave Veil Haven because nothing is out there except the windless plane of Void and stars.

I take out my phone and text Josie, *You have nothing to worry about.*

When she sees it, she instantly feels better.

And it's true. There isn't anything to worry about.

Except Veil Haven changing. Veil Haven burning. Losing control of my ability. Developing blind spots. The Forest Eye manipulating me. Chief lying to me. The director *gone*. And Lydia...

If I can't see what's happening, if I'm not allowed to know, if I can't ask Chief or the director for help—what can I do?

Out the window, on the western ridge, the Mysterious Mountain Lights burn to life. They wink at me deviously, hiding so much from me. And I keep repeating the same questions in my head.

When Director Capaldi let me work alongside him, he was preparing me for something, wasn't he? He gave me responsibilities no one else had. He told me how The Watchers work. He taught me how to protect Veil Haven. It was privileged work, and it doesn't have to be over.

The Mysterious Mountain Lights vanish.

My chest tightens as this familiar heat burns through me, flooding my cheeks and making my head spin. I clench my jaw. If everyone is trying to keep the truth from me, I'll find it myself.

CHAPTER 23
A DOORWAY OF LIGHT

I wish grief was easy to define. But grief can't be bound by simple explanations, no matter how much we want it to.

We want to soothe those who have lost someone. But some people don't want the reminder. They don't want check-in calls and condolences. Meanwhile others crave it. They need the attention, the distraction, to know they aren't alone.

Grief is as expansive as the forest. It's just as deeply rooted, harboring rot, and easy to get lost in. But grief burrows differently in everyone. There is no pattern.

In Veil Haven, funerals happen at sunset. We bury our dead as the light fades. And after, the Void adds a new star to the sky. It's already happened but no one can see it yet. Lydia's star rests faintly above the third star in the handle of the Big Dipper.

Death reminds people what they have to lose. So at funerals, they make the most of their life.

Everyone shows reverence in their own way. Some of them are cultural while others have familial traditions. This can be wearing your favorite outfits or dressing as your life's ambition in hopes of lightening the affair. After all, funerals are not for the dead.

I park behind the church, take a deep breath, and slowly make my way around.

I see someone dressed as a circus clown and someone else made up like an old timey movie star. I see a woman in a large, forest green ballgown and an antique scuba diver. Others are pastry chefs, park rangers, scientists, doctors, poets, shamans, and the list goes on.

The family wears the favorite color of the dead. You'll rarely see black here.

When I look inside the packed church, my mind's eye settles on the mourners' bench and her family dressed in hot pink. Lydia's mother is the older replica of her daughter, and she's sobbing into her husband's shoulder. Her pink business suit is as bright and pressed as she could make it. Mr. Boswell's pink foot-high top hat and matching gloves stand out even as the church packs with color.

Josie finds me outside the entrance. We remark at the low, heavy snow clouds, how we can see our breath, and how cold the earth seems without her.

As Josie's lips quiver, I pull her into a hug and brush her wavy hair down her back. "You're so beautiful, Josie. I've always loved this dress on you." It's her favorite, though usually reserved for the summer. The knee-length white dress is embroidered with sunflowers. But to stay warm she's wearing fur-lined leggings and her camo hunting jacket.

She takes in my outfit and laughs, her eyes damp. "Lydia hated this outfit."

"I know." I laugh back. I'm wearing iridescent leggings and a hot pink cowboy sweater. I untangle the tassels running across the chest and arms in a V shape. Paired with my usual turquoise hiking boots, I can almost hear her roasting me.

Together, Josie and I gather our strength and move inside the church.

The building is massive, but today's crowd makes it feel cramped. Half the town is here. Many stand in the back to leave space for those closer to Lydia. Josie made sure we had seats near the front, and we settle into the pews.

The entire cheer squad sits behind us. The captain made sure to wear her runniest mascara.

The football team is in the middle of the church, including Kane, though he's anything but serious. He attempts to telekinetically move the Bible from its shelf behind the pew into his hand, but sharp pains pierce him, and he grimaces. The Bible plummets to the floor, but you can't hear the echo over the deafening hums of the crowd.

Hayden holds his head low, his hands shaking. He wanted to get high before the funeral, but he couldn't do it. Lydia hated smokers. And now he regrets it because he can't shake the energy wafting off her corpse. He's fighting his trance, death begging to be witnessed again and again and again. He wants to retch.

The night he found her is on repeat in his mind—how he rocked her back and forth in the mud, how he held her the way he should've held her the night they broke up.

The only person on the football team who isn't here is Logan, and we understand why. Logan can't report the future, and he isn't supposed to correct it, but mourners still blame every future seer they can.

I watch Logan sitting on the side of his bed. He cups his head, his fingers running through his hair. His eyes are red from crying, and dark circles accent them. He counts his breaths and then texts me.

Is Shakira there? I know she wouldn't miss that. I haven't heard from her in a few days and I'm getting worried. Sorry.

Shockwaves course through my body as I stare at the message on both our phones.

The world grows louder.

My mind's eye pans through the roaring crowd of the church, then Shakira's home, then the shops, the streets, the abandoned dam—

I find her car parked along the road exactly where she left it, and my face flushes.

"Ash..." Josie rubs my arm, sensing me stiffen.

The sound in my head curbs at her voice, her touch, and the world sinks to my periphery again, even if only moving back like a snake about to strike.

I uncurl my fists and look up at the vaulted ceilings of the church. I ground myself in the sour scent of frankincense, the colorful mosaics of the stained-glass windows, the detailed stonework, the gothic design of the entire interior. Catholics always have the best architecture.

One thing at a time, I tell myself. *One thing at a time.*

Josie slides closer, our shoulders touching. She tucks my short black hair behind my ear, but for some reason, this makes me more aware of everyone around us. I can *feel* their assumptions.

They wonder why I didn't help sooner, why I left her in the mud all night, why I didn't pursue every obvious solution a person with my ability would come up with in a moment like this. *They were friends. Weren't they?*

A wave of nausea crashes into me, and I clutch Josie's hands, swallowing my bile. "I don't know if I can do this."

The building seems so small with everyone stuffed inside. I'm so cramped I might as well be rubbing shoulders with them. It feels like everyone is looking at me, blaming me, hating me. And I can't breathe. I can't breathe.

Josie squeezes my hands. "You're not alone in this, Ash. And you're far stronger than all of them." She wipes the tears from my lashes. "This isn't about them or what they think." She smiles somberly. "Plus, Lydia would want us to be here. She needs the attention."

I laugh a little before resting my head on her shoulder and taking a deep, shaky breath.

The ceremony is hard and heartfelt.

As the sun begins to set, the church's stained-glass windows glow, and slowly, the congregation moves to the street making their way to the Riverside Cemetery.

It doesn't matter who follows what faith or even if you knew them, when there is a body for a funeral, people bear witness. We have far too many empty caskets and hollow graves.

As we make it to Riverside, so does the snow. It falls in large, fast chunks. The attendants have marked a path leading to Lydia's gravesite with a red carpet.

She would've loved it.

The fresh earth is piled on a tarp beside the hole. Our breaths wrap around us like shawls as we stand near the grave and wait for everyone to arrive.

The world is silent, the snow falling like a sigh. My knees shake in the cold, but I wouldn't have worn anything different.

I keep my head down, my eyes trained on the hole.

She will be so far from the sun.

The pallbearers lay her gently on the pulley system. The white and rose gold casket is draped with flowers of every color.

I take note of every detail, every sniffle, every footfall, the biting breeze, how the snow freezes my nose and ears, where people stand, how they look, the prayers they utter. It's too much to remember, but still, I try. I want this moment to be immortal.

They lower her into the earth with a final prayer.

Hayden falls to his knees. "Lydia," he sobs, reaching out for her, "I'm so sorry, Lydia. I'm so sorry. I should've been there. I should've—" He cuts himself off.

Everyone stares. My stomach quakes. Mrs. Boswell looks away, cupping her mouth.

Kane lifts him up, though he looks rather embarrassed about it. I move toward them, wanting to soothe Hayden, but Kane guides him away from me as if protecting him. He glares at me, tightlipped, and I remember our last encounter.

I stop. The snow melts on my hair.

Josie turns me away, matching Kane's glare. "Ignore him," she says as we move off the grass. "He'll always be a jerk. We can visit Hayden later."

We meet up with Ford and Markus on the smooth, black asphalt lot of the cemetery. People shift around the graves. Their hushed voices carry on the wind as they linger near the cars. Shoes clack. The snow falls faster.

Chief is here, dressed in his best-pressed uniform. His wide-brim hat keeps the snow off his face as he looks for me. I duck behind Ford and Markus. I can't handle this right now.

Kane encourages Hayden to leave.

Ford suggests we go to Paulette's.

Lydia's family stirs behind their cars, talking and sharing well wishes of a beautiful service. Lydia's mom rubs her raw nose as I cross her line of sight. Without pausing the conversation with her sister, she marches toward me.

My jaw locks.

My friends pause as I stiffen, and then they see Mrs. Boswell. No one can stop her.

When she speaks, her strained voice pierces the bitter breeze. "Tell me what happened to my baby girl!" Tears line her angry face. "You saw something. Tell me!"

I stutter and stare at her manicured finger pointing between my eyes. She must be referencing one of the rumors. "I-I'm sorry, I—" My vision blurs, half-concentrating on her, half on the near-ing crowd. I shake my head, the words not forming.

"How are you going to keep this from me, you selfish little—"

"Sheela." Mr. Boswell grabs her from behind, which distracts her. He offers me an exhausted glance of apology.

They're all staring at me and the weight of their gazes makes the world tilt and spin. I see *everyone*. I hear *everyone*. They're shifting inside me and I can't catch my breath, I can't get out from under their gazes. And now Chief is approaching me, and I have to get out of here.

I feel Josie gently clutch my arm, trying to console me, but her touch compounds my panic and I tear away. I need to be anywhere else but here.

Without another breath, I turn and run.

I hardly hear Josie call my name. Ford suggests she give me space. Markus watches me leave with slacked shoulders. Chief paces up to them and asks what happened, but they ignore him. And I ignore them all.

The air is so cold I can't breathe. It suffocates me. Thoughts that aren't even my own leave tread marks across my mind. Everything piles up.

My throat burns. My legs ache. I don't know where I'm running until I see the downtown park. And once inside, trying to catch my breath, I pace through the snowy grass until I find it.

A doorway made of light. The portal to the other towns.

The noise is sharper now, matching the fast rhythm of my heart and the wheezy pitch of my breath. I wasn't built for running.

The portal is a large neon doorway. It's darker around the frame but filled by an ethereal green light that fills my white eyes and makes all the nearby trees glow.

I've never stood so close to it with any type of intention. I've watched others, though, seen their desperation, their loneliness, their exhaustion. How they've paced up to it, paused, reconsidered, or walked through. Those who choose to leave Veil Haven don't return. Either for the shame of it, because The Watchers don't allow them back, or because something happens to them. Maybe they become content with their new lives, or maybe they die trying.

We aren't allowed to know.

But this is where Declan came from. This portal marks the start of all my problems. If the director really is dead, he won't let me walk through.

I don't know how the portal works exactly. Do you get to choose where to go once you walk inside? Is there a room full of doors? Or does it just teleport you at random? I always assumed a specific alignment happens on game days, like a tunnel cutting through the Void. But these aren't questions we're allowed to ask. Let alone know the answer to.

However, this is the only place I might find answers. And if this isn't enough to get the director's attention, he really might be gone.

I hold my breath, keeping down the sting of vomit.

Static radiates from the portal. I never noticed it before. It shushes the back of my mind, weaving between the noise of Veil Haven. My arm hairs stand on end as I swear I hear a voice forming my name through the static.

"Ash... Ash..."

Is it familiar? Or am I just imagining it?

"Ash." A voice from behind makes me jump. I spin around to find Chief Mun gawking worriedly. "What are you doing here?"

I clench my jaw and tighten my fists. "You lied to me! Maybe you've done nothing but lie to me. Lydia is dead and I can't say why. It wasn't a cryptid. It wasn't natural causes. And you wiped the tapes from the Foodie Mart!" My voice cracks. "You told me you didn't investigate her death, and now the director might be gone, too? What else are you hiding?"

"Ash, come on... you just buried your best friend. You're emotional. We don't need to do this here." He holds his arms out as if I'm a wild animal, and if he gets any closer he might spook me into hurting myself.

"I know people lose people all the time. *I know.*" I tap my chest. Tears freeze my face. "But you're supposed to keep *my* people safe. I'm supposed to keep them safe."

Chief steps forward, cocking his head as if fighting off tears as well. "Ash, baby, please. You put so much pressure on yourself. This isn't your fault."

"I know it isn't," I scream. "It's yours! It's his!" I point at the portal.

The heavy snow falls faster and I wonder if it'll bury us.

"I need to see him," I choke out. "If this isn't enough for him to notice me, nothing is. Then he might as well be dead."

Chief cocks his head, his brows stitching together, genuinely taken aback. Genuinely afraid. But before either of us can speak, his cellphone rings. The silly tune devalues me, but his eyes widen with a new kind of fear. And what's worse is he answers the call.

"Yes?" He swallows, staring at me gaunt. "Yes, sir." I didn't think it was possible for someone to look like they're sweating in a snowstorm. And as Chief holds out his phone for me, I catch the slightest shake of his hand. "He wants to talk to you."

The snow covers the blades of grass at our feet. The portal makes the world glow brighter, especially after sunset.

Slowly, I walk forward. It feels like someone poured concrete in my boots. I can hardly find my breath, but when I do, my mouth is drought-ridden. I take the chief's phone, step back a little, and put it to my ear, trembling.

"Director?"

"Ash," Director Capaldi answers.

My relief is instant, tears cutting down my face. It's him. The weight of how he speaks my name. His mobster-movie voice. The man I've idolized. My dad. He's alive. He's alive!

I cover my mouth as I turn away from Chief, pacing. "I thought something happened to you, I thought—"

"Ash..." he cautions me like a child.

I freeze and swallow my fast-beating heart.

"You should know better than to test my limits. You've been given direct orders to be patient, to trust me. I know your friend's death has been hard on you, but you must remember to listen to us." He sighs, but I can't discern what it means. When he speaks next, he sounds as empathetic as he can. "I'm sorry about Lydia, Ash. There was nothing we could do. I know what she meant to you."

My knees finally give out. I crouch low, my butt touching the snow. My throat closes in as I clutch the phone. I wish I could be closer to him. There's so much I want to say.

I can feel my heart reaching out to him, wanting so much from him, *needing* so much from him, but I can't find the words. The last time we spoke, we were yelling. I was yelling. But he's been watching me this whole time, just like I hoped. Could it be enough?

The snow across town hushes the world, and the static from the portal still snakes through my mind. I can't think of what to say, every point of tension coming to a head and vanishing. But the only thing I care to ask is the thing that makes my voice break.

"Are you mad at me?" And just like that I'm fourteen again.

"No, Ash, of course not. But you really do have to listen. Andrew's orders come through me, and so do Winona's. When they tell you to do something, agree to it, you understand?"

"But, Director, why can't I see Declan?"

The silence I'm met with feels like a punishment. I can feel his disappointment through the phone.

"You can't rush these things, Ash. Don't you trust me?"

I stand up fast with a pang in my chest, my anger corrupting my relief.

"After everything I've done for you? Everything you've left for me to take care of on my own? When the town turned against me and you visited once? All the times I hoped you were watching me. The nights I *begged* for your forgiveness. Every time I wanted to talk to you but didn't because I felt shunned." I take a breath before screaming, "I still do the work for you! And *you're* asking *me* if I trust you?"

I glare at Chief who looks mortified.

"Can't I trust you *and* be tired of waiting?" I raise my voice. "Haven't I proven myself to you? Aren't I enough?"

"No."

His voice is almost drowned out by the noise pitching in my head, but the static of the doorway hisses louder.

I clench up, my eyes watering, the heat rising in my face.

"I'm disappointed at your immaturity, Ash. I had hoped you would be ready, but your insolence and demand to push me only shows me that you're not. If you can do better, and listen, maybe we can revisit this conversation at another time."

My ears ring as the call disconnects.

I don't move. I keep the phone against my cheek. My molars grind. And as Chief moves closer trying to catch my gaze while the portal's static gets louder, I snap out of it.

I scream and throw the phone at his chest.

He catches it in shock and stares at me, still gaunt. "What happened? What did he say?"

"I'm always being told to act like a kid, to act my age, to stop pushing for more," I yell, accusing him. "But how did I have more responsibility when I was eight than I do at seventeen?"

"Oh, Ash... I'm sorry."

"Is that all you can say?" I throw my arms down and face the portal. "The director is wrong. I *am* enough." I push away my tears and squint against the green light.

My cold damp hair sticks to my neck. I ignore the shiver in my legs, the chatter in my jaw, the numbness in my toes. "If no one will give me answers here, I'll find them myself."

Chief lurches forward, his hands out, still afraid to touch me. But the crack in his voice gives me pause. "Don't do this, Ash. *Please* don't leave through the portal."

"Why not? You let the new family in. You want all this change to happen. I was raised to believe I was some sort of exception, and I am. Aren't I? But maybe I've pushed my luck. And maybe this is my final straw."

I step closer, only a couple of feet away from the portal now. It's inviting, warm, but the static screams inside my head. I try not to flinch. It's never been louder.

"Ash, if you go, you won't come back. Don't put Josie through that."

I turn around, disgusted.

"Don't put *me* through that," he begs, taking his hat off. "Please."

"You've been pushing me out because of *his* orders! I finally realize that Director Capaldi wants nothing to do with me. And you're just his puppet, so you don't get a say." I lift my arms. "You raised me to do something I'm no longer capable of. So where does that leave me? Patiently waiting for nothing!"

"None of that is true, Ash. You were never something to push away. You're my daughter. I raised you. And I'm sorry I haven't been better to you. You have to understand I can't disobey him. You have no idea what he's capable of." He looks down. "You don't need to do this to get my attention, Ash. I'm sorry. I'm so sorry." He wipes his eyes. I've never seen him beg. "Can't we go back to how things were? You've never had a traditional family, but I thought we worked pretty well."

"Things change... apparently." I face the portal again.

In the back of my mind, that voice forms through the static again. *"Don't go, Ash... Ash..."*

Chills rise on the back of my neck. I clench my jaw to stop my teeth from chattering and tuck my hands inside the ends of my sleeves.

"Ash, if you leave, I can't protect you," he tells me plainly.

I laugh, though it comes out more like a scoff. "And you're protecting me now?"

"I am always protecting you." The weight in his eyes gives me pause. Those kind, sad, desperate eyes. I've never seen him so scared. He drops his hat on the snow. And when he reaches out and cups my shoulder, everything shifts into perspective.

I got to speak to the director. I got his attention. I have proof he's alive. Meanwhile Chief is here begging me not to take the leap. *He's* the one paying attention to me. He's the one who cares.

And across town, I see Josie being comforted by Ford. They're sharing our usual booth at Paulette's with Markus and Logan, who met up with them after the burial.

A type of dread floods my system.

I should be there. I should be with the people who love me and listen to me and believe me.

I refocus on Chief, who looks like he's about to cry.

"You are capable of so much, Ash," he tells me, laying his hands on both my shoulders. "But some things are too much for someone so young to handle. I don't mean that in a bad way. I know you can take care of yourself. But please..." I let him take my hands. "Believe me when I tell you that everything I've done has been to protect you."

He pauses and cups my cheek. "You don't want to leave town," he says, hoping it can be true. "Please don't try to leave, Ash. You won't find any answers out there."

Despite my anger, my pain, my plans, I listen to him.

My heart lurches in my chest and something inside me crumbles like the dam wall.

I squeeze his hands and rest my forehead against his chest, exhausted. He wraps his arms around me, both of us relieved, and I cry.

He isn't much warmer than I am but it doesn't matter.

If it was always a choice between Director Capaldi and Chief Mun, I was obsessed chasing a man who couldn't care less about me. The director is no better than the Forest Eye. Chief is the only parent in my life who treats me like a human being rather than a tool, a puppet, a cryptid.

Maybe the world isn't falling apart. Maybe I'm not losing my grip. Maybe I've just never lost someone before, and I'm looking for people to blame. Maybe I'm not supposed to have everything figured out.

And maybe I'm not supposed to save everyone, though that doesn't make Lydia's death hurt any less.

I shouldn't be freezing myself in the snow when I could be eating burgers with the people I love.

After Chief and I eat takeout, after we get warm in front of my fireplace and watch reruns of my favorite show, he leaves.

The snow hasn't stopped, but it's slowed considerably.

A new kind of darkness blankets the world as I sit at my kitchen table thinking about today.

I take something to ease my pounding headache. I've never had one so bad. Between the sobbing, the snow, and the fighting, everything hurts. I can hardly form a personal thought.

Despite all these emotions, all these resolutions, and the idea that things can change and heal and I can be okay, a small void has stitched inside my chest.

It's small, but it's there, and it's empty.

I stare out my sliding glass doors and look into the faraway darkness of the woods at the end of my yard. Snowstorms like this always make the world quiet. But while I am grateful for the hushed tones in my head, the lack of static, and the lack of even my own thoughts, this pervasive emptiness pokes at something that shouldn't be stirred. Something I hoped would've been satisfied by now.

The glow from my kitchen forms a doorway of light on the snow. I stare at it for a long time.

Even after my questions were answered and my fears were dashed, something doesn't feel right. But my headache begs me to rest, and instead of staying up to watch the snow blanket my deck, I choose to go to bed.

CHAPTER 24
The Few Moments We Have Left

When I wake up, it's Halloween.

I'm not sure I'll ever get out of bed. I can pretend to be okay in this pocket of warmth. I can ignore the sun reflecting off the snow outside.

The first thing I saw this morning was Lydia. Snug and shadowed, buried. They put her in a dress I haven't seen her wear in years. I pulled my mind's eye out of her casket before I could hyperfixate on anything else.

I can't stop hearing Hayden's wails. He can't stop thinking about her. The last night they were together. The last time he saw her. His endless teasing. How she stormed away at the carnival. He mumbles apologies to no one.

How do people live after losing someone? How do they get used to it?

I don't think I'll ever be okay again.

Veil Haven is tucked in white sheets made silver and gold in the sun. In the muffled noise of town, I am grateful to hear my own thoughts. Most people are asleep or slow moving because of the long holiday break. But all I can think about is how last night's chill made the last of the autumn colors fade.

Everything is moving so fast.

The town plowed the roads and cleared out downtown for the annual celebration of Samhain for the pagans and witches.

A giant bonfire sits at the top of Main Street. The rest of the road is lined with stalls and vendors decorated with lights, wreaths, sigils, and musky incense. Each stall is selling a different set of harvest goods: herbs, gemstones, animal hides, bones, spell services, final harvest veggies, meats, preserves, winter clothes, and so on.

Tonight, the fires will continue to burn. The tradition of dressing up to disguise yourself from harm and cryptids will roll out. It doesn't help against the really nasty ones. But sometimes, when superstitions bleed into wishful thinking, it generates just enough luck to keep you safe. Especially on nights surrounding Halloween.

I watch Markus and his sisters parade through downtown, surprised by the festival. They throw snowballs at each other in the park. They've never seen so much snow in their lives. It's only about a foot high.

Markus tries to keep up with his little sisters as Kyah and Jarissa speed from vendor to vendor. They're vastly over-bundled in new winter clothes.

After the girls talk to a young woman and decide she's a "real life witch," they become set on finding something they can get for their mom.

When the vendor asks Markus what ails her, he has a hard time explaining her illness and quietly admits there's probably nothing here to help. But still, Kyah and Jarissa have their hearts set on finding just the right potion or rock or herb to help her.

I lie back and let my mind's eye wander.

Someone is sewing for the first time. Someone is having an epic snowball fight. Someone goes to the abandoned carnival while it is closed and is killed almost instantly. Someone is making a deal with a Mothman to clear the Shadow Person out of their home.

Someone hears his front door open.

He sees someone familiar standing in his living room and it breaks his heart. The look in her eyes says everything. The gun in her hand says even more. He is guilty but not remorseful. He looks at his stained white tank top and blue striped boxers and says, "It doesn't matter what you wear when you die. Right?" She doesn't hesitate. It's over in a second.

Then it hits me. I roll over and groan into my pillow. Today is the séance. I volunteered to help them reclaim Dante's living memories.

Dante has been bothering Ford extra hard since midnight. All the ghosts are stronger today, more tangible. Some can even become visible. This time of year holds so many celebrations, but Ford and other ghost whisperers would rather sleep through it.

With Dante able to touch things, he hasn't stopped poking Ford, playing on his consoles, tearing the sheets off his bed, and messing with the lights.

Ford is counting down the hours to the séance this evening.

Something about the full moon rise makes the ghosts even stronger, thus more grounded in the realm of the living.

But for now, I still have a few quiet hours to myself.

I watch Josie as she goes about her day and tries to settle her nerves for tonight. She's never attempted to *touch* a ghost before. She isn't sure what will happen, but she can't let Dante or Ford down. They're counting on her.

She's hanging out with Miss Ava, helping her prepare her greenhouse for the winter.

Miss Ava might be alone in her cabin, but she keeps busy with her luscious garden and the various crafts that make her home colorful and warm.

The windows of the greenhouse fog and blur the world, and Josie is grateful for its warmth and seclusion.

I feel faint when I realize what's on Josie's mind. How could I have forgotten so soon?

She's thinking about Kimi's journal, what she saw, how she hid it from Ford, how she hides it now—this killing thing. Kimi's memories replay again and again. That blue sky.

"Whatever's troubling you," Miss Ava interrupts Josie's thoughts, her nails deep in the warm soil, "you have to practice restraint. The Void is telling me to warn you about that." Ava casts her dark gaze over her shoulder.

The color drains from Josie's cheeks. She takes a deep breath, about to explain something, but Miss Ava stops her.

She holds up a wrinkled, freckled hand. "Josie, whatever you've found, take it far away from here and bury it."

Josie hardly breathes, her heart beating fast.

I suppose this means the Void is just ignoring me. Or maybe the Forest Eye is shielding me from them. Maybe it threatened the Void like it did Mr. Boogle. But what can one god do to another?

Josie nods. Her eyes scan the floor as she tries to piece it all together.

"You gotta stop doing that, too," Ava says. She takes Josie's hands, neither of them minding the dirt. "You're a sweet, soft thing, Josie. Don't let them play that against you. If you want to be okay, forget. If you can't, hide it." Ava smiles but it doesn't reach her eyes. She pats Josie's hands before returning to her work.

Josie thanks her softly. She tries forcing Kimi's memories down, down, down. It's hard but she has to try.

Ava is right. What she saw, the implications... they're dangerous.

As Josie and Ava go back to their quiet work, a new thought passes through me, and I grab my phone.

I text Logan about Shakira. How could the funeral only have happened yesterday? Will the world ever slow down enough for me to catch my breath?

I watch Logan ignore his phone. He's lost in deep, cautious

thought. I do my best not to pry, but I've never seen him so serious. Has he seen another vision about Veil Haven burning? Maybe something about Shakira?

I don't often catch his visions. They happen so fast it's hard to keep track, but maybe I should be more aware. I'm supposed to see everything. Why does it feel like I'm finally realizing that was never true?

He'll see my message when he's ready. I have to leave it at that.

I park behind Shakira's abandoned car and the dread pierces me like an arrow.

Logan hasn't texted me back.

I don't know what's happened to Shakira, but it's my fault, isn't it? Bile rises in my throat. I wash it down with some water.

I grip the wheel and I tell myself to breathe slowly. Logan is playing video games ahead of a small Halloween party. He's dressed as Where's Waldo, and it's just silly enough to make me relax. Everything is fine. Shakira will come back like she always does. Nothing is wrong.

I fix my hair under my blue pom-pom hat and ignore the pimples on the side of my face. I wrap my ombre infinity scarf snugly beneath my patch jacket before fiddling with the plastic bags tucked between two layers of socks. Once comfortable again, I get out of my car and walk through the snowy glen toward the dam.

It feels strange to hang out with people or even go to a party the day after Lydia's funeral, but it's Halloween, and sometimes you need to be distracted from your grief.

Josie, Ford, and Dante are already here.

I'm surprised how visible Dante is. He's still transparent, but everyone can see him now. I can see his ghostly visage from across the field, floating between them and gesturing wildly.

Josie is using all her strength not to blush and turn away. I'm not sure she's made eye contact with Ford since Dante mentioned how cute they would be as a couple. Ford is growing more irritated by the minute.

"Ash!" Dante shouts, teleporting from the center of the dam to right in front of me. He sounds vaguely distant, like he's speaking through a phone with poor reception. *"This is so exciting! You can see me?"*

I laugh. "Yes, Dante, I can see you. Hi."

He tugs on his letterman jacket and grins. He brushes his hand over his close-shaven hair. *"It's nice that you can officially meet me. Being dead is wild, but this is great! I wish it was Halloween all the time!"*

"It's nice to meet you too, Dante. You've been pretty entertaining even without me being able to see you. You've really annoyed Ford out of his shell."

He follows me as we walk back to Josie and Ford. *"Ah, well, someone had to do it. You know what the best part about being dead is?"* he asks. *"I don't have to keep adjusting my glasses. They just stay put!"*

I look up at him. He's naturally tall but loves hovering about a foot off the ground. "I'm happy you like being dead."

"Oh, I recommend it."

I force a laugh and use Josie's hug as a distraction. She compliments my jacket while Ford gives me an apologetic look on behalf of Dante.

The snow out here hasn't thinned. The cool breath from the river chills us, and I bury myself inside my sherpa jean jacket.

Affectionately known as my patch jacket, it's decorated with patches and pins ranging from fandom references and band symbols to cute cryptids, quotes, and a whole bunch of eyes. Most I bought for myself but some of them were gifts.

One Christmas the girls and I gave each other something that represented each other. The glow-in-the-dark sunflower patch across my heart is from Josie, and the sparkly pink Starbucks cup pin is from Lydia. I moved it to my left sleeve so I could see it better. It's bittersweet.

This jacket makes me feel whole, and I'm grateful it's cold enough to wear again.

The abandoned dam isn't the warmest place to visit at sundown, but the privacy seemed like a good idea.

The peachy sky has darkened to orange as the sun dips behind the mountains. No matter what the current moon cycle promises, the moon is always full on Halloween. The rainbow stars seem extra bright as the final sun rays stretch across the sky. And finally, we spy the moon rising above the knitted blue peaks.

I'm nervous being so near the woods, but I'm praying the Forest Eye has some decency. I don't want to be interrupted. And I don't have the energy to explain my history with the long-lost forest god. Or why I never told my friends to begin with.

Josie, Ford, and I face each other as the moment dawns upon us. None of us are really sure what the procedure should be, but Ford has been researching this type of séance, and he tells us it seems as simple as we expect.

The pit in Josie's stomach deepens as she fiddles with her hands. But as Ford and I smile at her somewhat sheepishly, and Dante gives her an excited thumbs-up, she finds the strength to swallow her last-minute anxieties.

"Alrighty." She rubs her hands together, staring at Dante. "It shouldn't hurt or anythin'. And you shouldn't be able to see what I see, so, no worries about accidentally movin' on. What I see stays with me."

"*Good,*" Dante says. "*Because I like being here. I just... want to remember a little more about myself. And about that girl I was dating, too. Althea.*"

"From the yearbook," Ford reminds us, his arms crossed.

I ball my hands inside the ends of my sleeves and tuck into my scarf. Noises shift through the woods behind us as the cryptids can't help but lurk and stalk along the tree line.

A Black Dog howls and it echoes through the river valley. Everyone tenses. Josie jumps in place and backs behind me, clutching my arm.

"They won't bother us," I tell them, quickly. "They know better."

I think about the Shadow Person that taunted me in my house and swallow. I don't think they notice.

"Okay, well…" Josie can't find the words to finish her thought. It takes her a while to shake her worry.

"It's pretty stupid coming out here," Ford finally says, his arms by his sides. He scans the trees, ready for anything.

"Sure." I laugh. "But it's fine."

He looks at Josie.

"The cryptids never bother Ash," she explains. "We don't know why. But, well, yeah."

"Ah." Then, he swallows. He looks away, embarrassed, as if finally remembering the rumors suggesting I'm a monster. Literally.

I wish I had a real explanation as to why the cryptids don't bother me. Well, I do, but that would involve having to tell people about the Forest Eye, and how it cares about me. I don't want to separate myself from what's normal any more than I already am.

I stand with my back to the woods in a symbolic gesture, hiding my own nerves.

The moon bathes us in silver light as we watch our breaths rise toward the stars.

"Okay," Josie says abruptly. She steps closer to Dante who's as serious as I've seen him. "Y'all ready?"

Ford and I watch from either side of them.

Dante nods.

The action is as simple as grabbing someone's hand, but when Josie touches Dante, her trance sweeps over her instantly. Thrust back in time, her physical body stays with us while her eyes glaze over and her body tenses, almost statuesque.

This isn't like other times. Josie can usually shift around in the past and view the scene from the third person. But without a physical object or a death anchor, the only thing she can latch on to is Dante.

She isn't just witnessing his life. She's living it.

Josie looks down at herself and finds Dante's dark skin, his muscular arms. His fingers are interlocked with another's.

He's holding hands with a beautiful young woman, her darker skin radiant under the porchlight. She's been crying. Her lashes are damp as she begs him, apologizing. She takes his hand and touches it to her stomach fondly.

"They can't do this to us," Dante protests.

"They're going to whether it's right or wrong," the young woman says. "There's never any choice here. We both know that." They can't be older than eighteen. "That's how we operate. That's how they want me to operate." Her hand curves around her belly and she weeps.

"Then why can't we just leave right now? We're running out of time."

"I have to distract them or assure them we aren't doing this. That they don't have to kill us or take us away. I can do this, Dante. I just need a little more time."

"You're a good negotiator," Dante half-jokes, cupping her cheek, "but no one is that good. Some things you can't heal, Althea, and if The Watchers—"

She hushes him, standing on her toes to cover his mouth.

Dante takes her hand and kisses her palm.

She almost cries again, the pain swelling in her chest. "We have to try. We have to do everything we can for this baby."

"If either of us has to take the fall, it can't be you," he says. "Even if they come for me, you have to leave. If it comes to that, do whatever it takes."

"But it won't." Her dark brown eyes trace his. "We have to believe this will work."

Dante kisses her passionately, holds her belly, and promises, "Anything for you and Markus."

The scene is consumed by mist and shadows, rebuilding itself into something new.

Josie feels her chest tighten as Dante runs through the woods at full speed.

He saw The Watchers closing in around his house and he ran.

Nothing went right. Their plan failed, but Althea is waiting for him. Risking everything for a chance. He just needs to get there.

Branches snap under Dante's fast-moving feet. His panicked breaths fill the quiet forest as he sprints between the dark trees. It feels like they're closing in on him, but he can't be sure.

Maybe he really is outrunning The Watchers. Maybe they really can do this.

A bramble of thorns cut into his calves but he doesn't let it stop him. He's trained for this. Well, not for this, but he is the fastest guy on the team. He can outrun anyone. He can outrun them. He has to.

The creatures of the forest are silent. If The Watchers are behind him, they don't yield any noise. It's like the world is holding its breath, watching him.

Dante looks behind him before turning sharply off the deer path and shifting down a bluff without considering the noise of it. And before he can stop himself, he loses his footing at the base of the hill, slides into a tree with a loud thump, and splashes into a creek.

His ears ring. He readjusts his glasses as he crawls out of the water and presses his back against a tree. His throat burns as he stifles his loud breaths. Beads of sweat roll over his brow.

He waits, listens. Nothing. Maybe he lost them. Maybe they didn't hear him. Maybe luck really is—

The underbrush ahead of him shifts with movement as figures in black combat gear rise to meet him. The white symbols on their *shoulders seem to shine in the night. That's the only thing Dante can focus on. Those eyes like the setting sun.*

He tries to run or scream or—

But the bullets cut through him all the same.

Josie rocks into the present with a scream, shuffling wildly to get away from Dante.

I'm already in place to catch her as she trips over her feet. We fall together.

She holds her face and pats her chest where she felt the bullets tear into her. Her muscles ache as though bruised, feeling his death even now. She crumbles against me in her panic, her labored breathing piercing and loud.

We all ache at the sound of it. Dante most of all.

Ford kneels beside me and Josie folds against his large frame.

I stare at our imprints in the snow. My head is full of static. The periphery of the world is threatening to spill over, and I hold it back as best I can.

My own thoughts are finally louder than the rest of Veil Haven.

The Watchers killed Dante. But they don't... And if they killed Dante, then they killed Kimi and... They were both near the edge of town. Dante and Althea were trying to leave and if he didn't make it then...

"What happened?" Ford asks me. He dwarfs Josie as he shields her from the past.

My white eyes cut to Dante. The words weigh in my mouth as I swallow the bitter taste.

"Dante is Markus' father."

CHAPTER 25
STRANGE DEPTHS

Dante teleports away instantly, leaving us under the moonlit sky.

He reappears in the Jacksons' home and moves quickly to the master bedroom. Althea is asleep in her bed, alone. She's aged, and life hasn't been kind to her, but she's the girl from the yearbook without a doubt. Her hair is different. She's too thin now. She doesn't open her eyes, but it's her.

Dante doesn't know what happened, but new memories are beginning to flood through him. How he laughed with her, kept his arm around her shoulders, joked about her height, threw pencils at her in class. How he would pick her up and spin her around. How he would always run up to her in the bleachers for a kiss after a touchdown. How passionate she was for him. How grounded and confident she was. How devious her smile could be.

They were in love. They were going to be a family. But something happened. Dante can't remember what, and something in his gut begs him not to try.

His hands shake as he touches her cheek and gasps when he feels her. He remembers the magic of this night, the thinning of the veil.

Dante takes her hand and tries to stir her, whispering her name, but she doesn't wake.

Quietly, tears spill over his cheeks. Dante hangs his head and covers his mouth before collapsing in the nearest chair, staring at her.

He continues to remember her in little ways. Their bond, the light in her eyes, how she made him laugh. How her fingers moved, the way she stretched her arms, how she played with her hair, the way her hips swayed when she walked.

And finally it hits me.

A ghost without a death anchor.

Who manifested within the same lifetime as his death.

Dante arrived the same day the Jacksons moved into town. Dante is here because Althea and Markus are back in Veil Haven.

That's his purpose.

They're his resurrection.

We all stay on the cold ground. I feel swallowed by the deep orange sky.

Josie tells Ford about her vision now that Dante is gone. Talking it out is helping her catch her breath, but she's afraid. Ford holds her hands as he listens. Josie is grateful for the warmth.

I stare at the moon-bright snow and the grass blades that peek through our footsteps.

"Nobody leaves town... nobody returns..." My voice is buried in the back of my throat.

"Maybe they let her leave," Ford suggests. "Maybe the town is making amends by letting her come back."

I feel so far from myself. "Veil Haven is changing."

Josie stands up and holds herself tightly. We follow her lead, our butts numb from the snow.

I see something dark glaze over her eyes as she looks at me. Is she blaming me? "*They* killed him."

The ground is spinning. I begin to pace along the side of the dam wall to keep my balance. The fresh, cold air helps me fight off the noise from town.

Josie steadies her voice with a deep, shaken sigh. She walks up to me, making me pause. "We have to tell Markus."

Declan burns in my mind. That smile. That knowing look in his dark eyes. My body floods with chills. "No."

She rocks her head back. "No?"

We stare at each other. I can't find the words to explain myself.

"He deserves to know," Ford says.

I look down, clutching the dam. Somewhere far below, the Boy looks up at me from the Black River, observing my panic.

Does everyone have to witness me? Why does it suddenly feel like a million eyes are watching me?

A voice cuts through the static of my mind, a somewhat familiar voice—distant, humming, reverent. The Void?

"Ash..."

The hair on the back of my neck stands on end. I turn to face the sky, breathing fast. The worlds melts away.

"Ash, please be careful."

The stars twinkle in unison. The entire sky is aligned in this cosmic dance. The Void's gentle presence is gratifying, but their warning doesn't soothe me as it should.

In a breath, the Void's voice drifts out of my mind like a breeze, and the stars return to their asynchronous twinkling.

The riot of noise rises in my periphery. Josie and Ford haven't moved. And I'm still standing here. The static in my mind is swelling like a storm.

Someone is lighting jack-o-lanterns. Someone is kissing in the abandoned history museum. Someone spills glitter on their carpet. Someone is making popcorn.

Logan is laughing with his teammates at a party, and even though this is what he's done every Halloween, it feels wrong now. Hayden drinks alone in his room, watching a horror movie, feeling numb. Kane is tearing his room apart, frustrated that his telekinesis is slipping. Markus is trick-or-treating with his sisters. Declan is nowhere to be found.

I can barely hear myself speak.

"Let me tell Markus." I'm wide-eyed, my jaw tight. "And... for the record, we're safe. We're safe and I'm gonna keep it that way. We just... we shouldn't talk about this. Or think about it."

Josie and Ford share a glance before agreeing with me.

She steps forward, resting a hand on my shoulder. "Ash, are you okay?"

Someone completes a ritual. Someone is lured into the woods. Someone sees their grandpa's ghost. Someone honks at a Not-Deer and laughs when they scare it. Someone is passing out candy. Someone is dragged into the sewer.

"Yes. But I-I have to go."

Josie cocks her head. "You should stay." She looks at Ford who nods.

"We can go back to my place. It's big enough that we don't have to run into anyone. We can just chill and forget about this."

I don't meet their eyes. "Dante is with Althea at Markus' house. I'm so sorry. I have to go."

Someone is hit by a car. Someone is practicing for a musical. Someone drowns in the Black River. Someone is stargazing. Someone is practicing their fire manipulation in the woods.

"Ash, wait—"

I'm already hurrying back to my car.

Althea is from Veil Haven.

This is what The Watchers were keeping from me. But why? And why bring her back now? And why allow the true outsider in?

Ever since Declan showed up everything has gone wrong. Why are The Watchers siding with him and giving him a position that would cement him deeper into the government? Wait, wasn't Althea the mayor?

My head pounds as I turn the ignition. I stare at Shakira's car and feel both wired and exhausted.

Did Althea run away to Fox Falls? When did she meet Declan?

Why is she paralyzed and sick? Could that really be from a car accident? And what was her ability?

I slam on my breaks several car lengths from a stop sign.

If Markus is from Veil Haven, why doesn't he have an ability?

I continue driving. I only want to be one place in the world right now. Only one place can give me answers.

The Watchers killed Dante.

The Watchers killed Kimi.

Director Capaldi explicitly told me they don't kill people. Or did he? Did he ever actually say that?

The pleather squeaks as I wring my hands over the wheel.

Althea left Veil Haven.

Althea left and came back and now Declan is here. A new life. A new lie. But I'm missing something.

If the Jacksons came through the portal, what was Dante running towards?

At the end of a holler lined with antique cottages stands a stone castle hidden behind the trees.

It has an ivy-covered tower with green-copper roofing, parapets, dungeon-barred windows, and everything else you can imagine a stout, two-story castle to have. Everything that suggests there's an ancient cult in the woods.

This is the Keepers' Keep. And yes, it is the dumbest name they could've chosen.

I park along the road and take off my hat and scarf before sliding the extra pair of socks and plastic bags out of my boots. Then, I jog up to the castle's wooden doors.

The Keepers of the Coast aren't here. They're in the woods up in the mountains doing a big celebration ritual in the hopes that some of their dead past members will recognize them and return to reveal "the truth." Ghosts have been arriving, but most of them are just confused, and one is actually toying with them. None are previous members.

Still, the cultists are pretty eager.

And for some reason, they've left their keep entirely un-guarded. I don't need my omniscience to know they hide the key in a fake rock beside the entrance. I roll my eyes and enter.

The foyer is dark and reeks of musty fabrics. It's as dark academic as you can get—rich wooden panels, thick ornate picture frames, wall sconces and antique chandeliers. The Keep is one of those unwelcoming spaces that whispers, *You don't belong here.*

Director Capaldi told me so, at least. *"You hear me, Ash? Stay away. That kind of thinking isn't good for you. It isn't good for any of us, but especially not you."*

But his last sentiment reverberates inside my skull.

Aren't I enough?

No.

I clench my molars, my fists tight, and navigate deeper into the Keep as if I've done it a million times.

The inside is exactly what you'd imagine a weird culty castle to look like. Dark blue carpet lines dark wooden hallways, which are poorly lit with medieval sconces packed between obnoxious frames holding strange artwork. The entire place smells like old books, mothballs, and the vague hint of mold under the creaking, well-worn floorboards.

The castle itself isn't that big. Once you factor in the internal boxy architecture and poorly designed "hidden" rooms, it's not much bigger than a four-bedroom home.

If an outsider had to guess where their ancient para-religious book is hidden, I would hope they would choose the random door-sized wainscoting between two framed paintings of the ocean at the end of the main hall.

I push against the wall and the hidden door opens with ease, revealing a dark blue room draped with banners of the Keepers' symbol—an ocean wave crashing to the left over a sunken eye.

Bookshelves lay against the walls where said banners don't hang. The shelves buckle under the weight of massive old books I'm certain no one has read in decades. But against the leftmost wall, under a single delicate spotlight, stands a podium displaying a navy leather-bound book inside a plexiglass box.

The book is well-worn and has been restored at least twice over the years. It isn't thicker than an average fantasy novel and is about a foot long. It has no title, no author, and is almost entirely filled with notes and additions to the original text.

I pause, half of me wanting to turn away. *You're not supposed to be here.*

I steel myself. If Director Capaldi doesn't want me here, he'll have to stop me himself.

I take the plexiglass box off the podium and place it on the floor. Carefully, I open the book. I only need to see one entry—the text that inspired the cult.

They don't often read it directly from the book since most cultists have it memorized, and they just recite part of it in unison when recruiting new members. I've never been able to fully understand their impossibly poor chorus.

But in light of Josie's visions, I need to see the Keepers' truth.

The original text is on small, thin pages taken from somewhere else and transplanted into this book. Years of fingers tracing the text has made the handwritten words fade, but it's been laminated and transcribed on the following pages. Various records of the text appear in the opening of this sacred book, but I want the original.

At first glance, the passage looks more like a diary than a religious text or anything meant for an audience. It's personal, private, poetic.

With my heart in my ears, I read the ancient text.

In the creases of my memory I am sunken
beneath the waves holding my breath as the

current pulls me to the horizon. There I am, rubbed raw by the ocean, salty and sunbaked. There, I have sand between my teeth and toes and wedged so deeply in my hair that I take the beach with me everywhere I go.

But I've lost that and the ocean has lost me.

Here in the mountains my freckles have faded, my skin crawls with cold, and I ache knowing this very same sun beats somewhere else warming some past-me who will never know where this life takes her.

And they took me. It was horrible, and I'm not sure these scars will ever heal, but that's not what this is about. This is about the ocean and how my heart longs for its vastness.

There is a distinct before and a distinct after, and now I am living some third life. While not bad, it isn't the before.

I don't think I'll ever know the ocean again, that endless wine-dark water stretching until it kisses the sky.

I am a lighthouse with no sea, a ship on dry land, a beached whale without breath. If there is any way to die it is to sink beneath the waves and know the truth of this world; to be where life began. I thought it would be poetic. Now, I will never have my perfect end.

That thought was the only thing that kept me alive when the US first stole us. I promised myself I wouldn't die there but now that we're hiding here I fear I will never know the ocean again. I will never know the thick sea air, the froth and foam washed ashore, how the tides rise and fall like the Earth taking breath. How that current can pull you out, push you in, or hold you there like a child in the palm of their mother's hands.

That was life. This is survival. Or maybe this is something else entirely. I have yet to see how our haven unfolds. And even as this landscape changes, as we change with it, I will forever weep knowing that part of me is lost far beyond these woods. I hear it like some secret voice begging me to come home, home, home.

But I cannot leave. I can't risk everyone's safety. Valentine has done so much for us. We have to believe we can survive here. It would be too selfish to leave, and we are still being hunted.

But still, I cry.

These woods are deep, but nothing can match the depths of the sea. And in my grief, I know I will never again see the ocean or the world beyond these mountains.

I step away from the book with heavy breaths as the noise of the world crashes into me. It deafens me, makes my hands shake, but I close the book, cover it with plexiglass, and leave the castle in a sprint.

I dash into my car, my white eyes wide, and hyperfocus on everything around me. The stained fabric seats, the chill seeping through the glass, the humming engine. The pleather squeaking under my hands, my aching molars, my breath fogging the windows. The near-invisible listening device, the hair itching my face, the goosebumps covering my body.

My head pounds. My chapped lips ache in the cold. My throat is just as dry.

The ocean. That same thing I saw in Markus.

The world beyond these mountains. What's *US*? What happened to the author? Who is Valentine?

Was Kimi killed for leaving Veil Haven? That blue sky. But it's impossible. And Dante, Markus' real dad, he was killed for trying to leave. Wasn't he? But Althea left and she's back with an entire family. It doesn't make sense.

My headache from last night returns with a vengeance. I cringe and massage my temples.

Veil Haven is changing.

Everything started when Althea came back.

The night they arrived I was at the abandoned carnival. The six-eyed deer left. The Forest Eye reached out to me.

But no, they arrived after I left the carnival, well after it closed for the night. What would the Forest Eye know about the Jacksons before they even got here?

They moved in when I slept. I dreamed of Hayden doing something that didn't happen. I dreamed. And I dreamed the night Lydia died. And it was the Forest Eye. Wasn't it? Does everything in our world circle back to the Forest Eye and The Watchers? Why does it feel like I'm their central focus?

But I'm not. Thousands of people are doing thousands of things at any given moment. I have nothing to do with this mystery besides trying to unearth it.

Dante is Markus' father. Althea was the mayor eighteen years ago and she left Veil Haven. Dante tried leaving but The Watchers killed him. And they killed Kimi Kingfisher all those years ago, too.

Could the Keepers of the Coast be right?

I cover my mouth, my quick breaths like a symphony. I don't care if The Watchers have all their best telepaths trained on me. I can't help myself.

How could the Keepers of the Coast, our dumbest cult, be right? But why else would The Watchers kill people for leaving? Nothing lies beyond Veil Haven but the Void, and it would kill us if we entered it. The Void is inhospitable to anyone who's not a voidwalker. We all *know* this.

I send my mind's eye to the edge of the world. It's swathed in thick undergrowth and cryptids, some of which don't even have names. It's dangerous out there. It's beautiful, too. But there's an abrupt stop. The mountains kneed into the hills. The trees are wide and overgrown but there's a distinct line. An ending. An edge. Veil Haven is one giant bubble, and I see all of it. I see everything.

And nothing lies beyond that.

So why am I shaking? Why can't I catch my breath? Why am I consumed by a fear I can't explain?

The director's voice rings in my head. The hairs on the back of my neck stand up. I can almost feel his thick hand brushing my hair, how I laid against his large belly as he spent time with me in the early days. How we sat together, feeling like a family, back when everything made sense.

"You see this world for what it is, Ash, all its horrors and won-ders." He smiled at me. Proud. "You're my good girl, and I will do everything to protect you from this place. I can do it, you know. I can keep you safe."

"You keep me safe," I agreed. He gave me a house, nannies to raise me, people to shop for me. And when I was older he would pay me for my work, he would give me a car, he would provide me with everything I have. He loved me. I loved him.

"Let me protect you, Ash," he said, sitting me up, making me face him. His small mouth was tight, the lower whites of his eyes so prominent. He was serious and thinking of nothing but me. I loved the feel of it. "You're so curious but questions are dangerous. Knowl-edge is dangerous."

My brows furrowed.

"You can't follow your curiosity, Ash. That gets people killed. But you know that. You see it happen, how those people are killed by cryptids, why they're taken. Let me keep you safe." He grabbed my shoulders. "Understand? If you have questions, you keep them to yourself. That's how people live. Don't chase those feelings. Don't let them control you. You're my good girl. Right?"

I nodded, fixated on his every word.

"Good." He hugged me.

I grip the wheel tighter, heat filling my cheeks. My eyes sting as tears slide down my face. I stubbornly wipe them off.

How could I be so naïve?

But what am I supposed to believe? I was a kid. I still am a kid. When the leader of the secret military organization that controls our town, the man who happens to be your adoptive dad, tells you something, don't you inherently believe it? I can't blame myself for that. But then why do I feel so empty?

What I learned from our séance and the Keepers' book are only half-answers.

Why doesn't Markus have an ability? Maybe not everyone has abilities in Fox Falls, which could explain Kyah and Jarissa. It could even explain Declan if I ignore the possibility that his blind spotness is an ability. Even though it's not as intense as the homeless guy, uhm, Yona's brother, wow, why can't I remember his name? If that isn't Declan's ability, what is? None of this explains why Markus lacks one!

Why can't Director Capaldi just tell me everything? It's not like he doesn't know. It's not like he won't tell me later anyway. It's all part of his grand plan. After all, he was raising me to take his place one day. I mean, wasn't that the point of all this?

I'm quiet for a long time. Veil Haven is quiet for a long time.

That's it. Isn't it? He was training me to be the next director.

But what happened? I pushed him too far? I broke the law by asking for him to spare Logan? Why would Anthony Capaldi ever give up his power? I can't even imagine him sharing it with me. Not that I would want it anyway.

I don't.

I watch my breath form in the cold of my car and finally turn the heat on.

Veil Haven vibrates in the back of my mind. I feel just as distant.

I pinch my eyes shut and shake my head. It makes me nauseated. Then I scream into my hands.

I don't know what I want but I can't be his good girl anymore. I need more answers—with or without his blessing.

I lean my forehead against the wheel and let the dry, warm air ground me.

Despite the dangers, I want to tell someone everything I know. But Josie has too much on her plate. And I'm not ready to tell Markus because I can barely grasp it myself. I'm missing something.

I could go to Logan. I could go to him, and he would understand. I don't know how we could communicate any of this but—

I stare at my phone as it vibrates, transfixed. Logan just texted me.

Meet me at the dam tomorrow at noon. Please.

Did he see my breakdown in a vision? Does he already know what I want to tell him? *Do* I tell him?

I look out at the dark orange sky backlit by the full moon. I see a small shooting star burn across the Milky Way. Sucking in a sharp breath, I turn back to my phone.

Logan is alone in his bedroom. It's quiet. He sits with a heaviness, a hollowness. Whatever he harbors inside him, he buries it and keeps it away from any prying eyes.

I realize he never texted me back about Shakira.

The phone light stings my eyes, and despite knowing better, I text him back.

I'll be there.

CHAPTER 26
The Past Clawing After You

The snow hasn't melted much as I retrace my steps from yesterday, but the air isn't as dry, which helps my chapped lips. I lean against the dam's wall and let my head loll back, resting beneath the far-away noontime sun.

Again, I'm not afraid of being so near the woods. I guess that's what faith does to you. Because if Logan asked me here I know it's safe.

I can't figure out what the Forest Eye is planning or why they want me so badly, but that's one question I don't feel compelled to find answers to.

The celebrations of the dead are still ongoing. The ghosts aren't visible anymore but their presence is still stronger than the rest of the year. Even people who can't see them can feel them more than usual.

By the time Markus got back from trick-or-treating with his sisters, Dante was still enamored by Althea. Even though part of him wanted to reveal himself to Markus, something held him back. He chalked it up to nerves. It's already a hard task to introduce yourself to your long-lost son, but it's another thing entirely to reveal to him that his dad is dead. Despite wanting to take advantage of his opening, Dante sulked away, and before the night was over, he left their house entirely.

He's back with Ford now, though neither of them talk about what happened. Dante doesn't carry his normal pep or energy, but after the emotionally intense evening, Ford is grateful for a calm day.

They say October 31, November 1, and November 2 are when the veil between the living and dead planes are the thinnest. Thus anyone from the other side can poke a hole and walk through. It's hard for me to keep track of all the ghosts in Veil Haven, but there is always an uptick in loved ones long past visiting their living descendants. I guess that's why they give us three days off school. I'm grateful for the long weekend.

I rub my eyes. I can't believe it's already November. We buried Lydia two days ago. Will the world ever slow down?

When Logan arrives, we hug each other for a long time. We don't speak. It's so nice to see him again. I can't remember the last time it was just the two of us.

I have to bite my tongue from word vomiting everything that's happened to me. He looks even more tired than I do. He's wearing a maroon quarter zip under his letterman. And with his gray winter hat, leather gloves, and a cream scarf, I can tell he intends to be out here for a while.

I swallow and smile, hoping not to sound too eager. "A lot's been happening."

"Yeah." He looks down and kicks the snow. I spy the same plastic bag trick in his boots as with mine.

I try to sound like I'm joking when I speak, but it comes across hollow. "Why did you want to meet out here instead of some place warm like Paulette's or the Pancake Palace?"

He forces a laugh but doesn't say anything. He lays his hands along the dam wall and pushes any remaining snow to the ground.

"Should I tell you..."

"No," he says quickly, his eyes snapping to mine. He steps back. "That won't be necessary."

"I love hanging out with you, Logan, but come on, it's me. I know what this is about."

"I don't think you do."

I purse my lips, unable to withstand this electric silence. "Why did you bring me out here, Logan?"

He avoids my gaze. "I thought you needed this."

My words almost stick to my throat. "What about Shakira?"

He frowns, his jaw clenching. "She's... I don't know." His blue eyes seem paler than usual. His nose is pink and raw.

My mouth feels full of cotton. I can barely whisper it. "This is my fault. I told her to go."

"It's not," he says quickly. "It's no one's fault." He looks away, rubbing his eyes with his wrist.

"Logan." I touch his arm. "Whatever it is, I can help."

"You will in time."

"I can help you *now*."

Our eyes lock. It seems we're both rigid with everything we want to say, but even where no one is watching, it still feels dangerous.

Maybe we'll always keep secrets in order to save the other.

"I'm sorry." His lips quiver as he cries quietly. "I think you know better than anyone the kind of burden an ability can put on you. And I... I just don't know if I'm strong enough, Ash."

I shake my head, closing the distance between us as I take his hand. "Logan, you are more than enough."

He wipes his tears as they come, training his eyes on the magenta sky. I've never seen him so fractured or scared or sad.

"You are *more* than enough," I tell him. "You're Veil Haven's golden boy, and whatever is happening, whatever needs doing, we will do it together. Whether we're supposed to or not."

He squeezes my hand. And when he works up the courage to look at me, he sees me with a depth I wasn't sure was possible, even from an old friend. "There's nothing worse than being important."

A cavern forms in my chest as the director's words echo through my mind. *"You're important, Ash."*

My jaw tenses as every whisper of that phrase echoes through my mind.

"Sorry," he says after my reaction.

"No," I stutter, "I'm sorry you have to carry this burden."

He shakes his head and his wavy blond hair falls into his eyes. "I miss the days when we were just teenagers."

"We're still teenagers." My smirk fades fast. I wring my hands beneath my sleeves. "I haven't felt the same, either. I'm..." *Confused? Scared? Angry?* "Tired. But it can't last forever. Things always go back to the way they were."

"Anything is possible." He wipes his final tears and then laughs at himself. "God, I'm such a mess."

I chuckle. "We're a mess together, Logan. Whatever happens, it's together. We'll get Shakira back and everything will be okay again."

"Right."

I cock my head. "That isn't what this is about?"

I watch the color drain from his face, his brows stitching together, his eyes shifting around. He's recognizing something. The future ceaselessly melding with the present. And before I can ask him what he's seen, I feel myself choked by the sickly familiar pressure of an omnipotent presence.

I face the woods, my heart jumping to my throat. *No, no, no.* And as I back away Logan stands in front of me. He takes my hands.

"Please just wait," he cautions.

"Ash..." The Forest Eye sinks over my mind like a fog. *"It's time to come home."*

The unworldly pressure on my temples is enough to remind me that the Forest Eye could kill anyone without a second thought. Though it isn't threatening me. It's only telling me that I can't run away this time.

I tear away from Logan, hardly having the breath to speak. "How could you?"

"Please just trust me. Okay?"

"You have no idea what it'll do to me!"

"I don't want to embarrass you in front of your friend, but I will," the Forest Eye temps. *"You've had more than enough time to come to me willingly."*

The ground spins beneath me as I try to conceive a way out of this. I can't catch my breath. The thought of going back there, being face to face with the Forest Eye... I can't do it. It tried to corrupt me, change me, imprison me. It tricked me into thinking it loved me. It only wants to use me. I can't do this again.

Why did I come out here? Why did I think this was a good idea?

My posture changes. My shoulders high and back as it dawns on me. I look at Logan. "You *knew*."

"This needs to happen," he stresses.

For being Veil Haven's golden boy, Logan has never reduced himself to seem more average. He's desperate, but his red, puffy eyes hold little weight to me. He's not made for begging.

"Last chance to come on your own before I drag you here my-self."

I don't take my eyes off Logan, my panic hardening into something sharper. I walk slowly to meet him, my teeth bared. "You have no idea what you've done."

His soft blue eyes are like an apology, his voice small but steady. "You asked me what you could do to help. Talk to the Forest Eye, Ash. Please."

The cavern inside me grows. I came here because I trusted him, and I still have a dying glimmer of faith inside me. My belief in Logan barely burns brighter than my fear of the Forest Eye, but I suppose it's enough.

Despite every sense of my being begging me to run away, knowing I won't make it to my car, knowing I can't run from it forever but still wanting to try, I obey whatever future Logan promises me.

Bitterly and numb, I move toward the woods on the opposite side of the dam.

The scent of freshly tilled soil wafts through the air as snapping roots and shifting trees silence the world. The Forest Eye isn't here, but earthen tendrils rise from the ground. Leaves rain down like confetti. Trees part to reveal a path for my travels. The entire forest is opening up to welcome me home—to swallow me whole.

Roots and vines snake out of the forest and braid themselves into a hammock-like pod just like they would when I was little. It's so the Forest Eye can carry me quickly to the Heart of the Woods rather than expecting me to spend days attempting to hike there.

I look back at Logan, my heart in my throat, and I'm blinded by the sun on the snow.

This is it. This could be the last moment I'm fully myself. But if I don't go, I'm sure the Forest Eye will attempt to hurt him in order to punish me. After all, the cryptid god always gets what it wants.

As I slide into the hammock, I am greeted with colorful bioluminescence and a scent meant to calm my nerves. It doesn't work. Not really.

I want to scream, but I don't. I'm too petrified by whatever choices have led me to this living nightmare. And as the roots enclose the hammock with me inside, I begin to hyperventilate. What if Logan is wrong? What if this doesn't need to happen? What if the Forest Eye got to him somehow? What if—

Someone burns their wrist on the stove. Someone throws a plate against the wall. Someone knocks over a shelf of glass jars. A Skeletal Shifter mimics someone's dead best friend, luring them into the woods to eat them too. Someone slams their finger in a door. Someone drives off the road. Someone is mauled by their dog.

I cringe against the noise clawing through me as though the world itself were about to burst from my head. I can't fight it anymore, and as I prepare myself to face the home I once knew, I am given no other choice.

CHAPTER 27
LOOKING GOD IN THE EYE

I stall my sobs as the pod carries me through the woods at a break-neck speed. Staring at my shaking hands, I fold them into steady fists. I can't let the Forest Eye see me like this. I'm not a child anymore. Except a knotted pressure in the center of my chest is still choking me.

I flinch as the world rumbles in my ears, and I fold into my knees, holding myself as tightly as I can as the impending storm draws closer.

Someone finds a door that wasn't there before. Someone is tearing off yellow wallpaper. Someone is lost in the woods. Someone is pulled under their bed. A Plant Person is tearing the pine needles from their arms, desperate to look more human. Someone is thrown off their roof.

Someone is burning their partner's clothes, certain they'll stay dead this time. Someone keeps seeing shadowy figures that aren't there. Someone pops a pimple the wrong way and the pus keeps coming. It won't stop, and the hole in their face is growing wider, deeper until they're pulling at the edges, peeling the skin back until they see bone, until they slide out of their skin entirely, until they remember they are nothing more than a skeleton playing human.

The trees shift around me as I'm pulled deeper, closer to the Heart of the Woods. Even the earth is moved forcibly out of my way. Boulders and trees migrate to streamline my journey and are placed back as though nothing happened. The sound is reminiscent of a deafening waterfall.

In a matter of minutes my pod appears dwarfed by thick, massive chestnut trees and other giant species. The ground is blanketed by ferns, mushrooms, and soft earth. After all these years, I'm finally back in the Wildwoods.

This place is home to all the cryptids we rarely see. This is their haven, their respite from humanity. The seasons don't pass here. The air is always cool and humid, providing for the consistent bloom. We can't see the Wildwoods from town because of how it's tucked between the mountains.

Wedged in the center of this cryptid paradise is the Heart of the Woods—the home of the physical manifestation of the Forest Eye. You can only reach the Heart if *it* wants you to. It's surrounded by an ever-changing landscape and blocked by rows of trees so dense even the sky is sheltered. No one in. Nothing out.

I unfurl within the earthen hammock as it slows, preparing for my arrival. And as the forest moves around me in a maze not even I can follow, I am finally carried within the Heart of the Woods.

The hammock peels open as the vines and roots sink back into the earth. I am softly dipped out of it and welcomed by the sweetest, warmest air. The Heart is perpetually lush, green, and alive. My soul aches with a bittersweetness, grateful to know this meadow again. My childhood. My home.

Beds of moss cover the ground while bioluminescent plants light even the darkest shadows. There is no sky here, only canopy—a shelter from the world and the Void.

My heart fills the narrow walls of my throat as I step forward. The smell alone could make me cry. Safe. Quiet. Home.

It's exactly as I remember it. Not a new tree or bloom or vine out of place. All the spaces I laid, slept, played, danced, meditated. This is where I found peace for the first time. Where I felt the love of a family I never had. I was noticed and cared for.

But I can't fall into old habits. I have to remember what the Forest Eye did to me. What it might do to me now.

I stand with my back to the wall of pines and wait.

In a blink, the Forest Eye manifests, floating so I have to crane my neck. The giant eyeball glows slightly as it looks down on me, its hazel iris as beautiful and impossibly complex as the woods.

Despite it having no features or indicators of emotion, the energy rolling around me taps into my senses, and I can imagine the Forest Eye smiling at me. Its prodigal daughter has returned.

With a prideful hum, its words weave through the creases of my mind. *"Hello, Ash."*

My heart wedges in my throat as its raw energy drowns me. My body hums being so close to the god of natural creation. I feel goosebumps everywhere.

Its power is suffocating. Its presence is terrifying, and despite my best efforts, I am intoxicated by it. Warm and welcomed and safe, my guard tries to come down.

But my aching molars ground me. I refuse to be persuaded.

We stare at each other for a long time, our reunion souring by the second.

There is a softness to the sounds here, the gentle birdsong, the whispering creek, the silence of the world put to bed. So when I speak, my voice grates against the quiet world.

"Why am I here?" I tighten my fists and lock my knees to keep myself from shaking.

The Forest Eye hovers to my level, the eyeball three times my size. *"You've been in so many interesting situations lately,"* it hums, slowly looking me up and down. The colorful bioluminescence surrounding us reflects off its white sclera. *"You've been looking everywhere... asking everyone for help but me. How hurtful."*

A foulness overwhelms in my dry mouth. "Even the director offered me condolences." My heart pounds in my throat, choking me. I'm not playing with fire, I'm playing with creation and destruction personified.

"The director," the Forest Eye scoffs, floating further into the mossy clearing.

I'm expected to follow.

Despite my comfort against the outer wall of pines, I follow. My face contorts to fight the tears as I make my first demand. "Did you see Lydia that night?"

"Oh, Ash." My ears ring. *"I'm disappointed in you."*

My heart shrinks. I swallow it. "I know you are! You always are! Everyone is. But I've stopped caring what you think of me. I don't need you anymore."

It turns around quickly, a physical rage building in the air. *"You can lie to yourself, but you cannot lie to me. I know you, Ash. I raised you."* It hovers close to me, pale white light radiating from its body onto mine.

"A lot of people raised me." I bare my teeth. "None of them manipulated me to hate myself for being human."

"You don't think your precious director hurt you? You don't think you're being manipulated now?"

I clench my molars, the rising heat making me dizzy. "Just tell me what you want."

The Forest Eye turns away as if rolling its eye. *"I'm offering my help, and you speak to me this way? Your god?"* It slowly moves around, circling me.

I stand still, closing my eyes. My body vibrates.

"You forget your place."

"Please just—" I swallow the pang in my chest. "What do you know about Lydia's death?" I refuse to believe she died of natural causes, and even though I want to ask a million questions, this is the only thing I can bear to bring up.

"Oh plenty." It smirks, amused. *"All these years and you're still so blind. You should've stayed with me. I could've taught you how to navigate these... blind spots. Instead you chose the happy lie."* It turns away again, moving deeper into the glen. *"The prices we pay, I suppose."*

"It could've been me!" Tears bite my lashes.

The Forest Eye pauses, the air dipping. *I would never allow that to happen.*

"But you allowed this to happen! And you'll let me suffer in her absence." My throat burns as I yell. "How can I help people if I can't see them? Between Declan and The Watchers and Lydia—and Shakira is missing and I—" I push the hair from my damp face. "I can't do this. *I can't save them.*"

If a god could flinch, this sharp energy dip would be it. But it's quickly replaced by a warm breeze wrapping me like a hug. I feel pathetic for finding comfort in it.

None of what is happening is your fault, Ash. The odds were against you from the start.

"What does that *mean*?" I beg, my shaking hands reaching out. "Please just tell me about Lydia. That's all this was ever supposed to be about. *Her.* Not the new family, not Declan, not weird ghost journals, not the Keepers of the Coast, and certainly not the director. *Lydia.*"

The Forest Eye stares at me. The warm breeze ceases. *I'll show you what I saw that night. But I want something from you.*

My stomach twists. The moment I was sure would come. The promise, the pact, the deal.

"What do you want?"

Your presence. I don't want to drag you here to see you. I miss you.

My heart twists. *I've been a bad daughter.* Wait, that thought isn't mine. I grind my molars, glaring. "I don't want to make any deals with you."

It's not a deal, just something I'd like more of.

Everything is a deal. And I don't *want* to see the Forest Eye. I want my life to go back to normal. I want Lydia. I want my ability to work. I want to be confident again.

But Lydia died in the mudflats, and the Forest Eye knows

something. I need to know so I can convince The Watchers to listen to me.

In my gut, that's what makes the most sense. Everything else can fall away, all those secrets hinting at something beyond Veil Haven—*if we were supposed to know, we would know.* That doesn't have anything to do with Lydia. I need to know *this* truth.

"Okay. I can…" I swallow, feeling woozy and ill. "I'll try to visit you more."

The Forest Eye hovers closer, its white light glowing on my golden skin. *"You're sure you want to see what happened to your friend?"*

My nails bite into my palms. "Just show me."

The Forest Eye's pupil dilates as it worms inside my head, wedging its power deep within me.

My body goes stiff and I am no longer myself, not wholly. I become an extension of the Forest Eye, a puppet, a tool, and I choke on my panic. I didn't realize this was what I was asking for. I didn't realize. I don't want this. I don't want—

The Forest Eye's voice soothes me from within, *I will not change you, Ash. I only want you to see.* And because its magic tendrils have melded to my every nerve ending and synapse, when it tells me to calm down, I do.

CHAPTER 28
THE MARRIAGE OF GRIEF AND RAGE

I am numb and everything is bright.

I am floating in nothingness, or maybe I *am* nothing—just a dust mote passing through a spectrum of light.

I am nothing and I am heavy. I am unbound and I am floating.

I am within the Forest Eye, and it is within me. Together we float in this strange, timeless place where time and space have no meaning and only memory exists. Everything replays on loop.

Humans talk about muscle memory, how the hands remember, how a scent draws forth the past, but this is not how nature memorializes. It is constantly recalling. Steeped in the past, present, and future.

Humanity is a blip in the natural order. These mountains remember when the earth was new, when plants grew from darkness, when bones were forged, when life walked, when it ran, when it fell, when it stood taller.

There is no remembering here, only reliving.

The Forest Eye knows, ubiquitously, what was, what is, and what could be. Again and again and again.

In the creases of my human mind lies darkness. But with every visual outlet through the Forest Eye, through the woods, I see light, energy, divinity, wholeness, and absolute omniscience. This is where I am. This is *what* I am.

In millions of visual outlets inlaid in every root, leaf, bug, animal, cryptid, breeze, breath, heartbeat, I am not watching them, I *am* them. And it isn't deafening. It isn't overwhelming. It just is.

There is no sense of time, only sense of being. As existence reverses and we move backwards through memory, we narrow in on a single group of outlets—the dead trees of the mudflats. And now we *are* the dead and dying and hibernating.

Warblers, skinks, gnats, and everything moves backwards as the Forest Eye pinpoints the exact moment it happened.

As we slide into the past, or the present, or the future, everything slows. Maybe my breathing does too—

Am I breathing? Do I have a body? Will I stay this way forever? Has it always been this way?

I am neutral and analytical and calm despite the overwhelming riot of noise and color and movement. We have always been at the mudflats, we have always been witnessing, and now we will focus once again on the moment that changes everything.

It is night. The mudflats are cold and quiet. The closest light is a lamppost above the asphalt path that cuts through the land. And when a young woman—Lydia—comes into focus, the light from her phone illuminates her face. She walks unaware of what this moment is. Her guides and any higher beings are silent.

A figure approaches from the front but we can't make out who it is. It's a man, or what we assume to be a man. It is not one of our cryptids. It is different. Unknown. Terribly unknown.

He walks up to her with precise, controlled movements. A Watcher? But even we can see The Watchers. No, this is something else.

Lydia lifts her head when she senses someone approaching her but her senses have betrayed her. It's too late.

The man clutches her throat and she's instantly paralyzed. Frozen stiff.

Her phone lands face up on the asphalt.

She does not scream. Usually humans scream. Usually humans attacking other humans cover their mouths so they don't scream. But this man knew what would happen.

We home in on him, but he is shrouded in a darkness so dense and unknown he is more void than person. But this is not the Void. The Void would never harm a human.

A piece of the universe is missing where this man should be standing. It cannot be understood. Nevertheless, we are quite curious.

Lydia—the girl—begins sputtering in a seizure-state. Strange. What is causing this reaction?

The man closes his eyes as he lifts the frail girl off the ground as though she is feather light. Her seizure becomes violent, her head rolling back as her arms and legs flail.

The man, or not-man, shivers pleasurably. He is taking everything: her life, her energy, her power. And he is feasting. Consuming.

Lydia becomes pale and limp.

The not-man looks at her, suddenly aware of his actions. He lets go of her quickly and steps back in shock.

She falls hard and unmoving on the asphalt, the skin of her jaw, elbows, and knees, scraping on impact. Her neck and legs are bent at unnatural angles. Her eyes are open, but no light is inside.

The man stares at her for a long time. He kneels beside her and carefully searches for a pulse in her neck. When he realizes she is empty, he brushes the hair from her face with a shaking hand.

Curious behavior. Is it regret, surprise, shock?

The girl was dead before she hit the ground. This much is obvious. It seems as though he's done this before, so why would he be surprised by this outcome? Unless this isn't the usual result.

Interesting. If his intent wasn't to kill her, what was it?

The not-man, almost-man, maybe-man hangs his head as if in prayer. Then, he rolls his shoulders and shakes away the feeling. Sliding his arms gently under her body, they rise together. He walks to the edge of the path where his shoes brush the crabgrass and throws her into the mudflats.

She—Lydia—the human girl, now dead—lands hard on her side, slapping into the mud with a pop. Her back is to the path, one of her eyes and mouth are open below the mud.

The man—must be a man because a cryptid would have taken more—tugs on his shirt in an attempt to regain composure. Then he walks away.

The Forest Eye exits my mind and body like a snake, and I am thrown into myself, thrown off a cliff into the depth of my every feeling. I collapse.

The moss is damp under my hands and knees but the cushion is hardly comforting.

My vision blurs.

Every emotion that was stalled floods into me, and I can't breathe. I can't think. I can't stop the rising acid in my throat.

My gut quakes and I heave. Afterward, I scream until my throat tears and my shaking arms give out. Until blood vessels break. Until I heave again.

The world should be making my ears bleed but the Forest Eye holds it all back. Its soothing energy holds me.

I can't begin to think, to speak, to breathe and still I'm begging for an explanation. Begging to know, to understand. "Lydia!" I screech, "Lydia, Lydia, oh my god, Lydia."

I am a container for grief.

Soft, mossy vines grow from the earth and wrap me like the arms of a loved one. I sink against them. I hold them as I sob and scream and shake until I have no breath left in me. I am full of brittle things. I am empty, but it is ravenous and devours me.

Something fundamental has changed within me, but I lack the energy and perception to understand what. I just know I feel *different*.

The moss absorbs my vomit to feed the decay. The creek still sings. The birds do not.

It takes time for the pounding in my head and my heat-flushed cheeks to fade, but the Forest Eye gives me time.

I am cradled, and safe, and seen. But I am still a contradiction. Full and empty.

Finally, gently, the Forest Eye speaks. *"His entire existence was and continues to be redacted, but he was not always like this."*

I do not wipe away the layers of tears and snot. I sit up and clutch my knees, staring at nothing.

"He stole this void-state from another, I believe. A man who stayed in town. Someone who was not seen either but born that way."

I see Lydia in my memory. Shaking. Gagging. Freezing. Falling. Thrown. I witnessed that and I felt nothing. *Nothing.* And even though I am feeling it all now, something underneath this pain seems empty.

"I have never encountered this kind of power, Ash," The Forest Eye lowers itself to catch my gaze. *"This was what I wanted to warn you about at the carnival."*

I lift my head, my throat aching, my lips tight. I do not feel my heart. "I'm sorry I ignored you." I am distant. What is this emptiness? How can I feel lonely inside of myself?

"Ash, you must understand the dangers," it tells me. *"You must be careful."*

I think of the doorway of light in the snow, the bitter chill on my pink nose when I ran from the graveyard, how heavy the rotary phone was in my hands, the *ting* as I threw it down.

I think of that towering Victorian, the shadow in the window, the door opening to no one. And in the creases of my memory I see a front porch, a handshake, and a man I cannot see.

I rise. My fingers unfurled. I meet the mosaic gaze of the cryptid god who made a home for me in its heart, and I understand.

"There's only one person in town I can't see. It's Declan." The warmth crystalizes inside me like sugar—sharp, sticky, sweet. "Declan killed Lydia." I feel as distant as I sound, though I almost laugh. I was right.

I stare forward only hearing my own breath.

It was obvious from the start. Wasn't it? The stranger. The

only man I can't see. Why did I give up on that pursuit?

And then I remember. I trusted the government. I trusted Winona and Chief Mun and Director Capaldi. And when they told me: *No, not Declan, not the Jacksons, everything is fine. Listen to us. Everything is fine,* I believed them.

The heat curls inside my body like a starving animal desperate for one more hunt. I could do great and terrible things with this rage. I think I will.

The Forest Eye registers my hardened gaze. *"I don't want you near that man."* It isn't a suggestion but a demand.

I want to say, *But how else will I kill him?* I don't.

The warmth steadies me. And with a quiet, empty mind, I ask, "What is Declan's ability?"

"He has more than one, Ash. He hungers, devours, and takes whatever he touches. His ability is to collect other abilities." The Forest Eye does not ask me about my thoughts.

I taste embers in the back of my throat. "No one can have that much power." I feel outside of myself yet grounded.

"It appears this one does."

The Forest Eye warns me with the same phrase I've heard throughout my youth. This time it reverberates inside me. Even my marrow listens. And as if a new lens filters over my concept of Veil Haven, I understand it as though hearing this for the first time. Everything is finally so terribly obvious.

"Humans can be monsters too."

CHAPTER 29
How I Ruined Everything by Saying It Out Loud

The Forest Eye drops me off at the dam past midnight. We don't say anything else. It will give me space.

The sky is deep red, and occasionally a star will wink through the thick, yellow clouds.

I stand here and recognize the sickly grief and rage growing within me. Only one thing permeates this pain. One thought burns through me.

I don't care what it takes, or how much it costs, I am going to destroy Declan.

I shook his hand. Those hands that touched her. His hands that—

The Void watches me through the eyes of the clouds, and their presence weighs on my congested mind. After all this time, they're finally allowing me to witness them again.

It was just me that they hid from. Wasn't it? Miss Ava received advice and messages for Josie, after all. But when *I* needed answers, the Void disappeared.

When the Void speaks, a faint sound follows their words like rainfall or fireworks or the shimmering static of falling stars. They are kind, gentle, and pleading. *"Don't allow your anger to corrupt your sense of justice, Ash. There are many ways to achieve what you want. There are ways to manage this rage."*

"My rage doesn't need to be managed!" Tears sting my eyes as I bark at the sky. "He killed her! Declan killed her and I was too stupid to pursue my gut. Everyone lied to me. I'm allowed to be furious!"

Something catches the corner of my eye and I scoff, gawking at the far, dark peaks. The Mysterious Mountain Lights. It feels like they're mocking me. Just another thing I've always been blind to.

I watch the lights and instinctively step forward, my hands clutching the cold concrete wall.

She died of natural causes. We couldn't do anything. We're sorry. She wasn't murdered, Ash. You can't know everything. You're just a kid.

Why did I believe them so easily?

I can sense the Void's desperation, knowing what comes next when a person feels the way I do. They've watched humanity for eons. They've seen the same stories play out over and over.

The Void begs me gently to save myself. *"There are other ways. I know you believe killing is the only righteous solution, but you do not need to walk this path."*

My frozen fingers curl. The Mysterious Mountain Lights disappear. I lift my eyes to the sky and quake as I shout. "Where were you when *she* needed to hear that?"

A shooting star falls straight down between the yellow clouds, and the Void retreats from my mind.

I push away from the dam, fiddle with my keys as I cross the field, get in my freezing car, and leave.

When I return home, I take a shower to get the scent of sweet-rot off my skin. The warm water soothes my tense muscles, but I'm not comforted. While I usually rest in the shower for a long time, tonight I settle for a simple wash. I wish it made me feel better.

I draw my blinds and turn on the warm fairy lights that make my room glow. I sit with my legs crossed in the center of my bed, my back facing the window. Even though it's the middle of the night, I text Markus. I know he's awake.

We need to talk.

He's startled by the message, a dozen questions racing through his mind. But after looking at the time, he settles on his answer. *I can't right now, Ash. But we can hang out tomorrow evening. I have some family stuff to take care of first. Is that okay? Are you alright?*

I'll meet you at your house then.

I slip under my covers. There's nothing else to say. Well, I have a million things to say, but I need to find the words. I need to tell Markus everything but, carefully.

I stare at the glow-in-the-dark stars on my ceiling, feeling the heat still churning throughout my body. My mind's eye stays with me, no more aimless out-of-control wandering. Perhaps that's a temporary blessing from the Forest Eye.

In the reprieve of the world's silence, I begin creating a plan.

The pink sky holds rosy clouds. Only faint traces of snow remain on the ground now.

I never understood how the official start of winter could be December 21. We are in the first days of November, and the trees are brown or barren. The world is cold, dying, dead. But the sharp daylight softened by the clouds makes me almost hopeful for this conversation.

I meet Markus at the end of his street. I can't make myself go near his house. The thought of being in range of Declan makes me sick, and I can't mess this up.

Markus acts cautious when we meet, sensing something big about to be unearthed. He doesn't ask me about it.

We walk down the hill from his street, past the park, and stay on this side of the road. We need to talk privately and there's no place more private in town than the abandoned history museum. I don't want to go back to the woods.

There's never been any Watchers devices in the abandoned

museum house because people don't go there. History is nothing short of illegal. There are swift consequences for digging up the past and learning what is meant to be forgotten. So inherently, people stay away.

Markus sniffles in the cold as we walk away from downtown. He's upgraded from just his black hoodie to having an actual winter coat on top of it. I'm wearing my patch jacket and my grandpa golf sweater. We don't say much as we walk.

We stop before the long stretch of golden fields. The wild, glowing sunflowers are extra bright this time of year. The periwinkle and maroon wildflowers add so much depth to the grasses. But we aren't here for the valley's field, we're here for the final wooded hill beside it.

"This is it."

I pause at a set of barely noticeable crooked concrete steps built into the hill. Between the overgrown crabgrass and overhanging trees, it's an easy monument to ignore, which is sort of the point.

"You have to leave your phone here." I place mine on one of the steps hidden from the crumbling sidewalk. Markus gives me a stalled look, but when I ask him again, he follows my lead.

Carefully, we climb the steps and duck under branches until the small historic-looking house rises out of the brush. The brick foundation has kept this wooden home standing. The house isn't necessarily dilapidated, but it isn't brand new. Segmented into four rooms, a single small window in each, the open doorway is more of a hole than an entrance.

The porch wavers slightly with our combined weight and I pause, Markus hanging on my every word. "This is the only trace of our history anywhere in Veil Haven. People don't come here because knowledge of what came before is dangerous. This is the only place in town The Watchers aren't listening."

Markus' brows shift at the mention of the name. He's never heard it before, but with just enough context clues, he can imagine it's something dangerous.

"What is it, Ash?"

Without saying another word, I walk inside.

I suppose the museum is more of a shack than a house. The whole place smells like wet rot. The main room you enter into has plaques with vague historical facts like how this was the first legislative building in Veil Haven, and how "back in the day" they didn't have electricity, so they had to heat rooms with furnaces and hang blankets over the windows.

I think about Kimi and her abandoned, moldy house and wonder if this is from her time or if this building is even older. Veil Haven doesn't keep track of dates.

I stop in the farthest back room, the empty space nothing but dark boarded walls and a small window. The cool breeze pushing through the window helps with the smell. The light from the pink sky illuminates the center of the room.

The softly setting sun is too gentle for the things I have to say.

Markus shoves his hands in his jacket, his shoulders high, watching me intently.

I try to be stern and strong, but to be honest I feel ill. My heart is pounding, my hands are clammy, and my throat is so tense I'm worried I won't be able to speak.

"I've never seen you like this," he says.

"I have to tell you a lot," I say. "You won't want to believe me but please hear me out."

He shifts in place, tensing his jaw, ready for the hit. But before I can begin, he cuts the silence with his own rambling sentiments.

"I know about the rumors, Ash. About what you did or what they say you did to that guy's uncle or the coach or whatever. I know it made everyone hate you, but I don't care. That was the past and I know you *now*. You've been nothing but nice to me and you've kept me safe in this weird place. You even thought about my sisters. I appreciate that more than anything. So if this is about that just know... it's okay."

A smile carves my cheeks but I feel like crying. I curl my fingers and pop my knuckles as I steady my fast-beating heart. Can I do this? Can I really destroy our friendship?

But I would want to know. I would want Markus to tell me if the roles were reversed. So I have to tell him. Not just for that, but because I need his help.

"Thank you, Markus." I feel so far away. "That means more to me than you know. What a relief." I try to laugh. I sound hollow. "But that's not what this is about."

Markus swallows and steps in place as if preparing for a blow. His hands turn over in his hoodie pocket.

Without breath, I begin.

"Veil Haven thrives on secrets. The government is a front, the police are figureheads, and the only real power in town controls everything through hidden cameras and recording devices." The blasphemy, the disappearance-worthy truth, burns my lips. "And they're everywhere. Every room, every car, every bathroom, every street corner. If The Watchers see something they don't like, something that could disrupt the harmony and safety of Veil Haven, they send agents to kidnap said danger, which is what happened between me and Kane and his uncle."

I study each shift in his dark brown eyes as he hangs on my every word.

"The Watchers raised me, Markus... Director Capaldi took me in when I was a child and taught me everything I know. He gave me my house, my car, and money for providing information. That's why people hate me. That's why they're afraid of me." My frown deepens. "I might as well be the face of The Watchers." I rub my nose as it runs in the cold. "Even talking about them can make you disappear. Me telling you could make us disappear."

His face drops. "Then why are you telling me?"

I look at my boots. "The Watchers aren't inherently bad, Markus. They keep us safe, keep our lives easy and unbothered.

I mean, can you imagine if everyone just used their abilities freely in public? Sometimes, though, The Watchers overstep. Sometimes they ruin lives more than they help them. But they always have a legitimate reason for taking someone."

I swallow. "The Watchers are an organization and the person leading them is known as the director. Director Capaldi is a terrifying man but... he's the man who raised me, and..."

My voice cracks, telling him this is my greatest crime. It feels like I'm hardwired to do the opposite. I take a minute to regain my composure.

"Director Capaldi raised me through government figureheads like the chief of police and the mayor—not Winona but the man before her. I didn't have parents, so Director Capaldi took care of me. He kept me safe, kept the people I loved safe. But that's changed." I cover my mouth, my face contorting with grief and apology and horror. "He's now helping hide the man who killed Lydia."

Markus raises his brows, gawking, his eyes wide, and in my pause he realizes I'm only telling him this because it has something to do with him. I sense the idea run through his mind just before I work up the nerve to say it out loud.

"It's your stepdad, Markus. It's Declan. He killed Lydia."

Markus steps back like my words have physically struck him. "That isn't true. Declan isn't... he might be an asshole but he isn't a murderer."

He purses his lips as the thought of his mom's car accident weaves through his mind, and I see him remembering Declan's recount of it when Markus was only twelve, *"But don't worry, son. The driver didn't make it. I made sure of that."* And something bigger clicks, too, something larger than what we're talking about, though I can't conceive his fast thoughts. As he stalls, I continue.

"I visited the Forest Eye yesterday." I shake my head, realizing I need to explain this too. "The Forest Eye is the god of all cryptids and nature. It's a very long story, but basically, it's a giant floating eyeball with endless power, which also raised me for a little while."

His head rocks back as he scrambles for some sense of what to say.

"I know," I interrupt him, "and as easily as you got comfortable with the concept of cryptids, I imagine it'll be a lot harder for you to come to terms with living, physical gods. You're the first person I've told about my relationship with the Forest Eye. Seems so simple, doesn't it? Just a breath and the truth is out. Sorry, I'm rambling." I shake my head again and sigh.

I gather myself and continue. "When I visited the Forest Eye, it showed me what happened to Lydia through its memory. Before, I never saw what happened to her. The event was blocked from my mind's eye, just like how I can't see Declan through my ability. And... well, with the Forest Eye, I watched Lydia die." My jaw aches. "I saw the same nothingness that I see whenever I look at your stepdad."

He holds up his hand and steps back. "I'm confused." The sass in his patient voice spears me. "Are you saying you saw him or you didn't?"

I shuffle in place, having known this was coming. "When you first came to town I didn't know Declan was with you. He's blocked from my mind's eye and I can only see him if I'm physically looking at him. When I look at him there's this emptiness, like he's invisible... and that's exactly what I saw when he killed her and threw her in the mud."

Markus doesn't know what to say.

"Winona told me you came from Fox Falls, and that *everything is going according to plan*," I say with air quotes, "but that means they know he killed Lydia and they've been lying to me. Maybe they even allowed him to kill her. I asked Lydia to investigate him the night she died. She must've learned something and... I think something terrible is coming that's going to change Veil

Haven for the worse, and I think your stepdad is at the center of it. I don't know how else to explain it, but I think Declan is working with The Watchers."

He's quiet for a second. "Ash, Declan is not part of The Watchers. How does that make any sense? And again with this Fox Falls thing. I've lived in more states than I can put on both hands, but we've never lived anywhere called Fox Falls. We most recently came from the beach, but you told me not to talk about it for some reason. And... I mean... how can you believe my stepdad *killed* Lydia? He didn't. There's no way."

I hold his gaze for a long time. "But he's killed before."

Markus swallows, saying nothing.

"Your mom is Althea. Althea Freeman. She's from Veil Haven, Markus. She was born here, and she was the mayor. Then she got pregnant with you and I guess The Watchers didn't like that, so she ran away and somehow she left Veil Haven and survived. She's the only way Declan could've learned about us." I bite my lip, picking at the chapped skin. My every word is too heavy and too quick. "Your real dad was killed by The Watchers. His name is Dante Jackson and he's the ghost who's haunting Ford."

Markus stares at me, neutrally and distantly, like the first night I met him.

"It means you're from Veil Haven, Markus. And the reason you don't have an ability is because Declan must've stolen it from you. Because that's *his* ability." Saying this out loud for the first time makes my hairs stand on end.

Markus can only stare at me. He begins pacing around the room, saying nothing but feeling frustrated, confused, and attacked.

I suck in sharply. "I was raised to protect Veil Haven, Markus. And while I haven't done a good job in years, I know Declan is putting everyone in danger. Who knows what he and The Watchers are planning? You think I know everything, but I don't. I'm severely less important and less powerful than I previously thought, but that's why I'm telling you. I need you to help me. We need to stop Declan."

He pauses suddenly, looking at me with narrow eyes. My gut ties itself in knots as his mind roars with questions and defenses. His anger is pitched, his confusion is overwhelming, and when he finally speaks I feel the world shift.

Next thing I know I'm chasing him down the crowded sidewalks of Main Street.

"Markus, *please*." I grab his arm as the dinner rush moves around us with sharp looks.

He whips his arm from my hand and spins around. "No! Are you kidding me, Ash? This is a joke. It has to be one big joke to you. You're not my friend."

"I'm telling the truth," I stress.

"You wouldn't know the truth if it were standing in front of you. You admitted you don't see him!"

I huff as my anger carves through me, the winter air suddenly not so cold. "I'm trying to help you."

"You're trying to help yourself." He pokes my chest. He seems to loom over me, his dark eyes even darker now. "That's all you ever do. Those rumors were right. The people here avoid you for a reason. Don't bother me again, Ash. Leave my family out of your obsessive grief." He storms away, almost walking into traffic as he crosses the street back toward his home.

I stand here rubbing my face as people stare at us and begin to whisper conclusions. My head pounds as the world threatens to pour over my periphery but no—no I have to stay in control.

I watch the person I just told every truth I have walk away and go home to the man I warned him about. He chose Declan over me. Can family really be so blinding?

People give me sidelong glances as they pass, ducking into shops and eateries. I'm sure the town will know about our little break up before I can even tell Josie. Great!

But I can only stand here rubbing my cheeks and feeling every pimple along the side of my face. Everything I've known is slipping—has just slipped through my hands.

Everything I do makes things worse.

The world is spinning. Did I just blow my lead with Declan? Is Markus going to tell him everything? I want to laugh at myself. But as the heavy heat hollows me out all I want to do is scream.

So that's exactly what I do.

CHAPTER 30
SYMPATHY FOR THE DOOMED

By the time my senses return, most people on the street have decided to ignore me. *If you were supposed to know, you'd know.*

I'm fuming and begin to storm away when I see Logan up the street. I didn't expect to see him here, and he doesn't see me.

He's running some sort of errand, but something catches his attention in the second story window of one of the buildings. It's a boutique, and they store their overflow upstairs. But that's not what he sees.

The world washes over with blurs of gray as Logan's consciousness flickers from the present to the future. The brick building remains untouched, but someone is banging wildly on the cast-iron window.

The first thing he recognizes is her gold accented braids. He freezes with the sharp beat of his heart. He cranes his neck and finds horror painted across her face.

"Shakira?"

She pounds against the window. "Logan? Logan!"

"I see you!" he shouts back.

People around him look at the empty window, glance at him, and move on.

"I'm stuck," Shakira yells, her voice strained. "It's terrible here, Logan. I can't—Please, please help me." Tears round her cheeks.

"How?" The question bubbles fast in his throat. Blood pulses through his ears as he strains to stay in the future.

Shakira searches behind her as if she hears something, her handprints staining the humid glass. But the image of her flickers. Color bleeds through the corners of his vision. And Logan's panic sets in.

"Shakira," he stresses, reaching out for her.

When she looks at him again, her brown eyes pierce him, but her message strikes us both.

"Tell Ash."

Goosebumps rise on the back of my neck as I slowly walk toward Logan.

He shakes his head searching for answers. "Tell her what?"

Shakira bangs on the window in frustration. She tries to open it but it won't budge. She turns around again, scared.

Someone has entered the room.

Shakira backs into the window, her shoulders rising and falling like a symphony. Logan can't hear what she's saying, though it looks like she's begging. The person moves in front of her, shadowed and short.

As the colors of the present swarm the grays of the future, Shakira looks back at him trying to say everything in a single glance.

Logan's core temperature drops. Shakira keeps her eyes trained on him. They are just as close as they are distant.

She studies his face for a moment longer, smiling sadly before her gaze hardens. "Tell her everything."

Her request hits him like a thunderclap as Shakira is swept away in hues of the present just as the figure reaches out and grabs her.

He blinks, and she's gone.

Logan beats against the brick begging her to come back. Something whispers in the back of his head that she might be gone for good. He looks around half-expecting people to be just as morti-fied as he is but they're completely unaware.

Then his gaze sets on me.

I rush toward him but he meets me halfway, eyes hard, hand out.

"Ash, don't." He's stern.

"Logan—"

"Just go home," he barks.

I rock back, surprised by the demand and his undertone of hostility. People on the street seem to notice, too.

"Go *home*, Ash."

I clench my jaw and beg. "*Tell me.*"

He won't meet my eyes, and finally, he turns away. "No."

Before I can understand why I listen to him, I'm already half-way home, stewing with every step.

Shakira is trapped. She's afraid. She said it was terrible there. *Veil Haven burning.* Is that what we're doomed for? What does Shakira know? What does she want Logan to tell me? And who was stalking her?

Too much is happening to keep track. I can barely form my own thoughts. Why won't he tell me? Why won't anyone tell me anything? Why does it feel like I always come up short?

I'm almost home when my mind's eye wanders ahead of me. Josie is waiting on my porch, slumped over as fear sours her face. She presses her arms awkwardly against her chest, hoping to make it look like she's just huddling for warmth rather than holding something under her jacket.

I hurry down the holler trying not to dry my throat in the early night air.

Her brows furrow when she sees me, and she meets me halfway to her muddy red truck.

My pulse quickens. This isn't like her. I reach for her hands but she has them tucked away.

"Ash, I need to talk to you about somethin'. Can we go somewhere?"

What she means is: Can we go somewhere *safe*.

I answer without hesitation. "Yes."

We take her car to the abandoned dam in silence and park along the road as night burns above us.

I feel stuck in a loop. Back and forth. Back and forth. But where else can we go that's safe from The Watchers? I'm just relieved it isn't the abandoned history museum. And I'm glad we haven't run into anyone else out here. I guess people have been shooed away by the snow.

The stars are like torchlights across the deep blue heavens, and suddenly I feel bad about what I said to the Void but... well, they know.

The cold bites our fingers as we use pocket flashlights to walk to the dam, leaving our phones in her car. Josie thought of everything. I pale at the idea that I forgot when I talked to Logan earlier, though luckily we didn't say anything. Maybe that's why he insisted we didn't. Among other reasons. At least the Heart of the Woods naturally blocks out any Watchers tech.

The trees loom above us and creatures howl in the distance. She squeezes my hand and rocks close beside me. She isn't usually this jumpy. I tell her the Forest Eye will keep us safe. I say it loudly enough for the cryptid god to hear.

Her brows stitch, confused why I would invoke its name, but she has more pressing things she wants to discuss. Josie's face creases with worry. With a deep breath, as though about to reveal something, she instead just stands there stiffly and awkward.

"You're starting to worry me, Josie," I say with a short laugh. "You can show me the journal."

She flinches at the mention of it. "Oh god, was I obvious? Have I been obvious? Do they know I know?"

"Whoa, whoa, Josie. Everything is okay. No one knows. Not a soul but me. I just saw you that day, that's all." Quieter, I say, "This is probably the only thing they don't know."

My shoulders fall and the night suddenly weighs on me. I haven't slept much. My eyelids are heavy but Josie's fear keeps me focused.

When she finally pulls out the book, she looks at me as though she's revealed a horror. She swallows audibly. "I've been tryin' so hard not to think about it. I've been journalin' a lot about Ford and Lydia and you and Miss Ava and my family and just anythin' I can think of that's not this. Because, well..."

The journal is a worn black book not much bigger than her hand and about an inch thick. The edges are cracked and peeling.

Josie gently pats the cover. "I've been readin' this in secret out in the woods by my house." She flips it open, careful not to bend the brittle pages. "I don't understand a lot of it, but there's enough for me to know how dangerous this is. And after the séance with Dante..." Her voice trails off as she stops herself from crying. Her hands shake as she dabs her lashes.

"Oh, Josie, please don't be scared. No one knows about this. I promise no one's noticed. They have far more pressing matters to deal with than to spy extra hard on a girl who's just been journaling about her crush." I make her meet my white eyes. "You've done well."

She nods slowly and lets out a long breath. "I want you to read some things and tell me if they make sense. I feel like I'm goin' crazy, Ash. You know I hate keepin' secrets. I'm so bad at it, and this whole thing is terrifyin' me."

"I'm here and we'll figure it out together. It's us and no one else, always." I can feel my bones itching, desperate to tell her everything I've learned. And I will, but this is more important to her than brutal answers to questions we aren't even supposed to be asking. "Here, let me read it."

She nods solemnly, desperate and grateful, and she hands me the journal after flipping to a page labeled April 20. We hover our flashlights above the book, which makes the old, tanned pages look like they're glowing.

> Don't you find it strange that we don't have a history? We don't know how or why or when our town was created. People say it was always here but that doesn't make sense. How did they build a town? Where did the supplies come from? Who were our founders? They had to come from somewhere.
>
> Some of the older tombstones in the graveyard have the years scraped off. The rest don't have years at all. What are they hiding? Why is the past so dangerous?

Chills roll down my spine. How did I miss Josie reading this? These are the kinds of questions people instinctively know not to ask. This gets people taken, or I guess, killed.

"Her name was Kimi Kingfisher," Josie tells me as she flips deeper into the journal. She bites her thumbnail with her chipped front tooth and points to an entry halfway down the page marked January 8.

I begin again.

> There are massive divots at the edge of the woods. Or, I should call them craters. Some are overgrown, some even look like ponds. But most of them are barren. Nothing has grown there in years, maybe decades or even longer. What causes a crater that leaves nothing to grow? Why don't we talk about it?

Josie flips to another passage before I can react. This entry is labeled March 13.

> I found tombstones in the woods. How sad to be so forgotten. Most of them were unreadable and hard to reach on the steep cliffside, but the few I brushed off left me with more questions than I had before. The years and causes of death made me pause.
>
> Radiation poisoning.
>
> Bombings.
>
> They mentioned a war I've never heard of. How can there be war in Veil Haven? Against who?

I feel like the butt of some cosmic joke. Everything tells me I can trust Kimi, yet here I am completely unaware of any cliffside graveyard in the woods. Especially not with causes of death like she's describing. War? Radiation?

I don't know what to say, but Josie only turns more pages. We're getting to the end of the journal. The handwriting is messy. Scribbled in panic with slanted lines and unevenly sized letters as if Kimi was writing in the dark.

It's titled AUGUST 31 in large, underlined letters.

> I don't understand what I saw today. I walked through some briars in the eastern woods. I was just exploring. But when I tripped, I fell onto a ravine. Onto it. Not in. I was floating above the ravine as if I could fly.
>
> I patted the earth and watched the ground pulse with my touch. It was disguised by a hologram to look like a cliff or a ravine but it was solid ground.

It was meant to keep people away—
whether to keep them in or keep them out
I'm not sure.

I was more curious than scared. I'm an
idiot. They'll kill me for this. I know they will.

I walked on an old asphalt road in the
woods until I reached a gate covered with
warning signs.

DANGER. BRIDGE OUT. ROAD CLOSED. DEAD END.

I sprinted back, fearing the worst.

The sky was different there. It was blue.
And the air smelled different than I have
ever known.

When I pushed back through the briars I
saw the sky was purple again like it had been
all week. I knew in an instant I had left Veil
Haven. And what I found was no void.

I slam the journal shut and stare at it. "Did you show this to anyone?"

"No. Ford knows I have it but he doesn't know what's inside."

I cover my mouth, pacing as I shake the book. "She died for this, Josie."

"I know she did, Ash." She cries instantly as she picks at the fraying end of her sleeve.

I grab her arms and make her look at me. "Hey, you'll be okay. You're safe. You're okay." I let her lean against me as I rub her back. "I'm sorry for freaking out, I just... It seems like Veil Haven has been lying to us, Josie. Like they've lied to me about everything."

"I've tried to learn more from the book but with her spirit gone, there's no more energy. It's hard going back that far. It's hard to say how long ago it was."

I stare at her, my lips tight, my shoulders high. I have to tell her what I learned. There's no better time or place. I repeat the same sentiment to myself a dozen times until it feels real: *No one's here but us. No Watchers.*

I take her hands. My throat feels like sandpaper as my eyes water. I force myself to say it out loud. This blasphemy.

"A lot's been happening, Josie. I've been digging around where I shouldn't be and... I think the Keepers of the Coast are right. I think there's an ocean outside of Veil Haven. I think there's a whole world. That's why Kimi was killed. That's where Markus came from, not Fox Falls. That's where Althea ran to when she left, and where Dante was headed. Not the portal in the park, but the edge of the world. And somewhere out there, with the ocean, Althea met Declan and that's how he learned about Veil Haven. And..."

I pause and hang my head. I could stay in this silence forever. I don't want to tell her. I don't want her to carry this burden. Veil Haven hums in the distance. My frown deepens and I clasp her hands tighter.

"Josie... Declan killed Lydia. And he's working for The Watchers."

Josie gasps but I don't let her step away. Her pupils dilate hearing *The Watchers* said aloud for the first time in years. She shakes her head, her jaw tight, unable to string together a cohesive thought.

"I'm close with the Forest Eye, Josie. I'm sorry I never told you. I didn't want you to think of me differently. But it basically raised me. And last night, the Forest Eye showed me what happened to Lydia the night she died and it was... awful. I've never been able to see Declan and even the Forest Eye couldn't see him... but it was him. And I don't know what they're planning, but Director Capaldi assured me Lydia died of natural causes, just like Chief said, just like Winona and them telling me there's nothing to worry about with the new family."

Josie gawks without judgement, her thoughts racing a mile a minute.

I take a breath but keep going. "And I thought the director was dead because the Static Man told me, but then when I tried to leave through the park portal after Lydia's funeral, mainly just to get his attention, Chief stopped me, and then the director called me on his phone. And he was a jerk, Josie." I'm crying. "After all these years of never talking, never seeing me, hardly asking for me, he told me I wasn't enough. How could he say that to me? After everything I've done for him."

Josie continues to stare, unable to find the words, just trying to process it all, trying to keep up.

"But Declan killed her, Josie. Markus' stepdad killed Lydia and I feel so stupid for not realizing it sooner." I fight away the tears with shallow breaths, but when Josie pulls me into a hug, I break down instantly. "Why didn't I realize it sooner?"

"Oh, Ash." She pets the back of my head. "I'm just glad you're okay. You've been goin' through so much..." She takes my hands so she can look me in the eye. "I'm so sorry you had to see what you saw. I wish... Oh I wish none of this ever happened." Her voice breaks. "It's not your fault for not figurin' this out on your own. You can't possibly blame yourself. And it's okay, you not tellin' me. I mean, you bein' close with the Forest Eye. It makes sense I guess. For you. This is a lot, but it's okay. I'm glad you felt like you could tell me. We can figure this out together."

I squeeze her hands, finally feeling relieved, but something happens.

A warm, pulsing energy swarms through both of us, starting at our hands and moving up toward our heads as we're locked into a trance. This is her ability, and it's searching for something in my past.

Josie's stomach clenches knowing she's crossed a line, but a deeper, almost protective energy nags at her to lean into it.

And I don't stop her. I don't pull away. And in the same breath, eyes locked, we let it happen.

Josie's eyes glaze over as she sinks into her trance, allowing this power to push and pull between us. As she enters the past as a third-party observer, the energy soothes me like a late autumn sunbeam.

In her mind's eye she sees a vast darkness that she begins to fold around her like a blanket. There are many representations for the past, and she's been trained well enough to take them all with stride. She's always careful when witnessing living memories, out of respect, but there's a fear that comes with seeing *my* past.

As she nuzzles closer to the darkness, sneaks through like breeze-blown curtains. The moments shine. And I see myself through her.

I'm young. Back when my hair was long and I had bangs. It's hard to tell when this was but I'm at the station with Chief. I'm upset—no, furious. We're arguing. I witnessed someone in trouble that we could help, but Chief is holding me back, telling me no, telling me it isn't safe to get involved. He says something about the bigger picture and that I'll understand when I'm older. But I refuse, and I tell him I'll intervene on my own. He can't stop me every minute of the day.

Chief kneels down to my level and tries to convince me again, but I'm insistent. When I try to pull away, he tightens his grip, and he... he tells me I'm not going to intervene. He tells me everything is fine, and, "You won't remember I did this to you." And like a switch is flipped, I believe him, and I settle down.

Another memory. I'm older but not quite a teenager. I'm crying in his office. I've met my hardest consequence yet. Kane hates me. Everyone hates me. I am desperate to undo my actions. I want to tell the director I lied. I'll do anything to return things back to normal. Anything. A sinister tone laces my voice as I harden, conceiving some plan to save Kane's uncle, to tell the people, to rescue him. But when Chief takes my hands to comfort me he... he tells me to forget these ideas... these feelings... and to never consider something so dangerous ever again. And quietly, he tells me I won't remember what he's doing to me.

The next memory is only a couple of weeks ago. I'm in his office. I get up from the chair. I'm heated about the new family and feel like he's ignoring me. Chief walks around his desk to soothe my fears and he pulls me into a hug. Then he pauses, considering something, but holds me a little tighter anyway. He tells me to calm down. My shoulders ease. I settle against him. And he says, "It's okay to feel this way but you need to calm down. You have to believe me when I say the director doesn't want to burden you with more responsibilities. You're only a kid once. Don't rush that. And don't worry about the new family. Everything is under control." Quieter, he says, "You won't remember I did this to you, Ash. Please believe that I'm sorry, and I love you, and I'm protecting you."

Now I'm in his arms and I'm sobbing. Shaking. Screaming. He holds me in the hallway outside the morgue. He tells me to take deep breaths and I do, despite, despite, despite. He pets the back of my hair as I soak his uniform, and he whispers, "Know you'll survive this. You will get through. And for today, the sadness will not break you. You won't remember I did this to you." Next I know, I'm hollow. He leads me to Hayden and we discuss our plans for the day.

Josie continues to tug at the darkness so more light can break through, so she can see at least one more memory before this energy dissipates.

Chief Mun and I are in the park. Snow insulates the world and is falling fast. The portal glows green at my back. And I'm scream-ing at him. He's begging me to listen. "I've always been protecting you," he says, imploring me with his kind, sad, desperate eyes. I've never seen him so scared, but it still doesn't convince me.

Then, he cups my shoulder. "Ash, listen to me. You do not want to leave town. You don't have any questions about what lies out there. You will not go through this dangerous portal. And you won't re-

member I've told you any of this." And despite my anger, my pain, my plans, everything shifts into his perspective and I listen to him. He doesn't give me any other choice.

Josie drops the darkness like a heavy coat and we step out of her trance together.

It's impossible to put my emotions to words. To intellectualize them. To explain this overwhelming... everything. I stand here for a long time, my throat closing up, my mind racking itself over again and again. And my heart *aches*.

Josie says something, covering her mouth, shaking her head, taking a couple of steps back to give me space, but I can't pay attention.

Everything is very still. Then, I let out a long, shaking breath. And the world strikes me like a lightning bolt.

Someone knocks over a candle, catching their clothes on fire. Someone is locked out of their home, and they can hear the hungry cryptids coming. Someone steals their cousin's truck. Someone traps their partner in the basement. Someone is pushed off a cliff. Someone is calling out for help and watches their dad walk away from them. I collapse. Josie follows me.

"Oh... Ash..." She tries to read whether or not I want to be touched.

These were just snapshots. How often did he—

It's already hard to recall those memories. They're slipping through the darkness like secrets I was never supposed to know.

I harden. Josie sees it in my jaw, the twinge of my lips, the emptiness in my eyes.

She covers her mouth, watching my rage manifest. "Ash..." she cautions, afraid. Afraid for me, for the secrets *she* unlocked.

I flick my eyes to her, and although she can barely tell, she knows. "The Forest Eye was right." There's more vitriol in my voice than I thought possible. *Humans can be monsters, too.*

My words hit her like a flashflood. She's putting so much trust in me, but she's scared. Her arm hairs stand on end as she watches me rise.

"Have I always been their puppet? Is my apathy because of *him*?" My face burns. I could spit fire. "What parts of me are just orders?" I'm so tense I fear if I move too fast I'll sprain something.

Josie shakes her head, lost for words, and rises to meet me.

"He—" My voice cracks. "They've all been—" My vision blurs and in a breath I'm a child again. "Josie, he was the only one I trusted and he... he..."

Josie braces herself against me as I crumble, cry, and hyperventilate. "Ash, I'm sorry. I'm so, so sorry."

"I trusted him." I quake. "He's the closest thing to a dad I've ever had and he's been just as bad to me as the rest. I've never had anyone, Josie. I've never..."

My mind must be so full of panic and noise that Veil Haven doesn't have room to sneak in. As I try and fail and try again to piece myself together, Josie consoles me with gentle remarks.

She's back to worrying about what domino effect she's begun and how quickly it could catch up with her. I can't blame her, but I don't have the energy to console her either. I'm not sure my assurances have ever meant anything or ever will again.

She tells me, "This doesn't define you." But of course it does.

Andrew Mun has branded me and manipulated me in the name of love, safety, and protection. Am I really that much of a threat to myself? Do I really need to be policed? Stripped of my free will? Forced into a state of ease?

After what feels like forever, I'm finally strong enough to hold myself steady without Josie.

I recognize now that I've never been exempt from the dangers of our home. I need to stay away from Chief Mun. I need to stay away from all of them. But only until I'm ready to strike back.

I turn to Josie, unable to read her through the mess of my mind, and stare at her with deadly intent. I know neither of us has the energy to go through that again, but far more questions have yet to be answered, and there's more than one way to find what's hidden.

"What else can we unbury?"

CHAPTER 31
WHEN IS A DOOR NOT A DOOR?

We decide to stay at the dam and brainstorm. Josie tucks into her camo hunting jacket. Meanwhile I keep myself warm by pacing. I can feel the Void watching us from the dark blue sky, our only silent observer.

I tell her everything—from the Static Man to the director, the Keepers of the Coast, my fight with Markus, all I know about Declan, and everything I've experienced with the Forest Eye. For the most part I'm talking fast. She interjects with questions, but mostly she keeps her arms crossed and listens.

When I tell her about the Forest Eye, giving as brief a summary as I can muster, she pushes off the wall and holds me.

"I'm sorry you've been so alone, Ash."

I don't say anything as I close my eyes and let our bodies warm each other in the midnight chill.

"I think maybe that's what this place tries to do. Veil Haven can be so isolating. Especially if people don't like you."

I rub my face, trying to warm my runny nose. "I'm sorry, Josie, I never meant to keep so much from you. It's all been happening so fast, and I can barely keep it straight. When I'm not being made to forget it, that is."

Josie looks down, lost in thought, and I let the gears turn until she's ready to speak. It's a lot to sit with.

"I guess when it comes down to it, you have blind spots. The Watchers," she swallows, "have always been invisible to you in a sense. We don't really know anythin' about them, but we know they're powerful and they have all sorts of technology. But what if they aren't actually invisible? What if they're just hidin' from *you*."

She cups her mouth, trying to connect the dots. "It's a strange coincidence. Isn't it? All these people hidin' from you specifically? The only difference with Declan is that he stole somebody's blind spot ability, though he watered it down somehow. That's why you can't see him in person but you could see the director. It's like how you can see The Watchers when they're in town, but then they disappear when they go back to their base."

"Right. And they've always kept that a secret from me."

"So, when you try to see Declan, like if he was washin' dishes, would you see floating dishes?"

"No, not that I've noticed. It's like everything he even vaguely interacts with besides other people just disappear."

"Well, how's this." She steps closer as if to whisper a secret. "What if there have always been blind spots? Not like Declan, that seems different. But if The Watchers can cloak themselves from your mind's eye every time they close their van doors, or drive off to wherever their base is, who's to say they don't have more hidden spaces in town that you specifically can't see? And because you were always led to believe you could see everythin', you just never looked for them."

She clasps her hands together. "If you learn how to find these blind spots, maybe with a feelin' or somethin', maybe you can find other important things they're hidin' from you. And maybe with enough focus, you can find a pattern for how to find Declan. Or if not him, just stuff the director and Chief Mun and Winona are purposefully hidin' from you!"

I blink. "Josie, you're a genius."

She smiles ear to ear and bounces in place. "I know you've never really had a reason to go to the trainin' facilities, but practice is what it's all about. You meditate, and it starts with a feelin'. Then it grows and grows until you have an epiphany!" Josie stretches her arms out.

"Okay." I nod. "Okay, I can do that. That's easy enough. Right?"

"You know Veil Haven better than anyone. If anyone can find what shouldn't be there, it's you. You were born for this."

Josie is right. She has to be.

I clutch the wall and look at the Black River weaving toward town. Letting out a long breath, I send my mind's eye sweeping across Veil Haven in search of something unfamiliar.

We spend the next hour like this. I search every inch of town, as everything floods through me. I filter just about everything I can. And when nothing feels out of place or weird, I move on. I witness the night through thousands of different lenses. And not just people, but I investigate every object, every corner, every animal, and bug. I investigate every source of noise and movement, and even though my head is pounding, and I have to sit on the cold ground with my back to the wall, I keep going.

Josie stays beside me for a while before pacing the length of the dam, then she goes into the field to braid the tall grasses, then she leans against the wall opposite me staring at the stars. Now she's reading Kimi's journal again, flashlight in hand.

I rock forward, finally finding something. Josie's light makes my eyes look like they're glowing in the dark.

She jumps forward and helps me to my feet.

"You know the clock tower downtown?"

"The one that always chimes whenever you notice it?"

"There's a big plaque under it. Right?"

"Uh, yeah, I think so," she says.

I scoff. "Apparently not."

314

Wedged at the back of downtown stands the forty-foot-tall bell tower. As we approach the clock, the two-octave bells sound, singing our arrival only to us.

We stand under the bells and look down at the giant bronze circle in the concrete.

"I don't know how I never recognized this before." I crouch to inspect it. "I mean, it doesn't make any sense. I've looked at this plenty of times. I showed this to Markus when we went around town. I can't be *this* blind."

"Maybe it's just about your perspective. You weren't looking for anything weird, so you didn't find anything weird," Josie suggests. "Plus there's a lot more to focus on than a random plaque in a place no one bothers coming to."

The plaque reads, *If you see something, say nothing,* and has our town sigil in the center: a celestial map of the five towns across the Void, connected like a constellation, and forming an eye with Veil Haven at the center.

I move my hand over the plaque as my mind's eye suddenly flickers, assuring me that it isn't here at all. I try to remember what I thought was here before, but I guess I really did just see the plaque with my physical eyes.

A couple of Night Crawlers and Black Dogs are in the park as well as some unnamed cryptid eyeing us from the sewer, but they won't bother us. They all move along as my gaze scans the vicinity. The rest of downtown is clear.

The cold is sharp against my fingers as I trace the bronze eye, and to my surprise the pupil feels like a button, like something I can press. I readjust myself, goosebumps rising under my sweater.

I push hard on the pupil and something clicks under us. I step away from the plaque as it moves and grinds. It separates into halves and tucks under the concrete to reveal a chamber leading far beneath the earth. Warm lights flicker on one at a time to reveal a spiraling staircase.

No one is around, no one is watching, there are no Watchers devices on the clock tower, we even left our phones in the car, but Josie still looks around on high alert. I admit it's strange that no cameras are aimed on this spot, but there must be some reason.

I grab her hands, bringing her attention back. "Are you sure you want to do this? You don't have to come with me."

"I want to." She squeezes my hands. I watch her swallow and convince herself wholeheartedly that this is what she needs to do.

Something in the back of my head says I should make her leave, but if something is down there and she can look into its past, it will be infinitely more important than whatever I find in the present.

If they're hiding the past from us, Josie is the only one who can bring it to light.

I step onto the first metal step and slowly descend into the warmly lit hole. The plaque grinds closed over our heads once we're halfway down but Josie sees a button on the underside for our safe return. We keep going.

The stairwell is tight. If Josie and I were any larger, it might not be possible for us to descend. I didn't know a staircase could be this narrow. The lights are pushed into the wall to give us as much space as possible. The air is chilled and dry, not as musty or dank as one might imagine a hole in the earth.

It doesn't take long for us to get to the bottom, and when we do we're met by a cave. Though it's only ten feet in each direction, it's out of place compared to the obviously human-crafted stairs. And beyond this cave room lies an archway with a paved concrete floor that leads into a pitch-black tunnel.

My mind's eye is throbbing against the crown of my skull and I have to clutch Josie to stop myself from falling. I'm so dizzy. I've never had my omniscience bounced back on itself. It's claustrophobic down here. How is that possible? I been in caves before. I've been in basements, no problem. It can't be because we're under the earth, it has to be this place.

I really can't force myself to see above us. Whatever is going on in town, I'm blind to it. I'm stuffed down here. I feel clammy and strange and I close my eyes to hold down the sickly urge to vomit.

"Ash, are you okay? What's happenin'?"

I nod, and catch my breath. "Just, adjusting." I swallow again, and when I open my eyes, instead of my ability moving outward in every direction, I focus it down the dark tunnel. Somehow, though slow, I'm able to see what's ahead.

Clutching Josie tightly as we walk in tandem, we move forward.

The cave leads us to a large metal door. Cobwebs fill alcoves around us while a cold breeze kisses our ankles. My stomach twists at the idea of what I've gotten Josie into. Every fiber of my being tells me we aren't supposed to be here.

The chances of someone being behind this door are slim, and I don't see or sense any Watchers devices, but with my mind's eye partially blinded like this, anything is possible.

Clutching the handle, and with a thrust of my shoulder, I swing the door open. The air is instantly cold and musty as we stumble into what must be a large, open room. The dust that swirls up makes us gag. We cover our noses with our shirts and hold hands as we step deeper into the dark.

The lights lag as we enter, flickering on slowly. And when everything is lit with an almost blue undertone, we take in the strangely sterile room.

The room is wide but shallow, and the smooth concrete walls are covered with cardboard boxes stacked to the ceiling. Half of them are crushed under their own weight. But what really grabs our attention is the wall of retro TVs. They're dull but they're on. There must be at least a hundred, each stacked on metal shelves above a long control panel. On the desk ledge in front of the panel of buttons and switches are four swivel chairs, a few dusty clipboards, and an empty coffee cup with a ring stained inside.

"What is this?" Josie whispers.

"Don't touch anything," I warn as I walk up to the screens.

Most of them are just static but some are displaying images. I can't tell if they're recordings or live, but I know these places. They're random spots in town. I see Main Street, town hall, the park, outside the hospital, the rec fields, the high school. It goes on. But the images are monochrome and staticky. This technology is old. This room is old.

The only people in town who would even consider having cameras everywhere are The Watchers, but this is too primitive for their ever-reaching grasp.

Unless this place is as old as The Watchers.

"How is there electricity here?" Josie wonders.

"I guess they forgot it was still on the grid."

I move from the screens to the closest half-opened box not crushed in a ceiling tower. Lifting the cardboard arms with the careful precision of someone defusing a bomb, I find it full of paper. Reams of paper, the kind you have to tear the serrated edge off of. The pages are filled with some sort of numerical code, but the only numbers I find repeating themselves are twelve and thirty-one. I see no useful information here or at least nothing I can understand. I move to the next box and find the same.

Josie sits in one of the old office chairs and feels her trance tugging at her, whispering, begging her like an impossible itch. "Ash," she says sleepily, "I need to touch this button."

I turn around and see her finger hovering above a large red button, almost entranced. "No way." I laugh nervously, rushing to her side. I spin her chair away. "That could set off some alarm and we'd be trapped down here."

"I can touch it without pressin' it," she tells me. Her eyes are wide, and I can see the trance washing through her, begging her to dive into the past.

I push the chair further from the panel, which seems to pull her out of the trance. "Is anything else calling to you?"

She blinks a few times before standing and walking around the room. Something in the far-right corner pulses through her, and she's drawn there just like she was to the button.

We move a few boxes, and we discover a door. It takes the both of us to wedge it open. The metal-on-metal *shriiiik* makes our hairs stand on end.

Carefully stepping inside, the lights turn on as we enter the small room. It's dusty and cramped, filled with filing cabinets and shelves full of random things I can only describe as knickknacks. It feels like a weird janitor's closet, but the most confusing thing here is something massive covered by a beige tarp. It's so large it almost reaches the ceiling. How did they get it down here. A teleporter?

Together, as if on cue, we curl our hands around the tarp and pull. After we're done coughing from the dust, we see a bronze statue of a man.

Neither of us recognize him, but he must've been important enough to get a larger-than-life-sized statue made of his likeness. He's a handsome man with long curls and a soothing smile, but our attention is drawn to a plaque at his feet. We bend down and read it at the same time, gasping in unison.

"Valentine Marks. Town Founder."

Horrorstruck and confused, we stare at each other for a long time.

"Valentine. That's the name from the Keepers of the Coast's book. Whoever wrote that knew him." I gasp again, louder this time, clutching Josie. "They were there when the town was founded. That's an artifact from the beginning of Veil Haven!" Goosebumps cover my skin.

"Should I touch it?"

I stare at her wondering what she thinks she'll find. "Can you even go back that far?"

"Only one way to find out." She clutches the statue's leg before I can protest and is instantly sent into a trance.

Her eyes glaze over and her muscles stiffen, holding her upright. In an instant she's sent back in time. And with all my pent-up energy being bounced back on me, I direct it at Josie's subconscious as she dives further back than maybe anyone has ever gone.

She opens her eyes in her mindscape with a shudder, gasping for air as she's stretched thin. She feels as though pieces of her have peeled off and are left floating through time like breadcrumbs to the present.

Following the pull of the ages-old monument, every step feels like she's pushing against an invisible barrier. She aches as she stretches herself, sure she'll reach the limit of her ability. But with one final thrust, she pierces some time-membrane and manifests into the memory attached to the statue.

Josie is downtown but everything is different. There are only a couple of buildings including a modest, red brick town hall. She can see across the Black River to a freshly cut forest but there's no bridge or West Veil Haven in sight.

Several workers lower and align the bronze statue on a marble pedestal in front of town hall. A small crowd passes, but it feels like a moment of construction rather than the unveiling.

Josie hears a deep, male voice behind her and is struck to see the living monument.

Valentine Marks.

The statue is almost an exact likeness of him. He's young for such an accomplished man, maybe in his thirties. His hair frames his rich, brown skin and chiseled features, but the sculptor has left off a stunning amount of detail.

There are neon glowing eyes covering Valentine Marks from head to toe. The multi-colored eyes are stamped on his skin in varying sizes and shapes. They look more like drawings than actual eyes. Each glowing pupil moves independently except for the few that crown his forehead, arching above his pitch-black eyes.

As Josie stares at him, he turns his attention to her, and she freezes in place. He raises his brow and crosses his arms.

"It's a bit strange to be here. Isn't it?" His voice is indulgently smooth.

Panic fills Josie as she shrinks under his dark gaze, but when he turns to the man standing beside him, she realizes he was simply looking through her at the statue. She sighs in relief and moves closer to listen.

"It's fitting," the second man says. "Our fearless town founder should be front and center." He punches Valentine's arm, and the two men laugh. "But listen, you deserve this. You've given us a home when we were stripped of everything. Because of you we're able to survive."

"It was a team effort," Valentine says. He squints at the statue, crossing his arms. "I don't know why they didn't include my eyes."

"I don't know either," his friend says, cocking his head. "You look odd without them."

"If not for my omniscience, Veil Haven wouldn't be here."

His friend says he will talk to the artist and see if they can add the eyes before the unveiling. As he shuffles off, Valentine is approached by a different man wearing a black suit.

"Sir, The Watchers are ready for inspection."

Josie tenses at the name spoken casually around so many people, but none of them appear bothered. She steps closer to Valentine, close enough to touch him.

Valentine nods and unfolds his arms, "Of course they are. I'd like to test some of our new technologies as well. We need to strengthen the veil if we're going to continue to expand."

"Yes, sir. I'll set up a test of our latest cloaking devices."

Josie stands beside him feeling herself pulled both forward and back with every step. She's straining herself being this far in the past but her curiosity demands she stay. She watches Valentine study the statue as dozens of questions race through her mind. The tension in her chest grows with every pseudo breath as realizations begin sinking in.

"Good," Valentine says to the suited man, "I'd like to make something that rivals even my power. You never know who could be watching."

She can feel him about to leave, the vision peeling apart at the edges, but there's so much she needs to know, so much she wants to see. She isn't sure if she'll ever get this opportunity again.

Valentine straightens his back and turns from the statue, and without any reason or hesitation, Josie grabs his wrist.

Her core temperature sinks when she makes contact with solid mass. She didn't think she could do that.

And as Valentine flinches at her touch, all of his eyes lock on to Josie. He squints at her trying to understand the phantom he's witnessing.

As Josie holds on to him, she sinks into an endless dark room. A spotlight is centered on her and Valentine Marks. But she can't pull away. She feels stuck to him. And even though it doesn't make sense, even though it should be impossible, she's certain all of his ethereal, glowing eyes are pinning her here until he's done with her.

But despite her panic and attempts to pull away, images of Valentine's past wash through her like flickers of light, a thousand memories lacking context or order.

Deep red on brown hands. Hellfire falling from above. Blue-lit rooms with silver tools. Soft pink kiss marks. Heavy breaths through dark green woods. Golden fields of sunflowers. Black smoke bruising the blue sky. Dark water with cresting waves. Silver beneath rotting earth. Neon eyes splattered with something viscous.

Something tells her he senses her too, sees who she is, where she is, and why she's here. That he's seeing just as much from her as she is from him.

Valentine looks at her in a way that sends chills through Josie's incorporeal body. His dark eyes shine with something heinous. His smooth voice could pin her to the spot if she wasn't already feeling crushed under his gaze. With a curling grin, all he says is, "Interesting..." Then, he tears his wrist from her grasp.

In a breath, Josie is thrown into her present body gasping for air. Tears pool around her shaking lips. She clutches me and looks around wildly as I guide her to the floor. She keeps apologizing for some reason.

My nerves are shot. "Josie, it's okay. You're with me. You're back. It's okay. It's done." I push the hair from her hazel eyes as she shakes.

"He saw me, Ash. I didn't think I could touch people when I—" She cups her mouth, fears striking her like lightning. *Did I change the past? Did he tell anyone? Are they coming for us?*

I'm sick to my stomach, my anger knotting as I try to soothe her. "Nothing happened. He can't come for you. No one is coming for you. No one knows." I wipe away her tears. "You're so powerful, Josie. You went back further than anyone has ever gone."

She swallows, searching for something in my white eyes. "Valentine Marks was omniscient, Ash. Just like you, except he had eyes all over his body and his real eyes were black. I can't believe I touched him. I can't believe he saw me." She cups her mouth again, his distant untethered memories circling inside her mind. And that smile, that grin.

My mind shifts through all the promises I heard growing up that I was the only one, that I was the first omniscient person in our history, that they didn't have any record of how my ability works. How I would have to struggle for years before I found the Forest Eye, and even then, even after, even now.

"Why wouldn't they help me?" I'm distant. I feel the same burning emptiness as I did with the Forest Eye.

Josie tenses her jaw, not sure what to say.

"They lied to me about everything. *Everything*. What's the point? Why would they pretend I was the only one when the *town founder* was omniscient?" This rage makes me stand. I don't look at anything. Static hisses in my pounding head. "Why would they keep his statue down here? Why did they erase the past? What is this place?" I shout, looking around.

Josie rises and pulls me into a hug until I calm down but I can't. This won't settle. I'm choked by the fact that our founder was omniscient. Were there others? Were my parents? Why didn't they tell me? Why would they watch me suffer and struggle and try and fail for years?

"They talked about The Watchers like they were nothin'," Josie says, trying to pull me back, "like they were brand new. Downtown was hardly even built. It was the beginning." She collects her thoughts. "I think Valentine Marks was more than just the town founder, Ash. I think he created The Watchers, too."

"This is an old Watchers base. Don't you think?"

"It's the only thing that makes sense." We both look at Valentine's looming statue. Josie shudders. "Somethin' was wrong with that man, Ash. He played nice and normal but somethin' much worse was goin' on."

My eyes flick to her. "Maybe he did something so bad they wanted to erase him."

"Or he decided he and his Watchers needed to disappear." Josie pales.

"Hey, he's long dead."

Josie nods, looking down. "We need to keep goin'. We have to find somethin' more relatable to what's happenin' now."

I look at her, surprised, but even more surprised by my own reaction. I want to ecstatically agree with her. I want to tear through this place and unearth every secret they've kept from me. I don't care what the consequences are. I don't care what it takes. I stare at my best friend, and I want these things from her.

The better part of me stalls. "Are you sure you're up for it?"

"I don't ever wanna come back here. I wanna get it done."

CHAPTER 32
The Sins of the Father
and His Father and His Father and…

We leave Valentine's statue and stand under the screens in the main room. Their light casts strange shadows on us. My mind pounds in the silence as my omniscience continues to bounce back on me. My breathing is steady and low.

"Do you still wanna touch that button?"

Josie nods and sits in the nearest chair, pulling herself closer to the desk. She eyes me and hovers one finger above the button. "I won't press it. I promise."

I speak slowly and sound as distant as I feel. "Just don't wear yourself out."

With a deep sigh and a steady hand, Josie brushes the button with the gentlest touch, and her joints lock in place. Her eyes glaze over, and this time they close.

So much energy radiates from this button that Josie feels divided. In her mindscape, she feels herself drawn toward a particular moment close enough to the present that maybe she can learn something useful. Something to satisfy us. Something to get her out of this place.

Her mind pulses as she lets the past carry her away, and in an instant she's transported only a few feet back in the same room. Except decades ago.

Men sit in the chairs operating a fully functional panel, Watchers' symbols on their clothes. The room is filled with people instead of boxes and dust.

Josie is extremely uneasy in their presence, knowing instantly they're all Watchers, but she stands stiffly, careful not to rub shoulders.

There must be two dozen people here. She doesn't recognize anyone, but I do. I'd recognize those eyes anywhere.

The Director Capaldi I know is a large, broad-shouldered man with a big gut and an imposing aura. But in Josie's flashback he's young, thin, and with a head full of hair. He seems completely different. But still, I couldn't mistake the prominent lower whites of his eyes for anything.

He's only a teenager, maybe younger. Standing with his mentor. And all I can think about is how this is what I was supposed to have from the beginning. This glimpse into what I was promised from our relationship, but never received.

A slim, older man with salt and pepper hair stands beside young Capaldi. I thought my director was scary, but this man has a chilling air about him. He carries himself with a truly dangerous cruelty, not to Capaldi or anyone in this room, but something about this elder director frightens me to my core, something in his eyes. I could've had it a lot worse.

"You might need to do this one day, Capaldi, so pay attention." The man straightens his back and looks pointedly to a Watcher behind him. "Is everyone in their bunkers?"

The Watcher, dressed head to toe in black armor, steps forward to confirm they are.

"Good, good..." the man trails off. "Do it."

One of the men at the console presses the central red button but nothing changes. At least nothing inside the bunker.

Josie recognizes how everyone is glued to the screens, but she has to step closer to see it.

A couple outside of town hall are in the midst of an embrace when it happens. Both of them are frozen, and then the man falls, seizing. So much is happening on those screens Josie can't focus on them all. The cameras catch different scenes unfolding around Veil Haven.

Everyone has stopped moving like the cameras themselves have frozen. But she sees some people fall down, others lie still, some twitching, others having full seizures.

Nobody in the room seems to react, but Josie begins to panic, looking around for any sign of empathy. Pushing this button did something to these people and they're hurting. They can't all be apathetic.

The longer she watches, the more she has to resign that yes, yes they are.

"You see, Capaldi." The elder man lays his arm across the kid's shoulders. "The original director had this idea..."

The vision begins to wear thin, the conversation breaking apart. Josie turns in circles trying to recover it but she's panicking.

"Valentine—"

"—smart man—"

"—population growth—"

"—control—"

"—desire for freedom—"

She tries to focus on the conversation, but it's fading in and out with the rapid beat of her heart.

I talk to her, desperate to keep her there. She can't leave yet. I need to know what happens next. "Josie, you have to stay calm. This isn't real for you. Focus." I whisper closer in Josie's ear, coaching her softly to pinpoint what's in the room. If I can rebuild the setting as she's still there, maybe she can get a grip.

The room and people melt away as the world fades to black, but the older director and Capaldi stay illuminated in the center of her mindscape. She stands on the outskirts, distantly watching, feeling more and more out of her body.

"Now," the older director continues, "if you have a crowded populace where everyone has powers and you put them inside a small, safe haven it'll eventually become unsafe. That's common sense.

Naturally, we will outgrow our borders. And on top of that, with enough freedom, people will begin to wonder why we have a boundary, where we came from, what's out there. If they leave, they take Veil Haven with them. You see?"

Capaldi nods, infatuated with his mentor's speech.

"It becomes unsafe. Our purpose is to keep our people safe." He points at the screens that Josie no longer sees. "So Valentine said, if we control the narrative of where we came from, the people won't wonder about our borders, they won't want to leave, and they won't take any information with them. There will be no possibility of inviting danger into Veil Haven. We control the perception of our world, we control the population of our town, and we control the story they believe. You understand?"

"Of course, sir," Capaldi says, but he shuffles in place wanting to say something.

The director looks at him sternly and raises his silver brow.

Capaldi's arms hang by his side. "But we're erasing everyone's memories this time because of the mayor and the police chief. Aren't we?"

The older director tenses his jaw and looks forward, eyeing one of the screens specifically. "Yes."

Capaldi tenses too, nervous to have upset his mentor.

"This process is a last-ditch effort," the man tells him. "It takes a while to prepare, but that's why we study our predecessors. That's why I have you. You'll be an even better director than I am—if you pay attention."

"Always, Director."

"It's easiest to erase everyone's memories at the new year. You'll keep track of everything that way, and it'll be easier for people to explain that fresh start feeling. But the final result..." He raises both his arms, smiling under the TV light. "Is a thing of beauty."

Josie falls back into herself and pushes away from the console as though it's hot. She breathes fast and stands up, moving away as quickly as she can.

I stare at nothing. I stare at the floor. I catch my breath just as Josie is catching hers. And I realize a paralyzing truth.

I don't know anything about The Watchers.

I stare at the wall of boxes wide-eyed. The numbers I didn't understand. Twelve and thirty-one. It's New Year's Eve.

The Watchers wipe memories on New Year's Eve to make data collection easier? They can erase certain memories of everyone in town? How? Is it like Chief Mun's ability but amplified? But it doesn't happen every year. Only when they need to—or when they want to?—or when people start asking too many questions?

"Did you know?" Josie asks me. Her voice bounces between the walls.

I'm hollowed by the question. "Of course I didn't know." *I don't know about The Watchers at all. I've never known. I'm just another one of their tools.*

Josie's eyes are red from crying. She looks at me with the same terror she wore in her vision. She looks at me and she sees them.

"I told you everything, Josie. You think the director ever told me about this? That he ever brought me here? Or showed me around The Watchers' headquarters? He won't even pick up the phone when I call him." I have to temper myself.

Josie looks gaunt. Whether she believes it or not, her fear is making her connect dots she shouldn't be. I hear her quick panicked thoughts. *She's just like Capaldi in the vision. That's how she was raised. She was made to be this way. She was manipulated to be this way.* Josie swallows. "I believe you, Ash. I'm sorry you've been put in these situations."

I turn away and stare at the floor. My brows twitch. She doesn't mean it. She's just afraid. Has she always been afraid of me?

I take in the implications of this room. I imagine Capaldi standing here and what it would've been like to be here with him. I think about what it would've been like to truly be taken under his wing. Was that what I was promised? And slowly, I realize I was raised to want this.

I swallow the feeling and turn to face her. "You have to believe me, Josie. They've kept me out of the loop for so long... maybe there was a time when I would've wanted to be a part of this. But Capaldi has never kept me close." I wish he did. Some deep, desperate, childish part of me wishes I had known. "If anything, he's pushed me away."

Static fills my ears as I stand with this contradiction. Do I really want *this*? Do I want to know more? Then an idea comes to mind that grounds me in the present.

"Oh my god. Althea left under Director Capaldi's reign. What if he brought her back so he can properly mindwipe everyone to hide his mistake?"

"But how would Declan play into that?" She sounds equally tired. "Why would he kill Lydia?"

My heart sinks. "I asked her to learn more about him. What if her guides told her something, and The Watchers' telepaths found out while she was at work, and then... I don't know."

"Ash." I almost don't meet her eyes, but she waits until I do. "I think it's already too late to do anythin'."

"No. If they are preparing to do this, there's time to stop it. They said they only do it on New Year's." I take her shoulders but she backs away. My throat tightens. "I could talk to the director. I could convince him to stop."

Her shoulders fall slack. "He won't even pick up your calls."

Josie's words wound me. Her exhaustion wounds me. And I can't find the will to speak. What can I say to make this alright? What can I do to fix this?

"This was a mistake for me, Ash." Her eyes water. "I was wrong for comin' down here. I'm sorry. This..." She shakes her head, trailing off to stop herself from completely breaking down.

I cup her cheek. She doesn't pull away this time. "They don't know about us, Josie. If they did, they would already be here." I wipe her tears with my thumb.

She bites her shaking lip and I see the corner of her chipped front tooth.

I realize I'm able to hear her thoughts so easily because my mind's eye doesn't have anywhere else to go down here.

Josie wants to say, *I believe you,* but another thought is louder. *How can I believe you when you're one of them?* In the end, she doesn't say anything, and my heart breaks all the same.

I step away, blinking fast. With the world muffled and distant, no outside moments flood my mind. It's just me down here. Just me and my best friend who's terrified of me. I can't look at her.

"We can't tell anyone. We can't even think about this."

"I know," she says too quickly.

"We have to pretend like we don't know."

"It's hard for me, Ash! You know I love you and I trust you with my life but—" She thinks about Lydia.

I cover my mouth. My vision blurs with tears.

She seems to finally realize why, and she melts. "Oh, Ash…"

"No, please don't. You're allowed to feel this way. You're even allowed to hate me."

"I don't hate you," she presses, "but I'm scared and I'm confused, and I'm not safe like you are. Sometimes you get lost in your version of the world, and it's scary to be left so alone. I need to get rid of that journal. I need to throw it in the Black River or bury it somewhere in the woods. I need to protect myself, and you need to figure this out because I'm not supposed to know any of this. Just like Kimi wasn't supposed to know. Or Lydia…" She hiccups as she cries.

"I'm sorry, Josie. I asked too much of you. I'm sorry."

She cocks her head, her features contorting as she cries. "I know, Ash."

"But nothing will happen to you." I swallow, steadying myself. "Nothing will happen to you."

Josie clenches her jaw. "The Watchers are evil, Ash."

Her words graze me, opening a strange wound. She knows I don't have any part in this, so why does she keep acting like I do? I'm not lying to her. *They're* lying to *me*. But the way she looks at me has me rethinking everything.

If I was raised by The Watchers, if I've done everything they asked of me, if I still want to run to them now, what does that make me?

CHAPTER 33
THE FAST-COMING FUTURE

We ascend from the bunker feeling strange and new. I check for any peering eyes and assure Josie we're safe to leave. My mind's eye spreads across town like a pent-up breath finally letting go. For the first time in my life, I welcome the humming noise.

The sun will rise soon, but for now the world is quiet with frost. The clock tower chimes as we watch the hatch close.

"I have to go home." Josie looks as exhausted as she sounds. Between her sleepless nights from reading the journal, our all-nighter, and how far she's ventured tonight, it's no surprise she wants to go home. "I just need time to forget, Ash. I'm... sorry. We can regroup later but I need some time."

I don't say anything as we slide into her mud-stained car. I feel like a burden the entire drive home.

As she pulls beside my driveway, I get out and linger. My thanks is the first thing either of us has said since we left downtown.

I catch her desperate, hollow gaze as she wonders quietly, "How am I supposed to forget this?"

I stall in the cold air. "It's what we were raised to do."

"I'm scared, Ash." Her voice breaks.

I swallow, trying to find the right words to make this feel better. But some things aren't supposed to feel better. "Everything will be fine. I'm going to fix this. They'll listen to me."

"You say that." She looks ahead of her. There's a strange figure under the orange streetlight staring at us wantingly. "But does anything ever really change?"

My brows furrow but without anything else to say, I close the door and she drives away.

The figure under the streetlight pulls out a guitar and starts humming a melodic folk tune. Fitting. It's the same cryptid that mesmerized Markus the first night we met.

The night of the game. When Logan had his vision of Veil Haven burning... ash mixed with the snow, scorch marks across the torn-up field. I've missed any other visions he's had between then and yesterday but he's gotten progressively more shaken. And Shakira. Oh, Shakira.

I feel hollow as I stand where my grass meets the road. The siren knows his trance won't affect me. I guess he's just setting the mood, and I'm too tired to care.

A flash of teal light moves across the street toward the cryptid. I'm surprised to see a Being of Light out here. I watch them for a moment, trying to figure out if the cryptid is dancing with the siren or trying to chase him away. The humanoid shape of light giggles as it moves around the siren in large, swinging—

My mind's eye jumps across town and hyperfocuses on Hayden. I perk up, surprised by the sudden jolt in perspective. Something is wrong. Why is he driving around this early in the morning? My gut twists as I watch him.

He seems so thin and pale. His bloodshot eyes speak for themselves. Hayden takes a shaking breath and unbuckles his seatbelt.

Chills rack my body.

It isn't the first time he's thought about driving off the road, but it's the first time he grips the wheel with the determination to do so. Then, he closes his eyes.

I step forward, reaching out as I yell for him, but it happens so fast.

Hayden turns the wheel so sharply his car flips as it flies off the road. It twists at a terrible angle and falls hard on the front wheel, forcing it into a roll. His body is thrown inside. He hits his head on the glass, his arms and legs flailing. When his car crashes into the trees he is propelled through the window. The sound of it makes me sick.

His life flashes before his eyes as he's airborne. It happens in no real sequence.

He remembers heat, grass on the football field, golden leaves, the clang of a wooden stick on metal plates. He feels himself leaning against a doorway smirking, waking up to the sound of laughter, moving pictures on a screen, the tearing of skin, white smoke curling around his nose. He remembers the burn of sunlight, a different kind of burn in the moonlight, and the far too delicate touch of his first love.

He forgets the memories as fast as he remembers them. In the pass of two seconds, he hits the ground and rolls into a tree with a terrible crunch.

In the pass of two seconds he experiences everything about himself and then nothing.

My knees falter as he falls unconscious.

I scramble for my phone, but it slips from my clammy hands and cracks on the asphalt before I get a grip and dial for help. The teal Being of Light is staring at me halfway down the street. The siren still plays. And the world crashes through my periphery as I drown in the dial tone.

Someone stares at their sleep paralysis demon. Someone breaks their ankle. Someone can't wake up. Someone finds a corpse hanging from their shower curtain. Someone stares back at the glowing eyes. Someone forgot to put out a candle and the glass jar explodes. Someone bites their tongue as they sleep.

"Hello? What's you're emergency?"

"There's been a car accident on Hard to Find Drive. Hayden is dying. There's... god, there's so much blood. He isn't moving."

"Ma'am, stay calm." She promises me help is on the way. She wants to know if I'm injured. If I tell her I'm not there, she might think it's a prank call and cancel the ambulance. I pace across my road, barely able to breathe, and I lie to save his life.

"The ambulance will be there in five minutes."

This will be the longest five minutes of my life.

Someone forgot to lock their window, and a cryptid is slowly opening it, smiling, hungry. Someone is being suffocated under their pillow. Someone feels something lick their hand under the covers. Someone is overcooking their toast. Someone is running in the woods, but they'll never make it out. A Plant Person finds more ferns growing from their wrists. Someone breaks through the sewer grate gasping for air, covered in viscera, thanking the Void they survived that. Someone is dreaming of their crush. Someone isn't dreaming at all.

I fall onto my knees, helpless, and just watch.

You were made to watch.

Teal light illuminates my back as the Being of Light stands in my yard. It feels ethereal, but the cryptid's positive energy doesn't change anything.

It hurts to breathe. To see. To cry.

My throat closes as the cryptid walks closer to me. It doesn't do anything. It and the siren only add to the movement and noise of Veil Haven. I'm numb to it.

I am hollowed every second I focus on Hayden while the present rushes through me. I can't stop the visions. I can't quiet the noise.

Someone wakes up to their alarm, to their kids crying, to a blood covered bed. Ghosts pass through tombstones wondering why they're stuck here. Someone sneezes. Someone blows their nose. Someone picks the sand from their eyes. Someone is levitating off their bed. Someone dances to their favorite song because it's the only way for them to wake up. Someone lies in bed trying to grasp that they'll have to do this all over again today.

The Being of Light stands close in fascination. It wants to

soothe me. It wants to give me good fortune. But I don't need it. Hayden needs it.

Because Hayden is dying.

Other people are dying too.

Someone wakes up normally. Someone watches Jackalopes hop across their yard. Someone burns their tongue. Someone doesn't shut off their alarm, thinking they're alone so it isn't bothering anyone. But it's bothering me. I'm here. I'm listening. So make it stop! Make all this noise stop!

I cover my ears and scream. The Being of Light vanishes. I'm not breathing right and everything is spinning and the ambulance is arriving and Hayden is dying and I'm watching.

I'm watching.

I clutch my cracked phone and start a call. I'm kneeling in the middle of the road outside my house as the siren finally stops playing.

Logan rubs the sleep from his eyes, his blond hair messier than he would ever allow anyone to see it. He answers after the fourth ring.

"Hello?"

"Does he live?" Tears cut down my cheeks. I'm heavy in this husk of a body.

"Ash?" He sits up, racked with chills.

"Just tell me if Hayden lives. I can't do this again, Logan."

He pauses and my heart stops. The static between us is the only thing making the world still. He's seen this, right? He knows what happens, right? But he thought Lydia lived too. Is this any different? We should've been with Hayden, checked on him more, done anything, *anything*, but I've been so distracted and—

"You don't have to tell me," I say quieter, my lips shaking. "Just say anything if he makes it. Anything."

As if teetering on some ledge and this was his final shove, he answers. "Ash, you know the rules. Even if I knew, it isn't my place to share."

I rock back, cupping my mouth. The relief drowns me as I sob. The knot in my throat sinks to my stomach.

The paramedics handle Hayden in their ambulance. They will stabilize him. They will save him. And before I hang up, I tell Logan to meet me at the hospital.

My car idles in the empty lot beside the hospital. The large building towers behind me, most of its windows dark. It is taunting me, and I am bitter. My car's exhaust curls in the cold.

Before long, Logan is knocking on my window, huddled under his letterman.

I slam the door as I meet him outside. The purple fluorescents bathe us as we stand between our cars.

"There's a lot you aren't telling me."

He fidgets under my gaze, his eyes wide. "You're acting like I can talk about this."

"And what about Shakira?"

His eyes become glassy and he tenses his jaw. "You don't understand."

"But I could—"

"Maybe what you're asking is too much for me to give," he shouts.

I step back, my hands tight in my jacket.

He rubs his face and looks around before stepping closer, speaking quietly. "Ash, this isn't the time."

"When will it be?" My nostrils flare. "Do you have any idea what the Forest Eye could've done to me?" I look at the looming hospital. "Did you know this was going to happen?"

He holds my gaze. "I didn't have enough time to stop him. I don't see everything like you do. I don't even see the important things. But lately..." He looks away. "I don't know. There's been too much. This expectation. Ash, I can't even sleep. I can hardly catch my breath."

"Is it about your vision on the field?" I whisper. "Veil Haven burning."

He runs his fingers through his hair. I guess he forgot I knew.

"I haven't told anyone." We step closer. "But between what you've seen and what I know, Logan we could—"

"I *can't*," he stresses, shaking his head. "*Hear* me, Ash. I can't." His voice deflates.

My frown feels as heavy as his begging gaze. We step apart.

I lean against my car, and we don't speak for a while. My mind's eye takes me to Hayden's surgery. It's going well.

"He's been so sad," I finally say. My lips shake at the thought. "He loved her, y'know?"

Logan nods slowly. "Yeah, I know."

I stare at my turquoise boots. "Between the three of us, he was the only one who saw her. I was so focused on trying to figure out what happened I wasn't paying attention to the aftermath, to him."

"We're all struggling."

Our eyes meet.

"Shakira..." I begin. I don't expect to finish the thought.

He turns to face the sun glowing behind the mountains. He shrugs and shakes his head. "She's gone."

I push off my car. "What do you mean she's gone?" My stomach curls up like a dying animal.

"I can't find her anymore."

"But she's not..."

"I don't *know*." Anger backs his voice. I watch his blue eyes harden but the look fades with a breath. He hangs his head and wipes his eyes.

Silence wraps around us like our breath in the cold. The soft sun meets the blood orange sky as it rises over the mountains. We stand shoulder to shoulder, hands in our pockets, and let the cold November morning bite our cheeks until they sting.

When they wheel Hayden out of surgery I convince the hospital staff to allow Logan and me to stay in his room. His parents greet us at the door and tell us he'll be unconscious for a while. A nurse says that between the accident and the drugs in his system it's a miracle he's alive. It'll take time for him to get back to normal.

Logan and I stare at him. They had to shave half his head to drill into his skull. He has cuts and stitches everywhere we can see, and where we can't too. His face is so swollen it's hard to recognize him. His hands are wrapped in casts.

The machines tell us his stillness is restful, but I have to wonder if his ability still calls on him. Did his trance make him witness himself as he was dying? I couldn't tell.

I hear his parents thank me for saving his life, but it doesn't seem right.

I can't take my eyes off him. If I was awake last time, would this have been Lydia?

I know my answer. I can't tell if that makes it worse or not.

The hours pass as the four of us linger around him. For a moment, Logan and I have the room to ourselves as his parents step out.

I am somewhere in the back of my mind reviewing what Josie found beneath the clock tower, but Logan's voice pulls me from it.

"Is Veil Haven falling apart?"

I rub my face. So many secrets are housed within me. They're heavy and I want to get them out.

I need to see Director Capaldi. I don't care what I have to do to get an audience with him. Even if it means confronting Declan. We need to speak, and I can't wait on him like he asked me. I might disappoint him, but he still has to trust me. He has to care more about me than Declan. I don't know what they're planning, but even the Forest Eye called that man a stranger. The director has to trust me over a stranger.

340

My gut is full of lead. I'm not sure I believe that anymore. I just don't know what else to do.

"I've tried asking my trainers and teachers for help, but they just brush me off," Logan tells me. "They aren't listening to me."

My stomach twists when my mind's eye takes me to Chief Mun. For some reason, he stayed at the office and slept on his in-office couch. I look away, trying not to care.

I rub the sides of my face and pick at my pimples.

"It doesn't seem like anyone in power wants to help," Logan continues. "They don't care. They're happy to keep everything the same and pretend even when it's not."

I almost tell Logan what Chief Mun has done to me, but I don't. It's wedged in the back of my throat. I can't get it out.

"I'm barely keeping my head above water, Ash." The circles under his eyes look dark with these fluorescents. "Our world is falling apart in the worst ways, and I don't know if I'm strong enough to do what it takes to save it."

I drag my chair around Hayden's bed. Logan and I touch shoulders. We reach for each other's shaking hands. The machines whir deftly as we lock eyes, our jaws tight.

"You're not alone in this, Logan."

"I am, though." He squeezes my hand. "I know what I have to do, but it scares me."

I swallow, my words heavy and sour. "I'm scared too."

He nods slowly, closing his eyes. He rubs them and sinks into the chair. He keeps hold of my hand. "I can't bring Shakira back now but maybe I can give her a fighting chance in the future." His breath shakes as he holds back his tears.

I clutch his arm and make him look at me. "Let me help you. For real this time." We're both desperate, just in different ways. "I've made so many mistakes, Logan. I've hurt so many people. But you're Veil Haven's golden boy. The best quarterback in fifty years. The Mothmen's hero. If either of us are going to make a positive change, it's you. And I... I want to help."

"None of this is your fault." He tries so hard not to cry. "Do we really have to do anything, Ash? What if this time, doing nothing will save us?"

"Is anyone else going to save us?"

He forces a smile, but it doesn't reach his eyes. Everything he wants to say is seconds from spilling over but he can't. Now isn't the time.

He breathes sharply and stands, letting go of my hand. "I have to go to the bathroom. I'll be right back."

I try to say something but he's already out the door.

I look at Hayden, the humming machines setting me on edge. He's so bruised. And for some horrible, sickening reason I think of Myrah. I look at Hayden and imagine Myrah. How scared she was. How scared Logan is now. How he's begging me to do the right thing, begging himself. How we need to do something or nothing or find this balance between the two and how are we going to save Veil Haven and Shakira and each other if—*if, if, if.*

I see Myrah twitching under the Cryptid of Vapor and Flesh's tight, boney grip. Her neck crushed like a soda can. She's gasping for air. Her eyes glaze over. Her slow-beating heart finally stops.

I stare at Hayden. The world swells inside of me.

Tears burn my eyes as that cryptid's voice hisses through my mind. I cover my mouth and reach for Hayden's bruised arm like an apology.

You will never save them, child.

CHAPTER 34
WELL IF IT ISN'T THE CONSEQUENCES OF MY ACTIONS

Logan decides to leave around lunch. Hayden's parents are here, and I'm not leaving, so we just part ways. I want to say more. Anything. But I don't.

We can't.

I find a window seat in a vacant hallway and stay there. The cold shocks my skin whenever I lean against the glass. I close my eyes and meditate, shifting the noise of the world to the background.

I think about what Logan suggested.

Do nothing.

My head lolls to the side, my face pressing against the cold windowpane. But when's the last time I really slept? But I don't have time to sleep... not even for an hour... or two...

Hayden's parents find me asleep curled up against the window. When I stir at their gentle touch I'm met by the sunset. Bright red. Dread fills me, twisting like a knife, and I try to recall every minute of lost time.

Nothing changed. Everything is fine. The world and all of my people are accounted for. It was just a nap. Harmless. Except I'm more tired than before and with a foul taste in my mouth.

Hayden's parents tell me they're going out for dinner. The hospital doesn't stock his father's special diet. They want me to be with Hayden, *just in case*. I agree.

Fiery threads weave through the sky as evening meets night. As darkness swarms the town, my paranoia rises with it. I can't sleep again, knowing what I know—what Josie knows. *I won't.* Everything bad happens at night and Hayden is living proof.

I don't take my eyes off him, my stomach churning at the thought that if I do, I'll miss something. If I don't watch, something bad will happen. *I'm made to watch.*

And that's about when I jerk myself awake. I clutch the chair with sharp breaths and brush the hair out of my face. I look out the window and see the stars burning above the dark mountains.

A loud, quick burst of *everything* strikes me like a blow. Vertigo pulls me under, but after I swallow the noise, my body eases. That hasn't happened before. Strange. But that single blink was enough for me to know everything is fine. I tell myself I fell asleep because I'm tired not because any supernatural force made me.

Hayden is alive and I am okay. Josie is still in bed. Logan is staring at his ceiling unable to fall asleep. Everything is fine.

I check on Markus and watch how Dante haunts him.

He talks to Markus like a father, as a joke, but it slowly simmers into something more somber. Dante knows Markus can't hear him. The ghost doesn't know I told his son everything. I guess Markus has kept it all to himself, after all.

But how could Markus just stay in his room acting like nothing happened? Like I didn't tell him he's from Veil Haven, that his mom is from Veil Haven, that his real dad is dead, that Declan—

I perk up as Markus listens for the sound of his front door closing. He holds his breath as he counts to thirty and then leaps from his bed and quietly peers down the hallway.

Dante follows him with the same curiosity I have.

He's quiet for how large he is. He's memorized the loudest floorboards and avoids them as to not wake his sisters. Markus pauses at the end of the hall, his fingers quietly twisting the ornate doorknob to his stepdad's office.

Dante floats at his back. Markus assumes the chill is from this old house.

The office smells of dust and old books despite the lack thereof. Dante and I watch him move around Declan's bulky wooden desk and begins pulling drawers open, sifting through papers, and reading files. Not even he knows what he's looking for, but he takes his time.

I'm at the edge of my seat sure that something useful must be stored here. Why haven't I thought to check? How will Markus open those locked drawers? What is he going to—

Hayden stirs.

I clutch the side of his bed instantly, ignoring Markus.

Hayden fades in and out of consciousness. He isn't in any pain—the doctors made sure of that—but even looking at him hurts.

I scoot closer and quietly urge him to wake up.

His senses return to him in fragments. His muscles stiff. A filthy sourness in his dry mouth. His head pounds. His skin crawls. He feels death pressing its numb fingers into the crevices of his brain, every sensor lighting up. He's forced to be aware of the death around him. It calls him, forces him to bear witness, but he can't.

He can't open his eyes. He can't move. In his half-awake mind, he thinks he's dead. He thinks he's trapped inside his rotting corpse, stuffed underground, forced to feel this for eternity.

I squeeze his upper arm. "Hayden, it's Ash. You're in the hospital. That's why you feel this way. You're alive, Hayden. You just have to wake up. You were in a car accident. You didn't die."

It takes a few minutes of convincing, both our hearts racing. I run my fingers over his unharmed skin and narrate to him. "This is me touching your arm, your chest, your face. You're alive. You're okay."

He mumbles as I try to help pry him out of this half-conscious sleep paralysis.

"I'm touching your cast, your hair. Hayden, please wake up, it's okay. No one is upset. I'm sorry I didn't pay more attention. I'm sorry I couldn't help you sooner."

His eyes are watery as they open. His blurry vision moves from his hospital bed to the casts on his hands, to the IVs in his arms, and finally to me. But when he sees me, his swollen, discolored face contorts and he cries with this awful gagging sound.

"I'm sorry, Ash." His voice is so thin.

I shatter. I tell him he doesn't need to apologize but he can't hear me over his sobbing.

He rolls his head side to side with what little energy he has. He's inconsolable. His voice bubbles up in small coughs as he speaks. "They made me do it, Ash. I'm so sorry. They made me do it."

I feel outside my body. Static. Numb. "What are you saying?"

"A man visited me." His voice shakes as he compels himself to speak. "He told me he was the director of The Watchers, and he told me I had to die to keep my family safe." He breaks down, pushing the side of his face into his pillow. "And my friends would die, and you would die. And all I could think about was Lydia, and if I could've saved her, if we could switch places. I would do anything, Ash. Anything. And now I've messed this up too. He said he needed a distraction, and I can't even do that right." He pushes his head back, tensing his swollen jaw. "I can't do anything right. And now you're all gonna suffer because of me."

I stare at him in shock. I barely move. "Director Capaldi visited you?"

His brows furrow. "He said his name was Jackson. Director Jackson."

I shoot up, my chair skirting back. I stammer as the riot of noise pierces me.

Someone is being attacked in their dreamscape. Someone is hunting a Not-Deer. Someone is being dared to step inside the La

Bella's liminal doorway. Someone is helping feed an injured Bigfoot. Someone is having a rave for Beings of Light. Logan is sleeping. Kane is sleeping. Ford is sleeping. Markus is reading and taking notes. Dante is watching him. Josie is texting Ford a long message confessing her feelings for him. She's drowsy and full of love and eager for tomorrow to begin, eager to finally shout this unspoken thing into the world. It's the only thing taking her mind off everything else. Then, she too falls asleep.

Someone is smashing pumpkins. Someone is fighting a Mothman. Someone is making sacrifices to the Forest Eye. Someone is stargazing. Someone is hammering holes in their wall. Someone is digging a trench beneath their house. Someone is trying to seduce a Shadow Person. Someone is burning their sister's diary. Someone is clawing the inside of a buried, wooden casket.

Then, everything slows. The noise becomes muffled. I don't feel my body. And in the midst of this silence, a single voice whispers through.

Chief Mun's.

I transport myself into the bowels of town hall. Chief of Police Andrew Mun stands in Declan's empty office talking to no one. He stands at attention in the center of the room. "What can I do for you, sir?"

There's a short pause.

In the hospital room, Hayden is begging me to stay as I back away. He cannot clutch my hand.

Chief Mun responds, though seems confused by the question. "I can manipulate others with my touch, sir."

My mind's eye can't recognize Declan like it can with the clock tower. The Forest Eye saw a redacted space. I see nothing. The warbled noise of the world builds in my ears.

I walk around Hayden's bed, listening to them, watching them.

Chief Mun watches someone walking circles around him. When Declan stands in front of him the chief meets his eyes.

There's a knowing pause as he clenches his jaw, and then he says, "Yes, Director."

I lean against the doorway staring at the ground, at the chief, at Declan's office, at myself. I can't think. I can't breathe.

Hayden is saying my name, asking me what's wrong, calling for the nurse.

My vision blurs as the room spins, and the world tilts slowly. My knees are shaking. The heat that consumes me is suffocating, but I have to move. I tighten my fists until it feels like my palms are burning. Until I burn. Until I breathe again. And suddenly I'm in my car.

Director Capaldi can't be dead.

He's no longer with us.

I heard him. I spoke to him.

My heart wedges in my throat.

Don't call here again, Ash. Veil Haven is changing.

I'm clutching my steering wheel as my tires screech out of the hospital lot. I breathe. I focus. *He can't be dead. He can't be dead. That's my dad. I just talked to him. He can't be gone.*

But The Watchers are capable of anything.

I remember Chief Mun's surprise when his phone rang, how gaunt he looked. And weeks ago when I asked him about the director, he acted like he was keeping a secret. Or when I called him and he gave me a rehearsed speech. How long has Director Capaldi been dead? This is why everything has gone wrong, isn't it? This is why everything has been changing. It all makes sense now. It finally makes sense.

I take the bend too fast and swerve over the yellow line as I race down the hill toward town hall, screaming, spit flying.

I believed their lies. I *wanted* to believe he was still alive. I needed to. But the Static Man never had a reason to lie. I keep trusting the wrong people.

I beat against the wheel until I have to catch my breath. My chest aches. My vision blurs. I use my mind's eye to guide me because it's never steered me wrong. Not until *he* showed up.

Director Capaldi is dead. That's why he hasn't contacted me. That's why he didn't help me with Lydia. That's why they kept telling me to wait and be patient and let them have control.

Director Capaldi is gone—forever. All these years of waiting, and I never spoke to him again. My mind races for any last words we shared but there's too much anger, too much silence, too much sadness.

Hands around Lydia's neck. Paralyzing her. Taking her ability. Killing her.

Declan killed the director. He took The Watchers. And they just let him?

My sharp breaths help me swim through my panic as I hyperfocus back on the conversation in town hall.

"—and if I may," Chief Mun says, "I'm not sure injuring the boy was the best approach."

Even with every fiber of my being focusing on this office, I *still* can't see Declan.

The chief is listening to Declan—to his director, to the man who controls Veil Haven—with an even longer pause.

Andrew Mun looks down, looking less like the chief of police than I've ever seen him. He's broken. Distant. Choked up. Fear shifts through his eyes as he scans the ground. What is Declan telling him? Why did they hurt Hayden? Why do they need to distract me? Was Lydia a distraction?

Chief Mun nods, lifting his head. He swallows that suffocating ache and agrees to whatever Declan has said. He has to agree. That's the director.

"Where do we begin?"

My car eats the curb as I turn into the town hall parking lot. It's empty. It's night.

"Then we should go to the base," Chief says, opening the door for a phantom, a murderer, the director. "You never know who could be watching." He's surprised by whatever Declan says next.

Every hair on my body stands on end as I slam on the brakes in front of the towering marble steps. I know the doors are locked. I know I can't get in, but that's never stopped a blunt object before.

I watch Chief enter the main lobby, and I'm so close. For a moment I think they're going to walk out and see me, but instead they move to the side of the main staircase. Chief Mun puts his hand to the wall and something happens.

They walk into the wall and disappear.

My anxiety takes over, and before I know it, my boots are crunching on glass, a tire iron weighing heavily in my hand.

I run to the wall where they disappeared. It must be another blind spot.

I run my hands over the fleur-des-lis wallpaper until I feel a well-worn area. I lean all my weight against the palm sized area and the wall hums, shifting. It folds into itself revealing a set of coiling stairs just like the clock tower.

I grip the tire iron and charge down the wide, dark stairs. It's like a dungeon in here. Old stone steps, stone walls, and wall sconces in the shape of hands.

My mind's eye grows numb as I descend, and just like the clock tower, I become blind down here.

The stairs spiral three times before spitting me into the weirdest place I could've imagined. It's an incredibly white and uncomfortably sterile hallway. It hurts to look at. And it's empty.

My mind's eye pulses like a homing beacon trying to understand where they went. The hallway isn't long. It's like a foyer with an end.

Tall. White. Blinding. Empty.

My heart cuts into my throat. Where did they go? I can't see them anywhere. I can't see *anything*. My mind's eye is fuzzy down here.

"Where are you!" My scream is guttural. I clutch the tire iron in both hands as I pace up and down the hallway searching for breaks in the wall.

What's the point of being the Girl with Eyes Everywhere if I can't find the one person ruining my life?

My rage roots deep and I scream again. I kick the walls. I beat them with the iron. But nothing happens. Not even a scratch. My mind's eye pulses. I am dense and burning and everything is quiet and loud and I'm alone. *Where did they go! Where is he!*

I press my back to the wall, sure I'll finally pass out. My head is spinning. The town still tilts with what little I can see. I feel myself floating. I can't catch my breath. I slide down the wall praying I won't pass out but something *moves.*

The wall peels away at my back and I watch the sterile whiteness fold into itself and reveal a cave tunnel. I stand, the cold rushing to greet me.

My stomach vibrates as I stare at the cave illuminated with white lights mounted to the rock face. The floor is the same sterile white in this hall. I stare as far as my eyes allow because my mind's eye won't enter.

The tire iron is heavy in my hands.

I sprint up and down the hallway dragging my hands across the slick walls and forcing my weight against them. Before I know it, I'm standing at the base of the medieval stairs staring at my work.

Eight doorways.

Eight matching sets of underground tunnels.

It's a crossroads. It's the heart of something terrible and un-known.

Declan and Chief Mun vanished down one of them. But which one? I need to decide fast. I need to decide *now.* They're getting away.

He killed Lydia. He killed the Director. He almost killed Hayden.

I race to the center of the hall and my growl cuts through the static in my ears.

"Declan!" I grit my teeth knowing he must hear me. "I know everything!" I pace between the cave entrances like a cryptid stalking its prey. I want my voice to carry. I want him to feel the weight of it, the rage of it, the bitter promise that *I will kill him.*

"Declan! I know everything!"

I get no response. I imagine him smirking. Poking Chief Mun. Saying something coy.

I stand in the center of this incredibly white, uncomfortably sterile hallway, my mind's eye numb to each tunnel, and without waiting for a sign, I choose one.

CHAPTER 35
THE BEGINNING OF THE END

I move as fast as I can without running. The cave tunnel is about twenty feet wide with bright, sterile lights built into the rocky walls. I feel gagged down here as my mind's eye knocks against the crown of my skull. I become lightheaded if I focus on it for too long. Instead, I let the heat in my system temper me, my knuckles white around the tire iron.

I stalk the tunnel for a long time without any promise of catching up with Declan or Chief Mun, but it doesn't stop my nerves from rising with every step. He won't surprise me like Lydia. And the chief is with him. Would he stop Declan from hurting me? *Taking. Devouring.* My gut twists at the thought.

He killed Director Capaldi. The Static Man was right. But how is that possible? Are The Watchers really bound by some gladiatorial law? Kill the leader and you become the leader? I understand why Winona and Chief Mun acted so normal about the Jacksons moving in. They were ordered to.

I know I chose the wrong tunnel after hours of walking and finding nothing. And now I'm met with the end of the cave. The white flooring rises against the wall creating a sort of door.

I hold my breath. All my senses are numbed. What is on the other side of this wall?

Tensed, tire iron at my side, I slide my hand down the center of the door and it opens just like the others.

Daybreak blinds me. My mind's eye escapes out the tunnel like a breath, and before my eyes can adjust to the morning light, I see the world beneath me.

The Black River.

The Abandoned Dam.

I stare across the ebony water. The dying trees hiss in the wind. The sky is autumn brown.

I turn back to examine the ungodly long tunnel, its cold air sweeping my hair across my face.

Cave systems run the expanse of Veil Haven. Caves I can't see.

This is how The Watchers move around unseen.

Declan and Chief Mun are still gone. The town is still asleep. And I'm walking home trying to preserve the fire in my chest. Like a mantra, I repeat all the things that burn me.

The Keepers of the Coast, Kimi's journal, our omniscient founder, The Watchers able to mindwipe us, Hayden's near-death, Declan the director, cave systems I can't see beneath Veil Haven.

The police are called to town hall when someone reports my car and the broken doors. Detective Stevens recognizes me as the culprit almost immediately, but he tell everybody not to make a move without the chief. For once I am grateful for the detective.

I return to my thoughts. To the reality of our present. Declan is in control of Veil Haven.

Stay away from that man, the Forest Eye warned me. And when I mentioned the director all it did was scoff. Did it know? My fists tighten so much I'm sure I'll cut into my palm. Did the Forest Eye know Director Capaldi was dead?

I pause on my porch and lean against a pillar. The Forest Eye knew. Of course it knew. And of course it didn't tell me.

I enter my house and fall onto the couch with a huff, my body more exhausted than I realized. I drop the tire iron. My aching fingers uncurl. I rub my face until my cheeks and nose regain feeling.

I should've known these secrets from the beginning. The director raised me. The Watchers raised me. I was always going to work with them.

I think of that older director with Capaldi in the bunker. I think about how young Director Capaldi was and how much he was learning. Why wasn't that me? Why did Director Capaldi keep *me* at arm's length?

I bury my face in my hands as I come to terms with it.

I was supposed to be the next director. *I'm* supposed to be the new director. Not. Declan. But my god I am not ready for any of this.

My eyes search the floor looking for nothing. Static courses through my thoughts, memories interlocking all the moments Director Capaldi trained me, gave me passes, let me help the town. I was always supposed to know more, more, more.

My throat dries as a stray thought lingers to the front of my mind. *Just another thing Declan has taken from me.* I lift my head and swallow. It wasn't supposed to happen like this. Capaldi still had plans for me. He was supposed to train me more. I'm not ready.

My nails scrape against the couch.

Everything I had is destroyed. Lydia is in the ground. Hayden is in the hospital. Director Capaldi is gone. Chief is working with the man who killed my father and my best friend. Declan is going to mindwipe us because why wouldn't he? It would create a new normal. It would allow him to rule in peace.

I sit straight-backed, my pulse racing. If he erases my memories, I would work with Declan. I would still work with The Watchers, and the director, and I would follow Declan.

Nausea overwhelms me, and I'm sure I'm going to vomit when my mind's eye snaps me out of it.

In the mountains across town The Watchers exit their van marked with an eye like the setting sun, and I am frozen stiff. They secure the perimeter of the familiar home and enter the ranch with ease.

They choose their steps with practiced caution, avoiding all squeaky boards as they sneak through the home.

I don't breathe.

Josie turns blissfully in her sleep.

I'm scrambling upstairs, digging through my closet, tearing out the rotary phone, and racing to the corner of my living room. I can't breathe. My body vibrates. My mind aches with static, every inch of me screaming.

Josie doesn't hear them enter her room or walk to her bedside or inject her with a serum that instantly immobilizes her.

I'm holding the phone to my ear and screaming into the buzzing dial tone. "Hello? *Hello? Don't do this!*" I step back and stare at the near-invisible camera in the corner of my ceiling. "Declan, don't do this! *Don't take her!*"

I hear nothing in return. Not even the Static Man.

The Watchers unfurl her sheets and pluck her from the bed. Her limbs bounce limply as they carry her through her home. Her sisters and parents don't wake up.

Tears burn my eyes as I keep begging. "Declan! Don't do this. Please. Please!"

The cold air doesn't faze Josie's exposed skin and neither does being placed in the van.

"Please!" I ache.

The Watchers close the van door and vanish.

The phone hits the floor hard. So do I.

I can't catch my breath.

I am within and without.

They took Josie.

Josie is *gone.*

My ache is swallowed by a heat so intense I snap out of my panic. I'm on my feet. I tear the phone from the wall and throw it on the ground again and again and again until it shatters.

Finally.

My vision blurs at the edges. The world tilts to the left, turning, turning, turning. There's a steadiness to my heart and the world is quiet. Everything is so quiet. And I seethe, staring at The Watchers' camera, imagining Declan staring back.

There is nothing else to do now. Nothing else but burn through the woods, find The Watchers base, and kill Declan with my bare hands.

I tear open my front door but my anger hits a wall.

"What are you doing here?"

Logan pushes me back as he enters my home, closing the door behind him. His hands shake at his sides, his hair unkempt, the circles under his eyes darker than yesterday. He ignores how flush I am, the tire iron on my couch, and the shattered rotary phone in the center of the room.

Quietly but firmly he says, "I need to tell you something."

Everything burning inside me turns to chill. That apologetic desperation in his eyes. *Everything* about him is setting off alarms in my head.

"No." I shake my head, panic choking me. "Logan, no. They just took Josie. I can't do this twice." I begin to cry. "I never should've asked. There has to be another way."

"Ash." His blue eyes pierce me.

I'm nothing more than a whisper. "You can't."

"I already do." He's stoic. "If it's not this, it's something else." He steps closer and grabs my hands. "Veil Haven is changing. We can't let it change us too." He searches for something in my white eyes. "I have to do this for Shakira."

"Logan, please. I don't want to be alone."

The future is coming fast, and he has to decide whether he will step into it. We already know which path he will take. I beg him not to. I beg him to keep the future to himself, but I know he isn't listening. He's coming to terms with our destiny and what it will cost to save the people he loves.

The world sinks away. My ears burn in the humming silence.

It's easy enough to plan what you want to say in your head and another thing entirely to find the voice to say it.

"Ash." He swallows. "Someone is altering the fabric of our reality."

"It's Declan," I tell him instantly, squeezing his hands. "Markus' stepdad. And Dante is Markus' real dad. The Watchers killed him when he and Markus' mom were trying to leave Veil Haven. And Director Capaldi is dead. And the Keepers of the Coast are right and—"

"Ash, I know."

"If they take you, they'll have to take me too." *Maybe that's how I can get to Declan.*

"But they don't. Let me tell you what happens instead."

"Why are you doing this?" I beg him. Anything to prolong this moment just a little longer. I don't want to follow this fate if it means losing him too.

"Because it's you, Ash. You're their chosen one. But now you have to choose us."

Then, he tells me everything.

What they will do. What they do to me. What I become. What I'm doing to Shakira in the future as we speak. But he promises me that with one simple act I can change everything. That it starts and ends with me.

He tells me what it'll take to change the future.

And then he tells me to run.

CHAPTER 36
THE EDGE OF THE WORLD

I'm running down my backyard, running into the trees, and the cold air is already drying my throat. I'm panting, my legs are burning, and I am reminded with certainty that I was not built for this.

Logan stays in my house. He stands and waits for them to come.

When The Watchers arrive, it happens so fast I could've missed it.

Three soldiers break through my front door, and Logan doesn't go down without a fight. He punches two of them despite their helmets, and pushes another into the back of my couch. I guess they aren't used to kidnapping people who are expecting them. He's lucky they don't shoot him, but I guess he already knows they won't.

They tackle him to the floor, rugburn enflaming his face. He almost grabs the tire iron but they tranq him. Logan falls unconscious and they bind him before coming out. They toss him into their van with a huff, and when the doors close, I lose sight of him.

I'm hollowed. But I don't stop moving.

I've resorted to a walk-run, needing to put as much distance between me and the town as possible. It's a miracle the Forest Eye doesn't speak to me. Even though I sense its ever-present gaze watching me curiously, it knows I need to do this alone.

The air is cool but the sunlight warms me as I weave deeper into the woods, slowly hiking the inclines that lead to the east woods.

I think about Kimi's journal, everything Josie saw, and how Valentine's hope for Veil Haven has gone to shit.

He was able to save people. Why can't I? Lydia is dead. Shakira is missing. Josie and Logan have been taken. God knows what Declan will do to them.

My stomach curls. I can't think about it.

Everything Logan told me plays on repeat in my mind. The image of what Declan will do to me is sharp and sickening. What he forces the chief to do to me. And what I'll be forced to do to Veil Haven.

They will break me if they catch me. But first they have to catch me.

The sun traces across the sky as The Watchers are deployed into the woods. The Forest Eye does not kill them, too curious to see how they will manage to track me. It's always playing some game. Eternity has not been kind to its boredom.

While I hike, all sorts of cryptids scatter from my presence. Jackalopes, Beings of Light, Bigfoot, Mothmen, Chupacabras, even a group of the Floating Men. I wonder how Kimi must've traced through these woods to find everything she did. How did she survive out here? Did the Forest Eye know her? Did it help her like it's helping me?

I hike for hours. The further I go, the harder the terrain becomes. I pass milky blue streams and pools outlined with moss and glowing flowers. I distantly wonder if these are the ponds Kimi wrote about.

When I see wild glowing sunflowers, my heart twists. Josie would love these. She should be here with me. Has she woken up by now? Is she crying? Is she terrified? What does Declan want with her? What do The Watchers do with anyone they've taken?

I've never known the answer.

Forgive us for not wanting to share the horrors of our work with a child.

I swallow at Chief Mun's words. He still hasn't returned to town. What does he think of Declan kidnapping Josie and Logan? Can he be the voice of reason? Can he help them?

I was certain they wouldn't take her. It would've happened so much sooner if their only reason was the clock tower, or even that journal. What changed? What triggered Declan's new orders?

I stop and the forest stills, as if even the animals are holding their breaths with my terrible epiphany. I want to collapse.

"It was me."

I ran after Declan. I shouted for him in those tunnels. I told him *I knew everything.* He must've heard me. It must've pushed him over the edge.

But why is he punishing me? Why am I the focus of his torment? We've only had a handful of encounters. *He* killed Lydia. *He* killed the director. I've done nothing to him. Am I really that much of a threat?

I ball my fists and move forward, fighting the urge to collapse. My legs ache, my lungs burn, my throat is so dry I'm sure it'll crack. The woods chirp to life as I march on.

It's you, Ash. You're their chosen one.

I swallow and think about everyone who's told me I'm special. How important I am to the town, to the people, to The Watchers. I'm dizzy with the sentiment now. "After everything, I better be."

As the forest becomes denser, I keep repeating what Logan told me before he was taken—before risking everything for the chance to change the future.

I asked, "Where do I start?"

And he said it so simply. "The edge of the world."

The brink of Veil Haven isn't what I thought it would be. I'm squinting two feet ahead of me where my mind's eye promises an abrupt end, but I'm staring at more trees.

I move forward carefully, expecting the worst, but as I cross this boundary, my ears full of static, my mind's eye expands outward. I'm swept with a tailwind of new earth, more woods, an entire outer ring to Veil Haven I've never seen before.

I spin around, making sure I'm still here. I check the autumn brown sky, and it's the same as before. This can't be what Kimi saw. This has to be something else.

But wow, a whole new layer of the world? My gut shivers at the thought. I can't tell if I'm more excited or terrified. In reality, I'm exhausted. All this land was here all along. How didn't I see it before with the Forest Eye? Has it been keeping me away from this too?

My mind's eye speeds through this new outer ring taking in as much scenery as I can. My arm hairs rise when I find the vertical graveyard Kimi wrote about. The headstones are nearly worn flat and covered with moss and lichen. They're hard to read, but I can make out some general phrases like *love, radiation, hope, war.*

More abandoned buildings lie out here too, places completely untouched by humans. The most impressive of them is an abandoned factory—ancient and made of brick. There's no roof but its inner pillars reach toward the sky like a strange hand clawing from the earth.

These places haven't been witnessed by people since Kimi. She was an incredible explorer.

I've expanded Veil Haven, but there's a new edge now, and the sun is getting low.

When I find an area that almost looks like a path, I am mere yards away from the true edge of the world. An even heavier blankness pushes on my mind's eye. Except I'm met by the promise of more mountains again.

I slow down and take my time to study my surroundings. Briars have been broken here. Something big has cut through them where the saplings and vines haven't had time to regrow. Whatever happened here was manmade and fairly recent.

I glare forward as my mind's eye hits a wall, and my head fills with static—the promise of a forest that isn't really there. It looks like the terrain goes on forever, as far as the folding hills will let me see, but it has to be an illusion.

This is where the Void begins. The static in my marrow, the tingling in the tips of my fingers, the way my stomach shivers. Everything about me on a molecular scale is buzzing and telling me to go back.

I swear I hear the Void whispering, *"Don't do this."*

But I grind my molars and tighten my fists.

As I step closer, I can feel energy radiating in front of me like a wall. And when I squint, the forest ahead of me doesn't look right, like the light shimmers in a way it shouldn't. As I shift my weight, the image of the woods moves like a kaleidoscope.

This is the edge. This is where Logan told me to come.

The Keepers of the Coast's book assures me something lies beyond these mountains. Althea left and returned, and I have to believe I will too.

I feel the world bending around me as both the Forest Eye and the Void watch me, waiting. The static bends in my ears louder than the park portal, but actually, pretty similar to the park portal. Except the energy here is far more suffocating.

"Stay," the Void pleads.

But I can't help myself.

I inch closer to the invisible wall, the static raging in my ears, the world heavy at my back. Waiting. Watching. Wondering. As I slip between the fold of the woods. I see what lies beyond Veil Haven and it is no void.

The mountain melt into new shapes, still mountains and hillsides, just slightly different. And everything is duller. The trees are bare, and an asphalt road curves ahead of me broken by a ravine. The sky is blue.

But I have not technically left. I'm standing in the space between worlds. I'm standing within the Void. I'm a breath away from something entirely new.

Veil Haven pulses in the back of my mind like a strange heartbeat. Everything feels slow and manageable. But this isn't where my journey ends. I need to take just one more step. One more step and I'll officially leave Veil Haven, just like Logan promised.

I regret it instantly.

Struck with a weight I cannot explain, my knees buckle and my entire body goes stiff. Fire rakes across my flesh like I'm being cut open. I can't even scream. I'm paralyzed. I'm trapped in my body as something changes. As everything changes.

My mind's eye is split open and taken from me—no, not *from* me, not *taken*—I am sent further from myself than I have ever gone. Stretching, searching, seeing, reaching farther, farther, father. In an instant, I am consuming a world larger than any comprehension.

The noise, the light, the chaos. It's deafening. It's paralyzing. I'm trapped here but I'm seeing everything. *Everything. Everything!*

Forty lightning strikes. Five babies born. Two people die. Hundreds of thousands of celebrations. Millions of internet searches. Billions of people walking, sleeping, breathing, laughing, crying. Billions. Billions.

Nearly ten billion people. Even more cats. And everyone is like Markus—nearly everyone. A few million people have abilities, but most of them pretend they don't. Some people use their powers daily, some publicly. Some are revered, wearing golden capes. Others are feared.

I found the ocean, my god, I found the ocean. It's vast and beautiful and terrifying and deep, so deep. It touches everything. It's everywhere.

Have I just been pinged on some map?

There's a whole new map of the world. The world. There are several. There is no Void here. It's up there. It's unreachable, no, impassable. Fox Falls, Leiton, Railston, and Bescour do not exist. There are millions of towns and Veil Haven isn't the center. Nowhere is the center. Everywhere is the center.

Fifty lightning strikes.

What the hell are those? Atomic bombs? Why are there so many?

It's nighttime. It's daytime. This place isn't a Void plane. It's a planet, and it's round and massive and filled with oceans and mountains and deserts and forests and cities.

Thousands of history classes, thousands of museum kiosks. They're telling such different stories than our truth. There was a war a hundred and fifty years ago. What's a civil war? What's America? What's a world war? Wait, there were how many? How many?

What about Veil Haven? Where is Veil Haven? No one knows about my home. Where are we? Nowhere. Wedged in the mountains. Hidden. Somewhere called Appalachia?

Where am I? I've lost touch of myself and... Am I floating? Falling?

2170. What does that mean? The year? That can't be right. That feels too wrong to be a year. 2170.

Everything is so much more advanced than Veil Haven. Look at their tech—

Millions of gunshots. So many car accidents. So much love. Just as much hate. Airplanes landing safely. What's an airplane?

My skin is on fire. My mind is on fire. I can't breathe. Am I breathing? Falling? Floating?

What about cryptids? Cryptids roam these mountains. I found all our six-eyed deer. They were never too far away. There are cryptids I've never seen before. They aren't just here. They're everywhere, but they're a secret, they're hiding, they're scared, hungry, quiet.

The ocean is real. What's a tsunami? People live on boats? On the ocean? It's so deep. What's at the bottom of the ocean? Oh god—

What's a president? Why are there so many? How can you lead a place so big? How can you live somewhere so overwhelming? Countries don't make sense. How do you draw state lines? Where's Veil Haven?

Four more babies. Two people die. Forty-four lightning strikes.

Several missiles in a desert kill several people. What are satellites? So many women are screaming. So many toddlers are laughing. That's a lot of scraped knees.

What is this place? The world. The Earth. It's too big to be real. Yet—

What's an iceberg? That's a huge mountain. Oh god, there are bodies under the snow. There are bodies are everywhere.

Dogs are barking. Children are crying. People are falling in love. People are watching TV, watching their phones, watching their computers, watching their holograms.

People everywhere, everywhere, everywhere, making so much noise. So much light. My eyes ache, my muscles ache, my skin aches. I'm in so much pain, but I can't move, can't break free of this.

Ten billion human perspectives. Billion. Billion.

A superhero in a golden cape saves a child falling off a bridge. She's only a few years older than I am. She has the ability of creation, imagination. Her name is Animus. Superheroes are real and villains are too.

Everything is happening. Everything. Why are people dying like that? Am I dying?

Forty-five lightning strikes. I swear I feel them all.

I am definitely falling. When will I hit the ground?

The world cuts out.

It is not quiet, but it is dull in comparison.

My eyes are closed but light surrounds me. Neon light. And my skin burns. And my head is pounding.

I feel crushed under the weight of the world. My mind's eye bounces inside the dome that is Veil Haven. I want to scream but

I can't. I'm trapped in my body, my mind. I'm exhausted. I'm passed out.

Veil Haven world washes through me unfiltered, unmanaged, and buzzing. I have fallen backwards into my home. I'm lying on the forest floor. I realize how compact and small Veil Haven is, and I am relieved. I have left the outside world. It can't hurt me anymore.

I am home but I am not safe.

I see myself above my body for a glimpse before I fall further into my subconscious. I am not the same.

I am stained with multicolored neon eyes that look drawn onto my skin. They crown my forehead. They are the ethereal outline of eyes that Josie saw on Valentine. They hover just above my skin. Their pupils move independently. They're looking everywhere. They're seeing *everything*.

My vision has expanded infinitely and their reach is bouncing against the canopied sky, against the edge of the world. These eyes are taking note of every inch of Veil Haven, and I am more familiar with my home than I thought possible.

Then, I see Declan. As simple as that. He's cooking for his daughters and Markus, who are watching TV in the other room. Markus fakes his comfort. He's found something and he's worried.

But Declan is right there. I can see him. I can finally see him. And I'm not letting him escape me ever again.

Veil Haven presses me to the earth, and despite the pain, I welcome the stilled, muffled noise and know that when I wake, everything will be different.

Something new comes to me in this exhausted, vulnerable state. A memory. Logan.

We're in my house. He's holding my hands. "After you come back, it will feel like everything goes wrong, but you have to trust me. You're going to make it through this, Ash, and you'll find a way to save Veil Haven."

"Why do I have to wait to save you?"

He smiles gently and answers with a promise. "All things in time."

NOTE TO READERS

Veil Haven will return!

I genuinely hope you had as much fun reading this book as I had creating it. I would greatly appreciate a brief review on Goodreads, Amazon, or your preferred book website. For every author, reviews are vital. Even a few words or a set of stars can make a big difference. Please note, I do not monitor, reply, or read reviews. Know that you are safe to leave an honest review without any reaction from me, the author.

ACKNOWLEDGMENTS

To Grandma and Grandpa, who have been reading my stories since I first began writing. In my heart, this book's dedication reads as a list of everyone's names of whom I love, and it begins with "For Grandma and Grandpa." I'm always thinking about you, and I love you beyond words. I measure the years in "until I can see you again."

To Mama, thank you for literally everything. You are *the* example of endless love. Your love for me shows up in everything I write. Thank you for always allowing me to write over the summer instead of forcing me to get a temporary job. That led me here! You did everything right. Know that I'll always laugh at how you still excitedly talk about a poem I wrote when I was twelve. You're my hero.

To everyone in my family, know that you were on my mind the entire time I was crafting *Veil Haven*. So much of this story comes from my yearning to be home and to see you. I can't wait to be home again. All things in time!

To my best friends, Shelby, Sierra, Kate, Ciera, Katherine, Bishop, Alison, Vera, Cas, Sarah, and Forbes, who have been with me for so long I'm not even sure there was a time before we met. You have been reading my stories for years and are always excited to hear about my wild ideas. I will never know a better friendship than the ones we share. It's a crime we don't live near each other.

Shelby, you're my alpha twin. Sierra, you're my soul sister. You're my writing buddies, the first ones I run to with exciting or sour news, and you're my forevers. Thank you for everything you do for me, even just existing. I can't wait to share the rest of our lives together.

To Amber, who is the sweetest girl in the world and *Veil Haven*'s very first supporter. You inspire my heart to love beyond its capacity as you seem to do so with ease. I'll always remember our freshman year together.

The biggest, most grand thanks to my phenomenal editor, Amanda Brown. It's been the greatest pleasure to get to know you and to work with you. And to my wonderful formatter, Greg Rupel, who saved the day like the hero he is.

To my nearly endless string of beta readers, thank you for taking the time and being so passionate about the things I imagine. I can get lost inside my head, so because of you I was able to navigate my words into this final draft. I'll be messaging you soon about book two, so no need to lock the door because I'm already inside, and I have a new draft for you to read. Thank you to Shelby, Sierra, Kate, Vera, Bishop, Claudia, Ari, Jordan, Ciera, Katherine, Cas, Alison, Patrick, Harmony, Grey, Reese, Ian, Sarah, Forbes, and of course Mama, Grandma, Grandpa, and Aunty Laura.

To my incredible, unending online community, your patience and support are everything to me. I never realized something like this was possible, but somehow we formed a fandom for *Veil Haven* years before the book was even published. If you follow me on TikTok, have roleplayed on Discord, or have just been excited about *Veil Haven*, thank you! Your joy and passion about my ideas have gotten me through even my darkest days.

To my incredible mods, Reese and Blitz, a million thank yous. Here's to many more years together! I can't wait to see what the future brings us.

Thank you to my author friends, Shelby Elizabeth, Whitney McGruder, S. L. Cokeley, Ariella McCulloch, Camri Kohler, Kristen Reid, Claire Cutting, Asia Hamilton, Kelsie Gonzalez, Brayden Caswell, and Kaitlyn Sanders. I love being able to share the highs and lows of our writing and publishing journeys together. Thank you for answering even my most vague and silly questions. It's so fun to be your mutual. I wish you the greatest success with your novels! I can't wait to watch them all unfold.

Thank you to my spooky sister, Sarah, who is equally as obsessed with me as I am with her. You drew the first Watchers logo from some scribbles I had, and you brought it to life. Thank you for revising it last minute and grounding me when I felt overwhelmed. I am forever excited to watch our seemingly matched, creative journeys unfold, and to one day be in your presence again. Stay weird, my love.

Thank you to everyone who has signed up for my newsletter and who has been rooting for me for days or years. Your commitment and excitement have made all the difference.

A vague thank you to all the artists who fill my Spotify playlists. Nothing can be created in a vacuum, and I've certainly filled my void with your music. Often on repeat. Thank you for creating your magic.

For anyone I am forgetting who has helped me with *Veil Haven*, know I'll suddenly remember to write you in as soon as this goes to print.

To my brother, who has to read a book now—*ha!* You're the sweetest, funniest guy I know, and it's my life's greatest blessing to be your sister. I'm glad we're no longer teenage enemies.

To the love of my life who gives me the fairytale I've always wanted, you're my everything. Thank you for supporting me, being patient with me, going with the flow, and inspiring me to be my best self. You're one of the most creative people I know, and I will lovingly blame you for the cruel plot twists that are coming in the sequels. You're my partner in crime. Thank you for being my solid ground.

To Daddy, who we lost along the way. You are within everything I write. I love you and I miss you.

ANNE M. KELLEY

is an avid writer, daydreamer, and adventurer. When she isn't lounging with her boyfriend and her cat Rusty, she is in the woods, playing Dungeons & Dragons, or cosplaying. If you ask her where she's from, she'll tell you, "I'm originally from Ohio but I grew up in North Carolina." She is happy to live within a short drive of the Appalachian Mountains, where half of her heart is buried. Hopefully, one of these days, she can remember exactly where she left it.

Connect with Anne through her website:

WWW.VEILHAVEN.COM

TikTok: @annemkelley

Instagram and Twitter: @veil_haven, or on Discord.